γ

Rules of
Surrender

SURRENDER

Charlotte leaned forward, touching him now because she had to. Fascinated, she walked her fingers up over his chin and softly, gently caressed his lips from one corner to the other . . .

Startled out of her boldness, she tried to snatch her hand back. He caught it in his and pressed her palm back to his chest. She never even saw his other arm go around her—she only knew he picked her up by the waist and rocked her down on him, then slid backward on his cushions.

He was solid beneath her, too bare for comfort as their bodies pressed together. She'd never been so aware of her maidenly status as all along the length of her she felt . . . so much. His face was right there, if she dared look up.

"Charlotte." His breath whispered across her face and his finger nudged at her stubbornly bowed chin. "Look at me."

Cowardice wasn't her way. She glanced up.

And found his brown eyes shining with admiration and something . . . more. Something dangerous. Something she'd never seen before but she recognized.

CHRISTINA DODD

Rules of Surrender

AVON BOOKS ◆ NEW YORK

AVON BOOKS, INC.
An Imprint of HarperCollins*Publishers*
10 East 53rd Street
New York, New York 10022-5299

Jacket photo by Nesossi Photography
Published by arrangement with the author

ISBN: 0-7394-0819-4

This first book in my governess series
is dedicated to my teachers.

To the ones who taught me to read—
you've given me the world.

The ones who taught me to love study and research—
because of you, my head is stuffed with information.
Most of it useless, but I treasure it nevertheless.

And especially to Mrs. Knowlton and Mrs. Reed—
you taught me to see, to think,
and most important, to write.

To my teachers,
bless you all.

Rules of
Surrender

CHAPTER 1

ENGLAND, 1840

Lady Charlotte Dalrumple, Miss Pamela Lockhart,
and Miss Hannah Setterington
~~Are sick and tired of having their successful
endeavors~~
~~rewarded with dismissal~~
Invite you to visit

The Distinguished Academy of Governesses

~~Born of their determination to seize control
of their lives by~~
Offering the finest in governesses, companions
and instructors to fill any need
Serving fashionable society since March 1, 1840
~~yesterday.~~

ADORNA, VISCOUNTESS RUSKIN, LOOKED AT THE OR-
nate lettering on the calling card in her gloved hand,
then up at the tall limestone townhouse. In London's
overcast March sunlight, the place looked respectable,
if slightly shabby, and while this neighborhood had
been fashionable in the days of Adorna's youth thirty
years before, many of England's best families still
lived along this street. That information allowed her
hope.

Tucking the calling card into her pocketbook, she
mounted the steps and rang the bell. At once the door
opened.

A butler stood there, a proper butler of the old
school in a powdered wig and knee breeches. He
summed her up in a single, comprehensive glance. His
summation produced a bow so obsequious his corset
creaked, and in an accent that was almost more upper
class than young Queen Victoria's, he said, "How may
I help you, madam?"

"I am Viscountess Ruskin."

From his expression, she knew he recognized her
name, although whether for her wealth, her connections or her notoriety, she didn't know. Nor did she
care. Adorna had long ago grown into her role as the
most beautiful woman in England.

Taking a step back to allow her entrance, he said,
"My lady Ruskin, we at Miss Setterington's Distinguished Academy of Governesses are honored."

As she stepped inside, she smiled at him with the
admiration she showed every man, regardless of his
rank or age. "And you are?"

A dark flush started beneath his cravat and dyed his
cheeks and forehead, but his demeanor never changed.
"I am Cusheon, my lady."

"Cusheon. What a *lovely* name."

The creaky old butler's lips lifted ever so slightly. "Thank you, my lady."

"There's that smile. I knew you had one." Adorna enjoyed coaxing cheer out of the sourest puss. "Cusheon, I've come to speak to the proprietors of this establishment."

He snapped his fingers and a towheaded serving boy ran forward to accept her hat and coat. With her thumb, she rubbed a smudge off his chin. "You look very much like my son at your age," she said. "Right down to the flour."

"I've been helping Cook with the baking," the lad said.

"Wynter used to do that, too," she confirmed, and reluctantly let him go. So many changes had occurred in her life lately. Changes were good, of course. Of course they were.

"Miss Hannah Setterington is currently assisting a countess," Cusheon said, "but if you would allow me, I will see if they have concluded their business."

"Thank you. That is most acceptable." While the butler made his stately way across the foyer, she assessed her surroundings. Although the tables were old-fashioned, everything here sparkled with polish and smelled of beeswax. Impressive. Very well tended. She relaxed infinitesimally.

The butler rapped on massive double doors and, at a call from within, entered. He returned almost at once. "Miss Hannah Setterington and the countess have concluded their business. If my lady would come this way?"

As they neared the office, an elderly woman, stooped, heavily veiled and wrapped against March's chill, stepped into the foyer on the arm of a tall woman. In a creaking voice, the countess said, "Miss Setterington, I am delighted with the companion you found me. You may be assured of my continued patronage."

This was Miss Setterington? Startled, Adorna studied the young woman in black bombazine. She hadn't expected the proprietress to be so lacking in years, yet Miss Setterington's easy manner bespoke experience in dealing with the peevish and crotchety. Indeed, she patted the gloved hand on her arm as she handed the countess over to Cusheon. "Thank you, my lady. We are always anxious to be of service." With a smile and a curtsy, she turned to Adorna. "And we are anxious to be of service to you, too, my lady. If you would come into the office . . ."

Adorna studied the old woman as she hobbled past, then followed Miss Setterington into a well-appointed library. A fire burned in the fireplace, the Aubusson carpets were clean if well worn and oiled leather books filled the shelves. "I thought I knew every titled person in England," Adorna said, "but I don't remember that countess."

"Lady Temperly travels abroad extensively," Miss Setterington answered. "That was why she had difficulty finding a companion. So many young people today want to stay only in England."

"Lady Temperly." The name *was* familiar. "No, I don't think I've ever had the pleasure." Although it seemed Adorna had recently heard gossip about her. But she didn't have time to worry about the elderly Lady Temperly. Her own personal crisis beckoned.

Miss Setterington offered a chair set before a delicate walnut writing desk, and Adorna settled into it.

The desk, too, was old-fashioned, well crafted and well tended, with a bottle of ink, a penknife and a pile of well-made pens. Files of every sort stood in stacks on its surface. As Miss Setterington rounded the desk to her chair, Adorna cocked her head to read the notations. *Marchioness Winokur,* proclaimed one. *Baroness Rand,* read another. The knowledge that she was not the first to utilize the Distinguished Academy for Governesses offered comfort. "I rely on your discretion, of course, Miss Setterington."

Miss Setterington seated herself in a delicate chair and reached for an empty file. "Of course, my lady."

"I need a governess." When Miss Setterington would have spoken, Adorna held up her hand. "Not just any governess. I find myself in quite an unusual situation, and the woman I would hire must be of strong moral fiber and unyielding determination."

"That would be Lady Charlotte Dalrumple," Miss Setterington replied instantly.

Adorna studied Miss Setterington, wondering if she was a fool.

"You doubt me, my lady, for my seemingly thoughtless reply," Miss Setterington continued, "but if I were to espouse two phrases to describe Lady Charlotte Dalrumple, they would be the phrases you chose. I suspect you have heard of her through the success of her pupils. In the nine years she has been a governess, she has taken six incorrigible pupils and prepared them for their debuts. Surely you heard how young Lord Marchant wished only for dissipation and fought the necessity of taking his bow before the queen?"

"Oh, yes!" Adorna had indeed heard the tale, and for the first time in two weeks, hope blossomed in her bosom. "Was that Lady Charlotte Dalrumple? Miss Priss, I believe he called his governess."

"Her other references are impeccable as well." Dipping a quill pen in the ink, Miss Setterington lettered *Viscountess Ruskin* on a folder. "Miss Adler was one of her students, as well as Lady Cromble."

Adorna's brief hope died. "Lady Charlotte polishes young ladies and gentlemen for their debuts. My . . . that is . . . those I wish her to teach aren't adolescents."

"She no longer wishes to confine herself to the training of adolescents."

"Why?"

"She is upstairs. We'll call her for an interview and you may ask her." Picking up the bell on her desk, Miss Setterington rang it. Cusheon came at once, and she asked both for Lady Charlotte Dalrumple and for tea.

When he had disappeared, Adorna smiled with a great deal of charm and ill-concealed curiosity. "As we tarry, Miss Setterington, you could tell me about the founding of the Distinguished Academy for Governesses."

Miss Setterington, Adorna noted, smoothly covered an expression of . . . was it alarm? . . . by rising to her feet. "I would like nothing better, but perhaps we could make ourselves more comfortable as we wait for our tea."

As Adorna chose a chair on one side of the fire, Miss Setterington arranged a small table between them. "This is cozier," she pronounced, and sat opposite Adorna. "We called it the Governess School." She folded her hands in her lap and smiled with such satisfaction Adorna thought she must have misread her previous uneasiness. "It is a venture between Lady

Charlotte Dalrumple, Miss Pamela Lockhart and my-self."

Adorna gestured toward the desk with its folders. "You have a great many clients for so new a business."

"Yes, between us we have years of experience."

Adorna blinked. Miss Setterington hadn't really replied to Adorna's comment.

Yet Miss Setterington swept on. "We will place governesses, companions to the elderly and dance, pianoforte and needlework instructors. As we grow, we'll train our teachers ourselves. Soon, when the *ton* has a need, they will automatically think of the Governess School."

The idea seemed so fresh, yet so logical, Adorna marveled that no one had ever thought of it before. "Such commerce seems a difficult venture for three ladies. Had you not thought of approaching a man to lend a hand?"

Miss Setterington's smile slipped. "We are all un-married, and you know how people gossip."

Adorna had been the center of gossip her whole life. "I do indeed."

"Such a masculine influence would be interpreted incorrectly, I fear," Miss Setterington continued. "No, we will succeed on our own."

"You remind me a great deal of my aunt Jane. She is a famous artist and refuses to countenance the gossip of narrow-minded people."

Miss Setterington smoothed her skirt. "Perhaps, then, we worry for nothing."

"Oh, no. Your venture has already been misinter-preted. My friends said a great many unkind things when we received the calling card."

Miss Setterington leveled her brown eyes on Adorna. "Unkind?"

Adorna touched her chin as she tried to remember. "Unthinkable, unbelievable, absurd, they said." She removed her gloves in preparation for tea. "But my friends have grown to be a bunch of old wheyfaces."

Miss Setterington's eyes danced. "Have they?"

"To hear them talk now, one would never think they once dampened their gowns and waltzed the night away." Adorna smiled as she remembered the scandalous evenings of her debut. "To tell the truth, if I weren't so desperate, I would have done the proper thing and sought a recommendation for a governess from among my friends."

"We're glad you did not," Miss Setterington assured her.

So was Adorna. She harbored no illusions that anyone, no matter how dear a friend, could keep this delicate situation a secret.

Miss Setterington recalled her from her abstraction. "Here is the tea, carried by Lady Charlotte herself."

Lady Charlotte Dalrumple. Adorna could scarcely believe it as she observed the young lady enter the room burdened by a heavy silver tray.

Miss Setterington had described Lady Charlotte as having strong moral fiber and unyielding determination.

She didn't look big enough to contain either of those virtues. She, too, was young, surely not more than twenty-two, and dainty, with a curvaceous bosom and a waist a man could span between his hands. Her face could only be described as sweet, with lips too generous for anything but kissing. Her hair was a shocking copper which captured the fire's glow within its strands, but the length of it had been parted in the middle and smoothed away from her face to nestle in a net of black cord that effectively subdued the brilliance. And no matter how much effort Lady Charlotte put into repressing her naturally vibrant coloring, that dimple in her chin voided any attempt at severity.

Only after she had placed the tray, laden with small cakes and a variety of biscuits, on the table and turned her cool green eyes on Adorna did Adorna realize why Miss Setterington had recommended her.

Lady Charlotte was cold, untouched by human affection or need, and she would do her duty unswayed by appeals for mercy or arrogant demands for explanations.

Yes. She might do.

"Lady Ruskin, a pleasure to meet you."

Her low voice was perfectly modulated, and her curtsy, Adorna noted, was a precise illustration of what a curtsy should be. She remained erect, awaiting Adorna's permission to sit, and as Adorna studied that upright figure, she discovered in herself a wayward longing to leave Lady Charlotte standing indefinitely.

She didn't, but extended her hand, wanting to touch the lady's skin and see if the frigidity extended through her flesh. Lady Charlotte's handshake was firm and warm, and when Adorna held on to her hand the extended contact did not shake her composure.

Little did, Adorna suspected. "Sit down, Lady Charlotte. Let us have tea."

Lady Charlotte sat, but with such rigidity Adorna would have sworn her spine never touched the back of the chair.

While Miss Setterington poured, Adorna said, "Miss Setterington said you had nine years' experience, yet you seem too young to have worked for so long."

"I began my career at seventeen. Miss Setterington has my references on file for your inspection."

So Lady Charlotte was twenty-six. Older than she

looked, young and beautiful, yet strong and resolute. Yes, yes, she really might do. Adorna said, "I have been told you are the famous Miss Priss who has prepared debutantes to take their bow in society. Thus I find myself wondering if you would wish to take on my grandchildren. Robbie is ten, and Leila is eight. If you prefer working with adolescents . . ."

"Ten and eight. Robbie and Leila. What lovely names." Lady Charlotte smiled, and for the first time Adorna observed a softening. Then the chill settled over Lady Charlotte once more. "To answer your question, my lady, I'm weary of my unsettled lifestyle. I'm an organized, disciplined woman. I wish to live an organized, disciplined lifestyle. Why must I go from place to place, teaching young men and women the intricacies of dancing, table manners, flirting and pianoforte, only to have my astounding successes awarded with dismissal when they have no further need of me? I am not saying your grandchildren will not learn those skills, my lady, but only that I will start with them sooner and have the chance to teach other things, too. Reading, geography, languages . . . but the boy will have a tutor."

"Not yet." Adorna accepted her tea and confessed the least of her problems. "My grandchildren have lived abroad all their lives."

"Abroad?" Lady Charlotte arched her brows.

Adorna ignored the delicate inquiry as to the place. "They are, I'm afraid . . . savages."

Miss Setterington looked startled at such an ungrandmotherly statement, but Lady Charlotte said, "Of course they must be. The lack of a stabilizing English influence will have worked against them. As the eldest, I suppose the son is the worst."

"Actually, no. Leila is . . ." Adorna thought of that wild child and words failed her.

Lady Charlotte nodded. "The demands on a girl in the *ton* are much more extensive, while the freedoms are much curtailed. She's probably rebellious."

Her insights astounded Adorna, and Adorna began to see how this Lady Charlotte had tamed and trained so many defiant youths. "Rebellious. Yes. And angry, I think, to have left her home."

"Is there something she liked to do there she could do here that would help with her adjustment?"

"She rode horses, apparently very well, but not side-saddle, and she will not allow us to seat her without her legs astride. She says it is a stupid position."

Charlotte nibbled at her lip. "How about the boy? What does he like to do?"

"He likes to throw knives." Adorna pleated her skirt. "Into my imported French wallpaper."

"Why?" Miss Setterington asked, looking properly appalled.

"Because the decorative roses made a proper good target."

To Charlotte's credit, she didn't show a flicker of amusement. "He's good with a knife, then."

"Excellent," Adorna said gloomily. "As their governess, Lady Charlotte, you'll be in charge of explaining our ways to the children, helping them adjust, teaching them manners and, as you said, reading and geography, and"—Adorna took a breath—"all must be done quickly."

Lady Charlotte sipped her tea, her little finger crooked at the perfect angle. "How quickly?"

"Before the end of the season, I am to host a reception for the Sereminian royal family during their official visit to England, and the royal children will participate. Therefore, my grandchildren must participate."

Miss Setterington's teacup rattled as she set it down. "That's three months."

"So it is." Lady Charlotte set down her cup, also, but it did not rattle. "So let me understand you, Lady Ruskin. If I train your grandchildren to behave like civilized Englishpeople in three months, your plan is to keep me on as their governess until Leila makes her bow."

"That is correct."

"That's ten years."

"So it is, but this first three months will irrevocably try your patience."

The slightest of a patronizing smile touched Lady Charlotte's lips. "With all due respect, Lady Ruskin, I believe I am capable of handling two small children."

Adorna knew she ought to tell the rest. She ought to. But really, Lady Charlotte would find out soon enough, Adorna needed her too much—and besides, Lady Charlotte's vainglorious smile made Adorna itch to remove it.

Adorna knew how to salve her guilty conscience, and she did so by offering a magnificent salary.

In this matter, Miss Setterington proved her worth, asking for a finder's fee which took Adorna's breath away.

"This guarantees your complete discretion?" Adorna asked.

"This guarantees everything."

Adorna rose, and the other women rose with her. "Lady Charlotte, I'll send a carriage for you at eleven. We go to Surrey, so we shall arrive by late afternoon."

Adorna had not thought it possible, yet Lady Charlotte stiffened more.

But she said only, "I look forward to the journey, my lady." And she curtsied as Adorna took her leave.

Charlotte and Hannah stood silent and listening as Lady Ruskin's footsteps crossed the foyer. They waited as Cusheon fetched her wrap and bowed her out the front door. Even after the door shut behind her, they lingered, wanting to make sure she had truly gone. Then—

Hannah released a whoop. Wrapping her arms around Charlotte's stiff back, she danced her across the room in an excess of joy.

Charlotte laughed, a creaking and seldom-used reflex, and let Hannah whirl her around.

From the back of the house, they heard the patter of running feet, and Lady Temperly burst in. But while this Lady Temperly wore the same heavy clothing, she held the veil in her hand, and her face was that of a young and handsome woman. "Did we do it?"

"We've done it. We've done it!" Hannah sang.

"She hired Charlotte? She's going to pay the placement fee?"

"Yes, Pamela, she did and she is." Charlotte still smiled. "A hundred pounds! Hannah never even flinched when she asked for it."

Miss Pamela Lockhart tossed the veil in the air and joined in the dance.

Still sober and proper, Cusheon entered and when they halted, out of breath, he said, "If madams are ready, I would be happy to pour the celebratory toast."

"Yes, oh, thank you, Cusheon." Hannah's brown eyes sparkled as the old butler dusted off the bottle of brandy, opened it and poured them each a ladylike measure. "Please take some yourself. We never could have done this without your help."

Bowing, Cusheon complied. "Thank you, madam, but you know Cook and I are most hopeful your venture will succeed. At our ages it would be difficult to find another position."

"We will succeed. I know it," Pamela said.

"I know it, too, madam." Cusheon lifted his glass to them, then took a drink and slipped out.

They imitated Cusheon, lifting their glasses.

"Here's to the real Lady Temperly," Hannah said. "God rest her generous soul."

"Here, here." Charlotte took a sip and grimaced. "I hate brandy."

"Drink it anyway," Hannah said. "It builds blood."

Pamela laughed at Hannah. "That's an old wives' tale, and you are neither old nor a wife."

Now Hannah grimaced.

Charlotte's gaze grew troubled as it swept Pamela's deceptive garb, and she picked up the veil and fingered it. "Are you sure this artifice was necessary?"

Among the three friends, Charlotte was always a stickler for absolute truthfulness. Hannah and Pamela exchanged glances, then together went to work on once again convincing Charlotte they had done the right thing.

Pamela began. "You know we agreed on this. We simply gave the illusion of success to ease any uneasiness our first client may have experienced."

"We're starting a new venture, and we must succeed or we'll lose this townhouse." Hannah gestured around her. "Lady Temperly left it to me, but there's no money. Do you want me to have to sell from lack of funds?"

"No, but—"

"We have seized our good fortune." Hannah wrapped her arm around Charlotte's shoulder and walked with her toward the fire. "In this house, we have a place to train and place other women who have need of a position. As proprietresses of the Distinguished Academy of Governesses, we pass on our knowledge *and* entice the *ton* into paying us a placement fee for our students."

Charlotte sank into the chair. "But we're not who we say we are."

"We are, too. *You* are Lady Charlotte Dalrumple, also known as Miss Priss for your mastery in teaching adolescents the proprieties. *She* is Miss Hannah Setterington, companion to the much-traveled Lady Temperly until her death a mere month ago." Pamela struck a pose. "And *I* am Miss Pamela Lockhart—or will be once I'm out of these clothes."

Charlotte still looked doubtful.

"Charlotte, I have ten years of experience with children," Pamela said earnestly. "Hannah really was Lady Temperly's companion. We have the qualifications to do what we plan to do."

"Once we find employment for ourselves and build up a few fees, we'll be able to help other women who, like us, have nowhere to go when the term of their employment is finished." Hannah knew that would clinch the argument for Charlotte. It clinched the argument for all of them. "Such a small deception as we visited on Lady Ruskin is worth that, surely."

"Yes." Charlotte squared her shoulders. "When this business is established, everyone will benefit."

"That's right. And I'm sure your megrims are because—" Hannah broke off.

Pamela couldn't leave it at that. "Because why?"

Taking a gulp of the despised brandy, Charlotte said, "Because my new position is in Surrey."

"Oh, no." Pamela sat down hard on the footstool. "Of all the places in England!"

"It's of no importance," Charlotte said, although they all knew it was. "As always, I will do my duty, and all will be well."

CHAPTER 2

Cool, FRESH AIR BLEW INTO CHARLOTTE'S FACE AS THE open carriage bounced down the turnpike, and she inhaled the scents of Surrey's North Downs. Surrey smelled like roses climbing an ancient trellis, like laughter and comfort, like winters spent riding her hobbyhorse, like summer afternoons lolling on a branch of her favorite walnut tree reading. Like home.

Charlotte had hoped never to breathe the scents of Surrey again.

"Is this your first trip to the North Downs, my lady?"

Charlotte turned to her new employer and suffered a pang, just one, of envy. Without being told, Charlotte knew men still fought over the widowed Lady Ruskin. A stylish hat perched atop her blond hair, her voice dipped and rose in husky gentility and her complexion would have done honor to a much younger woman. Her large blue eyes were guileless, and she had been the most amiable of companions on the two-hour trip down from London. Yet Charlotte found it hard to believe she had two grandchildren in need of a governess.

And without railing against fate—Charlotte considered railing against fate a waste of time—she wondered what god had guided Adorna into the newly founded school with a position tailor-made for Charlotte herself. "I was raised not far from here, my lady," she said steadily.

"You *are* a relative of the Dalrumples of Porterbridge Hall, then."

The curiosity was inevitable, Charlotte knew, yet the truth tasted bitter on her tongue. "The Earl of Porterbridge is my uncle."

Lady Ruskin nodded. "I thought you must be *that* Lady Charlotte Dalrumple." Picking up Charlotte's gloved hand in her own, she squeezed it. "Your father, God rest his soul, was the earl before. My husband knew him and called him a gentleman of distinction."

To hear her father spoken of, and in such a kindly manner, gave Charlotte a wrench which she hastily covered. "It's pleasant to be back after so many years." Nine years, to be exact, since the occasion of Charlotte's disastrous and decisive seventeenth birthday.

"Yes, Surrey is pleasant, and so close to London. Ruskin and I purchased the estate not long after our son was born so he could be raised in a healthy country atmosphere. Austinpark Manor is a quiet spot."

As she spoke, a brougham barreled around the bend toward them. Their coachman swerved to avoid a collision, slamming Lady Ruskin into the side of their carriage and Charlotte into Lady Ruskin. Charlotte's trunk, hooked to the back, swayed dangerously outward, and Charlotte's precious carpetbag banged against her ankles. The brougham raced on. As they passed, Charlotte heard through the open window a woman's high, scolding voice.

Skeets pulled the horses off the turnpike onto the

grassy shoulder and turned to Lady Ruskin. "Beg yer pardon, m'lady. Be ye hurt?"

Charlotte, too, murmured her regrets as she untangled herself from Lady Ruskin's fringed shawl.

"Nonsense, don't apologize, either of you." Lady Ruskin's melodious voice turned tart, and she gestured to Skeets to go on. As the carriage jolted back onto the turnpike, she said, "Some people have more money than sense. Although truly, my lady, such incidents are rare in this neighborhood."

"If it would please you, Lady Ruskin, I seldom use my title. Call me Charlotte in private, and Miss Dalrumple in front of the children."

Lady Ruskin's eyes warmed, and she took Charlotte's gloved hand in her own. "Thank you, my dear. And you shall call me Adorna, because everyone does."

That was not at all what Charlotte meant to happen, although she suspected that in Lady Ruskin's vicinity, matters seldom happened as they should. "My lady, while I appreciate the invitation and the kindness that it represents, such a liberty would be misinterpreted as a lack of respect on my part, or even insolence."

"In private, then."

"Not in front of the children—"

"Not in front of the children, either, although I fear they will never comprehend the complexities of English society." Adorna sighed, a lift and fall of her generous bosom. Her spring-green brocade gown nipped in at her narrow waist and her crinolines spread wide, overlapping the smoke-gray of Charlotte's plain gown. "They were raised, you see, in El Bahar."

"El Bahar," Charlotte repeated in awe. The country existed east of Egypt and south of Turkey, and evoked images of camels trudging across the undulating sand, of Bedouins and Arabian nights. She couldn't imagine English children raised in such an environment, and for the first time she understood Adorna's use of the word "savages" to describe her grandchildren. "How did they get there? And how did they get home?"

"Rather, ask how my son Wynter got there."

She looked so forlorn Charlotte ached to comfort her. So Adorna had lost her son. What a tragedy. Then the unusual name struck Charlotte. "Wynter?"

A mental portrait rose before her, one she had not brought to mind since she'd left Porterbridge Hall. The lad Wynter at a country dance, tall and blond, so handsome the girls swooned. Aunt Piper had scornfully proclaimed, *He imagines himself a young blond Byron.* Looking back, Charlotte rather thought he had, for a hank of blond hair hung over his forehead, his odd, dark lashes and brows had set him apart from the crowd of obnoxious adolescents and his brown eyes had been alternating fierce and brooding. Twelve-year-old Charlotte had fallen desperately in love with him, but separated from her by the distance of two years, he hadn't noticed her, and she hadn't seen him again.

"Wynter . . . is your son?" Charlotte asked.

Adorna looked delighted. "Did you know him?"

"I suspect I once met him, yes. But I thought he had—"

"Run away. So he did. He took his father's death badly," she said. "Viscount Ruskin, you know, was my elder by many years."

Vaguely Charlotte recalled the gossip. Viscount Ruskin had been a shrewd man of business, just the type the aristocracy scorned. But in his old age, he had done a great favor for the crown and the king, assuming such an old man would not beget children, gave him a title. A title when Viscount Ruskin promptly passed on to his son by marrying the beautiful, aristocratic, youthful Adorna.

Viscount Ruskin had been ninety at the time of his death, his marriage a perpetual scandal . . . yet Ruskin and Adorna had been so wealthy no one dared snub them.

"And although my husband lived a full and happy life, he left us on the day after Wynter's fifteenth birthday. Wynter was so angry at losing him. He had a fight with some other boys after the funeral."

Charlotte remembered that, too. Her cousin Orford, as weaselly a creature as had ever lived, had come home bloodied but smirking, and he had snickered when Wynter had disappeared.

Adorna turned to look out the side of the carriage. "The next day Wynter was gone."

Charlotte could see only the wing of her bonnet, but she heard the pain of loss in Adorna's voice.

"He went looking for adventure." The bonnet shook from side to side as Adorna contemplated her son's foolishness. "He certainly found it. After many escapades, he was sold as a slave to some lowly caravan leader."

Charlotte didn't know whether she wanted to laugh or swoon. That young, brooding Adonis had been a slave? She paid little attention as another carriage raced past them. "Dear heavens, my lady, did you know what had happened to him?"

"Adorna," she corrected absently. "Not at all. Stewart—he is my husband's cousin's son—traced him to Arabia, then lost him. Years passed with no word, but I knew he wasn't dead."

Another carriage raced past them, and although Charlotte paid it little heed, Adorna's brow wrinkled in concern.

Then she turned her wide blue eyes toward Charlotte. "Aunt Jane says I'm a romantic, but I know that when someone you love dies, you sense the tearing of the curtain between this world and the next. Charlotte, I suppose you agree with my aunt."

"No. No, I don't agree with your aunt." Charlotte's parents had died not far from this very spot, and for a moment Charlotte was a bewildered eleven-year-old again, hiding under her bed at Porterbridge Hall, flinching with each flash of lightning.

"I didn't expect to like you." Adorna placed her hand on Charlotte's shoulder. "I feared you would be rather stiff and haughty, but beneath that you're quite sensitive, aren't you?"

Though Charlotte had been sensitive when she was young, she didn't consider herself sensitive anymore. "I believe the word you seek is 'sensible.' "

Adorna smiled and nodded, but before Charlotte could speak again, she saw beyond Adorna a landmark she recognized, the crossroads marker for Wesford Village.

Wesford Village. Charlotte had hoped that Adorna's home would be at the far end of the North Downs, away from Porterbridge Hall, Uncle Shelby, Aunt Piper and her cousins. Fate, however, had ruled against her.

And if—no, when!—the gentry discovered Lady Charlotte Dalrumple had returned . . . ah, that would put the cat among the pigeons.

Adorna look around and saw the signpost, and assured Charlotte, "Austinpark Manor is just ahead, so you needn't worry you shall be totally cut off from civilization."

"Such a thought would never cross my mind."

Adorna lavished a smile on her, the kind of smile

that would make pudding of the average male and produced in Charlotte the uncomfortable sensation of having been transparent. "Of course not, dear. You are the type of female who finds frivolity unnecessary."

"I . . . that's true." So true, but Adorna made a simple virtue sound . . . tedious. "But my lady . . . Adorna . . . you must tell me what happened to your son, how your grandchildren were returned to you. The children must be devastated by their loss."

Adorna shook her head. "They devastate; they are not devastated."

The children weren't devastated by their father's death? Charlotte's long-forgotten romanticism surfaced. Perhaps the children had been orphans for a long time, wandering the desert . . .

Just ahead, a carriage turned onto the road, and the coachman whipped up the horses. They drove past in a breakneck hurry.

Charlotte recognized the crest on the carriage—as if she could ever forget it!—and her face went stiff.

Adorna craned her neck to see who was within. "How odd! That was Lord and Lady Howard."

Charlotte managed to answer, "So it was."

Adorna patted her hand. "Of course. I remember. How dreadful for you. But they were coming from Austinpark Manor, and it looked as if she were striking him with her hat! No one should be at the house except . . ." Her eyes rounded in horror, and she clutched the lace at her throat. "Tell me he didn't invite anyone to visit while I was gone."

"Who?"

"He wouldn't dare. I gave him specific instructions . . ."

"What?"

Adorna leaned forward and said urgently, "Skeets, hurry!"

The carriage turned between two gateposts onto a country lane. Skeets obediently urged the horses past a large and handsome gatehouse. Gravel sprayed from beneath the wheels. Adorna clutched the side of the carriage in her white-gloved hand and strained to see forward.

Charlotte was missing a very important piece of information, but what it was she could not imagine. They rolled past magnificent old trees lining the road. She caught azure glimpses of a serene lake in the distance, a marble pavilion, a trellised garden alight with bobbing flowers of gold, lavender and pink. And finally, as they rounded a curve, she saw the aged mellow blend of brick and stone of Austinpark Manor. The house blended into its surroundings, hugging the earth and rising to the skies in a celebration of man's elegance. The classic style had been popular one hundred years before; Charlotte wondered what noble family had built it, and lost it, and why.

Then another carriage rolled toward them, and Adorna exclaimed, "That's Mr. Morden and his wife, and you know what a stickler for propriety she is! Oh, I hope he hasn't ruined everything."

The house disappeared behind a grove of trees, then when their open carriage rounded the curve, the house reappeared just ahead.

On the portico stood a man.

Even from a distance, Charlotte could tell he was tall and broad-shouldered, a monument to masculine strength. Or perhaps he could be better called an affront to English civilization.

As they drove closer, she noted that his hands, clenched in fists on his hips, were massive. His shoulders stretched broad, and the muscles on his chest couldn't be concealed by his white shirt and sober black waistcoat. His trousers did not conceal his potency; rather, they emphasized it with a trim cut that provided the concept of straining seams and popping buttons.

He gave the impression of a man who had staked a claim, yet Charlotte didn't understand how. Surely this was Adorna's new husband, although she hadn't mentioned one, or a relative. Perhaps Stewart, the distant relative Adorna had mentioned.

But Charlotte couldn't pull her attention from the brute's hair.

Barbarously long, his locks blew in the breeze— and they were blond. The same blond as Adorna's.

As the carriage pulled to a halt, the man smiled. He started forward. And Charlotte saw what she hadn't seen before. His poor disguise of refinement was not complete.

His feet were bare.

It couldn't be, yet Charlotte had to ask, "Who is he?"

"My son." Adorna glared at him as she waited for Skeets to place the step and assist her down. "My son Wynter, back from the grave to plague me."

CHAPTER 3

"*I* THOUGHT HE WAS DEAD," CHARLOTTE BLURTED. Charlotte never spoke without thinking, and that slip should have warned her of the impact Wynter would have on her life. But she was blissfully oblivious as Adorna descended from the carriage.

As Charlotte watched, Adorna mounted the shallow steps and enfolded Wynter in her arms. "Dear boy, what have you done now?"

He leaned down to give her a warm buss on the cheek. In an accent so faint and foreign Charlotte had to strain to hear it, he said, "I simply told the men that they should keep their women under tighter rein."

Charlotte's old infatuation died a death so painless she scarcely noted its passing.

"Wynter, how could you say such a thing in Mrs. Morden's presence? She fancies herself above reproach, and the Mordens are rich and high-placed enough that she may think whatever she likes."

He reflected. "Actually, it was Lady Howard who took the greatest offense. A viperous woman who flirted with me in front of her man."

Charlotte pretended not to hear.

"Ladies are not sequestered here," Adorna said. "Flirtation is allowed."

"Is it proper?" he demanded.

Adorna tilted her head as she considered the intricacies of English society and how to explain them to her son. "Not when one party is married, but—"

"What *but* can there be? If it's not proper, it's improper." He turned to Charlotte as she gathered her carpetbag and descended from the carriage with Skeets's assistance. "What do you think?"

Charlotte *thought* any man who went barefoot, wore his hair like a woman and couldn't manage to button his shirt all the way to the top should not be passing judgment, but her ingrained manners would not allow her to say so. Instead she folded her hands before her. "It's not what *I* think or *you* think that matters. What matters is the hospitable treatment of guests."

"Yes. In the desert, if a guest is not treated hospitably, the sand and the sun bleach his bones." He looked past her as if seeing the shifting dunes and blazing sun. Then, behind him, someone cleared his throat and Wynter's attention snapped back to the present. He moved away from the top step of the portico to allow Charlotte to ascend, and without inflection, said, "Speaking of guests, Mother, you have one."

Adorna faced the well-dressed gentleman standing in the open doorway. Her fingers fluttered at her throat, and she said, "Lord Bucknell. Dear Lord Bucknell, what a surprise! Always pleasant, of course, but I had no idea . . . and to catch me away! But you've . . . met my son?" Her usual husky tone held a note of consternation, yet a smile curved her lips, and she moved toward Lord Bucknell with both hands outstretched.

Lord Bucknell stepped into the sunshine, a fit, handsome man of perhaps fifty. His hair was sprinkled with gray, his carriage erect, and he took her hands in his as if he knew better than to indulge in such a greeting, yet couldn't resist. "Yes, I met your son. Quite a shock, after these years. But you must be happy, Lady Ruskin. I know his absence caused you no end of grief."

"It did." She gave a gurgle of youthful laughter. "But I told you he wasn't dead."

"So you did." His solemn smile contrasted oddly with Adorna's warmth. But perhaps Wynter's un-flinching gaze constrained him.

Charlotte stepped foot on the veranda, and as smoothly as some great-maned predator, Wynter again switched his concentration back to her. She stood still as he closed in behind her and proceeded to circle, examining her with the open curiosity he might show a zoo animal.

She did not lower herself to do the same, but neither did she turn her eyes away in a pretense of cowardice. Nothing intimidated Charlotte; the sooner he learned that fact, the less conflict they would endure.

He had truly grown tall in his sojourn away from England; he topped her by more than a foot. His bulk filled her gaze, but she kept her vision properly affixed to his countenance.

He might have been a geometry proof, for angles of every kind made up his face. His forehead was a handsome rectangle, his cheeks jutted out from the point of his chin, his nose was a sharp, beaked triangle. A long scar tugged at the edge of one eye and bisected his right cheek. His brown eyes, she noted, no longer contrasted with his fair complexion. The sun in El Ba-har had tanned him to the color of toast, and lightened his hair in streaks. He still sported those unusually dark eyelashes and brows, but he no longer allowed them to droop in Byronesque brooding. He looked at the world with such direct and avid interest, some lesser beings might find themselves discomfited.

"Mother, does she fulfill all our requirements?"

He directed his question to Adorna, acting as if Charlotte were either deaf or invisible. Notables did behave so to their servants, of course, but governesses lurked in that ill-defined domain of neither servant nor aristocrat. Charlotte, especially, as a doyen of deportment, tended to be treated with respect. But Wynter was obviously oblivious to the niceties.

Charlotte would be offended—was offended—except she wanted to hear the answer.

"Mother?" Wynter repeated.

"Hmm?" Adorna was still holding Lord Bucknell's hands in her own and paying very little attention to the scene at the edge of the veranda. "Yes, she's perfect."

"She's very young and very pretty." Wynter's years in the desert had apparently stripped him of artifice.

Charlotte's fingers tightened around the handle of her bag and she put a crisp edge to her voice. "Youth and prettiness are not a barrier to efficiency."

"No? We shall see."

A rush of blood flooded her cheeks. And for no reason, she assured herself. In every new employment, she had been initially disdained by *someone*. But to have this man, this *brute,* so openly doubt her . . . ah, that set her teeth on edge.

Adorna hastily provided introductions. "Miss Dalrumple, may I present my son, Wynter, Viscount Ruskin. Wynter, this is Lady Charlotte Dalrumple, the governess for . . . or rather, an expert in manners."

Lord Bucknell coughed, and Charlotte correctly interpreted that as censure. But she paid him no heed. It was Wynter, Lord Ruskin, who commanded her attention. Determined to behave as if the personal comments, the cross-conversation, the insolent inspection were quite normal, Charlotte curtsied. "I am delighted to make your acquaintance, my lord."

Lord Wynter just gazed at her rather stupidly. "What should I do?" he asked, apparently to the thin air.

Acting on reflex, she placed the bag on the floor beside her. "You bow and repeat, 'I am delighted to make your acquaintance, Miss Dalrumple.'"

"But you have a title."

"Only because my father was an earl, and besides, using one's title to excess is considered uncouth. Even Her Majesty Queen Victoria is frequently called 'Ma'am' by her attendants."

"I see." He bowed, a sweep of courtesy. "I should bow like this?"

"Exactly like that."

"And I should say"—he took her hand and bent over it, then looked into her eyes—"I am delighted to make your acquaintance, Miss Dalrumple."

At that moment, she realized he made a game of her. He knew exactly what he should do.

She didn't like the man. She didn't like him at all, but if he was similar to the other fathers she'd had truck with, she would never see him past this initial meeting.

Only he looked at her as if she were a person who now merited his full attention. The gaze that before had been analytical now searched her as if he wished to know her in some intimate manner. And when he brought her hand to his cheek and smoothed it across the skin, she thought she knew exactly why.

The slight growth of his beard caught at the cotton of her glove. She knew her eyes had grown wide. She glanced at Adorna and Lord Bucknell, but they were engrossed in a conversation of their own. So she tugged at her hand, and when Wynter released her, she said, "If you would allow me, my lord, to offer a critique of your conduct?"

He straightened, still watching her. "Of course."

"I believe I may have pinpointed the reason for Lady Howard's flirtatious manner. That gesture of hand to cheek is quite unusual in English society. She may have read into it interest on your part. Perhaps it would be best if you dispensed with such gestures until you once again regain your sense of propriety."

He tucked his hands behind his back and straightened his shoulders. "Actually, I believe my sense of propriety is alive and well."

Now she looked at him, seeing him as others would; a swaggering, powerful, experienced man of the world. "But it is not British."

"You think the British have defined propriety?"

"Certainly. In your situation, where you have been gone for many years, to be a paragon of British propriety would prove a social advantage."

Wynter laughed, a wholehearted bellow of amusement. "You are lovely, oh moon of my delight. Without you, my life has been as barren and cold as the night desert when the harmattan blows with its endless, sorrowful breath."

Charlotte wanted to respond, to somehow point out that such an unrestrained babble of words was indelicate and most improper.

Yet with his head lifted, his hair swung back. In one small, neat earlobe, she saw a gold loop.

She couldn't have been more shocked.

An earring. In his ear. Only low-class women and gypsies wore earbobs, and he was neither. Yet undeniably gold glinted in the sun.

"Come inside, you two," Adorna called gaily, her hand tucked into Lord Bucknell's arm. "Charlotte and I have been hours on the road, so we shall have tea."

Wynter padded behind Charlotte as she walked toward the door. His barefooted step whispered on the smooth, sunlit stone while appalled astonishment rioted through her mind. Had the Bedouins held Wynter down and forced the ring through his earlobe? Had they tortured him, withheld water, tied him to a camel? No Englishman would allow such a ring without extreme measures.

Lord Bucknell and Adorna had entered the shadowy interior of the manor when Wynter stepped around Charlotte and bowed again. As he stood, again she saw that earring, and she realized: Perhaps he had been forced to accept the ring, but he was back in England.

He didn't have to wear it.

Before Charlotte stepped into the manor's long gallery, Wynter laid his hand on her arm and, when she halted, stepped close. His accent strengthened as he lowered his voice. "Lady . . . Miss . . . Charlotte." He tried out each word as if confused, then smiled in delight, a stranger of obnoxious seductiveness. "Lady Miss Charlotte, in all fairness I must inform you—I did not bring Lady Howard's hand to my cheek, for I am not interested in the sensation of her touch on my skin."

Without a thought to the Governess School, to civility, to the respect due a man society deemed her superior, she drew herself up to her full height and haughtiness and stared right into his impudent, mocking face. "In all fairness, Lord Ruskin, I must inform *you*—I am not interested in the sensation of *your* touch on *my* skin, and if you imagine part of my duties to be to suffer such a touch, tell me now so I may catch Skeets and have him transport me back to London."

CHAPTER 4

*B*Y THE DUNES, LADY MISS CHARLOTTE DALRUMPLE was a fierce little thing! Wynter quite enjoyed the frosty bite of her glare and that ruffled indignation. Lady Miss Charlotte—how it amused him to call her that!—was passing every test.

"My lord?" she snapped, not backing off, although he towered over her.

Smoothly he stepped back and offered her an obeisance. "All shall be as you wish, oh sunshine most brilliant."

Lord Bucknell harrumphed—something he'd done frequently since his arrival—and, when Wynter glanced his way, turned his gaze aside with so much obvious discomfiture he might have been interrupting a prolonged session of lovemaking.

Lord Bucknell did not approve of Wynter. But this was Wynter's home. Wynter was not the one on trial here. With the impassivity he'd learned at Sheik Barakah's side, Wynter inclined his head to Lord Bucknell and gestured for Charlotte to enter. She hesitated, perceiving the risk she took by accepting his offer of shelter and sustenance. But with their stifling clothing and hypocritical decorum, his English countrymen attempted to cloak the basic, primitive urges. Urges that drove a man to master and protect an unclaimed woman.

Because Charlotte had been raised with, and believed in, that travesty of civilization, she failed to heed the cry of her instincts. She stepped over the threshold into his home.

Her naïveté made him chuckle, and at the sound she looked back at him. Their eyes met.

Her eyes widened and lit that smooth, cool face.

Then Adorna called, "Come in, Charlotte."

Deliberately, Charlotte turned her gaze from his and sank back into the artificial safety created by her beloved culture.

And, he admitted grudgingly, if she became his children's governess, she *was* safe. It did not matter that he looked at her prim-pressed lips and carefully trussed body and wanted to open them both to his mouth and his body. He'd been long without a woman, but he couldn't imagine why he was attracted to a scowl and a corset. Yet he'd lived with the fatalism of the Bedouin long enough to accept the attraction while knowing with English certainty that only a cad would seek to take her.

Speaking of cads . . . when Adorna introduced her to Lord Bucknell, Lord Bucknell's bow was swift and shallow.

Bucknell's behavior astonished Wynter. Since his arrival a few hours ago, Lord Bucknell had been thoroughly correct, yet he turned a fisheye on Charlotte. Admittedly, Wynter might no longer completely understand the complexities of English social structure, but his mother wouldn't treat a governess with such warmth if that behavior was unacceptable.

Yet Charlotte seemed imperturbable, as though

she'd suffered other such cuts in other households and considered them beneath her notice. "Lady Ruskin, you have a beautiful home," she said, as she looked around the long salon with its acres of shiny polished wood floors, the wall of windows that looked out onto the terrace and the gardens, the portraits and book-shelves and rugs.

"So it was on my first sight of Austinpark Manor, and I've changed little. One doesn't improve perfec-tion." Adorna indicated the grouping of chairs and ta-bles around one of the merrily burning fireplaces where the maids were assembling cakes and biscuits. "We'll take our tea there. For all the sun is shining, one is still aware of the bite of winter past in the air."

With a glance at Lord Bucknell, now studiously ex-amining some of the titles on the bookshelves, Char-lotte said, "That would be lovely, Lady Ruskin, but I would really like to meet the children."

"Yes, you are certainly going to have to meet them." A faint sigh quivered from his mother. "I insist you have fortification first."

Wynter's smile faded. While his son Robbie found England a fascinating adventure, Leila threw tantrums and begged to be taken home. Taken back to El Bahar, when in fact he'd left that place for her.

She didn't understand. How could she? She'd only known the wild freedom of being his little daughter, of riding and training horses, of traveling with the car-avans and ordering the skinny native boys about. Only the skinny boys were becoming men and Leila . . . Leila would soon be a woman. Whenever Wynter struggled with the restrictions of English society, he had only to think of Leila to know he had done the right thing.

Several footmen were bringing in the baggage from

the carriage, and Charlotte suddenly called, "Wait! I need that bag!"

Wynter watched with interest as she retrieved a large carpetbag from one footman. It was heavy, its sides bulging. Again he moved closer and studied her. She placed the bag against the wall and allowed the maid to help her from her coat. She seemed everything his mother had hoped to find: cold, impersonal, emotionless. He couldn't imagine a woman like this dealing with a volatile child like Leila. If Charlotte showed herself incapable of handling Leila, she was useless.

Charlotte untied the bow under her chin and lifted the hat from her head—and Wynter found himself fascinated. Fascinated as he had not been for too many years. "My God, woman," he boomed, "why didn't you tell me you had red hair?"

Charlotte froze, her arms raised.

With his index finger and thumb, Wynter took the strand that swooped from the peak of her forehead into her chignon. "I've never seen anything like this. A man could warm his hands by your fire."

Then he became aware of a muffled sound from his mother. A laugh.

When he looked at her, she hastily moved toward her seat—but not before he saw her hand pressed over her mouth or the dancing amusement in her eyes. Another fatuous English dictum broken.

Charlotte handed her hat to the maid, then took his wrist in her hand and moved it aside. "Actually, my lord, it is considered uncouth to comment so freely on another's physical attributes."

"But what is the point of a woman displaying her charms if a man may not like them?"

"I am not displaying my charms! My red hair is . . ."

She took a long breath. "You may appreciate a lady's attributes, only . . . more quietly."

Her fingers shook where she held him. While he could see her chagrin in the color that flooded her pale complexion, it in no way commanded her voice. Charlotte had a formidable facade, and he wondered at the need for it. "Then may I say—your coloring is most agreeable to me."

"That is better, yes, but it actually would be best in our roles of employer and employee if you give me no compliments at all."

"But I do not find that pleasing."

She dropped his wrist. "To conform to society's edicts, it is sometimes necessary to do that which does not please one."

He scowled at her. "This I remember."

She brushed at her gown, her gaze fixed on her hands. "I don't believe that you would make such a comment to a lady of the desert."

"I would not so regard a lady of the desert. Only girl-children are allowed to roam uncovered."

Curious, she drew her gaze to his, and her eyes, as green as the spring fields, rounded. "You mean the women are truly kept in a harem?"

His friends' women had asked such questions, but their queries had been made in shrill, scornful tones. Charlotte was fascinated, so fascinated she dropped her cool mask.

"The wives of wealthy men who live in the city are kept in a harem," he explained. "I spent my time with the Bedouins, the wanderers of the desert. Our wives walk among us, but with their heads covered."

"Your wife . . ." Charlotte hesitated. "Wives? Had to keep their heads covered?"

"My *wife*"—he emphasized the singular—"kept her

head covered, and usually her face, too. But so did I. The sand and the sun are relentless."

"Of course." Charlotte's generous lips were pursed as she assimilated the facts.

He assimilated the facts, also. Perhaps Charlotte's decorous demeanor hid an adventurous soul.

"Come and sit down, dears," Adorna called.

Charlotte looked startled, then guilty, as she realized that everyone stared at her. "Forgive me, my lord. I had no right to question you."

"Is that another rule I should know? English people in pursuit of knowledge must not seek it?"

"No! No, that's not what I meant at all. Only that you wish to take tea, and the time and the place was not right for such interrogation."

"Later, then." He turned away before she could respond, and went to take his leisure in the largest armchair.

Adorna had taken a seat behind the gilt tea tray, and like a dog on a chain, Bucknell came to her call. Still Charlotte hesitated.

"Charlotte"—Adorna gestured to the bar-backed sofa at her side—"would you assist me, please?"

As the younger woman moved toward her, Adorna poured tea. "Cream only, I believe, Lord Bucknell." She passed the cup to Charlotte, who delivered it to Bucknell. "With sugar, Wynter."

Charlotte delivered Wynter's, not meeting his eyes.

"While I pour yours, Charlotte, would you pass Wynter the almond biscuits? As a boy, Wynter was very fond of those particular biscuits."

Wynter accepted the plate and took two biscuits, valiantly resisting the urge to eat them all, and from the serving plate yet. Charlotte would be aghast. Perhaps so aghast as to allow her cool mask to slip and allow real indignation to show through. But while he found appeal in such exposure, he did remember the basics of English social graces.

"Sandwiches, Lord Bucknell?" When Bucknell refused that, Adorna offered, "Seedcake?"

Bucknell accepted a slice.

Adorna loaded a plate with sandwiches, seedcake and currant cake and handed it to the seated Charlotte. "Ladies are too delicate to experience something so vulgar as hunger, but Charlotte and I are feeling peckish."

Wynter chuckled, and even Charlotte smiled faintly as she stripped off her gloves and prepared to eat.

But Bucknell nodded. "Quite right. Quite right. Englishwomen are not like your savages, you know, m'boy."

Wynter still smiled as he asked, "What savages are those? The savages like my wife?"

Bucknell started; his gaze flew to Wynter's, and he looked, if not horrified, then appalled. "That was thoughtless of me, my lord. Forgive me." Bucknell balanced his cup and the saucer on his knee and gazed earnestly at Adorna. "I, for one, was quite startled to discover Wynter in residence, Lady Ruskin. I admit I'm not in the mainstream for gossip, but I hadn't heard even a rumor of his return."

Wynter blandly interrupted. "I've been back a little over a fortnight and haven't felt the need to start any rumors."

"No, of course not." Bucknell stared at Wynter, and his starchy accent grew even starchier. "But usually such news would have flown the length and depth of Britain."

"Mother believes it would be easier for my children if they first learn the rudiments of English civility before venturing into public, and so we remain anonymous." He cast a humorous glance at Adorna. "Or— almost anonymous. I swear, ma'am, when I was in town Howard recognized me and invited himself down."

"Howard is frequently without funds," Bucknell added. "If not for Young Wynter's ridicu, er, unique opinions, Howard and his party would be here until forcibly removed."

Wynter pretended not to notice Bucknell's slur.

"I hope while you were in London you didn't have to go into your company, my dear." Bucknell spoke to Adorna, but the comment was obviously aimed at Wynter.

"No," Adorna said. "With Cousin Stewart's help, Wynter has taken up the reins."

"You should never have had to sully yourself with such plebeian proceedings." Emboldened by Wynter's apparent good nature, Bucknell chided him. "Lady Ruskin is a delicate flower."

Wynter could scarcely contain his impatience. "If you believe that, you know her not at all."

Bucknell reared back, an elder statesman insulted by a young buck.

Then, from abovestairs they heard the racket of heels on the wooden floor and a faraway call. "Papa!" Leila's yell echoed down the long upstairs corridor. "Paaaapaaaa."

Wynter imagined her sliding down the banister.

"Don't go in there." Robbie was yelling as loud as Leila, fondly imagining his reprimand made the volume acceptable. "You're going to get in trooou-uublllle!"

But the lighter clatter of her boots outdistanced his stomping, and with a flourish Wynter's daughter came sliding around the corner into the long salon. She was skinny, a bunch of bones connected with skin and tissue, and tall, much taller than most children her age. She had her mother's dark hair pulled back in a braid and a beautiful olive cast to her complexion. Though her appearance was demurer, Leila's eyes were alive with mischief, wide, dark and sparkling as she giggled and wriggled, and the dust that covered her dimity red gown had not been there an hour ago.

Wynter held out his arms. "Come on, then, baggage."

She launched herself at him at the same moment Robbie raced in the door. "I tried to stop her!" Tall and broad-shouldered, with the same coloring as his sister, he was already showing the signs of the handsome man he would become—but his voice squeaked and broke as he pointed at his sister, snuggled in Wynter's lap. "She's been in the attic, and she made a mess again."

"Don't carry tales," Wynter rebuked, and gestured Robbie over. The boy came and perched himself on Wynter's knee, and Wynter embraced him, too.

Then he and his family of outsiders looked out at the others, those representatives of the pinch-mouthed English society.

Adorna stared at her son and grandchildren with mingled despair and love. Bucknell, predictably, couldn't mask his antipathy. And Charlotte . . . ah, Lady Miss Charlotte.

For the first time since he'd met her, her green eyes were not cool. She looked on his children with . . . assessment?

Wynter jiggled Leila and Robbie to get their attention. "This lady is the governess your grandmama promised you. Her name is Lady Miss Charlotte, she is clever and, as you can see, very beautiful, and she will teach you."

A smile crooked Charlotte's mouth as she gazed at Leila, and she nodded at Robbie in a comradely way. "I'm so pleased to meet you. It is always pleasant to make new friends."

Wynter jiggled them again, and both children murmured, "I'm pleased to meet you, Lady Miss Charlotte." But they didn't stand, and they didn't bow.

Adorna would have reprimanded them, but before she could, Charlotte said, "Robbie, if you would bring me my bag, I will find the gifts I brought you."

Ah, the magic word! Robbie stood at once, eager for his gift, and fetched the carpetbag Charlotte had so craftily kept near.

Leila shrank back against Wynter. In the past months she had met too many new people, struggled with too many new experiences, and occasionally she suffered from shyness. And tantrums. And nightmares, but Charlotte didn't need to know that yet.

Charlotte paid no heed to Leila's reserve. Instead, when Robbie delivered the bag, she patted the place beside her. As he sidled up and seated himself, she opened the bag and drew out a carving of a horse some twelve inches high. A master craftsman had shaped the polished wood; the animal seemed to be in motion, its hooves flying, its mane and tail fluttering with the speed of its passing.

As Charlotte set the carving on the floor by her feet, Wynter felt Leila lean toward that horse.

"This is Leila's gift," Charlotte said.

Charlotte was clever.

Again delving into the bag, Charlotte plucked from

it something that looked like a thin, three-inch pale ivory handle.

Wynter knew at once what it was. Charlotte *was* clever. Dangerously clever. He would remember that.

As Charlotte held the object out to Robbie, Adorna moaned softly and dropped her head into her hands. Robbie frowned and warily took the handle from Charlotte's palm.

It took him only a minute to unravel the mystery of his gift. "Papa! Look!" He extended the pocketknife, blades out. "I can carry it with me and I can throw it . . ." He paused and looked warily at his grand-mother. "Except not in the house."

"Then we'll have to practice outside, won't we?" Charlotte said. "We'll do that during our walks. I was hoping you could show me the correct way to throw it, and Leila would show me how to ride." She turned to Leila. Leila, who had not yet taken her gaze from the horse. "Leila, her ladyship tells me you are a mag-nificent horsewoman."

Leila glanced suspiciously at Charlotte. "Yes. But I won't ride sidesaddle."

"Oh, dear." Charlotte picked up the horse and stroked it. "I didn't know you couldn't ride sidesad-dle."

"I can, too!" Leila stood up from Wynter's lap in a sweep of indignation. "I don't want to."

Robbie didn't even look up from his labor of ex-tending and replacing the knife blades. "How would you know? You won't even try."

Before Leila could shout an answer, Charlotte stood. "Girls can do anything, Robbie. Leila, come and fetch the horse."

Leila marched over and took the carving, held it against her chest and stroked it. "It's beautiful," she said in tones of awe. "Thank you, Lady Miss Charlotte."

"Girls have better manners than boys do, too," Charlotte said.

Robbie understood the hint. "Thank you, Lady Miss Charlotte."

"You are welcome, both of you. Robbie, would you bring my bag? With your permission, Lady Ruskin, these two can show me to my bedchamber."

"Yes. Good. You have my permission," Adorna said faintly.

Charlotte took Robbie's free hand and Leila's free hand, and as they exited the long salon, Wynter heard her say, "Did you know it's more difficult to ride side-saddle than a regular saddle?"

Standing, Wynter walked to the door, stepped out and, hands on hips, stared after his children and the governess. Charlotte handled Robbie and Leila with such ease, they didn't even know they had been handled.

She would do very well. Yes, very well indeed.

CHAPTER 5

$\mathcal{A}$ FEW MOMENTS LATER, CHARLOTTE SHOOK HER HEAD at the irrepressible gamine dressed in one of Charlotte's hats, a pair of full-length gloves and a plain corset cover. "I struggle to maintain an orderly appearance, and that's what I look like?"

Leila grinned, not at all impressed by Charlotte's mock reproof, and donned Charlotte's spectacles. Her eyes looked bigger behind the curve of the glass, and she blinked as the world took on a sudden tilt.

"What's this?" Robbie pulled the long case of Charlotte's precious slide rule from her open bag.

"Bring it here and I'll show you."

Leila staggered across the floor of Charlotte's bedchamber, arms outstretched, lifting her feet high.

Charlotte accepted the well-worn leather case from Robbie. "Do you know how to add and subtract?"

"Yes, ma'am." Robbie's language was more strongly accented than his father's, but he spoke the queen's English without faltering. "And multiply and divide, too."

Charlotte lifted her brows at him. "Very good. I didn't know how much formal education you had had. Who taught you?"

"My father. Papa is . . . was the man of business for our tribe, and he says one had to be learned in all matters of commerce to earn respect."

Charlotte lowered her gaze to her hands as she pulled the slide rule free. "Your father is a wise man." She manipulated the shifting pieces of marked and polished wood. "You'll be pleased to hear that when you've mastered the slide rule, you'll have a way of doing mathematics without using pencil and paper."

Robbie frowned. "Oh, I never use pencil and paper. I just do it in my head, like Papa."

Charlotte stared. "Large numbers? Like . . . six hundred and thirty-two times four thousand four hundred and eighteen?"

"Two million seven hundred ninety-two thousand one hundred and seventy-six," Robbie said promptly.

"No, you can't do that in your head. You see the answer is . . ." Hastily Charlotte ran the calculations on the slide rule. "Two million seven hundred ninety-two thousand one hundred and seventy-six." She looked at the boy again. "How did you do that?"

"Papa taught me."

"Your father taught you?" Astonished, Charlotte wondered if the lack of civilization had so sharpened Lord Ruskin's innate wits. "What an extraordinary talent the two of you share!" She wanted to question him further, but Leila careened into the washstand and the porcelain pitcher and wash basin fell onto the hardwood floor. The basin cracked in two. Water from the pitcher splashed out in a wave. Leila wailed.

"That was dumb," her loving brother said.

Charlotte rose unhurriedly to her feet and went to where the child sat on the floor, clutching her shin. "Are you wet?" She plucked her spectacles off Leila's nose and tucked them into her own pocket.

"Yes, and I hurt myself."

"Not badly. Here's a towel; let's clean up the water. Can you multiply like your brother?"

"No." Leila grudgingly took the towel and swiped at the floor. "I can't do more than one hundred times a thousand."

"I'm very impressed." Charlotte knelt beside the girl and used a rag with more efficiency. "Has your father taught you how to read?"

"I know how to read," Robbie said.

"You do not." Leila's accent, too, was stronger than her father's, but the girl's high, clear voice could be trained. "You just recognize a word sometimes."

"I'm better than you."

"I can do it; I just don't want to."

Charlotte righted the table and stacked the broken pieces of porcelain on the surface. "Of course you don't. But I know how to, and I have a book you might like."

"Not if I have to read it," Leila said truculently.

"No, I'll read it to you." Charlotte yielded, setting her trap without a trace of conscience.

Rising, she went to her bag. Most of the contents were scattered across the floor. The clothes she brought in case the servants didn't get around to bringing up her trunks—until correctly trained, servants failed to succor the governess—her slate, her mobile secretary with her papers and quills and a few very carefully selected books. She picked up the one with the green leather binding and looked around the large, sunny, east-facing bedchamber.

The best place for the three of them would be in the window seat. The window popped out over the flower garden, and the seat boasted a padding done in the same pattern and luxurious material as the counterpane on the bed and the curtains at the windows. The extra cushions each boasted a different solid jewel color that picked up a thread of the pattern.

"Come, children." Charlotte led them to the window seat and placed herself in the middle so Robbie and Leila could snuggle on either side of her. While they struggled to appropriate a sufficient number of back cushions, she thoroughly checked out her bedchamber.

The room wasn't in the nursery wing which usually housed the governess, the nursery maid and the children. Charlotte's bedchamber was on the second floor, furnished in the height of elegance. The wallpaper was a pale green and gold stripe. Two large, fringed Aubusson rugs rested on the floor on either side of the tall bed so when Charlotte rose, her feet didn't touch the cold floor. Two chairs and a settle had been arranged to form a little sitting area in front of the fireplace—another luxury which Charlotte had not enjoyed since leaving her uncle's house.

If only Charlotte knew why. For some reason she felt as if she were being bribed.

But why? Charlotte couldn't imagine what further challenge she could face with these children. They appeared to be mathematically advanced, reading deficient, unmannerly, rebellious and very intelligent. Thus teachable.

"What's the book?" Leila asked.

"It's new. I have only just read it myself, and I've been told there are more stories to come." Charlotte smoothed the leather cover of her newest, most precious acquisition. "It's call *The Arabian Nights' Entertainments.*"

"What's it about?" Robbie had picked up the slide rule and appeared to be manipulating it with a fair amount of intelligence.

Charlotte guessed if left to himself, he would fathom the instrument she had so struggled to master. She could only hope he had not already learned algebra and geometry, or she would be burning the midnight candle to stay ahead of him.

Opening the book, she said, "It is about a very clever lady and the stories she tells."

"Mama used to tell us stories," Robbie said. "Leila doesn't remember Mama. She was little when she died."

Charlotte didn't know if it was proper to be interrogating a child, but she found herself inexorably curious. "How little?"

"She was three. I was seven." His mouth trembled for a moment, then firmed. "I remember her."

"Then she lives on in your heart," Charlotte said gently.

"What do you mean?" Leila asked.

"She means I can still see her if I close my eyes." Robbie sounded impatient, but Charlotte suspected the impatience was feigned. "Mama was little and fat and she smiled at me all the time."

"Did she smile at me?" Leila asked.

"You, too."

"She liked me." Leila sounded triumphant. "Where's your mama, Lady Miss Charlotte?"

Charlotte hesitated to correct the child about her title. It was wrong, of course, but it had a charm about it, and besides, it might be unwise to contradict the child's father. "My mother is dead, too." Foreseeing the next question, she added, "And my father. But they died when I was eleven, so I was lucky. I had them longer than you had your mother."

"Lucky," Leila echoed.

Charlotte pressed her hand on the clean white page with the crisp black print. "Now, shall we read?"

"I'm really not good at mathematics." Wynter stared blankly at the thick ledger his cousin Stewart had spread before him, then looked up at the group of black-suited gentlemen sitting on either side of the long table in the London offices of Ruskin Shipping. "Won't you explain it to me?"

Out of the corner of his eye, he saw Stewart's fingers clench the edge of the leather bindings. Mr. Hodges turned so red Wynter suspected apoplexy. Mr. Read made a roll of the papers before him. Sir Drakely stroked his mustache to cover his smirk. And Mr. Shilbottle suffered a fit of coughing.

Wynter widened his eyes and raised his gaze to Stewart. "Is there a problem?"

In only a week Stewart would be fifty-seven, and he showed every day of his age. His thin, tall frame was stooped, his brown hair was thinning, and the tip of his nose drooped over his thin lips. Yet Wynter's earliest memory of his cousin was not really much different. Stewart had been born old. Still his eyes were kind, if exasperated, as he answered, "Not at all, cousin. Only that . . . it's difficult to give an arithmetic lesson right now. If you'd told me sooner . . ."

Wynter beamed at his board of directors and deliberately played the fool. "But you can tell me about the profits. That's all that really needs to concern me. And you can advise me on what is happening in the company. After all, isn't that what you're here for?"

Drakely glanced at Stewart's white knuckles and apparently decided someone needed to take action. "Yes, yes, of course that's what we're here for. It's just that your mother took a little more active interest in the

workings of the company and we thought that you . . .
And of course your father!"

Wynter asked, "Oh. Was he good at mathematics?"

Now Drakely was reduced to shock. "He was . . .
Lord Ruskin was . . ."

Shilbottle, a gentleman of about sixty with a face
that looked like wadded cotton wool, decided to step
in. "It was well-known Lord Ruskin could glance at a
row of figures and cipher them immediately. Why, his
lordship ran this company single-handedly. When I
first signed on as a coal carrier fifty-two years ago, he
knew everyone's name and function, and he was the
first man to recognize my potential and give me a
chance. Your father was a saint, boy."

"A saint." Wynter possessed very clear memories of
visiting the office with his wise and wicked father, and
he knew that it had taken death to elevate his father
to sainthood, and then only among those given to delusion. "I never heard my father called that before. But
while he might have closely supervised the company,
things have changed since his day."

"I'll say." Hodges patted the belly that protruded
below his silk waistcoat. "I signed on not long after
Lady Ruskin took up the reins. What a time that was.
She so lovely and grieving the loss of her husband and
son—you weren't dead, of course, but she was suffering anyway."

Everyone around the table took a moment to glare
at Wynter.

He stared back blandly and wondered which of his
mother's ardent proponents had taken advantage and
embezzled from her.

Taking up the tale, Hodges continued, "There were
a couple of rotters in the organization then, men who
would have willingly taken advantage of such a beau-

tiful lady, but your mother fooled them." He waggled his finger. "She's not as fluff-brain . . . er . . . she's not the fragile flower of womanhood she appears. Those cads never suspected a thing until they were dragged before the magistrate!"

The man was clearly in love with Adorna, and from the fond smiles all around, Wynter knew his mother held the others in thrall, too. Thank God for Adorna's ability to cloud men's minds with her charm; it was that which had saved the family fortune when he'd been a damn fool boy and run off to seek adventure.

Yet he wondered at these men; did it not occur to them *he* was not as fluff-brained as *he* appeared? Did they really believe his sojourn in Arabia had diminished his intelligence? It seemed all Englishmen imagined one had to attend Oxford, dress in black and breathe the air of Britain to understand the workings of business. Business, he could have informed them, varied not a whit anywhere in the world.

He said nothing. Let them discover the truth at their peril.

"My mother is indeed a gem sparkling with color and grace in the wastelands of the English desert."

The black-frocked gentlemen shifted uncomfortably in their seats, and Wynter barely restrained a grin. The English were so pedestrian in their language; all he had to do was speak with a slight lyric license and the men snorted like geldings about to bolt.

Poetry was a useful tool.

Also amusing in a man who found too little amusing about British society.

"But Lady Ruskin, of course, is willing to trust my judgment completely and encourages me to take up the reins without bridling me with unwanted guidance." Wynter stood. The others scrambled to their

feet. "Just as I trust your judgment. To give you gentlemen ease of mind, I'll take these books into my
office, but in thirty minutes I have a rendezvous with
an old friend. I really can't be bothered to examine
the accounts closely." Deliberately he pushed his hair
behind his ears, flashing his earring, and in the
shocked silence that fell, he left the room. He had not
gone far down the corridor toward his office when he
heard the burst of laughter, hastily smothered.

It seemed the English businessmen thought not only
his intellect, but also his hearing were deficient.
Reaching the luxurious office which had formerly
housed both his father and his mother, he shut the door
behind him. Taking the ledger to his desk, he sat down
and began to page through, totaling each column in
his mind—just as his father had taught him.

Dear Hannah and Pamela,

*Lady Ruskin has graciously allowed me the privilege
of posting a letter to you, my dearest friends and con-
fidantes, and so I am writing to let you know of the
events of the past three weeks.*

*First let me assuage your worry. I have not had
contact with any of the inhabitants of Porterbridge
Hall, and have in fact even avoided attending church
in Wesford Village on the pretext of waiting until the
children are ready to be presented. This is, of course,
the grossest cowardice on my part. My only excuse is
the thought of meeting those familiar, contemptuous
faces makes me writhe, and my punishment is that the
fear of meeting one of my cousins or my aunt or, God
forbid, my uncle hovers over me like a miasma. You
are the only ones to whom I can speak of these matters. In truth it is difficult for me to breathe the air of*

~~Surrey at all. I know it should not be, but here I find myself rebelling against the hopelessness and loneliness stretching before me where before I was resigned~~. *I assure you all will be well and you are not to worry.*

The situation when I arrived at Austinpark Manor was much as Lady Ruskin had informed us. The children have been given freedom far beyond the age when English children had been introduced to the classroom, and the smallest and most seemingly simple situation must be explained to them. For instance— I had to tell Robbie and Leila that the proper way to sit in a hard-backed chair was not to lay on the floor and put their heels in the seat. Leila explained it was possible to learn in that position.

Dear friends! I do not want you to think she spoke in an impertinent manner. These children are not impertinent. Indeed, they seemed to have an innate kindness toward others that made their courtesy automatic, and their curiosity and good humor make them a joy to teach. Yet in the matters of which fork to use, how low to bow, and most especially in the subtleties of conversation, they founder. It seems odd that the subjects which I have so seldom taught—mathematics, the sciences, language, geography—I now teach easily, but the one subject for which I am famous I continue to fail.

But I digress. I explained to the children that while they lolled on the floor facing the ceiling, they could not see the map or the long strip of paper with its carefully drawn letters or the slateboard where I conjugate French and Latin verbs. Robbie agreed they couldn't see with their feet, so now the children sit correctly in their chairs. Yes, my dears, I am challenged, but pleasurably so.

Much to my relief, since my arrival, their father has spent most of his time in London with Lady Ruskin. Ah, but you didn't know the father was alive, did you? Or perhaps I made an assumption which you did not. He is very much in existence. I report to him once a week and he is most thorough in his examination of me. He is also most fond of Robbie and Leila, eating breakfast with them whenever he is here. While I am pleased to have a parent who so embraces his children's development, I am at the same time frustrated with their behavior after they dine with him. Lord Ruskin, you see, is a consummate barbarian . . .

CHAPTER 6

CHARLOTTE FINISHED THE LATEST STORY IN *THE ARA‑bian Nights' Entertainments,* shut the book, and leaned back in her chair. "Did you enjoy that one as much as the others?"

She already knew the answer. Wynter's children sat at her feet, seeing the world as a place of excitement and anticipation, where anything was possible, even flying carpets and magic caves filled with treasure.

Although Charlotte knew she was making a mistake, she occasionally allowed herself to share their excitement.

Rising, she tucked her book into her carpetbag. "It's a beautiful day, and it would be good for you to encounter the experience of outdoor dining." She straightened the plain starched white collar and cuffs that decorated her blue serge gown, and as she hoped, they imitated her, standing and straightening their clothing. Robbie looked neat and clean in his black trousers and small jacket, but Leila . . . Charlotte suppressed a sigh. When Leila wore an outfit, she *wore* an outfit. Her skirt of pink dimity was wrinkled beyond repair, and she frowned at the ink smudge that decorated her right sleeve. But she brushed at her skirt and poked stands of her hair back into her braid.

When Leila had finished, Charlotte held out a hand
to each of them. "After we've eaten, we shall go for
our constitutional while you tell me about El Bahar."

That had become a routine. Everyday they walked.
Robbie practiced with his knife. Leila chased butter-
flies and tumbled in the grass. And the children shared
tales of their desert home. They enjoyed reminiscing
about the place they had left almost as much as they
enjoyed teaching their teacher. Charlotte found herself
fascinated by the visions of undulating sand, of camels
that spit and smelled of dung, of bones bleached by
the sun, by the sudden vision of an oasis and the realization it was only a mirage.

"The outdoor meal can be part of celebrations in
midsummer," she instructed as they walked down the
stairs and traversed the corridor. "When dining out-
doors, one must be aware that the rules of civility remain the same."

Leila heaved a sigh. "I don't want to talk about
manners. They're stupid."

"Manners are what separate the cultured from the
provincial," Charlotte chided.

"I thought culture was," Robbie said.

A deep chuckle sounded behind them. "He has you
there, Lady Miss Charlotte." Wynter stood in the doorway of the long gallery.

"Papa!" Leila launched herself at him.

He caught her in his arms and kissed the top of her
head, then swept an arm around Robbie and drew him
into his embrace. He smiled broadly, but Charlotte saw
previously unnoticed frown lines between his brows.
His feet were bare, his shirt was open and, without
collar or waistcoat, his hair looked as if he'd been

using his fingers to comb it, his scar sliced his cheek, and that earring . . .

Exotic. He looked exotic. That was the real reason why she avoided taking breakfast with Wynter and the children in the mornings. For her, he embodied all that was exotic, unattainable and desirable.

Hastily she averted her gaze. "My lord, how good to see you."

"You're not lookin' at him," Leila observed from her perch in his arms.

"That saying is just a courtesy." Charlotte thought that a reasonable explanation, but by now she should have known better. The children were literal—at least in the English language.

"Why would you say something that is not true?" Robbie asked.

"Yes, Lady Miss Charlotte, why would you?" Wynter echoed.

She knew he was laughing at her. At her, and at everything noble and honorable and British. Swiveling, she looked him right in the eyes and said, "Courtesy eases situations that might otherwise end in misunderstanding, hurt feelings and even bloodshed. I cannot believe that even in the far reaches of El Bahar courtesy is not observed."

"As usual, Lady Miss Charlotte, you are correct. The courtesies are very important in El Bahar, especially that courtesy which I find so lacking in England."

"What might that be?" she asked.

"Tolerance." Before she could think of a retort, he smiled on his children. "Fruit of my loins, what treat has your teacher planned for you?"

"Supper on the terrace." Leila took his head in her

hands and turned it so he looked at her. "Papa, please say you'll eat with us."

Wynter cupped Robbie's cheek in his palm. "I prayed you would ask. Does your governess acquiesce?"

As if she could reject her employer.

But that wasn't fair. He had done the polite thing. He had requested the lady's permission to join in their meal, and few employers considered the governess enough of a lady to consult her wishes. So Wynter had shown more courtesy than most men of his station. Despite his strange appearance.

It was just that . . . the thought of eating with him set her teeth on edge.

Wynter seemed to have too much. Too much self-assurance, too much comeliness, too much of that air that staked a claim on any available woman should he desire. Not that he had indicated any interest in her since that first day, and that had clearly been a test. But just as her vexation in finding herself in Surrey was always there on the periphery of her awareness, so was her irritation with him.

Like now, when he smiled at her quizzically. "Lady Miss Charlotte?"

"I'll go instruct the servants to set another place." She went at once toward the kitchen, setting her feet down firmly on the floor, a calm, professional, unshakable woman.

As she passed the library, she heard Adorna call her. "Lady Ruskin . . . Adorna . . . how good to see you back from London."

Adorna was shedding her traveling garments, her smile as fresh as ever. "It's a pleasure to be back. London is nothing but stews, gossip and parties." She hooked her arm through Charlotte's and strolled with her toward the kitchen. "A dreadful place. Do you miss it?"

"Not at all," Charlotte said.

"Because if you need more time to yourself, you need only ask. I understand you haven't even taken your half day off."

A faint groundswell of panic swept Charlotte. "These first months are vital to the children's sense of security and will build their trust in me. I cannot indulge myself in frivolous pursuits."

"I hardly think a half day every other week—"

"I have nowhere I wish to go," Charlotte said with finality.

Adorna nodded slowly. "I understand."

Worse luck, she probably did.

"I appreciate your care of Robbie and Leila," Adorna continued. "I find them a trial, I admit, yet I see only too clearly how difficult this transition must be to them. Their father and I must spend time in London until we have the business settled, and I . . . I am considering a licentious affair with Lord Bucknell."

Charlotte blinked, wondering if her ears had deceived her. "An . . . affair?"

"With Lord Bucknell." Adorna's husky voice still sounded as placid as if she discussed the weather. "I haven't ever had an affair, so it is a course to be wisely considered."

She seemed to be waiting for a reply, so Charlotte stammered, "I . . . yes, I imagine an affair should not be rashly entered into."

They entered the corridor that led to the kitchen, and one of the footmen came barreling through the door holding a silver tray stacked with napkins. Tall, young and gangly, he came to a halt at the sight of them and bowed.

Charlotte had never been so glad to see anyone in her life.

"Harris!" Adorna poked at the tray. "Where are you going with all those napkins?"

"The children are eating out on th' terrace, my lady, an' if I know me children, an' I do, one of them'll spill th' milk."

"No doubt you are right," Charlotte said. "It's kind of you to think of them."

"My son is going to take supper with the children and Miss Dalrumple, so another place must be set," Adorna said.

Harris bowed and backed toward the kitchen. "I'll take care o' it, m'lady."

And some imp Charlotte didn't know she contained made her say, "It would be no work for him to set two extra places."

Harris paused.

Adorna immediately laid the flat of her hand against her forehead. "I would love that, but my son and I just arrived from London, and I'm fatigued."

Charlotte relented at once. "A tray in your chamber, then."

"That would be lovely," Adorna said.

Harris nodded and backed toward the kitchen.

In a thoughtful tone, Adorna said, "Charlotte, you are not as guileless as you would have me think."

Charlotte didn't pretend not to know what she meant. "Forgive me, Adorna. I cannot imagine what spirit got into me."

"The spirit of mischief, of course. It is to be expected when one spends time with children."

As they walked back toward the terrace, a maid

paused in her rush to pass them while balancing another place setting on a tray. She curtsied toward Adorna, then turned toward the terrace. Another came past at a more dignified pace, holding her tray high and taking care not to tilt the meal that resided beneath the covers. She, too, curtsied, then turned toward the stairway and Adorna's bedchamber.

Adorna nodded at the girls, but continued her discourse in a matter-of-fact tone. "This affair I'm considering is a very adult activity."

The perambulations of her conversation left Charlotte blinking.

"Have you ever indulged in one?" Adorna asked.

"One . . . ?"

"Affair," Adorna said patiently.

Uneasily Charlotte wondered if Adorna was testing her or if, perhaps, she had fallen into some strange, weird dream. "No, ma'am."

As they came to the corridor that ran between the terrace and the stairs, Adorna frowned at her. "You don't approve."

"Lady Ruskin, it is not for me to approve or disapprove your actions."

"You're calling me by my title again. You *don't* approve."

"My lady. Adorna. Really, I would not presume—"

Adorna held up her hand. "That's fine. I will go to my lonely bedchamber and there eat my solitary meal." She turned and walked away.

And Charlotte, with no understanding how she had offended, hurried after her. "Please, ma'am, I didn't mean—"

Halting, Adorna took Charlotte's hand. "Dear, I'm storming off in a huff. It rather loses its impact if you go with me."

"I . . . yes, of course it would."

"Besides, you know that business about eating a solitary meal is bosh." She patted Charlotte's hand. "I really am weary. You go ahead to the terrace, and I'll see you tonight."

"Tonight?"

She fluttered her fingers and as she moved away, she uttered words that made Charlotte's blood run cold. "I think it's time you knew the real reason I brought you here, don't you?"

CHAPTER 7

As CHARLOTTE STEPPED ONTO THE TERRACE, A SOLI-tary Wynter leaned against the balustrade and watched her. "You must have been talking to my mother."

Still dazed by her encounter with Adorna, she stared at the man caressed by golden sunlight and wondered if he could read her thoughts. "How did you know?"

He smiled, and good heavens, what a smile it was. His chin came up, his lips swept wide, the angles of his face became curves, leaving Charlotte in no doubt of his amusement and enjoyment. The children frol-icked on the lawn. She should reprimand them for their shouts and their wildness, but Wynter's smile distracted her.

Pushing himself away from the railing, he went to the small, square, white iron table, set with four places, and pulled back the chair for her. "Mother tends to engender a sense of wonder." As she seated herself, he spoke close to her ear. "And you look wonderful."

His breath whispered across the nape of her neck, and he sounded so sincere that for a moment Charlotte struggled with her composure.

Dear heavens, returning to Surrey was proving more of a trial than she had anticipated. But she was a strong and scrupulous woman, and higher morals must prevail.

Someone should tell Wynter that. He still leaned forward, his hands resting one on each side of the back of her chair close against her shoulders, his clean scent surrounding her, and he was watching her profile. True, she couldn't see him as she stared straight ahead, but she felt that gaze on her skin and she knew, she just knew, he was still smiling. Laughing. At her.

Confident, handsome, odious man.

Yes, higher morals must prevail, and she was just the woman to tell him. In truth, she would even enjoy delivering the set-down. Turning toward him, she wasn't at all surprised to find his face far too close to her own. Yet she didn't back up, or in any way indicate how impressive—that is to say, *offensive*—she found his nearness. "My lord, I am the governess. I am here for your children's well-being. I hope you understand me when I say I have no interest in you or your smiles or your earring or your endless flirtatiousness." Having said more than she meant to, she snapped her mouth shut.

Had she just said that to her employer? Dear heavens. That was unacceptable.

His smile grew even broader. "The thing I like about you, Lady Miss Charlotte, is that you tell truth. That is a very rare quality among the English."

Automatically she said, "Englishmen always tell the truth."

He chuckled, a rumble of contagious mirth that deepened his dimples and crinkled the corners of his eyes. "You are as fresh as the morning dew on spring grass, as delightful as a shower after a long drought. But you are not so great a fool as to believe that."

She stared at him, caught by the faint accent that

might be growing on her. "No. I am not."

He pressed his palm against her spine right between her shoulder blades. "Can you tell when a man speaks truth?"

"I pride myself on the ability to weigh the likelihood that a man—or a woman, or a child—is lying to me." She wanted, needed, to inhale deeply . . . but he touched her, he looked right in her face, and she didn't want him to see her indulging a physical need. Any physical need. Slowly, cautiously, she calmly finished, "The possibilities, when taken with a thorough knowledge of certain involuntary actions performed by a perjurer, discern their falsehoods." The last three words came out in a rush.

He watched her carefully. "So you can tell if a man speaks truth," he prodded.

She allowed herself to sigh, hoping he would think her exasperated. "Yes. Yes, I can."

"Then you will know that I not lying when I say you are wonderful."

Not only did the breath freeze in her lungs, but every other vital body function ceased. It was an amazingly complete shutdown brought on by a warm, insistent hand, two brown, insistent eyes, and a coaxing, blinding, insistent smile. He was just so close and so . . . close.

"Lady Miss Charlotte?"

"Yes. Oh. Yes, my lord, if you believe that I . . ." She cleared her throat. "That is, if you think that I am . . . er . . ."

"Wonderful," he said peremptorily.

"Yes. Wonderful." She leaned forward, trying to escape his touch. Useless. His hand followed her, a warm entity against her rigid spine. She groped on the tablecloth. Her fingers encountered the folded linen napkin; something to do with her hands. With elaborate care, she pulled it from beneath the silverware and into her lap. "Yes, if that's what you think, I would not dream of calling you a . . . of saying you were anything less than truthful."

"Ah." Slowly his hand slid up to her shoulder. He cupped it and squeezed, a gentle pressure that surely seemed more like friendship than caprice, and again she experienced that dreadful, betraying breathlessness. "You are most gracious."

From out on the lawn, Leila shrieked, "Papa! Papa, is it time to eat yet?"

The elegant, menacing barbarian straightened and looked over the balustrade. "It's time," he bellowed back. "Come before my stomach thinks my throat's been cut."

Charlotte glared blindly at the white tablecloth, the four place settings, the goblets and the silver salt server. She didn't see them; somehow Wynter had emblazoned himself on her vision, as if he were the sun and she had been staring without consideration to her safety or her vision. The children clattered up the stairs, breathless and laughing. She turned her gaze toward them, but still she saw their father's image in Robbie's boyish features, in Leila's gamine grin. They slid into their chairs, one on either side of her, and stared at her guiltily.

Then Harris whipped out of the door with a basin of water and a cloth over his shoulder and knelt by Leila. "Let's clean ye up a bit before ye eat, young master and mistress."

Guilty. Of course. They'd gotten dirty.

She looked down into her lap and saw the napkin, crumpled as if she'd twisted it. Why should the children feel guilty when their governess retrieved her napkin even before they were seated? An unprecedented breakdown of civilized behavior! And—she shot a glare at the still-smiling Wynter as he assisted Harris—it was all *his* fault.

She took the first deep breath she'd taken since she'd stepped on the terrace, and that breath quivered with outrage.

Wynter heard her, for he looked her way, and without pausing in his scrubbing of Robbie's knuckles, said, "Lady Miss Charlotte, you are short of breath. You must loosen your corset strings."

Harris choked and turned a quivering crimson.

Charlotte stared straight at the man with her steeliest gaze.

Picking up the basin, he bowed, bowed again, and hastily vacated the terrace.

Matters did not soon improve.

Wynter seated himself across from her.

"Lady Miss Charlotte, why do you wear a corset?" Robbie asked.

Charlotte struggled between her desire to answer any question the children posed to her, and propriety. "A corset is a proper undergarment for a lady, but it is not proper conversation at the dinner table."

"Why not?" Leila asked.

Wynter leaned his elbow on the table, cupped his chin in his hand and stared at her. "Yes, Lady Miss Charlotte, why not?"

Charlotte could see the servants hovering by the door, waiting to serve the meal, but she would not signal them to come. Not yet. "Undergarments, both male and female, are not to be discussed with the opposite sex at any time, and"—she headed off Leila's inevitable question—"with the same sex only in moments of extreme privacy."

Leila smirked at Robbie. "Ha, ha, she's going to tell me about corsets and she's not going to tell you."

"That's not fair!" he said.

"That's *enough*."

The children quieted long enough for her to ring the bell at her elbow.

"Do not fret, my son," Wynter said. "To tell you about this feminine instrument of torture will be your father's privilege."

Charlotte wanted to snap at him, but she held her tongue as a skinny footman approached, staggering under the weight of the heavy tureen. How arduous to remain serene as a maid carried a plate of steaming crumpets and another the individually formed pats of butter. They placed the food on the table, bobbed their courtesies and raced away, in a hurry to return to the kitchen, where Charlotte knew, Harris was regaling everyone with the tale of her corset.

As she lifted the lid of the tureen, the steam wafted across the table and Wynter inhaled audibly. "Oxtail soup," he said. "I love oxtail soup."

The children imitated him, inhaling loudly and agreeing noisily.

Charlotte subdued a reprimand. She thought it difficult to tell your employer he was setting a bad example, especially when she'd already in essence reprimanded him for mentioning her . . . undergarments. She ladled the soup, a clear broth with noodles and a touch of sherry, into the bowls. "My lord, would you start the crumpets around the table?"

"I'll just give them one." With his fingers, he took a crumpet for each child and put it on their bread plate.

But that was not the end of his poor behavior. He would have reached across the table with Charlotte's crumpet, too, but she held up her hand in rejection.

"Thank you, my lord, but if you pass me the plate, I will take my own."

"Oo, Daddy, you made Lady Miss Charlotte angry," Leila said.

"Nonsense. Lady Miss Charlotte is far too much of a lady to be annoyed."

Leila kicked the leg of the table until Charlotte laid her hand on the child's leg and shook her head slightly. She reached for the soup spoon. She'd taught the children to watch her, and they, too, reached for their soup spoons. She lifted it and dipped it into the broth. They lifted theirs and dipped them into the broth.

And their father said, "I like to break up the crumpets and drop them in and let them soak up the stock."

The children stopped watching her and stared, round-eyed, as Wynter fit action to words.

"Can we do that?" Robbie ventured.

"Of course!" Wynter said. "We do not have to be formal when it is just family."

Did he challenge her on purpose? Or was he only lacking a sensible thought in his head? She didn't care. She only knew that he'd flirted with her, he'd unsettled her, and now he was making her already Herculean task of civilizing these children even more difficult. And she didn't know which sin bothered her most, but she did know it must end.

In her crispest upper-class accent, she said, "Actually, my lord, *I* am forced to disagree. Family manners have their place, but only when the people employing them are able to exercise company manners when necessary. Robbie and Leila are not yet able to do so, so until they know without a doubt which fork to use, we always practice our company manners."

Wynter leaned back and hooked one arm around the

finial of his chair. "You put too much value on company manners, Lady Miss Charlotte."

His lounging infuriated her yet more. "The value I place is no less than the value any other Englishperson of the aristocracy will place on them."

Like spectators at a lawn tennis tournament, the children whipped their heads to him.

"The aristocracy also takes itself too seriously."

"Be that as it may, this is the world which Robbie and Leila inhabit." Charlotte leaned forward and tapped the table with her finger. "It is an unforgiving one and, my lord, one which will already look on them harshly because of their unorthodox background. Any unmannerly behavior will be noted and mocked by their peers, and this I know, my lord—their peers can be cruel."

Now Wynter leaned forward, too, his eyes flashing. "I will not allow anyone to mock them!"

"How will you stop it? Beat up other little boys like your son? Invade a debutante's boudoir and forbid her laughter?"

"Papa, I don't like this England. Can't we go back home?"

Leila's quivering voice recalled Charlotte to her senses. No matter how incensed she was, she had no right to pass her fear to these innocent children. Despite her own experience.

Taking Leila's hand, she held it between her palms. "Sweetheart, you're going to be so unique, other girls will want to be you."

Leila sniffed and attempted a wobbling smile.

But Robbie frowned as forbiddingly as his father, and Wynter . . .

Wynter sat with his arms crossed over his chest, glowering at her. "This whole scene is your fault."

Prudently, Charlotte placed Leila's hand on the table and gave it a pat. "I may have spoken unwisely, but you, sir—"

"I am reasonable. I am logical." His accent grew as strong as she'd ever heard it. "*I* am a man."

Charlotte had to take a breath before she could trust herself not to raise her voice. "In my experience, gender has little to do with logic or reason."

"Your experience! You have been nowhere."

How cruel to disparage her for that! For the misfortunes that had made her life a dull and constant duty. "You're right, my lord. I bow to your wisdom. Tell us—how do men and women in other countries differ from the men and women in England?"

She thought he might try to mumble some nonsense about foreign women knowing their places, but instead he announced, "You are insolent, Lady Miss Charlotte."

He was wrong, he was immoderate and he was upsetting the children. And she, the lowly governess, was expected to bend to him. She would, of course. She always did, but heat blossomed on her chest and her face, and she knew her fair complexion had betrayed her fury. In as reasonable a voice as she could manage, she said, "I have been hired to teach these children, and you are obstructing me. Unless we can reach some compromise—"

"I do not compromise," he stated flatly.

"Ah." Without volition, she shoved back her chair and tossed her napkin on the table. "Then there is no reason for me to remain. I leave you to your supper. I wish you good fortune in finding a governess who suits your exacting standards."

And in a move that Lady Ruskin would have admired, she twirled on her heel and stalked away.

CHAPTER 8

CHARLOTTE MADE IT TO THE STAIRWAY BEFORE SHE stopped, hand on the carved newel post. How was she going to explain this scene to Hannah and Pamela? She had lost her temper, her common sense, her equanimity because of one man and his . . . his . . . surliness.

It was not his charm which had so shaken her.

Not that it mattered. No matter what the provocation, she had never created a spectacle before. And in front of the children! If Miss Priss behaved in such a bellicose manner, they could certainly be excused for thinking they could.

Except they couldn't. She had kept herself awake at night worrying how to successfully integrate these children into English society. Now she wouldn't be there to guide them, and she'd set a bad example. She had betrayed the trust the children had put in her.

More, how could she have forgotten herself so much as to quit her desperately needed employment? She had tarnished her own sterling reputation. She had lied to Adorna when she had guaranteed she would succeed. She had lost the hundred pounds paid to the

Governess School as a placement fee, putting her friends' venture in peril.

With one hand, she clasped the post until the sharp edges pressed into her palm. The other she used to pull her handkerchief from her sleeve and swipe at her damp eyes. She hated knowing she had been a fool for any reason, but to be foolish over a man! Ah, that was the greatest humiliation.

The door from the terrace slammed so hard the windows quivered, and Charlotte stuffed her handkerchief away. Heels clattered lightly, hurrying along the wooden floor. Leila. Or Robbie. The thought of either of the children seeing her in this state started her up the stairs with what she hoped was commendable dignity. She wanted no one to see her crying.

But Leila called, "Lady Miss Charlotte, come at once! You must come and see."

Charlotte didn't turn, but spoke over her shoulder. "I can't, Leila. I have to pack."

Leila never had use for subtlety, and certainly could not comprehend the need for it now. She raced up the stairs and grabbed Charlotte's hand. "You must come! Now!"

Charlotte glanced at the child clinging to her. Hope and anxiety lit that thin face, and Charlotte's chest tightened. She didn't want to leave Leila. Leila was like a vine that needed support and training to one day be the centerpiece of the garden, and Charlotte knew no other governess could ever be as sensitive to the girl's needs. She took a few steps down.

But she wouldn't yield to that ape Wynter's coercion. She stopped.

"Come on!" Leila maintained a steady pressure, and for a small child, she had a powerful tow. Charlotte trailed behind, arguing with herself. She didn't really want to quit, but how could she face Wynter? In the sunshine he could view her and know he'd made her cry.

The door loomed before her, the sunny terrace showed through the paned glass and Leila must have suspected Charlotte's renewed reluctance, for she said again in an excited voice, "Look!"

All right. Charlotte looked, then her chin raised defiantly.

There he sat, napkin in lap, chin jutting out, arms crossed across his chest, staring straight ahead. Impatiently, as if *she* were at fault, he demanded, "Well, Miss Dalrumple? Are you done running away, or are you going to stay and teach us?"

She ruffled up, belligerent and defensive, taking umbrage immediately. Then what he'd said caught her attention.

Teach us. *Us*. With that one word, he indicated he was willing to do as she instructed, and she didn't care if he pretended that scene was all her fault—any insult would be amply rewarded by having him under her domination.

And of course she would have employment, satisfy Adorna, save the Governess School and help the children. Those were the things that really mattered.

"Lady Miss Charlotte?" Leila said in a small voice.

A very serious-looking Robbie was holding her chair. She took a moment to smooth Leila's hair, then she seated herself with a smile. "Thank you, Robbie."

The servants that had been nowhere in sight a few moments ago appeared, and at her command removed the soup and brought a platter of cold, sliced roast beef surrounded by broiled mushroom caps, a basket of warm, yeasty-smelling finger rolls and a bowl of oat pudding. If anything, they bowed themselves away faster this time; if possible, the servants always disappeared when the master was glowering.

And Wynter *was* glowering. Obviously, and not surprisingly, it was up to Charlotte to act in an adult manner.

In her most civil tone, she said, "My lord, since we didn't know you would be dining with us, this is a plain supper, created with the children's immature digestion and haphazard handling of silverware in mind."

"I like plain food." Wynter sounded faintly sulky.

Leila whimpered. "Daddy, are you still mad?"

He glanced at his daughter and saw the tears in her eyes. With visible effort, he changed his manner. "Not at all! I was just telling Lady Miss Charlotte that I'm a simple man who has much missed plain English food."

Charlotte smiled at him, a mere stretching of the lips. "Of course, my lord, I knew that."

He smiled back with equal effort. "If you would, Lady Miss Charlotte, please pass me the roast beef."

The atmosphere was subdued as the plates were filled, and the children tried hard to handle the forks and knives without clattering them against the china. They didn't do well; too many years of eating with their fingers had left them inept. But they handled the utensils with more skill than they had a fortnight ago, and for the first time, they were trying—because their father was complying. His cooperation was all she needed. All she'd ever needed.

When everyone had started on the meal, Charlotte decided she should guide the children—and Wynter— a little further down the trail of etiquette. "At this point in our dinner party, you are allowed to make a personal comment, to tell something about yourself so the others can respond." She considered them impartially. "You may start, Leila."

A frown creased Leila's forehead. Then she brightened. Sounding as refined as Adorna herself, she said, "Nurse says the reason my bottom itches is because I sat in nettles."

Charlotte found herself unable to speak, choked by an instantaneous, inappropriate desire to laugh.

Robbie rose to the occasion. Perhaps because he saw nothing wrong with Leila's comment. Perhaps because he was curious. "Does it itch as much as sand?"

"Oo, yeah, a lot more." Leila rolled her eyes and rubbed at the affected part of her anatomy. "You can wash the sand out."

Charlotte didn't laugh. She would not laugh. But for one moment, her gaze met Wynter's and understanding passed between the two adults.

Smoothly, Wynter lobbed the conversational ball. "That's very interesting, Leila. I myself haven't sat in nettles since my youth. Nettles don't grow in El Bahar, Lady Miss Charlotte. The land is too arid for even those weeds."

With only the faintest tremor in her voice, Charlotte replied, "How fascinating, Lord Ruskin. You must have seen many different climates and vegetation on your travels."

"Indeed we did. Children, have you told your governess about our passage through the Mediterranean?"

His bright children caught on without any further guidance. In between bites, they chatted about the sights they had seen on their trip back home, what impressed them most about the English countryside and how much their lives had changed in the last months.

Then Robbie, as mature a boy of ten as Charlotte

had ever met, turned to Charlotte politely. "But we've been talking only about ourselves. What about you, Lady Miss Charlotte? Why aren't you married?"

Lulled by the enlightened conversation and Wynter's domesticated behavior, Charlotte again cast him a glance, expecting to meet his mirthful gaze. Instead she found him studying her with such somber concentration that she realized he wondered, too, and her amusement hastily faded. "If I were married, I wouldn't be able to teach you," she said. "It would be a shame if I didn't have this chance to get to know you. Now, shall we have our sweet?"

She signaled the servants, and they carried off the empty plates and brought a fancy jam tart with a section of apricot, raspberry and orange marmalade.

Leila sighed with anticipation and tucked her napkin up a little closer to her waist. "Can I have all the raspberry?"

"No," Robbie retorted. "I get part."

"Since your father is our guest, perhaps it would be mannerly to first ask him which he would like," Charlotte suggested.

The children's expressions varied from horrified to hopeful, and Charlotte held the knife hovering over the tart while she waited for Wynter to reveal the wisdom of Solomon.

"We shall all have a little of each," he decreed.

Charlotte began the torturous process of evenly dividing the much contested raspberry.

Leila said, "Maybe Lady Miss Charlotte has no male family to make a match for her."

Charlotte jerked and broke a little piece of crust off.

"Like Mama?" Robbie scratched his head, then at a reproving glance from Charlotte lowered his hand. In a tumble of words, he told Charlotte, "After my mama's father died, she didn't have anyone to make a match for her. If Papa hadn't wed her, she and her mother would have starved."

"That's very melodramatic, Robbie." Charlotte passed the tart to Wynter.

"No, it's not. It's true!" Robbie said. "Without a man, a woman is worthless."

Charlotte leveled a look on Robbie, one she'd perfected over the years to deal with insolent young men.

Robbie realized his mistake at once. "I didn't mean you were worthless, Lady Miss Charlotte, only that in other countries like El Bahar a woman can't . . . doesn't . . ." He gazed pleadingly at his father.

Wynter took pity on him. "In El Bahar, a woman cannot speak for herself in the councils of men, so if she is unwed and without a father or brother or any other kind of male relative, she is unable to make the match which would gain her a husband and financial safety."

Charlotte's mind sprang to her circumstances, to Hannah's, to Pamela's. They thought themselves ill-used in England, but . . . "That's cruel! They would really starve?"

"Not always," Wynter said. "Sometimes someone takes pity and takes them in."

As Wynter had. Charlotte eyed him with the beginnings of favor. She hadn't thought of him as an excessively compassionate man, but to marry a woman to save her life! That was surely admirable.

"Dara needed a man." Wynter applied himself to his tart. "I needed a woman in my tent to cook for me. It was a fair exchange."

Charlotte's charitable conviction faded.

Leila shot up out of her seat and leaned across the table. "I have an idea!" she shouted.

"A lady's voice is low, gentle, refined," Charlotte began.

Leila took no notice, and this time she not only shouted, but her voice rose an octave. "We can have a new mama. Papa can marry Lady Miss Charlotte!"

CHAPTER 9

"*P*UT THE SOFA HERE, AT AN ANGLE TO THE FIRE-place." Adorna stood with her hands against her hips, directing the footmen. "Place my chair here, and put the candelabra on the tables at either end of the sofa so I can see properly."

Since she'd reached the venerable age of forty, she'd noticed a blurring of her vision and found that good light helped her discern those telltale signs of discomfort or pleasure in her visitors. Each situation in her life she read by those signs.

She frowned as she thought of Lord Bucknell. He had proved a most vexing challenge, always there but insensible to her advances. But she would surely be equal to the game. The man hadn't been born who could long resist her.

"Place a decanter of brandy and one of ratafia on a table by my elbow." She approved the sparkling crystal with its golden liquids, then lifted one of the empty glasses, smudged with a fingerprint.

Without a word, she passed it to Miss Symes, who handed it to one of the footmen. "This is not accept-able in my lady's chamber!"

The footman rushed away, the glass clutched to his bosom.

The only times in her life Adorna ever had trouble was when she disregarded her instincts. She was in a bit of a pickle with the family business now, but as Aunt Jane was fond of saying, there was no rest for the wicked.

Of course, she usually said it about her husband, Uncle Ransom, and he invariably replied, "Then you must be very wicked, my love."

Adorna had done quite a good deed by getting them together, if she did say so herself.

The footman came back with another empty glass, which Miss Symes approved, and a plate of almond biscuits, which should put Wynter into an amenable frame of mind. Nothing so simple as food would work with Charlotte, of course. Men's bellies, conceits and organs controlled most of their reactions. Women were more subtle and less driven by the physical. Indeed, if Adorna guessed correctly, Charlotte had *never* been driven by the physical. So Adorna knew she would have to depend, in part, on liquor and its insidious effects. For the other part, Charlotte's rigid propriety surely couldn't resist the challenge Adorna would offer.

Miss Symes crossed her hands across her ample belly. "Will that be all, my lady?"

Adorna took a final check of the arrangements. "That will be all." She smiled at each of her servants in turn. "You have pleased me greatly."

Predictably the footmen blushed, even old Sanderford, who had served Adorna's husband long before she'd arrived. Miss Symes smiled back, an amiable tyrant.

"Oh, and Wynter will be wanting a cup of that coffee he so adores." Adorna made a face. She didn't understand why Wynter wouldn't indulge in the occasional spot of liquor. But wines and spirits held no interest for him. "Bring the coffee after he has arrived."

"As you wish, my lady," Miss Symes answered.

The servants bowed their way out, leaving Adorna alone. She seated herself, opened a book and placed it on her lap and waited for the two moths to arrive so she could entice them to circle her beckoning flame.

With most people there would be no problem; she could persuade almost anyone to do almost anything without them even knowing they had been maneuvered. But Wynter was her son, with a mix of her insight and his father's acumen, and she would have to tread carefully or he would balk.

And after this afternoon, Charlotte would be wary of being with Wynter. Miss Symes had given Adorna a report of the tumultuous tea. What was it Leila had shouted? *We can have a new mama. Papa can marry Lady Miss Charlotte!*

Adorna couldn't withhold a chuckle. Damn the child for being so forthright, but . . . how like her to shout out her desires as if volume would bring them to fruition! Of course the match was unsuitable. Getting Wynter accepted into English society would be difficult enough, but for him to wed a woman hampered by infamy . . . no. No, Charlotte would not do.

Thank goodness Charlotte had seemed appalled by the notion.

Yes, Leila had made Adorna's work more difficult, yet Adorna's plan made so much sense that it had to be implemented. Summer would come only too soon.

Charlotte arrived first, tapping softly at the door and entering in a smooth glide. Her attire was perfectly appropriate for the honor of taking refreshment with her employer. Her dark blue gown had been freshened by the judicious use of a sponge and an iron. She'd replaced her plain cuffs and collar with starched white lace, very expensive if rather old-fashioned, and her onyx cameo broach neatly pinned the collar together. It truly was a shame Charlotte's circumstances had stripped her of her rightful place in life. With her looks, grace and impeccable manners, she would have married well.

Adorna smiled in private amusement. Actually, Charlotte needed no more than her looks. Her ingrained reserve presented a challenge most men would be unable to resist.

"Sit down, my dear." Adorna indicated the sofa. "While we wait for my son, would you care for a drink?"

"No need to wait, Mother. I'm here."

Charlotte turned to face him, and came nose to chest with Wynter dressed in his desert costume.

Adorna had seen him wear it before, and in her honest opinion the outfit looked remarkably like bedsheets tied at the waist with three gold cords and a scarlet sash—symbols, he told her, of his rank in his tribe. However, she couldn't argue that the flowing white was more comfortable than an Englishman's rigid garb, or that Wynter shouldn't have the right to dress as he wished in his own home. Furthermore, the outfit admirably displayed his broad shoulders and allowed fascinating glimpses of his bare ankles and feet. Fascinating because Adorna suspected he was naked beneath those drapes.

Did Charlotte suspect that, too?

Wynter halted, placed his fists on his hips and glared forbiddingly at the governess, daring her to make a comment. "Is something wrong, Lady Miss Charlotte?"

Charlotte held her ground while barely controlling a flinch. "Not at all, my lord. I was just admiring your costume. I have heard about them, of course, but never seen one. A djellaba, is it not?"

Wynter touched his fingertips to his lips and in his deep, accented voice said, "You are, as ever, as wise as a crone of the tribe."

For a brief moment, Charlotte seemed caught unawares. Then she recovered herself to say, "You're very kind, sir."

Adorna repressed a giggle. Most women would have aimed a kick at his head. Charlotte assumed he meant it as a compliment. And perhaps he did, but . . . no. No, Wynter couldn't be exaggerating his ineptitude. What would such a tactic gain him?

Charlotte glided to the sofa and seated herself.

Wynter strode to the liquors. "Mother?"

His terse one-word inquiry broke the stillness, and Adorna artfully filled the quiet with a burble of random thoughts. "I want a brandy. Of course, ladies never drink brandy, or at least not in public, but the journey today was long, and Wynter has been laboring at the business. Haven't you, Wynter? While I have been hard at work trying to discover what rumors have been floating about in society about his return. As you can imagine, Charlotte, since their visit here his friends' wives have not been resting. With so many juicy bits of gossip, they have been spreading the story that Wynter is an ignorant lout. La, the cheek of those women! So a brandy will be very comforting. Would you like one, also, Charlotte?"

Charlotte hesitated, torn between the propriety of asking for a lady's drink and setting Adorna at ease with her unladylike choice of spirits. It proved no contest. "A brandy, please."

A slight smile played around Wynter's mouth as he poured a good amount of the golden liquid into two snifters and presented them with a bow to each lady. Then he sprawled on the opposite end of the sofa from Charlotte. There was space between them for another body, yet the odious boy took as much room as he could. He spread his legs, flung one arm across the carved back so his fingertips lingered close by Charlotte's shoulder, and he turned to face her, considering her without any seeming conscience.

Charlotte returned the favor, watching him out of the corner of her eye as she took a sip of the brandy—and shuddered.

"Dreadful stuff, isn't it, Lady Miss Charlotte?" Wynter drawled. "Yet your Englishmen make it a point to overindulge at every chance."

Charlotte took another, larger sip, and Adorna realized the two had reached a stage of combat, fighting in silence with raised chins and stern demeanors.

"Wynter, your coffee will be here at any moment," she interposed hurriedly. "You both must be wondering why I asked you to attend me tonight."

That got their attention. Both gazes focused on her, razor-sharp and vigilant.

"When I hired you, Charlotte, I confess I did not divulge my total intentions. The children do need to be trained in courtesy, but with them we have time." After a single sip, Adorna placed her snifter on the table by her elbow. "As I'm sure you realize, it is Wynter who is facing society every day, and who needs guidance."

Comprehension slammed into Wynter. So that was his mother's plan. He had known she was cooking something up, but this . . . Anger rose in him.

From Charlotte's open dismay he deduced she knew nothing of his mother's scheme. In matter of fact, she stared at him as if he were a tiger crouched for the kill. He allowed himself the pleasure of frightening her yet further by watching her with unfeigned hunger.

She looked away, her gesture as unconfined as her voice was calm. Taking another sip of brandy, she said, "While I certainly understand your concern for Lord Ruskin's conduct, I believe I'm unsuited for the job. Why not hire a tutor for him?"

Charlotte's ready agreement that he needed instruction raised Wynter's ire higher yet.

"Can you imagine any man being willing to place himself under the tutelage of another man?" Adorna replied. "It would never work."

"It works with boys," Charlotte argued.

"But Wynter is a man. Look at the way he responds when Lord Bucknell suggests the least improvement!"

Bucknell. Wynter snorted. Proper, pompous old geezer.

"You see?" Adorna gestured toward her son. "Gentlemen do not snort."

Wynter snorted again.

"There are a great many masculine places I have never visited—the clubs, the racetrack, even the dining room after dinner." Charlotte seemed to be swallowing the brandy very easily now, and color rode high on her cheeks. "How can I successfully instruct him?"

His mother was convincing her, Wynter thought, for her voice was faintly pleading. How did he feel about that? To have Charlotte telling him what to do and how to do it? It had taken a great swallowing of pride to have her brought back to the terrace today, and if not for his children's sorrowful faces he would never have given in.

"You've been around him enough, Charlotte, to know it's not truly his manners that are the problem." Adorna must have seen something in Charlotte's demeanor that indicated disbelief, for she added, "Oh, there are a few things that could do with correction. But he grew up in England. He remembers the basics."

"If that were the case"—Charlotte turned her cool gaze on him—"his endless impertinence would be nothing but a boy's grab for attention and rather than a governess he would need discipline."

"Or perhaps"—Wynter spoke through bared teeth—"he would need someone who could successfully explain to him the reason for the constant and silly posturing demanded by noble English society."

Adorna interrupted before they could fling any more insults at each other. "Charlotte, dear! You must realize it's the subtleties he's not grasping. How to wear his clothes—"

"Uncomfortably," Wynter interjected.

"—what to say and when to say it. He is far too—"

"Honest," Wynter interrupted again.

"—open in his appreciations and his dislikes." Adorna glared at him.

"I have just started making progress with the children. To take time away from them now would cause irreparable harm," Charlotte said firmly.

Ah, Charlotte. If she only knew how irresistable she was making herself to him! Her dimpled chin and softly rounded cheeks belonged to a woman of tender character, but her cool gaze and staunch independence renounced such spineless attributes. Yet when she spoke of his children, she couldn't hide the truth. His children were not duties to Charlotte, but treasures to be cherished. Did she realize how attractive her kindness made her?

No, she couldn't, or she would bury those characteristics deep inside and never allow him a glimpse. In fact, that must be what she had done on her previous posts or she would not be here for the plucking.

"I have kept him away from entertainments for fear of what he would say, but soon he must go out into the *ton*! The gossip has started and unless we take action soon, irreparable damage will be done. But what more damage can he do by telling a young lady who is flirting with him that she should return to her father for guidance? Or by pointing out the absurdity of whist? Or by scolding a lord for overworking his kitchen help?" Adorna gave a delicate shudder.

Wynter stared at the appalled ladies with wide, innocent eyes. This began to grow amusing. As he struggled with the proof of past embezzling within the business, he could use some amusement. The amount that had been embezzled, he'd discovered, was not enough to cause harm to the prosperity of Ruskin Shipping. But still, until he found the culprit, he couldn't rest easy.

And his mother was right. He *could* learn from Charlotte without resentment, for she cheered him with her endless tact, the seriousness with which she presented society's foibles, and that dimple in her soundly upraised chin. "I go into the city every day now. Any lessons would have to take place after the children were in bed."

Adorna flashed him an approving glance—well, of course she would, she had handled him—but addressed Charlotte. "Which sounds as if we've doubled your duties, and in a way we have, but we would allow you an extra half day off a week and raise your salary."

The high color left Charlotte's cheeks. She looked down to veil her thoughts, and she visibly struggled with temptation. Money meant much to a woman who made her way alone in this world. Wynter comprehended that very well.

In her husky, persuasive voice, Adorna said, "Charlotte, dear, this was why I came to the Governess School, to find someone like you for Wynter. As merchants, we are on probation with good society anyway."

How that irritated him! That constant insistence that people who worked were less valued than those who were idle, and those of ancient lineage were sacred, regardless of their worth. If his Bedouins had thought so, he would be nothing but bleached bones buried in the sand—but he supposed he couldn't expect the aristocratic English to display a tenth of the intelligence of a man of the desert. A man who earned his place by his wiles, his strength and his will to live.

Adorna drew breath, then continued, "If he sustains his present course, not even my good connections can save him from utter ostracization—and that will harm the children's future."

"Unfair," Charlotte murmured.

She meant the use of the children as a persuader, but Adorna pretended not to understand. "It is unfair, but it's true. And it's not as if you'll be teaching him forever. Only until the Sereminian reception has come and gone."

Charlotte caressed the rim of the snifter. Such graceful fingers, Wynter mused. Thin and well-kept, with a plain gold band on one index finger. A keepsake from a lover? He spoke his first thought. "Where did you get the ring, Lady Miss Charlotte?"

Even his mother was taken aback by the seemingly random question. "Wynter, don't change the subject."

"No, it's quite all right. This was my mother's wedding ring." Charlotte smoothed it with a fingertip. "I didn't steal it, if that is your suggestion."

Shocked, he said, "No! Thievery is not your way."

"If you truly believe that," Charlotte said, "then perhaps in the future you might refrain from interjecting a personal question in such an accusatory tone."

Gravely, he nodded. "You are right, Lady Miss Charlotte."

Adorna giggled with delight. "See? I know this will work. Oh, please, Charlotte, if you don't have a care for my name, please think of England's reputation. We mustn't fail to present our best foot forward to the Sereminian delegation!"

"I doubt if the Sereminian delegation will comprehend the complexities of English society any better than Wynter does." But Charlotte had obviously weakened.

Adorna added the final fillip to Charlotte's banquet of dismay. "Queen Victoria will be our guest along with the Sereminians."

Charlotte's fingers tightened in her lap. "Her Majesty? Here?" She gazed on Wynter in open consternation. She looked at his bare feet, the legs protruding from beneath his djellaba, his untidy sprawl. "With him?"

Solemnly, he bowed his head—and wiggled his toes. "I am sure I would impress the queen with my forthright manner, for she is surely wise and strong."

"No," Charlotte blurted. "Her Majesty wouldn't be impressed. Very well, Adorna, I will try, but only in the evenings, and . . . and I wish my salary to double during these months."

"Double?" Adorna, ever the businesswoman, looked taken aback.

But Wynter gave one quick nod of the head.

"Double, then." Adorna gave in with a brilliant smile.

Charlotte drained her glass, then stood. She listed slightly to the right, and Wynter put out his hand to steady her. But she shook him off. "If that's all, then I will retire to my chambers."

"That's all," Adorna confirmed.

Moving with the immense dignity of the tipsy, Charlotte made her way out of the room, still holding the glass. Mother and son watched her go.

"Dear me," Adorna commented when she was gone. "It would seem Charlotte has little tolerance for brandy."

"It would seem not." Wynter leaned toward at his wily parent. "Perhaps in the future we should limit her consumption."

"Yes . . ." Adorna picked up her own glass and sipped. "Unless we need to convince her of something more."

"Someone should make sure she finds her way to her bedchamber."

Adorna picked up the bell. "I'll call Miss Symes."

He stopped her with a gesture. "Let me take care of this matter. I want to clarify to Miss Priss what her duties are in regards to me."

Adorna smiled at him coaxingly. "Now, Wynter, you're not really upset with me for my little ruse, are you?"

"Mother, you are full of little ruses. This one scarcely surprises me." But Wynter was his mother's son. He would accept Adorna's scheme because it would conceal so well his own rapidly forming plan— a difficult endeavor, given his mother's remarkable intuition. But he had something most people did not. He had experience in fooling Adorna. It had been a necessary skill in his boyhood. "I'll cooperate, but she needs to know her place."

He saw Adorna's ire visibly rise, and her blue eyes snapped. "It is just that kind of statement that makes it necessary to engage a governess for you."

"I don't know why." He stood and bowed. "I must catch my new teacher. Good night, Mother."

CHAPTER 10

*W*YNTER LEFT HIS INDOLENCE AT ADORNA'S DOOR. HE knew where Charlotte's bedchamber was; this afternoon after their tiff he'd made it his business to know. If he hurried, he could net her in the portrait gallery, which was large, dim and exactly suited to his strategy. Catching a glimpse of her skirt ahead of him in the corridor, he slowed down and took care that his bare feet made no sound. He didn't need to apprehend her yet. The gallery was around the next corner.

He'd never before met a woman willing to quit her livelihood for a principle. He had never met a woman so dedicated to that which she believed right. He'd never met a woman who gave him such a pain in the bum.

He'd never met a woman he wanted so much.

He could see her moving through alternating bands of light and dark as she glided past each wall sconce in a stately progress. She gave an impression of serenity, yet beneath her facade of composure lurked a lady of passion.

She didn't know it. She didn't comprehend the tension that shivered between them like a winter mist, and that in itself intrigued him. A woman of her age couldn't be completely untouched . . . could she?

She rounded the corner toward the portrait gallery, and again he picked up his pace.

He never thought of her without wondering how she would look deprived of the gowns of blue and misty gray she so favored. The petticoats would have to go, also, and the corset she insisted on wearing despite his assurance she did not require it.

How long would it take him to melt that spine, to ease her backward on the cushions, to uncover her breasts and to kiss his way down her stomach and between her legs? What tactics would he have to use to ease her trepidation, to make her forget her ever-present manners and her inbred constraint? Would she fight him? Try to freeze him? Chide him?

Yes. Charlotte would try to combat primitive urges with civilized behavior. After all, he himself had tried to do just that while in the desert.

It hadn't worked. Domestication could never win out over savage instinct.

Rounding the corner, he entered the portrait gallery. Although the far door was directly opposite, he could see only the outline through the shadow and across the distance. But he knew the room; it hadn't changed since his childhood. Chairs clustered in groups around the few tables. Small, seldom-used guest chambers hid behind closed doors. The walls of the long chamber rose out of sight in a gloom candles could not ease. On one side velvet curtains of a rich crimson covered the tall windows. On the other, pictures of men on horses, of ladies posed with their children, of landscapes foreign and familiar covered the wall from floor to ceiling. There was even a portrait of the youthful Wynter with his spaniel.

If one were sensitive, one might grow uncomfortable under the scrutiny of so many watching eyes.

Charlotte glided along unperturbed.

Until Wynter got close. Then somehow she sensed his presence and whirled to face him, hands up in ready defense.

He stopped at once, taking care not to approach too close too quickly. He didn't want to alarm her—yet. "Lady Miss Charlotte." He bowed. "I have sought after you."

She placed her palm to her chest as if to contain her heart. He liked to think because she thrilled to see him, but he considered it more likely he had frightened her.

Sounding faintly breathless and looking annoyed, she asked, "My lord, what assistance can I render you?"

If he told her the truth, she would chide him. "I thought it would be good if we discussed our plans without the restrictive presence of my mother."

"Our plans?" Charlotte sounded alarmed.

"Where we should meet, how much we should do, how late we should remain together . . ." Faced with her wide-eyed horror, he had to relent. "For the lessons in English manners which you will give me."

"Oh!" She glanced around at the paintings that lined the walls as if they could speak and get her out of this predicament. "I knew what you meant."

Offering his arm, he said, "Shall we walk?"

Obviously, she didn't want to place her hand on his arm, but what could she do? Be rude and say *no*? He'd discovered just that afternoon that maneuvering Charlotte required only a subtle mind and the judicious application of courtesy.

She stepped just close enough for her ungloved fingers to flit onto his sleeve.

"Your hand settles as lightly as a butterfly." He

pressed his hand over hers. "And like a butterfly, you are shy and unaware of the jeweled beauty of your femininity." Before she even absorbed the compliment, he started pacing along the wall. "I want to meet in the old nursery. Do you know where that is?"

"Um." She cleared her throat delicately, and again like a butterfly, her fingers fluttered beneath his. "On the third floor?"

"The second. It was my nursery when I was a child. The furniture has been removed, which I find much more to my taste than the overrigged chambers of modern society. Chairs, sofas and tables enough so a man can't move without banging his shins! Drapes and tassels in every conceivable color! And every surface covered with gewgaws." He slid a glance toward Charlotte.

With her eyes downcast and her hair pinned up, she might have been the perfect lady. Except she was smiling.

He pounced on that. "Ah. You agree with me!"

"I myself prefer a plainer style than is currently fashionable." That she admitted anything about her preferences told him she was indeed under the influence of the brandy. "But I don't allow myself to be caught in a criticism of anyone's taste."

It almost seemed a shame to take advantage of her intoxication. Almost. "Nor do I. I would share my thoughts only with one such as you, whom I know to be compatible."

She stiffened again, overreacting to the mere suggestion of their affinity. Yes, good. She was far too aware of him and unable to hide her discomfort. Just as he was far too aware of her, and the sight and scent of her brought an ache to his groin. Because he had

been too long without a woman, yes. But also because
. . . she was Charlotte.

"Is that not the right word—'compatible'?" he
asked in feigned misgiving. "I meant only that you
and I think in a like manner."

"You most certainly used the word correctly." She
gave assurance easily. "I don't know that I would
agree."

"But you must!" he protested. "You believe that the
education of my children is the most important task
facing this household."

"Absolutely."

"So do I." The portraits moved slowly past as he
led her along the gallery. "For that reason only did I
ask you to remain when you humiliated me today."

She tugged at her hand. "You didn't ask me to remain, and I did not humiliate you."

"I agreed to lessons which must be given after a
long day in London and a punishing ride home."

"My day is long, too."

"I promised to pay you many pounds when already
you receive lodging and food while under my care."

Coming to a halt, she jerked her hand violently
enough to pull it from beneath his. "I am not under
your care. I am an independent woman."

He stopped, too, and faced her. "And I did not yell
when my daughter demanded I marry you."

He couldn't tell in the dim light, but he thought she
blushed. "That was not my fault!"

"You did not tell her to intercede on your behalf?"

"I beg your pardon, sir." She placed her hands on
her waist and glared at him balefully. "I most certainly
did not!"

He took one long step toward her. His legs pressed
against her skirt, and he held himself very tall, very

imposing. "Are you sure you did not tell her?"

"Am I sure? Of course I'm sure." Then her gaze ran over him, taking in his height, his breadth, his foreign clothing and his stern expression. She swallowed. "How could I forget making such a suggestion?"

He allowed his face to droop. "That saddens me."

"Wha . . . what?"

He had her full attention now. "At my daughter's cradle, the eldest of the tribe lifted her and laughed, and prophesied Leila would be wise and strong, gifted in matters of the heart, and she would bring luck to her family and honor to her husband. I had hoped that Leila heard what your heart could only dream."

"What?"

"This is not so?" He pressed closer yet.

Charlotte took a step back toward the wall. "I never . . . she never . . . such a thought never crossed my mind." She added hastily, "Or my heart."

"You will think on it now."

"It would be better if I didn't."

"I would like you to."

She so didn't want to ask. If she could, she would have turned tail and scurried away. But the wall was behind her, he stood before her and she had had enough to drink to doubt her ability to escape but not enough to comprehend the very real danger she faced. "Why?" She voiced the single word tentatively.

With the dint of good acting, he managed to look shocked. "I do not think you would do well as my mistress!"

Her horror was not in the least bit feigned, nor was it flattering, but he now knew she was aware of him in a physical sense. Her eyes were big and dismayed, and she kept her gaze fixed on him without blinking, as if vigilance would help her out of this disconcerting situation. Her nostrils quivered as she breathed in his scent—a scent he knew to be clean and masculine since *he* bathed every day, something no English dandy did. And his voice he took care to keep at a low hypnotic rumble, for he'd found it possible to say almost anything as long as he said it in a soothing tone.

"I wouldn't . . . dream of . . . doing something so . . . improper," she said haltingly.

"Exactly." He beamed. "I'm glad you agree with me. So you will think about all these things."

"No. I . . . no." Putting her hand out to the side, she touched the chair rail and used it as a guide as she sidled away.

"Lady Miss Charlotte, before you go . . ." He extended his hand, palm up.

She looked at it, then at him. Once again he had discarded the facade of the foreign simpleton, and allowed himself the freedom to demand. More, she understood that demand, and she feared the results if she refused.

With halting uneasiness, she placed her hand in his. He wrapped his fingers around hers and held them, feeling the warmth, the delicacy, the pure femininity of her slender digits and the fine-grained skin. He was used to women with calluses from hard daily work, women who labored alongside their men to scratch an existence from the desert. He admired those women. He had thought English ladies would benefit from such a dose of reality, and he had never thought to understand why any man would want a useless woman.

But when he held Charlotte's hand, he wanted to preserve its softness. He wanted to lift Charlotte above her struggle to survive. He wanted to give her the life she was meant to live—one of ease and pleasure. Much, much pleasure.

She was changing his thinking, and he didn't like that. Yet he had learned one thing in the desert. Sometimes destiny held him in its grip. He could fight this attraction. He could keep his thinking. But then he could not have Charlotte. And she he would have.

What was Charlotte thinking as she stared at their clasped hands? Did she want him to provide for her? Did she imagine her life as his wife?

Or was she a woman caught in the turmoil of confusion?

No matter. He had done what he wished. She would think of him in a new way now.

Lifting her hand to his mouth, he kissed it, a slow, tender kiss pressed into the palm. Carefully, he folded her fingers over the kiss, and released his grip.

She looked at her hand as if, should she decide to open her fingers, his kiss would fly away. She lifted her gaze to his in bewilderment, and when he smiled mildly, she seemed to come to her senses. She walked away—perhaps a little more quickly than usual. Perhaps with a little less steadiness.

But he was pleased to see she hid her hand in the fullness of her skirts. He knew why. She still held his kiss.

CHAPTER 11

THE NEXT EVENING, CHARLOTTE STILL NURSED A SLIGHT headache as she walked toward the old nursery. In the future, Adorna could drink her brandy alone, for Charlotte was convinced she would not be making this journey to meet Wynter if she'd had her wits about her.

Tutor a grown man, indeed! And a man such as Wynter, especially. What could Charlotte do with him? There was more to becoming a civilized man than knowing when to wear gloves.

How to wear shoes, for instance. Resolutely she turned her mind away from the memory of his arched feet.

Or not to sneak up on young women as they walked darkened corridors. And certainly not to make personal comments about becoming a man's mistress. Or his wife.

His wife! Charlotte fought a compulsion to snort just as Wynter had done. *Leila* had the excuse of ignorance when proposing marriage between her father and her governess. *Wynter* had only the excuse of lechery.

Oh, yes. It had taken some thought, but Charlotte

understood his nefarious plan. This extraordinary man didn't want marriage. He wanted the same thing every other gentleman thought he could get from any halfway attractive woman living under his roof.

Well, he wasn't getting anything from Lady Charlotte Dalrumple. She had already proved to everyone she would not sell herself. A shame Wynter didn't know the story.

A shame? She shook herself. She didn't ever want him to know her story. He was so uncouth he would question her, and she tried never to talk about that painful episode.

Uncouth. Yes. Lady Ruskin didn't realize what truly separated a gentleman from a chimney sweep. It was demeanor. Wynter had the wrong demeanor. He acted as if, given a battalion of men, he could conquer the world. Such arrogance was bound to grate on those Englishmen who had no experience with wild seas and golden deserts and fierce fighting warriors.

Stopping for a moment, she leaned her hand against the wall and fought her nonsensical tendency to romanticize Wynter's adventures. Obviously, she'd been reading too many adventure stories to the children. In truth, the sight of Wynter in his djellaba fueled her imagination. The garb was improper to the extreme, of course. Loose and free, without the constraints of enlightened nations' costumes.

When at first she'd seen the djellaba, she had been stunned, unable to form a coherent thought. After that initial jolt, she'd found her mind wandering. How would it feel to be shed of her corset? To have only material flowing over her body? After that, it had been a short step down the slippery road of sin, for she'd speculated on what undergarments one would wear under the garb. And when she'd looked at Wynter, she'd thought . . . well, never mind what she'd thought. Such a vision could only be explained as the fever produced by strong spirits.

No, no more brandy for her.

Straightening her shoulders, she again moved toward the old nursery where she had been instructed to meet Wynter.

She knocked lightly, and when no one answered she poked her head inside. The large, airy chamber was empty and dim except for an island of light by the fireplace. There flames crackled on the hearth and candles flickered on a long, low table. A clean white cloth draped it, some square cushions were strewn about in brightly colored stacks and wool blankets were folded nearby. Beneath the sparse furnishings rested a carpet glowing with gold, green and scarlet tangled into an intricate design.

But no lordly figure lounged about, challenging her with his insolence, so she called, "Lord Ruskin?"

From behind an almost closed door in the back wall, his voice replied, "Welcome, Lady Miss Charlotte." He said her name warmly, each syllable lovingly wrapped in the faintest of accents. "Come into my humble abode and grace it with your most exquisite presence."

His tone made her forget that she was a lowly governess and he was a viscount and her employer. She instead became mindful of her femininity and his admiration, and knowing such awareness was dangerous only made it all the more attractive.

This man could seduce her if she was not wary. "My lord, if, as I suspect, these are your personal apartments, it is improper for me to be alone with you here."

"My personal apartments? This is the old nursery!"

His amazement was faint but definite. "I will be only a minute. Be comfortable."

"Humph." She didn't quite believe him, but she felt she had made her point—that she was no fool, and she didn't wish to be alone with him.

Now, how to make herself comfortable in a room with no chairs? She contented herself with wandering toward the table, so low it came no higher than her knees, and examining the tray containing a loaf of bread, a small round of cheese and a bowl overflowing with purple grapes. There were no eating utensils, she noted, nor any place to sit, and she wondered uneasily if her suspicions about Wynter's intentions would prove true.

She could smell the scent of spring wafting up from the fruit. Leaning down, she inhaled, taking in the fresh smell rising from the clusters and, beneath that, the homey odor of bread.

The sound of Wynter's voice made her straighten hastily. "Please, Lady Miss Charlotte, take some."

He stood in the doorway, the light shining from behind him, and to her relief he was dressed in a proper gentleman's garb—except for his feet, which were bare. "No, thank you, my lord, I've already partaken in supper."

"Take, take, take! I cannot eat so many grapes or I will have wind."

She almost strangled herself trying to subdue her gasp of horror—or her spurt of laughter. Under Wynter's influence, she could no longer tell the difference. To give herself a moment, she broke off a grape and popped it in her mouth. It was sweet, wonderfully fresh, and full of seeds, and in the time she spent discreetly removing seeds from her mouth, he had taken the momentum.

Like a force of nature, he swept into the room. He wore his black waistcoat, black trousers and white shirt, and one should have been able, if one ignored the bare feet, to see him as an ordinary nobleman. But the shirt was open at the neck, revealing the slightest hint of curling hair, his thighs bulged with muscle and she couldn't ignore those feet. She just couldn't.

He stepped into the circle of light and took his usual stance, feet apart, fists clenched at his waist, chin tilted at an imperious angle. "So. We begin."

Hastily, she tossed the seeds into the fire and composed herself. "Indeed we do. I wish to say that, although I didn't want to take on the task of polishing you to fit society's setting, I will do my best to—"

"Yes, yes, I know that. You are a woman who always does her best. That is not a matter which bears discussion. Now, what should we do first?"

She was annoyed that he'd interrupted her well-thought-out speech of welcome, but maintained a placid demeanor. "Of a certainty, the first thing we should discuss is your penchant for discussing personal matters."

He cocked his head. "Personal matters? I should not discuss my children?"

"No, personal matters as they relate to your body. We don't mention . . . your internal workings, at least not in mixed company." She waited while he thought about her euphemism.

Light broke over his face. "Ah! I should not speak of my wind."

"Most definitely not your . . . no. And no discussions of illness or physical discomfort."

"But the *proper* ladies and gentlemen ask me how I am."

She ignored the faint hint of sarcasm. "A rhetorical

question only. When someone asks how you are, the correct reply is, "I feel well, thank you, and you?"

"That explains why most of the ladies no longer greet me by questioning my health." Striding to the low table, he seated himself on a large cushion.

Her heart sank. Exactly as she feared. He was showing her his barbarian ways, perhaps to tease her, perhaps as a protest against the tutoring which he had not sought. Certainly not because he thought it would attract her to see a man loafing about on the floor.

"May I inquire about the health of the ladies?" he asked.

"Only in the most general way." He faced her, his back to the fire and his legs crossed loosely at the ankles, and he looked very at home on his cushion, not at all recalcitrant. Perhaps, she admitted, this was nothing more than a man relaxing after a hard day at the desk.

He plucked at his lower lip. "Lady Scott recently gave birth, and I asked about her new son."

"Perfectly acceptable."

"And about her labor."

Charlotte closed her eyes briefly in pain. "Women seldom discuss such details between themselves, much less with a gentleman."

He nodded. "In El Bahar, the women speak of such things, but the men do not."

At last! A moment of concord, however brief. "There, you see, even in El Bahar the same rules apply."

"But I'm interested!" He protested like a little boy.

"Your interest should not supersede custom and protocol."

"In El Bahar, a man's interest supersedes all other practice."

Because he was spoiled like a little boy.

"You will say I am not in El Bahar any longer, and here protocol rules all." Much as she had, he sniffed the bread and grapes. Noticing she had edged outside the circle of light, he said, "I beg your permission to eat, Lady Miss Charlotte, for I have not yet dined."

"Of course, my lord. It's late. You must be hungry."

"As hungry as a camel seeking a date palm." At her expression, he reconsidered his more colorful language. "Yes, I am hungry." He gestured over the table. "You would do me honor if you would join me. You are too thin, although the lushness of your breasts brings to mind an oasis abounding with date palms and sweet libations."

She was shocked and . . . she was shocked. "You must not say such things!"

"Only to you, Lady Miss Charlotte. Most women are not so thin. But if you will not eat, then sit."

Dithering was not an activity in which Charlotte normally indulged, but she couldn't bring herself to explain to Wynter that her breasts were not a fit topic of conversation. Her breasts, or any other woman's breasts, although she couldn't rid herself of the notion that somehow he should know that. Still, he looked so unruffled. Later, when they were no longer speaking of *her* body parts, she would find a way to suggest he not mention such intimate topics.

"Please sit," he snapped. "I cannot learn if you tower over me."

Obviously, he wasn't thinking of her in any amorous context. Although what his purpose had been the night before in the portrait gallery, she still could not decipher. But then, she seldom understood men. "I could bring in a chair . . ."

"Still you would tower. I bid you to come here because I am weary, and here I can be alone. Cannot an Englishwoman find comfort on a cushion?"

"Not easily," she said wryly, but she couldn't explain to Wynter the trouble three stiff petticoats presented to a woman seeking to lower herself to the floor. As she placed one wide, flat pillow on top of another, she turned aside to hide a suddenly irrepressible smile. In many ways, Wynter was a man untouched by society's hypocrisy, and she had to wonder how the sophisticated ladies and gentlemen reacted to his observations. She would almost have paid to see the look on Lady Scott's face when he asked about her labor.

But by the time she turned back to Wynter, she had her facial expression under control.

He frowned at her hemline, although what he could see there she didn't know. "You have removed your shoes, of course."

"Removed my . . . ?" She barely refrained from calling him a barbarian. "No, I haven't removed my shoes!"

"But you tell me to do what is proper at all times."

"That does not include—"

"Lady Miss Charlotte, this is my sanctuary. I brought this carpet and these cushions back from El Bahar as a precious remembrance of my days there. I have no way of replacing them, and I shudder to think that someday they will be worn out and threadbare, leaving me no tokens of the home I found so precious."

His soft, rich voice spoke both lyrically and reproachfully. She couldn't rid herself of the suspicion he was manipulating her, yet . . . well, she knew he had loved El Bahar, and she surmised he missed it. If these were indeed his only momentoes, he was surely within his rights to ask that she do what she could to preserve the vivid weave.

But to take off her shoes . . . she stared at him for a full minute, waiting to see if he was jesting.

He was not.

"Very well, my lord"—she spaced the words precisely—"when I am seated, I will remove my footware."

"As always, you honor me with your courtesy."

If he were laughing about his victory, he hid it well, for she could not perceive even a twinkle in his eyes, and she thought she might make herself mad seeking mockery in his every word. Wisely, she let the matter drop.

The earthy, roasted odor of coffee reached her, she noted the ceramic pot placed close to the flames. "Would you like me to pour you a cup?"

He paused in the act of peeling the rind from the cheese. "Will you join me in that, at least?"

"If you'd like." She dragged her stack of velvet cushions close to the table, then brought the pot and the two cups, comfortably warm from the fire. It took a few moments of arranging her skirts before she was able to gracefully sink, and the cushions, when she reached them, gave more than she expected. She was almost seated on the floor, with Wynter across the narrow table. Not directly across—she sat near the end while he sat in the middle—but only a few feet separated them. She didn't know how to arrange her legs. Straight out? Feet flat on the floor and knees raised and pressed together? At last she decided her skirts provided ample camouflage, and she sat as he sat— with her ankles crossed and her knees wide. When at last she had settled, she found he observed her with fascination.

He said softly, "You make a performance of such a simple act."

It almost sounded as if he were chiding her, as if she should know how to sit on a cushion, to loll on the floor in absolute relaxation as he did. But she hadn't sat on the floor since she was twelve, and she didn't miss the freedom of rolling about, or listening as her mother read her a story, or just lying there looking at the ceiling and dreaming.

"And your footware?" he prompted.

She leaned forward and, without showing so much as a hint of stocking, unlaced her ankle-height shoes and slipped them off.

He watched as she placed the worn black shoes off to the side of her cushion, and with his hand on his chest over his heart, said, "My thanks to you, Lady Miss Charlotte."

Torn between annoyance at him and the pleasure she felt at ridding herself of the pinching leather, she could only smile tightly. With a steady hand, she poured the coffee into dainty cups and presented him with his. "I trust your day in London went well."

He sliced the cheese cleanly and efficiently with a knife of the type she'd given Robbie, except the blade was longer, curved, and the honed edge glittered in the light. "London spreads across ancient land, land that sings of its history and its royalty. The palaces and the churches rise in splendor, each different, yet each proud of its place in the city. The docks and tenements rot and smell, a decaying underbelly that roils with deceit." Picking up the cheese, he examined the marbled veins and said matter-of-factly, "London is a city that reflects its people."

When he spoke, it was almost poetry and much too

much truth—two sins the *ton* would not easily forgive. She hated to chide him, but . . .

When she hesitated, he chuckled. "Of course. I forgot. The question is for appearances only, for empty conversation with no content or depth. The correct answer is, 'My day went well, Lady Miss Charlotte. How was your day?' "

"Very well, thank you," she began, but she couldn't ignore his observations without answering them. "My lord, conversation is an art, one that allows two people to meet and in the slow dance of words become acquaintances and then, if one is lucky, to become friends. One surely does not wish to bare one's soul to every passing visitor, unless one wishes to have the precious secrets of one's soul distributed about to provide amusement to the spiteful."

He paused in the act of tearing the bread with his fingers, and she thought he would comment on her earnest and revealing remark. However, he only said, "As always, you are ever wise. It pleases me to hear your day went well. If you would be so kind, could you tell me how my children are progressing?"

She smiled at him, sure that this conversation, at least, was without pitfalls. "Your children are a joy to teach, my lord. Both are much advanced for their ages in mathematics, and their ability to pick up languages is nothing less than astonishing. They are rapidly learning the sciences, elocution, penmanship, sketching, and Robbie is progressing rapidly in his reading."

Wynter had been smiling much as any man who heard his children praised would smile, but now he sobered. "And Leila? Is she not progressing rapidly in reading?"

Reluctantly, Charlotte shook her head. "Leila will not read."

"You mean she cannot learn."

"I mean she will not try." Charlotte hated to discuss her own inadequacies, but in all fairness she thought she must. "I blame myself, my lord. I am not as experienced at dealing with younger children as other governesses may be, and I don't know why Leila crosses her arms and refuses, or how to coax her into wanting to learn. I have pointed out to her that when she can read, a whole new world will open up to her."

"She likes to hear you read." Wynter took a bite of the bread and a sip of coffee.

"Yes, the children and I have particularly enjoyed *The Arabian Nights' Entertainments*. I've told her that when she can read, she will not need to wait for me to know the stories. She can read to herself. But she is adamant."

His eyes gleamed as if he knew something she didn't.

"What is it, my lord? Is there something about Leila I should know?"

He smiled and shook his head. "Leila will read when the time is right."

Worry still pulled at Charlotte's brow, and he reached across the table. Startled, she leaned away. With his hand still outstretched, he stared at her reprovingly until she relented and sat forward again.

Then he smoothed the lines of her forehead with his thumb. "You must not worry. Before your arrival, my concern was that a governess would hem the children in with restrictions and lessons, slap their hands when they were naughty and despise them for their heritage. You think I do not see, Charlotte, but I have observed you with my children, and listened to their praise for you, and I thank you for guiding them into these strange ways with such skill and grace."

She let him stroke her forehead and temples because

she thought he didn't know such affection was frowned upon. She let his words stroke her pride because . . . well, she needed to hear his praise. Always before, her competence had been taken for granted. Now, when she worried her competence had failed to serve those who she most wished to help, Wynter reassured her.

Silence enfolded the old nursery. The flames crackled as they consumed the wood. Night pressed in at the bare windows, crept along the hardwood floor, played with the fringe of the carpet. The flickering candles cast a cape of light around the two figures seated, staring at each other intently. His fingertips slid down her cheek, over her nose, brushed the tips of her eyelashes as if the planes of her features brought him pleasure. And she found herself fascinated by the rough calluses on his skin and how his touch ruffled and soothed at the same time.

Then he removed his hand and settled back, and Charlotte found she could draw a much-needed breath. He drew such heretical reactions from her, she might have believed him to be a necromancer such as lived in the Arabian Nights. But Lady Charlotte Dalrumple didn't believe in necromancers.

"You haven't touched your coffee," he said. "Probably you drink it sweet."

"No, I don't drink . . . I don't require sugar." His brows lifted in disbelief, so she lifted the cup and took a sip.

Vile stuff. Burned and bitter, more different from its aromatic scent than any beverage had the right to be. She gritted her teeth and swallowed, barely restraining a shudder.

His intent concentration changed to amusement. "Lady Miss Charlotte, you do not like coffee."

It would do her no good to lie. Not unless she learned to dissemble better. "Well . . . no."

"You do not like brandy, either."

"Most definitely not."

"Yet you drink with me to set me at my ease, and drink with my mother to support her in her rebellion. I think you are too kind, Lady Miss Charlotte."

Right now she didn't feel kind. She felt bedazzled at being alone with a man she had suspected of base intent, yet who displayed nothing more than a sincere, if foreign, courtesy.

He'd touched her, yes, but not salaciously. Wynter made her uncomfortably aware that too many restrictions and too little hope bound her to her plebeian existence.

"I fear few people would agree with you, my lord," she said.

"I do not seek agreement among dilettantes and fools. I have eyes to see." He tapped his forehead. "A mind to think. And I think as I wish, not as others would have me do."

In that moment, she realized she *liked* Wynter. Liked his forthright manner, his informality, and most of all his assurance. If not for the Sereminian reception, he might never have made the effort to fit into society, for he was satisfied with himself and all he had accomplished in his life.

She was alarmed, for she knew it to be a dangerous thing, this liking of a man.

He pushed her cup away from her. "Tomorrow night, I will arrange to have tea for you. Now, Lady Miss Charlotte, I must ask you whether it is permissible for me to carry my father's old card case with the castle top. It was fashionable in its day, but as I move through the drawing rooms in London, I have noticed people eyeing it askance."

As Charlotte began in earnest to teach Wynter, in another part of the house the newest scullery maid sidled toward her bedchamber on the third floor. Normally Frances went to bed with everyone else, when the housekeeper carried a candelabra to light their way down the corridor that housed all the maids. But Trev James, the finest lad Frances had ever seen, had enticed her to visit him in the stable, and now she found herself returning to her dark room down a dark corridor. She could make out the contours of the hallway, but strain as she might, she could see nothing more.

All kinds of horrors flitted through her impressionable fifteen-year-old mind. She'd heard the stories. She knew old houses were rife with ghoulies and ghosties, and this manor was older than her granny, and her granny remembered the mad King George. Not the one who came before Queen Victoria, God save her, but the one even before that.

A board creaked beneath Frances's foot. She jumped, clutching her apron and swearing she would never again view Trev with longing, no matter how sweetly he smiled.

Who knew what crimes had been committed here, and what ghosts walked the hallways looking for peace or vengeance? Certainly not a quaking scullery maid newly come from her granny's cottage. And for the last few nights as she'd lain in her bed, she'd heard sounds from above. Spooky sounds, like hushed footsteps. Once, there had even been the clatter of something as it hit the floor. Something that sounded like metal, like the chains forged in hell for the damned.

Putting her back against the wall, she crept along,

counting the doorways as she passed. Her bedchamber was the last one on the right, just before the corridor took a crook and headed toward the access to the fourth-floor attics.

Frances had been in the attics. First good day in the spring, Miss Symes had marched an army of housemaids and serving boys up to clean out six months' accumulation of dust. The big attic wasn't bad, with windowed dormers that let in the light, but smaller attics tumbled off in every direction, and some were barely more than closets. It had given Frances the shivers to crawl inside and sweep them out.

Now she wished her bedchamber was closer to Miss Symes's. No ghost—or mouse, for that matter—would dare disturb the formidable housekeeper.

With only one door to go, Frances had almost reached her goal, when she heard a long, thin creak, like hinges on a door. She froze, barely breathing, hoping she was wrong, that her hearing had fooled her. But no—ahead she saw a dim light from beyond the crook in the corridor, almost as if someone, or some *thing,* had opened the attic door.

Faintly she heard a scuffling, then a heavy sigh as once again the hinges creaked.

As she told the bevy of wide-eyed maids the next day, her hair stood on end from ear to ear. She slid back one step, then another, her gaze fixed on the dark square where the corridor turned. The light was growing stronger, and Frances could hear the slight patter of feet.

It was someone playing a joke. Or someone hiding in the attic to avoid Miss Symes and her everlasting beeswax. Or—

Something rounded the corner. Something short in

a white flowing gown, holding a candle close to its hideous face.

Frances screamed at the top of her lungs. Screamed again, then turned and raced down the corridor as tinderboxes clattered, doors opened and the ghostly figure scampered out of sight.

CHAPTER 12

*T*O REFRESH HER MEMORY ABOUT THE EVENING'S LES-
sons, Charlotte flipped open the notebook filled with
her rules for gentlemen. "Ah, yes." She settled deeper
into the mound of cushions placed before the fire, trying to make herself as comfortable being proper as
Wynter looked lolling about on the carpet. "Tonight,
we'll discuss the conduct of the gentleman in the city."

Wynter grunted, stuffed a pillow under his armpit
and leaned his head on his hand.

She dug her stockinged toes into the carpet. "A gentleman always walks between a lady and the street, for
in that way he imposes his body between her and any
runaway horses."

"What if I don't like her?"

She kept her gaze fixed on her book and pretended
not to notice how close his bare foot came to the stocking that peeked from beneath her skirt. Was he at last
trying to take advantage of their isolation?

Not that he could. Or that she would let him. But it
was a puzzle. During the past week he had seldom
even given the appearance of listening to her lectures,
much less desiring her. He ate, he lounged about, he
fixed the fire and trimmed the candles. Yet she found

no reason for complaint, for when she quizzed him on his duties as an English gentleman, he always answered correctly. The suspicions he had aroused in the picture gallery had slipped away, to be replaced by . . . well, a sense of flatness.

Tonight was different. He watched her without appearing to, he moved closer under the guise of restlessness. He was argumentative.

"I don't understand your question, my lord."

"You say, Lady Miss Charlotte, that I should impose my body between a lady and a runaway horse, but such an endeavor seems fraught with danger. The lady must be very special to me before I would risk my life for her."

Why she imagined any of this signaled an interest in her, she couldn't understand. Perhaps it was because his behavior caused a similar rebellion in her own self. Tonight, when she occasionally allowed herself a glance at him, the flickering of the candles illuminated a man of solid build. Tonight she noted he had left off his waistcoat as well as his shoes, his stockings, his necktie, his cuffs and collar . . . the man was wearing virtually nothing but his trousers and his shirt, hanging white, wrinkled and loose. And of course he wore his undergarments. Surely he did. "A true gentleman will risk his life for any lady."

"How many true gentlemen are there in this country of England, Lady Miss Charlotte?"

She lifted her head at last, because she had to, because she couldn't avoid looking directly at him any longer. She had to glare at the impious man, and she did *not* contemplate his undergarments or lack thereof. "A true gentleman would not even think about his own jeopardy, but would show courage and fearlessness even unto his own death."

"Me, I would think first." He scratched his neck. "Maybe push the lady out of the way instead of imposing my body in front of the rampaging horse."

With a jolt, she realized he was laughing at her. He wasn't hooting like a lad, just pointing out the absurdity of the ideal. Very well. Probably he was right. Probably there were no gentlemen alive who would imperil themselves for a chivalric model, but she didn't have to admit it. Determined to regain control, she made a point of leafing through her book. "Pushing her out of the way is acceptable, also. The other reason a gentleman walks between the street and a lady is it's likely to be cleaner against the building."

"Yes, the maids are always throwing stinking slops out of the upper windows in your London." He flopped flat on his back, stared at the ceiling and threaded his fingers together across his stomach. "Must a gentleman impose his body between a lady and *that,* too?"

Right now she rather hoped the slops would hit him straight on, so she gathered her book to her chest and half rose. "I sense this is a bad night for a lesson, my lord. Perhaps we should postpone until tomorrow evening."

Rolling to his side, he slapped the carpet with the flat of his hand. "No! Tonight!"

She jumped. For a moment, in the firelight, he looked fierce, savage, not at all the torpid pasha she had come to expect but the desert warrior she had imagined. By Lady Ruskin's demeanor, Charlotte had judged that all was not well in the city, but whether in their business or socially, Charlotte couldn't begin to imagine. If it was the business, Charlotte could do nothing. But socially . . . With a delicacy she could not help but be proud of, she asked, "Is there some etiquette query I could help you with?"

"Etiquette. Does no one in this godforsaken society think of anything else? The ladies, they say I do not know etiquette, but I say they do not know manners."

It would seem Charlotte had found the source of his disturbance. "What are the ladies doing?"

"They are spreading rumors around London, false rumors, that I am a ruffian."

Charlotte grew indignant on her pupil's behalf. "That is indeed a false rumor, my lord! You are not conversant with all forms of etiquette, but you are not a ruffian!" Or perhaps. But only a little bit.

"Lady Howard and Mrs. Morant are wicked."

"Soon your etiquette will be the envy of all the wicked ladies in London."

"Etiquette! Even you! Do you think of nothing else? Every night we talk about me." He tapped his chest with his forefinger. "What I should say and how to say it. How high to tip my hat and when. To make morning calls in the afternoon, and what I must wear on every occasion. By the dunes, you have stuffed more rules into my head that the desert skies have stars!"

"That was Lady Ruskin's desire."

"I respect my mother. I adore my mother. But her desires are her own. So now—we will talk about you."

"Indeed we shall not, sir. I am a governess, not an entertainer. You have already approved me as a fit teacher and companion to your children, and as you just said, I am more than capable of helping you freshen your manners. That is all you need to know about me."

He reared back with every appearance of astonishment. "You do not wish to tell me about yourself?"

"I do not wish," she said firmly.

"But women always like to talk about themselves."

Nothing irritated her as much as these sweeping generalizations men, even the most civilized of men, were prone to make. "I don't know what women you have been associating with, my lord, but most women never get the chance to speak because of the constant and self-important conversation of men."

"I do not like these sweeping generalizations women make about men."

Had he plucked the thought from her head?

He demanded, "Have I told you anything about myself?"

"Very little," she admitted grudgingly.

"But perhaps this is what you wish. You wish to think me a barbarian, stupid and uncaring." His free hand played with the fringe on his cushion, and he watched her ceaselessly. "It is easier than getting to know me for who I am."

"I assure you that is not true."

"I will tell you now." He sat straight up, and when she would have interrupted, he pointed his finger at her admonishingly. "You will listen."

She didn't want to listen. She didn't want to raise the level of their intimacy, not when she had already conjectured seduction from ridicule. "We have much more ground to cover, my lord"—she showed him the pages held between finger and thumb—"and very little time until the Sereminian reception. If you don't wish to discuss life in the city, perhaps we could discuss horses and hunting. That would be more to your taste, I believe."

He ignored her as regally as a potentate from *The Arabian Nights' Entertainments.* "You've heard the gossip behind my escape to El Bahar."

"I believe you left after your father's death."

"You have been curious about me?" He sounded rather pleased. "You needn't be ashamed, Lady Miss Charlotte. I am also curious about you."

This familiarity is what came of conversing when she should be teaching. She bent her head to her book and read the first heading aloud. " 'A Gentleman in the Hunt.' "

"You do not wish to talk about you. Very well. When my father died, I was fifteen, and his passing caused me much pain."

She quoted, " 'A gentleman picks his steed for endurance and speed, and trains to jump with him until both move as one.' "

"My father had always been older than other fathers, but he shook off every illness. I thought he was indestructible."

She lost her place on the page. Or rather—the words before her eyes no longer made sense. "One does think that about one's parents."

"So your father also sings with the angels?" She shook her head, and he leaped to his next conclusion. "Or your mother?"

"The hunt," she said desperately.

"I comprehend. Both sit on the right hand of God."

Wynter spoke so gently, she found herself admitting, "Both are gone."

"Never truly gone." He blessed her with a beatific smile.

She didn't trust him when he looked so guileless, and she waited tensely to tell him again she would not confess her own story.

"Lady Miss Charlotte, I have told you before. You should leave off your corset."

Taken by surprise, she glanced down at herself. The

whalebones were sticking her, but nothing of that showed.

"As you have left off your shoes at my command. Look at you," he scolded. "All stretched up tight on those comfortable cushions. If you left off your corset, you would perhaps smile and not look as if you have a bellyache."

She closed her eyes in mortification. "I'm sorry if my countenance displeases you, my lord, but as your governess I must warn you not to use the word 'corset.' "

"Yes, yes. You told me this already."

"Not 'bellyache,' either."

He nodded. "As I do not mention my wind."

"That is correct."

"And your countenance is most pleasing to me."

She pounced on that. "Please don't speak without reserve to your governess about her looks." Tapping her notebook, she added meaningfully, "Or any body parts which might attract your attention. In fact, even when one finds a lady one wishes to compliment, one mentions one's approval only in the most general manner. One never mentions the specifics."

"In public. I know this. In the privacy of my dwelling, I do as I wish."

"I believe we are meeting here for its neutrality," Charlotte retorted.

" 'Neutrality,' " he mused. "That is a strange word to use between us."

That stopped her. She didn't want to spar with him, nor did she yearn to explore the meaning behind his strange manner. With innate caution, she said, "We have the same goal, so I don't believe we're enemies."

"I do not know what we are, Lady Miss Charlotte. I suspect we will discover that soon enough."

CHAPTER 13

"BUT YOU WERE CURIOUS ABOUT MY PAST," WYNTER said.

She was not curious, and what in the world did he mean, *I don't know what we are . . . I suspect we'll discover that soon enough*? What kind of comment was that?

Wrapping his arm around his knee, he looked out the dark window into his past. "After my father's funeral, I left here on a mail coach for London. A freighter out of Marseilles bobbed on the Thames, and I imagined myself Jason seeking the Golden Fleece." Briefly he dropped his head into his hands and laughed. "I signed on as a hand. I spent a week spewing my guts into first the Atlantic, then the Mediterranean. I scrubbed decks until the blisters on my palms burst. And do you know, I had never eaten weevils in my bread before?"

The sound she made was composed partly of compassion, partly of nausea.

"Yes, dreadful! Made worse by the fact that the other sailors were French, coarse and tough. They called me a milksop and made me miserable. When I went on my quest, I never imagined I would suffer *tribulation*. In those days, I was given to great dramatics, but I flatter myself I was not a fool. I'd led a life of privilege, and I quickly realized that." Wynter lost the twinkle he'd had when describing his younger self. Soberly, he said, "Worse, I had failed my first test as a gentleman."

She didn't mean to, but the question just popped out. "How so?"

"At the very time my mother needed me most, I thought only of myself."

Charlotte wanted to plug her ears. If he continued in this wry and self-deprecating vein, she might come to like him!

"Even the boy I was knew that running away would not bring my father back. In fact it would have disappointed the man I had worshipped. But I used his death to do what I wanted. To seek adventure."

Go back to being a barbarian, she wanted to urge him. *Go back to being appalling and rude. Stop this attractive candidness so I can again become a proper governess with no interest in my employer.*

Especially not this kind of interest. Her gaze slid unbidden down his lounging form. No, never this kind of interest.

"I imagined an odyssey. I got catastrophe. I resolved to run back to England as soon as the ship put into port." He grimaced. "And I would have, too, except . . ."

He paused, and she capitulated. "Except?"

"Except for the pirates." He sat up, his eyes dark and dramatic. "They loomed out of the night and rammed the ship. They forced me to help them steal the cargo and then took me when they left. I was a pretty boy."

"Yes, I remember," she murmured.

Instantly diverted, he inquired, "Had we met?"

She had almost betrayed something of her past, the past she would keep private. "I saw your portrait in the gallery."

"Ah . . . yes."

He didn't look as if he quite believed her, so she said, "Please, my lord, what about the pirates?"

"The pirates. They planned to sell me in the market in Alexandria. I ruined that scheme when I cleaned a knife and cut a gash down my cheek."

She stared in fascination as he traced the scar on his face. "I could never be so brave."

"You? Yes, Lady Miss Charlotte. You would be so brave." Getting up on his knees, he leaned toward her and stared intently. "You would do whatever was needed to save your honor, I know it."

She wasn't so sure. "But you, my lord. What happened to you?"

"The pirates vowed revenge." He came to his feet and raised his fist. "I had cheated them out of a great fortune, so they sold me instead to a Bedouin as . . . his camel keeper."

He dropped his fist and spoke so drolly, she had to smile.

"I was to take care of five disgusting, smelly, spitting camels. What a blow to a rich English lad who come seeking adventure. The old man Barakah and I—and the camels—started off across the desert. The second day out, I ran away."

She leaned forward to catch every word. "My lord, I have read that the desert is an unforgiving place."

Shaking his head at his youthful folly, he said, "You have read correctly, Lady Miss Charlotte. The heat in the daytime . . . you cannot imagine. The sun beating down, the sweat drying on my brow even as it formed,

the sand rippling on forever and ever, each dune the
same as the next, the same as the one before it." He
cupped his hand over his eyes and pretended to look
all around. "I thought I knew how to get back to the
harbor, but I was lost, hopelessly lost, when—" He
seemed to run out of breath, and he sprawled on his
stomach on the carpet. "But Charlotte, I have spoken
of myself for too long, and this you have taught me
is not gentlemanly behavior."

"Don't be silly. You can't stop now!" The moment
she heard those words out of her mouth, she knew he'd
cozened her. She also knew she didn't care. She had
to know the end of his tale.

Propping his chin on his fists, he looked up at her.
"Have you no relatives left to care for you, Charlotte?"

Charlotte. He was calling her Charlotte. Not that
pretty sobriquet which indicated respect, but her first
name. That could bespeak intimacy or insolence. Neither was acceptable. Clenching her fist atop of her
book, she stared at the strained white knuckles. Her
reserve and her caution ran deep. "I have no family
who matters. Please, my lord, what happened to you?"

"No attachments whatsoever?"

"Friends. Good friends."

"No lovers?"

Oh, he sounded innocent, but she knew better. He
was as innocent as the snake in the Garden of Eden.
He even slithered on the ground like a snake. Gathering up her book and her shoes, she stood. She
walked around his reclining form toward the door.
Away from the warmth of the fire, the scent of melting
beeswax and the deceit, the deviousness and indolence
that was Wynter, Lord Ruskin.

Just as she reached the threshold, he said, "I was
almost dead when the old Bedouin found me."

Charlotte slid her stockinged feet along the hard-wood floor.

"Actually, the most revered Barakah had never lost me," Wynter said. "He had just followed me through the desert until I rid myself of the notion I could escape on my own. Then he retrieved me."

She shouldn't turn back. Her every suspicion about Lord Ruskin had just been proved true.

"He tied me that night to the camel's saddle and told me he had done me a favor, for the desert lets no one depart unscathed."

She had no illusions about Wynter. If she didn't listen now, he would never speak of his history again. He was ruthless in getting his way.

She was not. She capitulated, all her restraint done in by curiosity. "What happened next, my lord?"

"I entered the Bedouin camp. Do you know much about the Bedouins, Lady Miss Charlotte?"

His ploy to snoop into her life had failed, so he returned to the formality of her title. He also sounded mildly curious, as if it were quite normal to carry on a conversation with a woman who stood in the doorway with her back to him.

"The children have told me of their lives," she said.

"Then you know the Bedouins are proud wanderers and fearless warriors. They travel the caravan routes across the Sahara, carrying goods from one port to another, and in that way they make their fortune." He seemed to notice nothing amiss about her behavior. "A goodly fortune it is, too, and there were others who coveted our route and our wealth. Barakah was the chief of his tribe, a princely ancient with an instinct for finding his way after a sandstorm had obliterated all markings. He also had an instinct for taming rebellious slaves and rearing them to be worthy men."

She leaned her shoulder against the doorframe, then rolled around to face Wynter. The wall supported her, which she thought was good, for obviously she lacked upright moral fiber.

He wasn't even looking at her. He had made a mound of all the cushions—all except hers, which were still stacked and waiting for her return—and he had crawled into the midst of them. He faced the fire, and she could just see the top of his raised head.

Funny, but she still thought he knew she was yielding. Inch by inch, and reluctantly, but yielding nonetheless. She crept forward, placing her book and her shoes at the edge of the carpet.

"By the time we had traveled the whole caravan route, I had a few whip marks on my back, I knew how to saddle a reluctant camel and I was the old man's devoted son."

"Son?" she exclaimed.

"I saved his life. Remind me, Charlotte, to show you the mark of the knife I took for him."

Charlotte surrendered completely. She walked around the cushions and knelt in front of Wynter like a concubine begging a favor from her reclining lord. "You were hurt?"

"I almost died. But when I recovered—I was a man." The firelight played on him lovingly, seeking the cornsilk of his hair, smoothing the golden brown of his skin. Moving with a slow, steady fluidity, he sat up and eased his shirt over his head.

Charlotte saw the brown of his skin and his blond body hair extended all the way to the edge of his trousers. All except in one place over his heart. There, a scar glowed with a pale sheen. He hadn't exaggerated to make his story more dramatic or to make himself sound courageous. The knife had sliced deep and long, and she found her hand hovering over the scar, attracted by the proof of his pain as she had not been by the arrogance he had gained from it.

The prudence of a lifetime seized her. She started to withdraw, but he caught her wrist and carried it to his chest. Beneath her fingertips his skin was warm. The scar was smooth and unyielding. And beyond that . . . He released her wrist.

She leaned toward him, touching him now because she had to. The hair on his chest was nothing like the smooth shining mass on his head. Each strand was stiff with stubborn curl, and invited the comb of her fingers. Beneath the hair his muscles bulged, delineating his strength. His chest rose and fell slowly with his breath as her palm stroked up toward his collarbone, then circled his throat, or as much of his throat as her small hands could encircle. There in the crease between his neck and his face the skin grew rough with the stubble of his beard. Fascinated by the sensation of harshness, she walked her fingers up over his chin and softly, gently touched his lips from one corner to the other.

A rumble started in his chest.

Startled out of her boldness, she tried to snatch her hand back. He caught it in his and pressed her palm back to his chest. She never even saw his other arm go around her—had he had it at the ready all along?—she only knew he picked her up by the waist and rocked her down on him, then slid backward on his cushions.

He was solid beneath her, too bare for comfort, a body alien from any she'd ever seen or touched. She'd never been so aware of her maidenly status as all along the length of her she felt . . . so much. They pressed breastbone to breastbone. His face was there, right before her, if she dared look up. She didn't dare. She tried desperately to think what to do. How to extricate herself. How to make herself *want* to be extricated.

"Charlotte." His breath whispered across her face, and his finger nudged at her stubbornly bowed chin. "Look at me."

Cowardice wasn't her way. She glanced up.

And found his brown eyes shining with admiration and something . . . more. Something dangerous. Something she'd never seen before, but she recognized.

Fear . . . it must be fear . . . brought a clutch deep in her womb. She thought to push against him, but before plan could become action, his lips swooped to hers.

In a moment of madness, she'd stroked his mouth with her fingers. Her fingertips still tingled, but that sensation was nothing compared to the commotion those satin lips caused against hers. Dry, warm, gentle, they pressed against hers firmly, a meeting and a declaration.

His eyes fluttered shut, so she let her eyes close, too. She concentrated on the way he angled his head. The tensing of his muscles in the body beneath her. The power of his shoulders held in her clutching hands. Just as each perception grew slightly familiar, she found something else changed. His hand flattened on her back and pushed her closer. His fingers plucked at her hair in little searching forays, and she heard faint pings as several somethings hit the floor. Her hairpins, she realized vaguely.

One tug pulled at her roots, not hard, but enough to wake her from her tumultuous haven. Her eyes flew open and she grabbed his hand. "Ouch!"

"I'm sorry." He was saying it even before she was done exclaiming, and he rubbed the sting in slow, soothing circles. "I'm sorry. I'm clumsy. Charlotte . . ." He came back for another kiss.

She covered his mouth with her hand.

He nuzzled her palm. Then, for some reason . . . he licked her.

Yanking her hand back, she scrubbed it against the cushion, but the sensation of his tongue, soft and wet, lingered.

She had never been this close to a man before. She had never seen a man from this angle. She needed to remember that only a few weeks ago, she had considered Wynter a savage. Even tonight, he had shown himself to be overbearing and opinionated.

He didn't kiss like an overbearing man. He didn't try to force her or sweep her away. He just kissed as if their meeting of lips was both a voyage and a destination.

"Charlotte. Again." He lifted his face toward hers.

Unwillingly flattered, she bent to him. Her lips settled easily on his, at home already with his warmth, the texture of his skin . . . and his taste.

Taste. His lips had opened, just slightly, yet enough that she . . . well, she had opened hers, too. She didn't know why; what madness urged her to meet him halfway, what curiosity nudged her along the path of dissipation. Maybe her attraction to the exotic, an attraction she had always feared, had led her to sample his flavor as if he were a dish for her delectation.

A savory dish. Smooth, warm, sensual, alive with the flavor of coffee and grapes . . . and Wynter. Her eyes slid closed again as she sampled his breath in her mouth. She wanted to moan with delight. Then she wanted to moan because his tongue skimmed along her teeth. Shocking.

She was shocked. She really was.

"Charlotte." He spoke without moving his head

away, as if he couldn't bear to part from her, and his lips moved beneath hers. "Kiss me."

"I am." Maybe, maybe if she didn't lift her head, didn't allow herself a moment of sanity, she could remain on top of him, her hands kneading the muscles and sinews of his bare shoulders.

"More." His voice was guttural, demanding, but his caresses in her hair, along her spine remained gentle and tender.

More? Ah, she knew, or rather, she could guess what he wanted. Ignoring the flutter of good sense within her enfeebled brain, she leaned into him yet further, and slowly slid her tongue into his mouth.

He groaned as if pierced through the heart. His arms tightened on her, and the pleasure of being in his embrace opened her like a rose to the spring sun's caress. Her arms went around his neck, her fingers slid into his hair . . . and her legs opened around his thighs.

Later, she blushed at her impetuosity, but now it felt right. Her heart pumped in a smooth, strong rhythm, her blood sang with sybaritism and her tongue slid against his like a maiden dancing her first waltz. If this was temptation, then no wonder so many women fell beneath its allure. She liked kissing. She adored having a man beneath her, not seducing but seduced. She loved his hands, one petting the side of her face, one firmly stroking her back and shoulder.

His knee rose, pressing between her legs. The material of her skirt and starched petticoats crinkled, and the pressure made her breath catch. Head swimming, she lifted herself above him and stared down into his face—and realized he had deceived her. Each touch, each caress, had been strong and controlled, but his brown eyes kindled with fire and a flush colored his tanned cheeks a ruddy crimson.

He wanted her. He wanted her badly.

Imagine that. A man, and he wanted her enough to give her a tumble.

Sanity returned in a rush. This was nothing special. There was no magic at work here. Men were always seducing governesses. She jerked herself free and rolled from the cushions, landing with an audible thump and a vague thought of bruising on the morrow.

"Charlotte." He grabbed for her.

She rose and backed away. "No! No, my lord." Her hair tumbled half out of its chignon. "This is what I feared. This proves I was right."

"Right?" He crouched among the cushions and stared at her through narrowed eyes. "What do you fear?"

"We must not allow ourselves to become familiar. You insisted on telling me about your life, and you insisted I tell you about mine."

He half rose. "I somehow think there is more to your life than the inkling you allowed me, Lady Miss Charlotte."

"No!" She backed away again, rubbing her forehead with her palm. "There's nothing more that you need to know, and we must never permit ourselves to be alone again for fear of repeating our folly."

"I can almost promise we will repeat our *folly,* as you call it."

"Never. I will tell Lady Ruskin"—Charlotte's voice trembled alarmingly—"that I can no longer be your governess."

He didn't say anything for the longest time. For so long, she forced her hand away from her eyes and steeled herself to look at him.

He wasn't watching her. He had relaxed back on his cushions and was staring into the fire as if the flames could give him answers. "You needn't bother my mother with this. I agree—maybe it would be best if we no longer played the role of student and governess."

Did he mean . . . oh, heavens, did he mean she was discharged? She stared at him and tried to form the inquiry into words, but all her courage had evaporated. If she was dismissed, tomorrow would be soon enough to know. With one last glance at his serious expression, she fled.

Wynter finally rose from his cushions, stretched and wished the Bedouins hadn't been so moral a people. Five years without a woman was a very long time, and such abstinence was putting a strain on his normal good nature . . . especially now that he'd determined who his next wife would be.

Charlotte. Lady Miss Charlotte. A virgin of good breeding with an impeccable reputation. A woman with no family to tear her apart with conflicting loyalties. She would be his wife and the mother of his children, and she would dedicate herself to his happiness. Just as it should be.

He smiled as he gathered her leavings—the book, and the shoes which she so self-consciously removed every evening. He would return them—when she returned to teach him again.

Unfortunate that women in England had the right to refuse a man. A vile arrangement, in his opinion, especially now when his hunting instinct had been subdued by his mating instinct.

Striding into his bedroom, he stomped his feet into his riding boots and headed downstairs.

His first wife had not required a courtship such as Englishwomen demanded; indeed, his first wife had made her needs clear when she sneaked into his tent and slept at his feet. It had been a bold move, for he could have rejected her. She would have been branded a whore and cast out of the tribe. Yet Dara had chosen her mark wisely. He had wed her. He had taken in her dying mother. He had had children with her.

As Wynter descended the stairway, the footman straightened from his station in the corridor and moved toward the outer door to open it.

On the terrace, Wynter took a breath of the fresh, dark, cool air. Barakah had always told him he had the eyes of a hawk, and it was true. As Wynter strode to the stables, he sensed and saw all that moved in the air and on the ground, and each footstep fell firmly. A good night for riding—and remembering.

He'd never loved his wife, but, Barakah had told him, love was a Western delusion. A real man did not love his woman. A man lived with his woman, he allowed his woman to pleasure him and in turn pleasured his woman, he ate what his woman cooked and listened when his woman scolded. But a real man found his fellowship among dogs, horses and other men.

Wynter had discovered all that to be true, but when Dara had died, he mourned her sincerely. He had lost a wife who was not only a good cook and an accomplished scold, but a shrewd helpmate and a good mother. More, he had lost the anchor which tied him to the tribe.

The night sky glimmered with stars. The stables were lit by a single lamp, and as Wynter entered he waved at the hostler who worked by its light.

"Back again, m'lord?" Fletcher called.

"Yes." Wynter went to his mount and allowed the stallion to sniff him, then entered the stall and stroked the mighty animal. He'd had to leave his favorite horse in El Bahar, and although this creature was in its way as mighty and spirited, still Wynter mourned the loss of Jabir, just as he mourned the loss of his friends and a way of life so free and vigorous it had made a man of him.

On her deathbed, his wife had told him that when Barakah died he would have to leave. She had been right. In the next four years, Barakah had become infirm, and one night he had escaped into the desert and nobly welcomed his death. The new leader, young, intolerant and a native man of the tribe, had considered Wynter a threat. Yet knowing the trials his children would face in England, Wynter had tried to stay.

Leading Mead out of the stall, Wynter accepted the bridle from Fletcher and worked it into Mead's mouth. Gathering the reins, he leaped onto the animal's back.

"Ye've got a way wi' th' beasties, m'lord." As always, Fletcher held an unlit pipe clenched between his teeth. "Hardly ever seen the like."

Wynter was not so foolish as to dismiss Fletcher's praise as flattery. The gnarled hostler had been in charge of the stables for as long as Wynter could remember, and Wynter valued his opinion.

Moreover, Wynter knew it was true. He did have a way with horses—and camels, although he doubted he'd ever find a use for that skill again—and he thanked God for the affinity he had for the noble creatures. "My children have the way, also."

"Aye. That I know." Fletcher nodded, then turned to his work. " 'Tis a good night for a gallop, m'lord."

Wynter urged Mead outside and walked him through the paddocks, taking care to avoid those enclosures where the mares were gathered. Mead was a lusty stallion. Wynter noted the kinship between them.

Stewart's letter had arrived in El Bahar, and it told Wynter of his mother's business problems. Wynter had had to recover from his astonishment, for he still couldn't comprehend how his mother, as shrewd as any person he had ever known, had come to such a pass. But he had begun his plans to leave.

None too soon. The new leader made demands Wynter could never fulfill. When the caravan had ended in the port of El Wajh, the little family had slipped away.

The return to England encompassed all the difficulties Wynter had foreseen, and more. All except in relation to this woman, this Charlotte. What man could have imagined a woman like her, filled with virtue, stuffed with learning, and blessed with a dimpled chin, an upturned nose and a body that brought tears to his eyes if he contemplated it for too long? He had seen better bodies beneath the swirling veils of the dancing girls, but Charlotte's body looked right. It looked as if it would fit.

This woman would not sleep at his feet. This woman understood almost nothing of the skills Eastern girls imbibed with their mothers' milk. So she was surprised at his passion, horrified at her own and did not accept the fire between them with any amount of grace.

In short, Wynter would have to court her. He grimaced. It could be done, of course. Like mares, women were easily led if offered the right enticement. But how much better when a woman accepted a man's wishes without such an arduous process!

Before he gave Mead his head, he turned and looked at the house, trying to find the window lit by Charlotte's candle and hoping she was finding the discomfort in her body as acute as he found the discomfort in his.

The drapes were drawn on most of the upstairs windows. He could catch no glimpse of the red-haired and difficult lady, although he longed to see her, even from a distance. But he did see lamps flickering on the third floor where the servants were housed, and above that ... His eyes widened.

A light moved slowly across the attic.

Very dangerous to have a lit flame up there, and there was no reason. If they had so many servants they could no longer find them chambers on the third floor, then they needed less servants, and so he would tell the housekeeper tomorrow morning.

Tonight he had desire to abate, and so he would ride.

CHAPTER 14

*A*RM IN ARM WITH HIS MOTHER, WYNTER STROLLED into Lady Howard's crowded soiree.

"Strictly speaking, you shouldn't be here, since you haven't received an invitation." Adorna wiggled her fingertips at an acquaintance.

"Lady Miss Charlotte would not approve." After more than a week of nightly lessons, he knew that much, and more. Much, much more. He knew Charlotte's breath was sweet, her body firm and lush. He knew she wanted him, and knew she didn't comprehend how dangerous that wanting could be or how far it could lead her. He knew that when he took her—

"Charlotte is a good girl, but she's a governess. A governess without a reputation is a governess unemployed." Adorna smiled into the milling crowd in the Howard drawing room. The long, large chamber buzzed with conversation, the scent of candles mixed with a hundred colognes, and many appreciative glances followed in Adorna's wake—and in Wynter's also. "In truth, I hadn't planned to reintroduce you to society until the Sereminian reception, but if that wretched Lady Howard thinks to dine out on the tales of your barbarity all season, she will have me to contend with. We shall give her this occasion to face you, and a chance to feed on her own putrid gossip."

He noted that while his mother seethed like a tigress defending her cub, she didn't deny his barbarity. "If this does not work?"

"Then I've lost my touch."

"And have you?"

She turned her amused gaze to his. "No, but I had toyed with the thought of calling in Aunt Jane and Uncle Ransom. Unfortunately, Uncle Ransom took Aunt Jane to Italy to view the artwork."

Wynter dredged a bit of gossip out of his memory. "I believe last time Uncle Ransom took Aunt Jane to Italy to view the artwork, she came back increasing."

"That was a long time ago, and Aunt Jane said it was the direct result of viewing Michaelangelo's David." Adorna's blue eyes rounded. "It must be a very impressive statue."

"I have heard that it is."

Adorna pondered the powers of such a statue, then shrugged a dimity-covered shoulder. "They would be annoyed at having to come back, but they'll do it for you."

Wynter recalled his alternately fond and fearsome memories of his uncle Ransom. And Aunt Jane, for all her distracted artist's air, could call down the wrath of hell when she chose. "I would hate to be Lady Howard facing them when they're annoyed."

"It's almost worth calling them in just to watch." Adorna burbled with pleasure.

Wynter realized she loved this: the social whirl, the games, the constant challenges to her supremacy. Adorna skated atop the scandal broth as lightly as a fairy.

He—he was more like Uncle Ransom. He could go

to Austinpark Manor and be satisfied to raise his children, ride his horses and take lessons from Charlotte. Lessons that had nothing to do with her beloved etiquette.

Every day he came into London, visiting the clubs, the prizefighting parlors, the theater. Anywhere his board of directors might be, there Wynter went and put on an act of indolence and stupidity unmatched in thespian circles. He smiled foolishly at Shilbottle, slapped Hodges on the shoulder, wagered with Sir Drakely and downed a bottle with Read. And when he had asked enough foolish questions that he had them convinced of his idiocy, he went to the office and checked their work.

Still he couldn't yet pinpoint the bastard who, in Wynter's absence, had been draining money from the firm. Now it was worse than that. Now the books showed an occasional, unexplainable increase. He understood embezzling, but why would someone put money *into* the business? Was it being done to confuse any auditor? Or did it signal the fear his return had caused?

His mother urged him to take Cousin Stewart into his confidence. Stewart knew more about the business than anyone, she said, and wasn't it Stewart who had sent the letter that had reached him at last? The one that told him about the confusion of finances and begged him to come home?

But to Wynter's way of thinking, Cousin Stewart had reason to resent Wynter's intrusion, perhaps even more than the others. Wynter trusted no one. He had abandoned Adorna at his father's death and left her to deal with the business, so this he must do—set a trap and catch the culprit.

As he had already set the trap to catch Charlotte.

He had spent hours working on it so far, and all for one small kiss.

Ah, but those hours were time well spent, for in that one kiss he had tasted the desire, doubt and dreaminess of an untouched maiden. He doubted that Lady Miss Charlotte fully comprehended how her life was about to change, and so much to the better.

"Wynter, I want you to meet Lady Smithwick," Adorna said. "You remember playing with her children at Fairchild Manor, don't you?"

He did, and a more raucous bunch he'd never met. "Lady Smithwick." Taking her hand, he bowed low and raised her fingers to his lips, taking care to give her his best smile.

Lady Smithwick was about his mother's age, but she hadn't aged well. Fat smoothed the lines from her face, and she jiggled when she giggled. She giggled now, and blushed up to her hairline and down to her bosom. "Adorna, you didn't tell me little Wynter had grown up to be such a handsome devil."

Adorna tapped her cohort on the arm with her fan. "But surely you heard the rumors."

Lady Smithwick's blue eyes bulged. "Well . . . yes. Do you mean to say they're true?"

"That he's become a barbarian?" Adorna laughed softly. "The sort of barbarian who breaks a lady's heart without even trying."

He knew without being told he should play to his mother's coaching. Ducking his head with simulated boyish allure, he cast upon Lady Smithwick a smoldering look which admired and seduced.

Lady Smithwick clapped her hand over her heart. "Yes. I see. Would you wait here?" Her gaze clung to his. "My daughter is quite lovely. Young. A maiden. I'll bring her to meet you." Pointing toward his feet, she commanded, "Stay here. Don't leave."

Adorna watched her scurry through the crowd and, ignoring her instruction, led him farther into the chamber. "Martha, how good to see you. Your cap is divine. Lady Declan, I can tell by your air of savoir faire that you have just returned from the continent. Why, Lord Andrew, you've gone and grown up!" She fluttered her lashes at the young man. "How handsome you are. Come, dears, and meet my son. It's so thrilling to have him home at last. He has been quite the world traveler, you know. He . . ." Her voice faltered, then returned. "He has so many tales to tell. Wynter, why don't you tell them?"

Wynter sought the cause of her disquiet and saw Bucknell on the fringes of the gathering crowd, watching Adorna and frowning.

What was the matter with the man? If he loved Adorna, why didn't he take her? His mother had certainly indicated her willingness.

"Tell them about . . ." Adorna tugged him down to her level, then said, "You've got to keep them enthralled until Lady Howard arrives. We need her to scotch the rumors that are destroying your reputation." She drew away as if she'd imparted a suggestion for a story.

Wynter smiled and nodded. He wanted Lady Howard here, too, but for a different reason.

Looking around at his audience of wide-eyed ladies and jaded men, Wynter knew he could keep them entertained. With every intention of fabricating a whopping lie, he said, "My adventures are so slight as to be almost negligible. Saving an English ship by fighting off a shipload of pirates is not so great an accomplishment."

"Lord Ruskin, this is my daughter, Miss Fairchild."

Lady Smithwick had returned with the most gorgeous blond girl Wynter had ever seen. She was exquisite, she was smiling at him—and she left him cold.

He really only had interest in one woman, and she was at home with his children.

"Won't you tell us your story?" Miss Fairchild asked.

"Because you have asked." Wynter sent her a smoldering look, too, and when she simpered he wondered if English ladies had an unlimited capacity to believe themselves adored. "The pirates of the Barbary Coast are powerful and ruthless, especially Abdul Andre Kateb. None dares speak his name without respect or he will have your head separated from your body." Lady Declan gasped, and Wynter bowed to her. "Ah, it is as I suspected. This tale is not for the drawing room."

"No, no," Lady Declan protested, aware she was the object of some glares. "I was momentarily overcome. Please, tell us all."

"As you wish, dear lady." He held out his hand to her. "But only if you take the precaution of sitting down. Such a delicate constitution might not withstand the shock."

All the women suddenly discovered a delicate constitution, and seats had to be found for them before he could begin again. "The first I knew of the pirates was their black flag fringed in red—the symbols of death and blood. They came on us like a hammer, ramming us with their ship and boarding us even as we foundered. The captain, as stalwart an Englishman who ever sailed the seas, urged us to fight for our honor and the honor of Britain, and every one of the brave lads aboard did their duty. You would have been proud of English warriors if you could have seen it, my ladies." Wynter beamed on them.

Enthralled, they beamed back.

Lady Smithwick asked, "Did you fight?"

"I was young and had no experience, so although I begged to fight, the captain ordered me to stand aside."

"Oh." Lady Declan sagged in disappointment.

"But our lads, they fought so bravely Abdul Andre Kateb himself came out of his cabin, where his slave girls had been servicing him—"

Bucknell stepped out of the fringe of the crowd. "Surely not a topic for the drawing room." His sardonic gaze made it clear that he, at least, didn't believe the preposterous tale.

Wynter placed the flat of his hand on his chest and bowed. "My apologies, my lord and ladies. I forgot myself."

"Of course you did." Adorna smiled at Bucknell, her innocent, guileless smile. "It's good to be swept into improper behavior occasionally."

"No, it's not," Bucknell snapped.

Wynter wanted to watch the tussle between his mother and her suitor, but his audience stirred restlessly, so he began again. "Abdul Andre Kateb stepped onto the deck, bare-chested, ugly and evil clear to the core."

"You could tell that just by looking at him, could you?" Bucknell asked.

"Yes, he could," Adorna answered.

Lady Smithwick turned on the quarreling sweethearts. "Shh!"

They quieted, but Wynter observed an exchange of glares. "The other sailors were engaged, fighting for their lives, and that wicked pirate came slashing through them with his cutlass"—Wynter slashed in demonstration—"headed right for our wounded captain."

"He was wounded?" Lady Declan asked.

"Wounded. Yes. By a shot from a cowardly pirate too frightened to face him in hand-to-hand combat."

"I have extensive contacts in the Admiralty," Bucknell said. "I could recommend this captain for commendation."

"It was a merchant ship." Adorna moved toward him until they stood face-to-face. "You know that, my lord."

"What I know, my lady, is that you—" Bucknell stopped and glanced around. Every eye was fixed to them. Taking Adorna's arm rather forcibly, he said, "We'll talk elsewhere."

As they left the chamber, two ladies put their heads together and began to whisper.

Wynter raised his voice to recapture their attention. "Beardless boy that I was, I knew not how to fight, but I knew what to do. I picked up a saber from a dying sailor's hand and advanced on Abdul Andre Kateb."

Breathlessly, Lady Smithwick asked, "Is that how you got that scar?"

"This scar?" Wynter traced the mark on his face and thought furiously. "Yes. Yes, and one on my chest which modesty forbids me to show." From the rapacious expression on young Miss Fairchild's face, he could have bared his chest, or anything else, for her inspection. But looking over their heads, he saw Lady Howard's head bobbing through the crowd, so he executed a thrilling finish of his tale, which coincided with her arrival.

He hoped the sight of him enthralling the ladies and gentlemen with fanciful tales, made romantic by his deep voice and deeper imagination, would dismay Lady Howard.

Indeed, she pushed her way in without finesse.

She wasn't a stupid woman, Wynter would allow her that. She knew she had only moments to rescue herself from disaster. "Lord Ruskin, you imp, you took Howard up on his invitation. Let me take you to him."

"Of course. I would be happy to greet my old friend again." To once again tell the henpecked husband how to keep his wife under control. He bowed to his audience. "If you would excuse us . . ."

The ladies, young and old, murmured their dismay, and Lady Smithwick trilled, "Don't forget to return, Lord Ruskin!"

"To you." Taking her hand, he kissed it again. "And to your lovely daughter."

While Lady Smithwick sighed, Lady Howard tucked her hand in his arm. The lacy gloves she wore had the fingers cut out. Her gown showed bosom and bare arms, attributes a lady displayed only in the evening. But she had proved herself no lady, only an amoral brunette with a voracious appetite and a salacious wit.

He despised her.

She knew it. She didn't care. After today, he was well on his way to becoming the Byron of the age, and the hostess who had him had cachet. As Lady Howard guided him through the drawing room and down the corridor, she said, "I've told so many of the really nice people about our little visit to Austinpark Manor." She projected her voice with theatrical flare, including anyone who was milling about. "Everyone's been panting to meet you."

Bending his head so his mouth was close to her ear, he said, "I came as quickly as I could, but first I had to take lessons in courtesy."

"Lessons? Really? Real lessons with a teacher?"

She smirked, convinced that tidbit would propel her into the upper reaches of the gossip grapevine. "You can't go wrong there."

"I'll give you the name of my governess. You, Lady Howard, would benefit by her expertise."

Her mouth opened, then closed, as she realized how he had set her up. She hadn't expected the savage to have a wit. In a deadly voice, she said, "Oh, do give me her name. I'll write her a letter of commendation."

He smiled blandly.

But he'd forgotten Lady Howard's phenomenal memory. "Wait. I heard that Lady Ruskin went to that disgraceful little Governess School and hired Miss Priss for her grandchildren. But it wasn't for her grandchildren, was it? It was for you!" Tossing back her head to better display her long throat, she laughed huskily. Taking a quick turn into the smoke-choked cardroom, she dragged him along to the table where Lord Howard was playing whist. And losing, if the pitiful pile of coins before him was any indication.

"Howard," his wife trilled.

Wincing, Howard raised his head.

"Look who's here. Your old friend Ruskin."

Howard squinted at Wynter through red-rimmed eyes. "Ruskin. What the hell are you doing here?"

"Darling, he's come because he's been to manners school."

She almost sang with mockery, Wynter realized, but it wasn't him she was mocking.

She ran a fingernail around Howard's ear. "And do you know who this big, strong, handsome man has for a teacher?"

Howard jerked his head away and swatted at her hand as if she were an annoying midge.

Too many gamblers were straining to listen, and too

many grins blossomed at the prospect of Howard's humiliation at the hands of his wife. So Wynter intervened. "Lady Howard, at this moment, discretion would be the better part of valor."

She glared venomously.

He stared back impassively. And won, of course.

"His governess is . . ." She leaned close to Howard's ear to whisper Charlotte's name.

Howard glared at the space in the middle of the table where the cards would land. Lifting the deck, he shuffled, then with the overdone care of a drunk, he dealt the cards. "So?" he asked. But his hands were shaking.

Lady Howard smiled a brilliant, well-fanged smile, and stroked her husband's hair with feigned sympathy. "Don't forget to visit the children in the morning. Their holiday is almost over, and they're going back to school Monday."

Howard ignored her. Taking Wynter's arm, she led him back into the corridor.

"What was that all about?" he asked.

She opened her mouth to explain, but a glance at him made her change her mind. "It's not important. Old history, if you will. Personally, you've made me very happy. If there is anything better than knowing you're under the tutelage of Lady Charlotte Dalrumple, it is knowing that nose-in-the-air snob is back in the North Downs."

Effectively distracted by this chance to know the details of Charlotte's past, Wynter's mind raced. "Back?"

"They have long memories in the country." Digging her nails into his arm, she leaned against him so her breast pressed against his arm. "Tell me, what did the

Earl of Porterbridge do when he saw the ungrateful chit after all these years?"

On full alert now, Wynter gracefully steered Lady Howard toward the nearest empty chamber. "Just what you think he did."

"Turned his back on her?" She shook her head. "But no, he hasn't a subtle bone in his body. Slapped her? Bellowed at her?"

"Her transgressions were scarcely worth that."

"You jest." She looked around the library with interest. "Now, I know you didn't bring me in here because you want to read. And I can't believe you want to seduce me. You're too . . . upright . . . for that. So you must want all the gratifying details about our dear Lady Charlotte." She traced a manicured fingernail down his cheek. "What will you give me for them?"

Wynter made it a point to know his adversary's weaknesses. "You gamble a great deal," he said, catching her wrist.

She sucked in her round, rouged cheeks. "So?"

"You will give me any information I seek, my lady, and in return I will not call in the vowels you owe."

"You? You don't hold any of my vowels!"

"But I do." His warrior's eyes narrowed on her. "I bought them for a fair price, and I will have my value from them. Tell me all about Miss Dalrumple, and tell me now."

CHAPTER 15

"*T*ELL ME AGAIN WHY YOU CAN'T MARRY PAPA."

Charlotte looked down at Leila's earnest face and suppressed a sigh. A steady spring rain had sluiced down the schoolroom windows all through the morning, teacher and pupils could not go for their usual walk and Robbie and Leila were like caged kittens. "Noblemen do not marry their governesses," Charlotte said.

"But you're Lady Miss Charlotte. Aren't you noble?"

"Yes, but I'm poor. Rich men do not marry poor women."

"But why would a rich man marry a rich woman?" Robbie interposed. "A rich man doesn't need more money."

The children didn't understand the inequities of the English marriage mart, and the more Charlotte clarified, the less logical it seemed, even to her. "People marry other people who are like themselves. Just like—birds marry birds, and horses marry horses."

"Horses don't marry, they breed," Leila said scornfully. Her words gave way to thought, and she swept Charlotte with a measuring gaze.

Oh, no. That the child even knew about breeding was bad enough, but Charlotte was not in the mood to deal with whatever Leila had in her shrewd little mind. Charlotte could scarcely deal with the memories of her . . . and Wynter . . . two nights ago . . . alone and close and kissing.

Kissing. Madness. Kissing sweetly, gently, their lips pressed together, their bodies intertwined . . .

The recollection should embarrass her and humiliate her, but at night when she was alone in her bed, it was not humiliation that kept her awake. It was the coiling in the pit of her stomach, the temptation to touch parts of her body she had ignored for years. Every moment of the day should be spent in anguish, wondering if she would be dismissed when Wynter returned from London. Instead she found herself smiling at nothing, allowing the children untold liberties, wearing her best shoes, since her second-best were in the old nursery, and thinking of love, marriage and all those ineffable items that Lady Charlotte Dalrumple had lost the right to imagine for herself.

Discipline. She needed discipline. Employers *didn't* marry their governesses, most especially men like Lord Ruskin, who was titled, rich and handsome. Lady Ruskin worried he would perform some *faux pas* which would destroy his reputation among society's hostesses.

Charlotte had worried about it, too. But now she realized that his foreign adventures added the romantic flavor of scandal to his reputation. That, combined with the way he looked at a woman, made her blood heat and her imagination fly to long nights filled with those slow, delicate kisses.

"Lady Miss Charlotte, why are you so red and blotchy?" Robbie asked.

Discipline. She needed discipline, and some way to distract her charges from her blushing countenance. "You children are progressing so well in your lessons, I think we should have a celebration. Perhaps read a story from *The Arabian Nights' Entertainments.* Would you like that?"

Robbie beamed.

Leila yawned.

Startled, Charlotte asked, "Don't you want to hear a story, Leila?"

"Yes!" Leila shouted.

"A lady always speaks in a modulated tone." Charlotte had said the bromide so often it came without thought while she scrutinized Leila. The child was heavy-eyed and hollow-cheeked. Charlotte placed her hand on Leila's forehead. "Didn't you sleep well last night?"

"No. Yes." Leila dragged her toe along the crack between two polished boards in the floor. "I don't know."

She was cranky, but she wasn't running a fever.

As casually as she could, Charlotte said, "You're not afraid of the ghost?"

Leila got an expression of . . . oh, Charlotte didn't know how to describe it. Appalled slyness, for lack of a better term. "Is there a ghost here at Austinpark Manor?"

Immediately sorry she'd brought up the subject, Charlotte dismissed it casually. "A silly kitchen maid said she saw something up near the attics."

"Really? A real ghost of our own? I heard so, but I thought it was drivel. How smashing!" Robbie crowded close. "Did it rattle a chain? Did it hold a severed head? Did it moan and drip blood?"

"Robbie!" Charlotte was appalled. "None of those

gruesome things. Where did you hear such nonsense?"

His enthusiasm undiminished, Robbie said, "Everybody knows that's what ghosts do."

"Everybody? As in your new companion from the vicarage?" Charlotte asked.

Robbie had found the vicar's son a week ago while roaming the estate, and since, the boys had been together every chance. Alfred seemed a decent sort, and his father was a stellar example of all that was obedient and decent. If he had not always been kind, well . . . he was a vicar, and a man, and he had a family to support. So she approved of Robbie's first friend in this foreign land.

But her brother's distraction had been hard on Leila, and it appeared the boys had been talking of matters better left unsaid.

"Alfred says lights have been seen in the attic. Oooo!" Robbie ran his finger up Leila's spine.

Leila backhanded him with her fist.

Charlotte caught him by the collar when he would have exacted revenge. To Leila she said severely, "Violence never solves a quarrel."

"He started it."

"Did not."

"You children are lucky to have each other." Charlotte looked at their two hot and irritated faces and thought how much she would have liked to have a sibling, and how much loneliness a brother or sister would have assuaged. "Not one child in England has shared the life you two shared in El Bahar. You cannot tell another soul about your adventures and expect they'll offer anything but vulgar curiosity. But for all your lives, you'll know one person who remembers how it was to live in the desert. That is your bond. Don't waste it on silly quarrels."

The children stared at her. For a moment, she felt the thrill of triumph.

Then Robbie poked Leila in the ribs with his elbow. "Alfred says the spook likes to scare skinny girls."

And Charlotte realized they had scarcely comprehended a word. She didn't give up, exactly, she only chose her battles, and right now she chose to address the issue of the ghost. "Someone suffers from an overheated imagination," she said as if her disapproval could dampen the rumors. "There are no such things as ghosts, and if there are, they wouldn't have the audacity to move into your father's house."

"Not with Grandmama living here," Leila declared. "She'd scare the ghost!"

Both children giggled.

"That's enough," Charlotte declared sternly, and their giggles subsided. Charlotte didn't know what to do about their blatant disrespect for their grandmother. Adorna had no idea what to do with her newly acquired grandchildren, nor did she try to learn. Mostly she watched them as if they were curiosities to be examined. Until Lady Ruskin decided to become a part of their lives, she would be an object of fun to the resentful children.

"Bring the candles, Robbie," Charlotte commanded.

A fire burned on the hearth to chase the chill away, and she led the children to the settle placed to catch the warmth. An hour of leisure would do them all good.

The hearth rug lay between the settle and the fire. A nice, large hearth rug . . . temptation. Charlotte stared at the thick, brightly woven floor covering and saw Wynter as he was in the old nursery every evening. Lolling on the cushions, smiling, handsome and indecorous. Sometimes, when she looked at him so relaxed and content, she was reminded of how, in the years before her parents' deaths, she had had the confidence to do what she wished without worry of reprisal. So many years ago, and yet she remembered.

"Lady Miss Charlotte, what are you doing?" Robbie asked.

Charlotte came out of her reverie to find Leila and Robbie staring at her. "I was thinking that we should lie on our backs to read today." Her own audacity astonished her, but when her gaze rested on Leila, she excused herself. The child was obviously tired; perhaps she would drift off for a nap.

"Yes!" Robbie plopped onto the carpet, feet extended toward the fire. Leila followed him, sitting close. He shoved her and said, "Lady Miss Charlotte is sitting there."

Leila shoved him back. "You make room for her."

"Children." Just that one word, but Robbie and Leila recognized the tone in her voice. They hurriedly separated, leaving Charlotte just enough room to place herself. As she sank down onto the floor, second thoughts assaulted her. After all, governesses had been fired for lesser infractions. But Adorna and Wynter had stayed in London last night, and no one expected they would travel through the rain to get home. She could relax; she was safe from discovery.

She wouldn't see Wynter today.

She lay back with a sigh, and when her back rested on the carpet she waited, expecting the sensation of foolishness to overwhelm her. After all, choosing to rest on the floor was not the same as being captured and forcibly held there. And then lulled with kisses.

No, this wasn't the same, but neither did she feel foolish. The floor supported her, the fire toasted her

feet, the ceiling had been ornately plastered and decorated at some earlier era and entertained her eyes. She
found herself smiling.

Robbie's sharp elbow bumped her. "Read, Lady
Miss Charlotte."

"Yes." She opened the book and found their place.

Robbie lay with one knee bent and foot flat on the
floor. He crossed his other leg so it rested on the up-
raised knee, and he wiggled his foot to some inner
rhythm as she read. Leila snuggled close, resting her
cheek against Charlotte's arm. The story unfolded in
a far distant land, and as always Charlotte found herself swept away from the drab day and into an adventure where she was a fleet-footed thief who discovered
a treasure trove and saved the beautiful lady.

The schoolroom, when she finished, was quiet, and
she turned first to Robbie and smiled. The boy grinned
back at her, laughing at some child-thing she didn't
understand. She glanced at Leila, and found her slum-
bering peacefully at her side. With a tender smile she
brushed a lock of hair off the girl's forehead, then
eased herself away and reached toward the settle for
a cushion—and jerked into a sitting position when
someone at the back of the classroom began a slow,
deliberate applause. She knew who it was, even before
she looked, but like a spectator at a carriage wreck,
she had to see.

A very large, rather menacing Wynter sat in her
chair in the shadows at the back of the classroom.
"Very entertaining, Lady Miss Charlotte. I have enjoyed this very much."

The lover she had last seen in the old nursery had
disappeared. His heavy-lidded gaze seemed almost
sardonic, and she watched mesmerized as his big

hands collided again. Applause, done not to praise but to intimidate.

He'd kissed her once. Possibly he'd been bored, probably he'd decided to entertain himself by checking to see if she could be seduced. She had proved to be weak, and now he would judge her behavior ever more harshly.

Worse, Miss Priss had been caught in improper behavior. She was backsliding, and all because of one meaningless kiss.

She was to be dismissed, so she would go with dignity and in the pursuit of her duty. "Hush, my lord. You'll wake Leila." Catching Robbie when he would have raced to his father, she said, "Quietly and like a gentleman, please."

As Robbie semi-sedately greeted his father, she tucked her feet under her and rose as gracefully as any woman could who had not sat on the floor for at least thirteen years. Taking a cushion from the settle, she tucked it under Leila's head, then covered the child with a rug. With an equanimity she didn't feel, she said, "My lord, we didn't expect you back today. Did you ride through the storm?"

A foolish question, perhaps, but a quick glance showed he wore dry clothing. He must have already changed, for his hair was damp and, as she expected, his feet were bare. How else could he have sneaked up on her so completely?

"I had to come," he said. "I could not wait to tell you of my triumph."

"What triumph, my lord?" she asked warily.

"I went to Lord and Lady Howard's soiree yester-eve, and rescued my reputation with my good manners." He smiled. "And my charming ways."

"Marvelous, my lord." She pressed her damp palms

together and directed an approving glance near his face at the place just over his left shoulder. "I knew you could do it."

"I owe it all to you, Lady Miss Charlotte." He put his arm around Robbie and turned him to face her. "You see, Robbie, if you listen to your governess, you will be a proper English gentleman soon."

Robbie wiggled, not understanding the undertones. "It's not hard to be a proper English gentleman. Just follow a bunch of dumb rules."

Wynter rumpled his son's hair. "Is he doing well, Lady Miss Charlotte?"

"Very well indeed." She smoothed the wrinkles out of her skirt. "Your children are bright and eager to learn. Even Leila has admitted she will learn to ride sidesaddle, if I will teach her."

Wynter's eyes narrowed on Charlotte. "I will have to see you ride, Charlotte, before I will give my daughter into your hand for training."

He would have to see her ride. He spoke of the future. He wasn't going to dismiss her. Perhaps he didn't despise her. Charlotte sagged with relief—but only inwardly.

Wynter swept on, imperiously trampling on her budding gratitude. "Since the children's manners have improved so much, it is time to take them out in public. Ah, you look dismayed, Lady Miss Charlotte, but I think—no, I know—the neighbors must be gossiping about our failure to attend the church in Wesford Village." Wynter was watching her much too closely. "Tomorrow is Sunday. What better place to go and test our skills than at a church, where all will be in a charitable frame of mind?"

CHAPTER 16

On Sunday morning, as Wynter, Charlotte and the children entered the nave of the ancient stone church, the congregation cranked their heads around and stared at the newcomers like a pack of wolves eyeing a few stray sheep. Wynter almost rubbed his palms together with anticipation. He would learn much today about the stubbornly elusive Lady Charlotte Dalrumple and why she lied to him about her background.

Ah, there were those who would say she had not lied, but Wynter had told her of himself, his travels, his youthful indiscretions.

And what had she told him? Nothing. Nothing, but her very silence had led him astray. He believed she had no family, when her family resided not five miles from Austinpark Manor. In fact, the Norman church with its square steeple was on the hereditary lands held by the Earl of Porterbridge—Charlotte's uncle.

Wynter smiled at the toothless old lady who stared at him so forbiddingly. His charm didn't move her. She continued to stare, her black gloves folded in her lap, her black cap pinned firmly on her gray hair. "Friendly place," he muttered in Charlotte's ear.

She ignored him. Of course. She could never have
been more proper than she was right now, with her
chin tilted high and her back straight, even under the
weight of her stiffly starched petticoats and gray wool
gown. He could have never guessed the shadow that
had blighted her life—but everyone in this church
knew.

Most pews were marked with a family name. Each
person seated therein had the look of someone who
had been forever sitting in the same place every Sunday, as if the seat fit them only. Disapproval weighed
heavy in the air. Even the saints glittering in the
stained-glass windows stared as Charlotte made her
way down the aisle.

His children could tell, too. Leila tucked her gloved
hand in his. Robbie moved closer to Charlotte and
took her arm as if he could protect her from hurt. The
lad had good instincts. Wynter was proud of his son.

Wynter wondered how long Charlotte would have
made a fool of him if it hadn't been for Lady Howard.
Knowing Charlotte and her everlasting discretion, she
probably would have duped him forever.

Not that he'd been fool enough to believe everything that lying jade Lady Howard had told him. At
first opportunity, he had cornered Adorna and ques-
tioned her. That had been a mistake, for in questioning
his elusive, maddening mother, he'd come to wonder
what other things she had "forgotten" to tell him. He'd
been so busy trying to hide his intentions from
Adorna, it hadn't occurred to him before, but—what
was Adorna trying to hide from *him*? For she was
hiding some secret, he could tell.

Wynter and his little group made their way down
the aisle to the front pew. On the left, Wynter remembered, sat the Viscount Ruskin and his family. And on

the right since the dawn of time, or at least since William the Conqueror, sat the Earl of Porterbridge.

Porterbridge sat there now on the end. His wife and eight of their fourteen children were strung out beside him. Wynter viewed him in profile. The earl stared straight ahead, perfectly still, his gaze fixed at the pulpit, scowling as if his unspoken command would bring forth the vicar to get the sermon preached. He exuded impatience but not importance, wealth but not culture. His graying hair and eyebrows had been touched with pomade, but a cherry-red razor burn marred his lowest jowl. His jacket was clearly London-made, but nothing could make his shoulders broad or keep his paunch sequestered within his waistcoat. He was, in truth, the picture of a petty, insecure tyrant placed in a position beyond his capacity. He might not have noted their appearance at all, but like a train, silence fell behind them as they walked.

Everyone heard Lady Porterbridge's exclamation of, "My heavens!"

As they were meant to. Wynter judged Lady Porterbridge to be a woman who enjoyed a disturbance as a way to liven up her life. Pathetic.

Lord Porterbridge turned his head slowly, taking care not to break the starch on his upturned collar or ruin the knot on his black satin cravat. He stared at Wynter without recognition. Then his gaze moved to Charlotte, and his fair complexion went from pale to ruddy in a moment. His boots hit the flagstones with a thump.

Wynter took one look at Charlotte's still, pale face and realized his mistake. He couldn't fling this woman to the wolves for any reason. She'd been hurt too much, and by the very man who now pointed his finger and in stentorian rage bellowed, "You!"

There was nothing civilized about her relationship with her uncle, and there was nothing civilized about Wynter's feelings for Charlotte. He would protect her.

But she didn't step back, or take Wynter's arm, or do anything a woman in need of refuge might do.

Damn the woman.

She stood her ground, trembling but calm, and watched as her uncle rolled toward her like a belligerent barrel.

Wynter stepped between them in a smooth move, and as if Porterbridge had been talking to him, said, "Yes, my lord, *me*. How good to see you, too, and how surprising that you remember me after so many years." Porterbridge stopped, but Wynter thought if he hadn't been so much taller, the older man would have plowed right through him, if he could have.

Porterbridge didn't waste respect or courtesy on the younger man. He blared, "Who the—"

"I am Ruskin, my lord." Wynter forcibly took Porterbridge's hand and shook it. "Your neighbor from Austinpark Manor. I am back from El Bahar. But while we have much to talk about, we should do so after the service. Look, the holy man enters." And was hurrying up onto the pulpit as quickly as possible. The vicar wanted no scene in his church. "We should seat ourselves and set an example for the congregation." Who were craning their necks unashamedly at the spectacle unfolding before their avid gazes.

Porterbridge's face flushed redder, and his gruff voice rang out, "Sir, there is one person here who would benefit from an example!"

Wynter allowed his accent full rein. "Yes, I know my deficiencies, my lord, but I am an Englishman and would challenge any man who says I am not!" He smiled. "Your choice of weapon, of course."

For the first time, Porterbridge looked, really looked, at Wynter, and obviously what he saw convinced him Wynter was both insulted and dangerous. "I didn't mean you, sir!"

"No offense taken." Wynter glared from his full height. "Not by me, nor by my children, nor by my governess, for I know you by reputation, my lord, and you would not be so asinine—is that the correct word, Miss Dalrumple?"

From beside him, Charlotte said calmly, "Correct, my lord, but impolite."

"—Asinine as to challenge *me*."

Porterbridge's gaze darted between Wynter and his niece while his color fluctuated alarmingly. He wanted, so badly, to humiliate her. Yet his desire to browbeat Charlotte couldn't compete with the fear that his unknown, foreign-sounding neighbor would smash him like a camel's hoof crushed a scorpion.

Bristling with obvious rancor, Porterbridge nodded to Wynter and prepared to take his place.

But not before Charlotte curtsied and said, "Good morning, Uncle."

He turned a choleric red and half turned toward her, but Wynter took her elbow and shoved her into the pew, and the vicar began his sermon—on the return of the prodigal.

Leila had never been so miserable in her whole life. She hated this place. All of it. This church with all these people who stared at her and whispered with hissing sounds. Austinpark Manor with all its silly rules and the servants who called her and her brother and her papa foreigners right in front of her as if she were deaf. The whole stupid country of England, green and rainy all the time. She was cold even with an overcoat and a velvet dress and petticoats, and she was skinny, she'd heard an old lady say so.

And her Grandmama hated her.

Standing behind a pillar, Leila glowered at the people milling about the churchyard. Everyone wore stupid hats and stupid dresses and the stupid English shoes hurt her feet. They smiled at each other as if they liked each other, but she'd heard two women talking and they didn't like anybody. They said nasty things in soft, gentle voices like Lady Miss Charlotte wanted Leila to use, and that made the nasty things sound even worse.

And that man—he hated Lady Miss Charlotte. He was ugly and he had a big belly, and Leila had thought he was going to strike Lady Miss Charlotte before church. Now he glared at her from a safe distance because he was afraid of Papa. The lady-voices thought that was funny. They said that man was mean and that they loved watching him try to avoid a confrontation with Papa.

But then they said why were Lady Miss Charlotte's old friends talking to her? Didn't they know she had been bad and deserved a good snub, and why was she clinging to Lord Ruskin in such a pathetic display? (Leila thought her papa was following Lady Miss Charlotte around. She didn't like that any better, but she didn't like the women talking in that snotty tone, either.) Had Charlotte finally come to her senses and decided to grab the first man who would have her? But she was a little long in the tooth (Leila thought Lady Miss Charlotte's teeth were beautiful), and surely she didn't imagine she could get Lord Ruskin. He was a good catch. She didn't deserve him.

Leila didn't understand any of it, except she understood she was more and more unhappy and no one cared. When she had suggested Lady Miss Charlotte marry Papa, she had imagined Papa and her governess sitting together with her in the middle, reading to her and kissing and hugging her and talking to her.

Instead, Papa and Lady Miss Charlotte were only paying attention to each other! Papa watched Lady Miss Charlotte openly. Lady Miss Charlotte pretended not to watch him. And all the while they were focused on each other. That wasn't right. That wasn't the way it was supposed to be.

Shouts of boyish delight drew Leila's notice. Her lip trembled and her eyes filled with tears.

Robbie was her brother, but he didn't care that she was sad. He was swaggering through the churchyard arm in arm with Alfred, his stupid new friend who called her a stupid girl and wouldn't let her play.

Nobody loved her, and she wanted to go home.

Home. To El Bahar.

Mr. and Mrs. Burton walked through the drying puddles in the churchyard toward Charlotte, and she braced herself for who-knew-what kind of greeting from her parents' dearest friends.

But Mrs. Burton held out her arms to Charlotte. "Dear, how long have you been back?"

Stepping into the capacious lady's clasp, Charlotte returned it with a tentative squeeze of her own. "Several weeks, ma'am."

"And do you have a hug for old Burt?" Mr. Burton asked.

"Of course I do." As she embraced him, a sense of fantasy swept over her. For years she had had nightmares about the day of her return. Yet Mr. and Mrs. Burton hugged her in front of the whole gossiping congregation, and not one, but two of her old girlfriends came up and exchanged greetings.

"If you'd written us, Charlotte . . ." Mrs. Burton frowned at her as she spoke of the days past, then straightened the bow on Charlotte's bonnet as if she were still a child. "I wish you'd written."

But the Burtons had never offered to help her on her flight. No one had. In her youthful hurt and fury she had thought herself abandoned. Now, for the first time, it occurred to her that events had unfolded so quickly, perhaps people had been paralyzed with surprise. Or perhaps they had disapproved of her actions, but would have helped her anyway. Or, even more likely, they had waited to be asked.

Looking at Mr. and Mrs. Burton's somber faces, she realized she might have been wrong when she thought herself completely alone.

"I'm sorry, ma'am," Charlotte said. "From now on I will do better."

"From now on, you'll be here and I can talk to you. So you're governess to this comely young man's children?" With her usual merry smile, Mrs. Burton pinched Wynter's cheek. "I'll wager you don't remember me, young Ruskin!"

Wynter captured her hand and bowed over it. "Indeed I do, madam. How could I not remember the lady who glows with the gilded light of sunrise across the dunes?"

Her laughter boomed out, and heads turned from their intent and excited conversations. "Ah, young Ruskin, you've changed. You used to be all brooding melodrama."

Wynter shook back his hair so that his earring caught the sunshine that blinked in and out from the clouds. Charlotte noted that his accent grew more noticeable—more romantic—as he said, "Now I am only . . . how do you say? . . . outrageous."

"Good God!" The razor-thin, impeccably dressed and old-fashioned Mr. Burton guffawed when he caught sight of the circle of gold. "With that hair and that bobble in your ear, it's hard to tell if you're a lad or lass."

Wynter extended out his hand to the older gentleman. "The lasses seem to know."

Mr. Burton shook it and glanced slyly at Charlotte. "I see they do."

The proper side of Charlotte could scarcely contain her embarrassment. "Sir, he didn't mean me!"

Both the Burtons chuckled.

Wynter put his hand on the small of her back in a manner that seemed to Charlotte most proprietary. She stepped away from his touch, and he smiled at her as if she were prey. As if he could rein her in at any moment!

Charlotte caught herself as the memory of his kiss began again to play in her brain.

Discipline. She needed discipline. And dignity. And equanimity.

She needed to stop thinking of his kiss, and think instead of her gratitude to him, for his propinquity kept her uncle, aunt and cousins at bay. No one else had ever cared enough, or been brave enough, to stand up to the Earl of Porterbridge. Uncle was simply too un-pleasant a character to challenge.

She glanced over at her uncle and the group of self-important friends that surrounded him. Uncle never forgot a slight. She ought to face him now.

Gathering her courage and her skirts, she walked toward Uncle. He turned his back.

Charlotte halted, courage withering, as the group

around him broke into shocked whispers.

Behind her, Wynter muttered a curse and stepped past her. Charlotte caught his sleeve and exclaimed, "No!"

He stared down at her, his brown eyes golden with fury.

"No," she repeated. "You'll make matters worse."

"She's right, young man," Mr. Burton said. "That shabby old wind-breaker is getting worse all the time. There's no use paying him the compliment of wrath."

Wynter glanced down at Charlotte. "He hurt you."

"No. Really. It was unpleasant. Nothing more." To Charlotte's surprise, it was true. Her uncle's slight left her mortified, but unbroken.

"Burtie's right. The spiteful old blackguard feeds on it." Mrs. Burton patted Wynter's back, then skillfully changed the subject. "Charlotte, which children are your charges?"

"There's one." Charlotte indicated Robbie, playing with Alfred and some of the other boys. But her first scan of the churchyard failed to find Leila. Alarmed, she looked again, and found the girl alone, leaning against a pillar on the church portico. "Leila is over there."

"What beautiful children!" Mrs. Burton exclaimed.

"Yes, they are." Her mind and gaze still on Leila, Charlotte absentmindedly accepted the compliment herself, and never noticed the smile Wynter exchanged with the Burtons.

Mrs. Burton pressed her hand against Charlotte's cheek. "Now that the drama's over, people are leaving and we, too, must go. Cook gets irate when we're late for our meal. But, dearie, it was good to see you. When you have your half day off, use it to visit us."

As always, Mrs. Burton wore too much rose cologne and wore a hideous bonnet trimmed with pink satin roses. Her dedication to rose scent, rose-shaped handbags and rose gardens had always made the youthful Charlotte giggle. Now nostalgia gripped her by the throat, and she could only nod.

As Mr. and Mrs. Burton left, Charlotte again looked for Leila, and again found her standing alone, watching her brother play with his new friend. "If you would excuse me, my lord, I must fetch Leila."

Leila straightened as Charlotte approached, and the hopeful look on her face made Charlotte's heart wrench. Leila was feeling abandoned, and that was a feeling Charlotte well understood. She knelt beside her.

"Are we going home soon?" Leila asked.

"Indeed. And this evening, perhaps we can read a story from *The Arabian Nights' Entertainments*."

Leila moved close to Charlotte's side. "Yes, please. I like to read about my home."

Oh, dear. "That's not your home, darling. This is."

"No." Leila leaned her head against Charlotte's shoulder as if she were weary. "My home is where the magic is."

Home. Magic.

When had Charlotte last felt that?

But she would do better for this child. She kissed Leila's forehead, and resolved to find some special something that would help Leila find the magic in England.

"Come on, then." She stood and took Leila's hand. "Let's go."

Magic. She was beginning to feel it again . . . and it terrified her.

$\mathcal{A}$s THEY BUMPED ALONG THE RUTTED ROAD, CHAR-
lotte's fright faded. Yet every time she looked at Wynter, seated across from her, the panic returned, stifling
in its intensity. She didn't really understand. He wasn't
doing anything magical. Indeed, he held Leila in his
lap while he explained the Anglican service to the
children, and most people would have said he was the
very portrait of an enlightened family man.

Yes, he had kissed Charlotte. Some might say he
had wooed her. But he hadn't demonstrated savagery
in any of his dealings around the estate. Really, his
barbarism consisted of nothing more than a pierced
ear and bare feet.

Yet she argued logic with herself to no avail. She
wanted—needed—to get away from him, for she
sensed in him an intent to learn her secrets, and to
work his magic. As the carriage pulled up to the terrace at Austinpark Manor, Charlotte began to chat.
"The Burtons reminded me, I haven't taken any of my
half days. Since I've seen them and they were so kind,
perhaps I should visit them right away."

"Now?" Robbie asked. The footman opened the
door and he jumped out of the carriage in one long

leap. "But you just saw them," he yelled as if a great distance separated them.

"You promised to read to me," Leila said.

Charlotte patted Leila's hand so quickly it betrayed her nervousness. "So I did. And I will, as soon as I get back this evening. Your nursemaid, Grania, can watch over you. You can have your dinner and, if the ground dries out enough, a walk."

The froth of words spilling from her should have overcome any objection, but Wynter still hadn't said a word. His reticence reverberated over the maroon leather upholstery and slid like ice down the glass windows.

If only Charlotte made a habit of chatting . . . but she detested chatting women. She did it so badly even Leila watched her with wide eyes as Wynter picked up his daughter and handed her out to the footman. He tweaked Leila's chin and smiled at her until she smiled back, then waved the footman away.

And shut the door.

Charlotte stared at his hand resting on the door with equal amounts of horror and, to her chagrin, excitement. The interior of the carriage was luxurious, but too small to contain one jittery woman and one large man exuding demand and determination.

But surely she was misinterpreting his actions. He was probably being excessively protective, "My lord, it is not necessary to drive with me to the Burtons'. I can easily find my way alone."

Wynter settled back on the seat opposite, crossed his arms over his chest and stared accusingly at Charlotte. "You haven't given me the explanations I am owed."

"I don't owe you any explanations." Outside, she heard the low buzz of the servants' voices as they tried to puzzle out this odd behavior. Glancing out, she saw them huddled on the steps, glancing toward the carriage and gesturing. "Are you, too, going somewhere?" she asked hopefully.

He ignored her as if she hadn't spoken. "The Earl of Porterbridge is the head of your family."

The coachman broke away from the little group to tentatively tap on the door. "My lord? Where did you wish me to drive you?"

"Nowhere. Go away."

"That was rude." The rebuke was not automatic, but an attempt to shift the balance of power and, even better, change the subject.

"Skeets?" Wynter called.

Skeets shuffled back. "Yes, my lord?"

"*Please* go away."

Charlotte couldn't look, but she writhed as she imagined Skeets's confusion before he replied, "As you wish, my lord."

She didn't have to think, she *knew* he was on his way to the kitchen to spread the gossip. "Open the door," she demanded softly. "What will the servants think?"

Obviously Wynter didn't care, nor would he follow her conversational leads. He would discuss what he wished, and she would not escape until he was satisfied. "You, Lady Miss Charlotte, are one of the Dalrumples of Porterbridge Hall."

It wasn't warm in here, exactly. The recent rain and the intermittent clouds kept the temperature down. But beads of perspiration formed on her upper lip, and she fumbled for a handkerchief. "If I answer, will you let me out?" He paid no attention to her attempt at a bargain, but pursued his line of questioning with a hard glint in his eye. One would have thought he was angry with her.

"Women should be protected," he said, "yet your uncle allows you to go from house to house unchaperoned, a prey to any man who wishes to have you."

Could he be any more high-handed? Ignoring her wishes, trapping her here, insinuating she had been helpless?

Insinuating she had been a loose woman? This was what came of sharing a kiss with him. Dignity. Grace. Equanimity. She needed all of the disciplines, and this was the proof of it. "I am not prey, my lord, and there is not a nobleman in England who dares imagine I am."

"So you have taken care of yourself."

"Exactly!" She blotted her upper lip.

"That is the right and duty of your uncle. You are twenty-six. You are unmarried and unfulfilled. You are miserable."

"I am not!"

He took a deep breath. "Very well. Even in El Bahar, there are those who fail in their duty."

Slowly, she relaxed back against the seat. He didn't appear angry now. He appeared to be reflective, and although one might wish he would pick an emotion and stick with it, perhaps this signified the beginning of the end of this interrogation. If she humored him, surely she wouldn't have to listen to any more insults. In a soothing tone, she said, "I'm sure there are."

"But I know my duty. I hereby assume responsibility for you."

She sprang forward in the seat. "You? Responsibility for me? I do not grant you permission!"

"I do not need permission." He leaned forward slowly, until their knees met and they were eye-to-eye—with him looking down on her, of course. "You are a woman in my employ."

"That doesn't give you the right—"

"Sometimes a man does not wait to be given rights. Sometimes he must take them."

Frustration bubbled up in her, and she almost shouted at him. But she didn't doubt some servants lingered near, and if she shouted, Leila would hear about it, and how could she convince the child to maintain a reasonable tone if her teacher couldn't even do so? So she regulated her tone until it was polite, well enunciated and so frigid he should have dropped to the ground stricken by frostbite. "The trouble with you, my lord, is you say these things and you don't seem to realize how inappropriate they are."

He thought for a moment, his handsome face a blank. "But I do. I simply do not care."

He was so much taller than she was, blessed with the confidence a handsome face, money and masculinity gave in a world run by men. The sense of being stifled grew in her again, and a trickle of perspiration ran down her spine.

"Am I so wrong, then? In England, is it not a man's duty to care for his female relatives?"

How she hated this! "Men usually support their daughters, but it's not required for a man to care for all his nieces and aunts. That would be a very great burden."

"For a poor man, yes. I see girls working here in the house and understand that they are helping their families to live. But your uncle is a wealthy man."

" 'Wealth' is a comparative term. All of my father's possessions were entailed to the male heir—"

"Your father was the eldest son and the earl before the current Porterbridge."

He was annoying her now. He had to know the truth

of this, but she answered courteously, "Yes, that's why I'm Lady Charlotte."

"All the money and all the lands went to your uncle. I still do not understand why you say he is not wealthy."

"He is very wealthy and very . . . he has many children."

"Ah." Wynter nodded. "His manhood is potent."

She snapped out, "Why is it that if there are many children, the man is potent, but if the marriage is childless, the woman is infertile?" Then, appalled, she shut her eyes. What madness moved her to voice what she had always thought? And, oh, dear, would Wynter assume because of her bad example, he could discuss fertility as he wished? Opening her eyes, she looked earnestly at him. "That was extremely improper of me. Please realize you may not ever refer to the . . . ah . . ."

"Making of babies?" he proffered helpfully.

"Fruitfulness," she said firmly. "In proper society, you may not speak of or in any way refer to any man's or any woman's fruitfulness for any reason."

"Lady Miss Charlotte, I do not know what I would do without your tutelage."

Could he be making mock of her?

Before she could question him, an idea seemed to strike him. "You object to me taking responsibility for you. You say you are capable of standing alone, without the guidance of a man. If I knew your story, I might agree."

Enlightenment arrived in a rush. "You're holding me hostage!" She grabbed for the door.

He caught her arm and held her. Not tightly—he wasn't hurting her. He wasn't letting her go, either. "Lady Miss Charlotte, I wish to know why you are so alone."

She should have recognized that look on his face right away. She'd seen it often enough. From the moment Wynter walked in yesterday from London, he had been stalking her, not because he wanted her, but because of vulgar curiosity. Someone in London had been gossiping. "I would wager you already know."

"Not enough about you, Lady Miss Charlotte." He watched her hungrily. "Never enough about you."

Now he hungered for details. And what difference did it make, really? He wanted to know. She would tell him. Then, maybe, he'd leave her alone to do her job.

Yanking her arm out of his grasp, she settled back on the seat, her arms crossed over her belly and her mouth unsmiling. "What do you want to know? Everything? Or just the information about my ignominious departure from Porterbridge Hall?"

He leaned forward as if he still feared she would bolt. "Everything, I would think."

She looked down at her fingers, and absentmindedly straightened their clawlike curve. "I was an only child. I was very spoiled. I had a nursery, a nanny, a governess and many toys all to myself. The corridors of Porterbridge Hall were mine to run through. The lands were mine to ride my pony across." Her youth had truly been a golden time, and the only way she could talk about those years was in a monotone, shutting herself off from the memories by sheer determination. Because when she allowed herself to remember . . . She would not remember. "Papa and Mama were killed by a lightning bolt when I was eleven."

Wynter tried to take her hand, but she flinched away from him. "You want to know. You can know. Just don't touch me."

He didn't like that, she could see. His wide brow puckered and the skin around his scar turned white.

But as she suspected, he wouldn't do anything to jeopardize this engaging gossip, or at least not until she had told every last juicy morsel.

She held his gaze until he nodded and sat back, then she continued, "The land wasn't mine anymore. The manor wasn't mine anymore. My uncle and his family moved in, and there were so many of them. They said I didn't need the nursery, I wasn't a baby, and they placed their infants in the cradle where I'd rocked my dolls. The older ones invaded the playroom. My uncle said he didn't need to buy toys, because I had so many. My nanny resigned, and my governess. Uncle didn't want to pay them more for caring for and teaching all his children than they had been paid for just me. I had to share my bedchamber with two of my cousins. One wet the bed. They fought. There was no place I could go to be alone, and no one cared for me." That sounded like self-pity, so she added in explanation, "Why would they? They didn't even care for each other."

Wynter stripped off his gloves and tossed them aside. "What did you do?"

"Do?"

"Did you throw tantrums? Did you demand your toys back?"

"No. Of course not. I was so bewildered . . . I look back and I think, poor child. So confused. Just on the brink of womanhood and no one—" She snapped her mouth shut. She didn't want to give him insight into the troubled girl she had been. He would enjoy it too much, this retelling of her pain. They all enjoyed it, all the seekers after scandal.

"You were frightened."

His soft tone and kind eyes couldn't fool her. This was an inquisition of the most brutal kind. "Of everything," she agreed harshly. "I think that annoyed the whole family. They'd shout, stomp around, kick each other and fight. I didn't understand that kind of display. I didn't know how to act like that."

"Do you understand now?"

"I have lived with many different families. Some are happy, some are not. Some are boisterous, some are not. Some make it their mission to make each other miserable—like my uncle's. I don't *understand,* but I know all that is true."

"I think my family is happy," he said reflectively. "At least, my mother is happy to have us home, and the children will be happy when they've adjusted. Don't you think so, Lady Miss Charlotte?"

"I think your children are charming."

"Don't you want to know if I'm happy?"

She smiled, but it was a difficult, unwieldy curving of the lips. "You must be happy, my lord. You must be positively ecstatic."

He didn't like her sarcasm, and his accent grew pronounced. "Not . . . yet."

Her toes curled in her shoes, and reluctantly she practiced circumspection, telling herself that was wise, for he was still a barbarian. "I tried to make myself invisible. I did whatever my uncle and aunt told me, but the other children used to get me in trouble when they could. So Uncle would yell at me, and I hated that. The problem is he looks so much like Papa. But Papa was Papa. He loved my mother and he loved me. If the present Earl of Porterbridge loves anyone, he keeps it well hidden. He has the spirit of a raging toothache."

She finished speaking, and Wynter realized with a jolt she had no intention of telling him the rest of the story. He was stunned. He was most empathetic and insightful, and she was talking to *him,* the mate of her soul, the man who would wed her. She didn't know that yet, she ought to know he could be trusted.

Nevertheless, he would not reproach her. He knew she had been hurt—everything in her contained manner warned him that this was a woman who had been maltreated again and again, until every kind word was suspect. "Your story is much as I thought."

"Is it?" she asked crisply.

Undoubtedly she was annoyed with him, for she guarded her privacy most assiduously. But when she heard how her tale affected him and what a favor he would confer on her, she would be soothed. "This also tells me I am right in my plans."

"What plans are those?"

"We shall marry." His pronouncement left her, he noted with pleasure, speechless. Also immobile and wide-eyed with the honor done her. He kindly continued to give her a chance to recover. "You are suitable. You're well-bred, you're handsome, you're exceptionally courteous"—he paused, but she didn't smile— "and you are in need of a husband."

She didn't exclaim, or thank him, or throw herself into his arms in an ecstasy of joy. Perhaps she didn't truly understand, or perhaps she thought him indifferent or uncaring about the attraction she felt for him. So he clarified. "Also, we both feel desire for each other. Our bedsport will be most satisfying."

Now she responded. Color swept into her face and she lowered her head like a camel about to charge. "My . . . lord." She spaced the words carefully, as if he might be unsure of his title. "I am not in need of a husband."

He chuckled. "Do not be absurd."

The rim of her bonnet began trembling, and the

trembling worked its way down her arms to her fingers.

Alarmed, Wynter tried to gather both her hands in his to chafe them.

In a tantrumlike motion as unrestrained as any Leila had ever produced, she knocked him away. With a staccato delivery, she said, "I have heard your speech before." She took a gulp of air. "I have been told before that I was suitable, well-bred and virtuous, and therefore the privilege of marriage would be conferred on me despite my poverty, and I would have the chance to express my gratitude and my undying devotion every day for the rest of my life."

The words she spoke forced him to realize he had expressed himself badly. "I would expect—"

"I don't care what you expect." She wasn't shouting or in any way sounding less than civil, but that shaking continued as if emotions bubbled within her that she couldn't contain. "When I was seventeen, I was an obedient young female who would do as she was told, even if it meant she would be a nothing, the keeper of an empty place men call a wife. But I changed my destiny." Her eyes froze him with their intensity. "You can't delude me, my lord. You know everything. Whoever told you my story wouldn't leave out the best part."

Trying to express his sincere sympathy seemed the only way to calm her. "All parts seem to me to be a tragedy."

But his sympathy seemed only to insult her. "Not this part." Her trembling halted. "This part was a triumph, because I . . . walked . . . away. I left my uncle's house with a single bag and caught a public conveyance to London."

He winced. To think of Charlotte at seventeen,

alone on a coach and traveling to the city, terrified him. Even though he knew her story ended well—or would once she accepted his proposal—he wanted to protect her from the terror and loneliness she had suffered. Such was the influence she had on him.

"I went to the house of a female acquaintance," she said, "a commoner who wished badly to have her son become part of society. She hired me. Hired me for the same reasons I had been suitable wife material. By the time she heard the tale of my rebellion, her son was well on his way to being acceptable, and she allowed me to finish the job."

The tightness in his gut loosened a little. "She was kind, then."

"She was a swine who lowered my wages, citing as a reason the price of scandal."

He had wanted Charlotte to tell him this, to share the trauma of her every experience so he could assure her of his tolerance. Yet for reasons that he didn't understand, she was not responding with the relaxation of her ever-present caution.

When Barakah had told him about women, he warned him of this, too. He had said that sometimes women failed to grasp that their man had only their interests foremost in his heart. Wynter had never personally experienced such behavior, so he had discounted it as a myth. Now he sent an apology to Barakah, who as he sat on the right hand of Allah was no doubt laughing at Wynter's folly. "I am grieved that your situation at that time was not ideal, and I still grieve that your situations since have left you unhappy."

"I am not unhappy," she said coldly.

He ignored that, as it deserved. "But I am a man.

You are a woman, and you must trust me to know what is best for you."

Her shaking began again.

"You will wed me. It is the right and proper thing to do."

"I will not walk up the aisle even if it means security and approval from the society which has scorned me." Her vehemence was all the more convincing for being subdued. "I have stood alone for nine years, my lord. I will stand alone until I die."

He studied her in astonishment. "Are you refusing me?"

"This is not a refusal, my lord, this is indifference."

He allowed her to place her hand on the door and open it. The step had been put below, and she used it to descend as the footmen rushed to assist her.

Wynter waited until she stood on the ground before he called, "Regardless of your indignation and your . . . er . . . indifference, Lady Miss Charlotte, I think you love me."

She turned her head toward him, but he couldn't see past the rim of her bonnet. "I think, Lord Ruskin, that you do not know what love is."

CHAPTER 18

LOVE HIM. CHARLOTTE HEADED DOWN THE CARRIAGE-way for a walk to the far reaches of the estate. Toward the oak tree in the meadow. Or the bench in the formal garden. Or to the Americas, although the Atlantic would present a bit of a challenge for a woman no taller than she was.

Yes, she should have gone to the nursery, sought out the children and proceeded about the business of being a governess as if nothing untoward had happened.

Nothing *had* happened.

In the inner reaches of her mind she had been prepared to be disappointed in Wynter. She was. Her infatuation was over. She would proceed as if their brief interlude had never happened.

Love him. As if she would love a man like him. A man who had abandoned his mother, his country and his manners. Who did he think he was, some pasha too lofty for ethics? She couldn't love a man like him.

She found herself swinging her arms and putting each foot before the other in excessively firm movements. Movements that, if nature had comprehended her mood, would have shaken the earth.

Dear heavens, why had she told him the truth of her life in such detail and with such passion? She knew how to relate her story—in a dry tone, as if the past had ceased to wound her and she didn't care that she lived in exile from the place where she'd grown up. When she pretended indifference, she at least saved her pride. Now she had no pride. And he thought she loved him!

At least when she'd refused that first proposal, her suitor hadn't accused her of loving him. Indeed, he would have been surprised and offended if she'd offered such emotion. And she never would have. Even if he had gone to the trouble of courting her, she'd had too much sense *then* to imagine the courtship to be prompted by anything other than expediency.

Love him. Wretched Wynter thought she loved him. Probably he had proposed marriage with no intention of going through the ceremony and every intention of performing the consummation. But Charlotte was no dewy-eyed fool. No, she was too old and wise to fall for that hoary trick.

"Miss Dalrumple?" the hostler called as she hurried past the stables.

Reluctantly she halted. "Yes, Fletcher?"

"Need t' talk t' ye."

She didn't want to speak with him. She didn't want to speak with anyone, especially not someone of the male gender, but Fletcher was a man of few demands and fewer words, so when he communicated it was with purpose. "Is there some service I can render to you?" she asked.

"Me t' ye." The knotted, gnarled hostler gestured toward the fenced stableyard with his unlit pipe. "D'ye know th' little girlie is ridin' yon mare?"

"The little girlie?" Charlotte was bewildered. "Not . . . Lady Leila?"

"Th' very same."

"That's . . . that's not possible." Charlotte strode to the paddock. The horse he indicated was no pony, but fifteen hands high and sleek with the spirits of a healthy young animal. "When?"

Fletcher had been around for so many years he knew she wasn't really expressing disbelief, only consternation. Speaking as calmly as if he'd been gentling a horse, he said, "Knew someone was ridin' Bethia. Saw th' evidence. Didn't know who or how. Stableboy told he'd seen a teeny sprite who flitted along on fairy wings."

"What nonsense!" Leila was no sprite, and for a moment Charlotte's spirits rose. Perhaps the hostler was mistaken.

"Aye. Seen me share o' sprites, don't none o' them ride worth a damn. Beggin' yer pardon, m'lady. So I kept watch." Fletcher placed his pipe between his lips and sucked on it as if it were lit.

"You're sure it's Leila?"

"Skinny girl, six hands high, good bones, nice mane. Aye, it's her."

Charlotte placed her hand on her racing heart. What if Leila had been hurt while riding, and no one had known where she had gone? At the thought of the child lying helpless, unconscious or crying in pain, Charlotte had to lean hard against the white-painted fence.

Fletcher watched her until she'd recovered her first fright. "She's ridin' after supper when ye've given yer charge into th' hands o' th' nursemaid. Best chide Grania."

"I would suppose." Charlotte narrowed her eyes at

the hostler. "You've stopped Leila, of course."

Fletcher snorted. "Nay. Not I. Can't stop a girlie who slips in wi'out bridle or saddle an' rides th' beastie. Never seen a girlie ride like her, m'lady. Never seen a child commune wi' a horse like that. 'Tis a gift an' an inspiration t' this old man." He tapped the pipe against the fence. "Just thought ye ought t' know."

"Yes," Charlotte said faintly. "Thank you."

Her walk forgotten, she turned toward the manor. She had to talk to Leila at once. She had to make her see the danger she courted. Charlotte placed her hand on her own forehead. This was her fault. She hadn't done as she had promised the first day she arrived and taught Leila to ride sidesaddle. She hadn't acknowledged the child's love of horses at all, and Leila had taken matters into her own hands.

Worse still, Charlotte had been distracted lately, imagining all manner of romantic drivel. Never mind that teaching the children in the day and Wynter in the evening had occasionally made her bleary-eyed. She was being paid, and paid well, to perform both duties for the limited time until the Sereminian reception. Moreover, she understood that Leila craved attention. The poor child was homesick and trying to find something to replace the life she had lost. Charlotte understood that, and her. Everything else in Charlotte's life was nothing but smoke and distraction.

Entering the house, Charlotte went at once to the nursery. She found Robbie cleaning his muddy boots on the hearth. "Stop that, Robbie," she said mechanically. "Send those downstairs for the footman to clean."

Leila stood holding the wooden horse Charlotte had brought her as a gift and staring at it as if at this very moment she were contemplating a ride.

Grania was nowhere in sight. Heads were going to roll.

Torn between the desire to hug Leila and the desire to shake her, Charlotte squatted before her charge. Leila looked up inquiringly, and Charlotte asked, "Dear, can we have a little talk?"

"You're in trouble," Robbie muttered.

Charlotte ignored him, intent on making Leila feel at ease with her. "Let's sit down on this bench, shall we?"

Leila sat down where she stood, right on the hard floor.

Obviously, she was still perturbed at Charlotte. "This is a good place, too." Charlotte sat down beside Leila, ignoring the discomfort of her corset, and slipped her arm around Leila's shoulders. "I would like to go riding with you."

Leila's dark gaze slid toward her, and she examined Charlotte suspiciously. "Why?"

"You said you liked to ride, and I want to train you."

Leila contemplated her wooden horse, then her earnest governess. "I don't need to be trained; I already know how."

Robbie sidled over and stood above them. "She's going to teach you to ride like an English miss, fool."

"She's not a fool," Charlotte reprimanded. Then, aware she had been too sharp, she thumped Robbie's arm. "She's so smart, it's immediately obvious she's *your* sister."

Robbie's face contorted as he tried to decide if he'd been insulted or praised.

Satisfied she had silenced him for the moment, Charlotte said persuasively, "When you learn to ride sidesaddle, Leila, we can ride together."

Leila hunched her shoulders.

Charlotte's vivaciousness faltered under such disinterest. She had truly failed the child if Leila didn't care to ride with her. "Every morning."

Leila narrowed her eyes.

"When your father is home, you could ride with him."

"Papa doesn't ride sidesaddle," Leila retorted.

"He could if he wanted to," Robbie said.

Grateful for that answer, which would never have occurred to her, Charlotte replied, "I don't know if he could or not. Boys ride the easy way."

Leila pulled her knees up and wrapped her arms around them. "Can I stand up?"

"Now?" Bewildered, Charlotte looked around the nursery.

"No, on the horse!"

Charlotte blanched. "Why would you do that?"

"We always do," Robbie said enthusiastically. "We stand up, and we hang off to the side, and we practice shooting between the horse's legs." He swaggered and for a moment he looked so much like his father Charlotte blinked at the illusion. "I'm really good at hitting a target."

"So am I," Leila shouted.

"A lady's voice is always low . . ." Charlotte trailed off. How did one tell a child not to raise her voice when she had been rehearsing for a desert battle? "Guns? You shoot guns?"

From his wide grin, it was obvious Robbie comprehended Charlotte's consternation and fully intended to enjoy himself. "Papa can shoot a bow and arrow, but he hasn't taught me."

Charlotte still couldn't—didn't want to—fully comprehend. "Your father lets you shoot guns while riding on the horse's side?"

Leila looked at Robbie, and Charlotte saw the silent communication that passed between them.

"Papa made us practice with the rifle before he let us ride with it." Leila paused dramatically. "He was afraid we were going to hurt the horse."

Charlotte stood and paced across the room. "This is worse than I thought."

The children burst into giggles.

She fixed them with a stern look. "Are you children teasing me?"

"No, Lady Miss Charlotte," they said in unison.

"I'll have to talk to your father." She had known all along she was going to have to have a conversation with him anyway. She had to inform him of her failure to monitor Leila and the child's escape to the stable. But now . . . now she would have to find a way to tactfully wrap her hands around his throat and demand what he'd been doing, teaching children of such tender age to shoot and ride like gypsies.

She had also hoped not to see him so soon after the scene in the coach, but she was not so weak-minded as to delay for the sake of her own composure.

"When are you going?" Robbie asked.

"As soon as I speak to Miss Symes about getting a nursemaid up here who understands her duty."

Leila scowled.

Charlotte knelt beside her. "Leila, I must ask for your word that you'll not go riding without a companion."

"Told you you'd get caught," Robbie said.

Leila shrugged one bony shoulder.

"Leila, please." Charlotte lightly stroked her hand over Leila's hair, then under Leila's chin. "I love you, and I would worry if you rode out on your own."

"I won't get lost." Leila allowed Charlotte to lift her chin. "Do you really love me?"

Charlotte looked into that thin little face. "Very much."

Oh, God, it was true. She had broken the first rule of governessing. She had come to love her charges as if they were her own children. But what could she do? While she hadn't been looking, these imps had stolen their way into her heart. If Wynter had been shrewd, if he had truly wished to disturb Charlotte, he would have accused her of loving his children. It wasn't Wynter who squeezed her heart into painful little knots of anxiety, or sparked pride at their accomplishments. It was his children. Of course.

Flinging wide her arms, she held them open . . . and waited for one very long second.

Leila launched herself first, coiling herself around Charlotte like a vine which had found the necessary support. "I love you, too, Lady Miss Charlotte."

Robbie was second and made up for it by hugging her to the point of pain. "I love you a lot, Lady Miss Charlotte."

They offered up their faces. She kissed them both, and hugged them again, and accepted noisy smacks on her cheeks. She came away from their embrace with tears of tenderness and the desperate hope that she hadn't done wrong by declaring herself. After all, governesses were easily replaced, especially when they'd spurned the master. But Lady Ruskin had promised she could stay through all the children's formative years, and so Charlotte would remind her. Charlotte would fight for these children.

Leila touched the tears on Charlotte's cheek. "Aren't you happy?"

"Very happy. Happier than I've been in so many years." Charlotte smiled at them and rose. "You've gladdened my heart."

"Are you going to see Papa now?" Robbie asked.

"Absolutely." It would be easy, for she didn't love *him*. *"After* I find you a nursemaid."

$\mathcal{T}$HE NEW NURSEMAID DISPATCHED AND GRANIA REP- rimanded, Charlotte strode along the corridor toward the old nursery. She was not completely at ease at the thought of seeing Wynter, but it would take more than a marriage proposal and the unfounded insinuation that she loved him to make her timorous. Her dismay had been nothing more than an instinctive recoil against another heartless and unwished-for proposition.

The door was open. Standing in the corridor, she stared at it as she straightened her bodice and stiffened her spine. Dignity. Grace. Equanimity. Those were the keys to dealing with Wynter. Indeed, those were the very foundations of her character.

Stepping inside, she found the nursery empty. Sunshine shone through the windows on the worn floorboards and old draperies. The carpet, cushions and table huddled against the empty fireplace. Charlotte realized that night's shadows and the flickering firelight had lent atmosphere to a barren chamber. The magic she had experienced here was nothing but a necromancer's trick.

"Lord Ruskin?" she called toward the almost-closed door at the back of the room.

No one answered at once, and relief niggled at her. If she was unable to locate him, then she didn't have to immediately face a possibly unpleasant scene. Or rather, the continuation of the last unpleasant scene.

Sternly she banished her discomfort. Dignity, grace, equanimity, she reminded herself. She need only re-member those qualities and Wynter's derangement could not disturb her.

"Lady Miss Charlotte?" His voice halted her. Framed in the doorway, he wore his usual outfit—trousers, a collarless shirt and no shoes. He also wore a most obnoxious and delighted expression. "I didn't expect you so soon."

Even without knowing exactly what he meant, she bristled. "Expect me? Why would you expect me?"

He chuckled indulgently. "Already you have changed your mind. You wish to accept my proposal and live blessed as my wife for the rest of your days."

Dignity? Grace? Perhaps. But equanimity failed her. She wanted to rant at him, to demand to know why he thought her such a spineless creature that she needed a man such as him. "No."

"Ah, you have some other excuse."

"I suppose you could call it an excuse, my lord, if you believe the news that your daughter has been rid-ing out alone is not important."

His grin disappeared. His eyebrows shot up. She noted with profound satisfaction that this was the very portrait of a man affronted. Good. One of the two of them was always agitated. It was about time he took a turn.

Stepping aside, he gestured her in. "Here. Now."

She marched toward him, appalled at her tactless

breaking of the frightful news and at the same time delighted by the fact she had knocked him off his manly perch and down to the level of the rest of humanity. As she passed him, he placed his hand on the small of her back and propelled her forward.

Unlike the nursery, this room was small, smaller even than her bedchamber, and she realized with a start that this had once been assigned to Wynter's nursemaid. The gewgaws he detested were manifestly absent, but this room contained a large carpet covering almost the entire floor, glowing in gold and emerald and fringed in scarlet. Scattered about were tables with shortened legs, some with papers stacked on their surfaces. Vermilion and gold velvet cushions were arranged according to his whim. Under the windows, a feather mattress rested on the floor under a wrap of netting suspended from the ceiling.

She had suspected; now she knew for sure. This was his bedchamber.

He slammed the door behind her. Fulminating, she turned on him, but he pointed his finger toward her nose. "Do not complain, Lady Miss Charlotte. If you are going to throw such a report at my head, you take the consequences."

She was not the kind of woman who quailed at the voicing of a threat. Instead she narrowed her eyes and gave him the glare that had reduced adolescents to cowering wrecks. "What consequences are those, my lord?"

"You will tell me why Leila has been allowed to ride without supervision!"

Her knees gave way. Hoping that it appeared intentional, she sank onto a fortuitously placed pile of cushions. "She was not *allowed* to, my lord. When I . . . I broke my promise to teach her, she took matters in her own hands. She sneaked out to the stable and rode without saddle or bridle." The impropriety of her own situation faded from her mind as she once again paled at the thought of Leila, alone, on a horse so strong some men might be overwhelmed. If she had been thrown . . .

"Dear Lord, and she rides like an *afreet*." He looked down at Charlotte. "A demon," he clarified. Then he, too, sank down on the floor. "I have taught her to ride as the desert people do, and while I am proud of her courage, her tricks make her unsupervised riding a father's nightmare."

After hearing the children talk about their feats of daring, she had half feared Wynter would scoff at her concerns, but the nightmares which haunted her also occurred to him. She felt obscurely comforted, and tried to console him. "There was no harm done, and I have asked her not to ride until I can accompany her. But we don't want to put a strain on her honor. I wish to start teaching her sidesaddle tomorrow."

He sat on his heels, stroking his forehead. "I did not save her from matrimony with that runt of a camel turd to have her killed by an English horse."

"I take full responsibility, my lord. I should have made sure that a nursemaid was with them at all times . . ." She paused, suspended by astonishment. "What do you mean, you saved her from matrimony with a . . . I assume you mean with a man?"

"Hamal Siham." He said the two words with such venom Charlotte was taken aback. "The son of a goat who took over after the death of Barakah, my revered Bedouin father. Hamal was less than a rabbit's droppings. He wallowed in his own stupidity and if I had not guided the people to safety, they would have perished in the sandstorm."

"This Hamal Siham . . . he was younger than you?"

Wynter crossed his arms over his chest. "Much."

She had not been a governess of immature men for years without gaining some knowledge of the way their minds worked. "You humiliated him."

Wynter's accent deepened and his sarcasm blossomed when he grew agitated. "What tactful way would Miss Priss have suggested I use to tell him he was an incompetent who almost killed a hundred of my dearest friends?"

"There is no way, my lord. It is a futile endeavor."

His voice dropped almost to a whisper. "Are you making fun of me?"

She answered with equal quiet and a great deal of care, for she thought him poised on the edge of savagery. "No, my lord. A youth given undue power is impossible to train. He speaks with unearned authority and believes himself invincible, and woe to the one who reveals otherwise."

Wynter watched her warily.

"You led the people to safety. He hated you for it—and he tried to marry Leila?" She could scarcely speak the words for horror.

"That stinking pile of sheep dung dared to demand that I give her in betrothal as a sign of my good faith, to be wed to him at the onset of her moon cycle."

Her dismay at his predicament overcame her embarrassment and her ingrained formality, and she breathed, "Oh, Wynter." And immediately hoped he hadn't noticed her familiarity, and prayed he would never again mention a woman's menses, for she hadn't the nerve to chide him about *that*.

He seemed not to have heard her use of his first name. "He already had two wives."

That confession left her speechless.

"I knew I had to come home. My mother needed me. I should have come to England earlier, but I thought it better that the children live in the fresh air and with an absence of torturous restrictions. Yet Hamal forced me to choose, for Leila's sake." Wynter stared at a place beyond Charlotte's right shoulder and spoke as if to himself. "I would never surrender my daughter to such a culture. For me, for Robbie, life in the desert offered unlimited freedom. For Leila, even sidesaddle is better."

She hadn't realized the reasons for his return, nor could she have imagined the sacrifice he had made for his daughter. Yet she didn't wish to dwell on that; she didn't need to admire this conceited boor. "I wish you would convince Leila that sidesaddle is better."

Brought back to the present, Wynter focused his gaze on her, a gaze that sharpened with wicked delight. "That is not possible. Leila is a sensible child. She quite correctly views the sidesaddle as an inefficient, unbalanced method for riding a horse."

Arguing that point would be futile. Instead Charlotte directed his attention to the obvious. "That's as may be, but it's the only way a woman is allowed to ride in England."

She could almost see him lay the kindling of flattery. "I cannot believe you, a sensible woman, submit to such barbaric torture. Woman must strike a blow for freedom and ride as God meant us all to—with one leg on each side of the horse."

She refused to allow him to light the match. Not with her. Not ever. "Perhaps so, my lord, but that someday has not arrived, and that woman is not me. If you will recall our discussion of earlier in the day, I am disgraced and outcast. Likewise your daughter may not be seen riding with her legs astride." A dreadful thought occurred to her, and she rapidly added, "Nor should she be seen standing on the back of her horse! That would be daring to the extreme."

"Bah!" Grasping the edges of his shirt, he drew it off and tossed it aside. "Lady, you have no courage."

She was alone in a man's bedchamber, and he was undressing. She would have said she had too much courage, or too little sense. His shoulders undulated with motion, his ribs rippled smoothly down his torso, the golden hairs glided to the waistband of his trousers. Her mouth dried, and the room seemed abruptly smaller. She tucked her feet under her and prepared to rise. "I will leave you to your ablutions, my lord."

"Ablutions?" Grandly unaware of his near-nudity, he glared in irritation. "Even I, consummate barbarian that you think me, know better than to think it acceptable to ablute with an audience." He leaned toward her meaningfully. "But if I had a wife, I could ablute with her."

Sinking back, she stared in utter confusion. Then comprehension burst on her in all its jarring glory, and she stammered, "I believe you misunderstand, my lord. Ablutions are not . . . that is . . . 'to ablute' is not truly a verb, but ablutions are . . ." He watched her with such eager anticipation, confusion touched her. Was he mocking? What did he know? She'd had too difficult a day to deal with such immature teasing! "Then we are agreed. I'll start Leila's riding lessons tomorrow."

His grimace might have been either disappointment or disagreement. "I did not say we are agreed. I trust you with my daughter's education, but not with my daughter's riding. Tomorrow you will show me your skill on horseback."

She didn't want to. Since she had left Porterbridge

Manor, she had ridden only intermittently, and she hated to have Wynter see her as anything less than competent. But she admitted he was justified, and more importantly, she had no choice. She rose as gracefully as she could, considering how off balance she felt. "I will leave you now to your—I will leave you now."

He stood, too, and his hands went to his trousers.

"No." She held out her hands as if to ward him off. "Not while I'm in the room!"

The way he smiled at her dispelled any notion she might have had of his ingenuousness. Catching one of her wrists, he accused, "Lady Miss Charlotte, you are shy."

"I am proper." She twisted her wrist.

"Stop. You'll hurt yourself." Bringing her palm to his chest, he laid it over one of his male nipples.

"Why does a man insist on blaming the woman when he is trundling her about and she resists?"

"It is the nature of man."

His freely given admission surprised her, but it made no difference in his actions. He still clasped her hand to his chest and he moved it slowly in a little circle. She held herself stiffly and glared into his face. He smiled at first, but as the motion continued his smile slipped away, to be replaced by an expression of expectation. His lids half lowered over his eyes, his nostrils flared, his lips parted slightly.

The hair prickled her palm, and the nipple, at first smooth and soft, puckered under the stimulus. She knew that, for as she grew aware of the physical sensations, she found she couldn't look into his face any longer, and the response beneath her palm was echoed on his other side.

And on her. She didn't understand it. She didn't like

it. But her nipples tightened, rubbing against her chemise, poking toward him as if demanding attention. He couldn't see them. She wore all the suitable garments designed to protect her modesty. Yet she had the uncomfortable perception that he knew, and the more uncomfortable perception of pleasure.

The necromancer's tricks were not so insubstantial, after all.

She could hear his breath, a rasp in the silence.

His free hand rose and hovered an inch above her breast in a cup formed to fit. The warmth of him radiated across the minuscule space. His thumb moved. She inhaled in anticipation. But he didn't touch her; he only moved his thumb in a little circle, and she knew almost what it would feel like. Almost. And she wanted to know completely.

She had to stop this madness before it went further. "Lord Ruskin, your behavior is not acceptable."

"But I don't mind when you touch me."

Intense with purpose, she narrowed her eyes at him. "Perhaps you would if I did as I wished."

He released her captive hand at once. "Do as you wish."

She meant to slap him. He knew she meant to slap him. God knew he deserved it. But even with permission she couldn't convince herself to do it. She told herself it was a lifetime of ingrained civility which did not allow her such a violent display. She didn't care to examine any other motivations.

"Charlotte?" His accent was smooth and seductive as silk, and his hand, the one close to her chest, slipped back to his side. "You're still touching me."

Her hand. Still on his chest. She snatched it back and cradled it against her. She wanted to glare at him, but she couldn't even look at him. Odious, overbearing, commanding beast. She'd walked into his bedchamber under her own power and he'd immediately seized his advantage.

He was probably grinning with delight, but he sounded completely respectful and positively indifferent as he asked, "What time do you wish to ride?"

What time do you wish to ride? As casually as if this whole incident had never happened. "I have arranged for a drawing mistress to come in tomorrow"— she had to stop and clear her throat—"so eleven would be a good time for me. If that is agreeable to you?"

"Perfectly agreeable."

Either this scene, or the one preceding it, must be a delusion. One could not so swiftly slip from incipient passion to indifferent courtesy. Could one?

Perhaps *he* could. Perhaps a vast experience made the return to normal life less jarring. But she still couldn't bear to look at him, so his mood was impossible to fathom. "I want you to know I spoke with Lady Ruskin before hiring this young lady," she said.

"What young lady?"

"The drawing mistress. Sketching is not my strong suit, so I advised hiring someone with more expertise. Yet I don't want you to think that because I am not accomplished at drawing and because I'm having difficulty teaching Leila to read that I am incompetent."

"Of course not." Now he sounded entertained.

Which made it easier for her to overcome her inertia and raise her head, and besides, she had something she *had* to say. She began, "By the by, I wish to reply to that accusation you flung at me from the coach." She looked right at him, and he was watching her. Watching her with hungry, blatant intent. She prided herself on her intelligence, and she knew she'd escaped only because he allowed her. If she told him . . .

But she would not allow him to intimidate her. This was too important.

"Yes?" he encouraged.

Did he expect some slavish declaration? The man dripped certitude, and that gave her the courage to say, "It is not you I love, but I very much love your children."

His eyes widened. Then he gave off fresh waves of absolutely insufferable amusement. "I'm glad to hear you love my children. That is indeed one of the points I consider essential in my wife."

How had her knife thrust gone astray? "I have refused your offer, my lord, if it could be called that."

"So you have." He nodded. "So you have."

For the second time that day, she turned to walk out on him.

"Lady Miss Charlotte, I believe I have something you want."

She turned back in a fury—and saw that he held out her shoes. Snatching them, she marched away, resolved that in the future, she would avoid him when at all possible.

CHAPTER 20

WYNTER KNEW CHARLOTTE WOULD HAVE AVOIDED him if she could, but he made it his mission to keep her close . . . and aware. At the stables, he insisted on aiding her into the saddle of the gentle gelding, and his hands lingered on her boot as he looked up at the woman who loved his children—and him. "You have a natural seat," he said.

"Aye, that she does." Fletcher knocked his pipe against the fence. "But a little out o' practice, I deem."

Charlotte flushed, and Wynter hid a smile. His Charlotte was a know-it-all who hated to admit she had not mastered every situation. The idiosyncrasy charmed him, as so many of her idiosyncrasies did. She was well on her way to charming herself into a wedding ring, although she said she didn't want one. She needed to trust him; he knew what was best for her.

Fletcher looked up at the sky. "Good day fer a ride, m'lord. The sun's come out wi' a vengeance an' she's dried up th' puddles."

Wynter, too, examined the sky. "A good day," he agreed. Charlotte hadn't removed her vigilant gaze from him, watching him so warily he knew she must be worried that his hand would rise up the length of her boot and under her skirt. So he asked, "Don't you think it's a good day, Lady Miss Charlotte?"

"*I* think we had better hurry, Lord Ruskin, or the drawing lesson will be done before we return."

"This is of great importance," Wynter agreed.

She couldn't have sounded more austere when she said, "Children thrive on a regular schedule, my lord."

"I agreed with you," he pointed out.

Her gaze flicked again to the hand on her boot, and she urged her horse forward.

Grinning, he stepped back. "We'll travel the main road, then cut through the hedgerow to the meadows," he called.

She lifted her hand to indicate she'd heard him, and rode down the drive.

"What do you think, Fletcher?" Wynter asked.

"I think if ye're no' careful, m'lord, ye'll be ridin' that filly full time," Fletcher answered.

Wynter slapped the hostler on the shoulder. "That's the plan." Hurriedly, he mounted Mead and galloped after Charlotte.

Fletcher watched Wynter ride away, and said to the open air, "Ye've a way wi' horses, m'lord, but ye don't know a damned thing about women. After that one's kicked ye in th' head a few times, I'll wager ye'll be a little more humble."

Wynter would have laughed at Fletcher's prediction, for on this morning he felt invincible. The sun was shining, the air was fresh and washed clean and he commanded a high-spirited animal with saddle and bridle. It was a perfect day for hunting the wariest of prey.

He could have caught up with Charlotte easily, but he hung back to watch her with the horse. Her lack of practice showed, but she fell into the rhythm of the canter and gained in confidence as she rode. She sat straight in the saddle and held the reins properly, controlling her gelding without use of a whip. She was strong, for all her delicate appearance, and the old-fashioned smoke-gray riding habit hugged her figure much as he wished to.

At the end of the drive, she halted to wait for him. Without looking directly at him, she asked coolly, "Will I do?"

"Very well," he answered.

He wasn't talking about her riding skill, and from her dour expression, she knew it.

"I find riding horses is the most fun one can have with one's clothes on," he said.

Now she acknowledged him with a glare that could have fried a sensitive man.

"Or perhaps it would be more proper to say—with one's shoes on." Laughing aloud at her very proper indignation, he turned right on the road toward Wesford Village and London. She followed, catching up to ride at his side. That made him laugh, too. She didn't want to talk to him; that he knew. But she refused to ride behind him, even if it meant a chance to avoid his odious company.

Ah, what a woman she was!

A closed coach rolled toward the two riders, and they edged to one side of the road. Wynter frowned when he saw the crest, and Charlotte gave a gasp.

The coach bowled past—and stopped.

Damn. What was Howard here for? Did he want to borrow money? Or to pay back his wife's vowels?

Had he brought that harridan of a wife with him? Her comments about Charlotte had been marked with a tinge of rancor—had it been personal, or simply the cruelty of a female on sighting a fallen foe?

The door of the coach opened and Howard himself thrust his head out. "Ruskin," he called heartily. "Fancy meeting you here!"

Wynter walked his horse toward the man who had long ago been his friend, and who he now wished to Gehenna. "Yes, fancy. Right here outside my own estate."

Howard chuckled self-consciously. "I did think there was a chance I might see you. I'm escorting my children back to school, you see."

"You?" Wynter didn't know the man well anymore, but he thought it unlikely Howard would stir himself for such an unprofitable reason.

Yet two young, thin faces were pressed against the windows, and Howard nodded with enough vigor to persuade even the most doubtful of companions. "Yes, they attend at Buriton in Hampshire." His gaze moved behind Wynter, and he said warmly, "What luck, Charlotte!"

Charlotte? He called her Charlotte? Not Miss Dalrumple, or even Lady Charlotte?

"My lord." Charlotte's voice was as cool as Howard's was warm, but that made no difference to Howard's obvious appreciation.

"I haven't seen you for years," Howard said.

"Nine years, my lord."

Howard wore a starched collar with silk cravat, a matching silk waistcoat, black coat and trousers and perfectly shined boots. Rather a formal outfit for traveling.

Howard ran his gaze over Charlotte in a discreet but completely uncalled-for manner. "You're looking well."

"I am well."

The two spoke across the space, for Charlotte had not moved forward, and while Wynter did not always understand the niceties of courtesy, he imagined Charlotte's behavior was not polite.

Why did she choose to be rude to Lord Howard?

Howard hesitated as if unsure what to do next, when one of the children's voices came clearly from inside the coach. "Father, are we almost there?"

Howard smiled back into the interior, a genuinely fond smile, if Wynter's instinct was correct. "Not quite, sweetheart, but soon." Turning back to the road, he asked, "Would you like to meet my children, Charlotte?"

Her hostility could never extend to a child. She brought her gelding forward. "That would be delightful, my lord."

"Absolutely delightful," Wynter grumbled.

Howard didn't pay the least attention to him. He had eyes only for Charlotte, and for the girls who opened the windows and greeted Charlotte in polite, wary voices. "These are my daughters Lady Mary," Howard said. "And Lady Emily."

Howard adored his children, Wynter realized, and more than that, he gazed at Charlotte with a more licentious variation of the same adoration. Wynter didn't know what connection existed between his governess—his future wife!—and this pathetic, gambling blowhard. But he knew he didn't like it.

And Charlotte . . . she took each thin hand extended to her and shook it, and spoke to the girls in a gentle voice. She set them at their ease and chatted with them, but her smile trembled and Wynter thought her eyes were damp.

"Your children are charming," Wynter said to Howard.

Howard could scarcely drag his gaze away from the captivating scene of Charlotte and the girls. "Didn't think I had it in me, heh?"

Wynter badly wanted to answer that, but Charlotte's training had had its effect. Or perhaps Wynter could see the pain beneath Howard's elegant, overdressed exterior. "Your daughters are weary. They wish a respite. Take them up to the house for refreshments. My daughter and son are in the classroom now. An interruption would please them."

"That's good of you, Ruskin."

Wynter didn't feel good about it; he didn't ever want to welcome Howard to Austinpark Manor again. "It is. Now go."

"Yes, Father, please. I have to *go,*" the littlest girl wailed. She couldn't have been more than six, and her demand couldn't be denied.

Howard pulled a face. "I suppose we must," he said to Charlotte. "Will you be returning to the manor soon?"

"No," Wynter said. "Come, Charlotte."

Charlotte didn't argue, or glare a reprimand for his rudeness. Instead she submissively nodded and said her good-byes to the children.

Howard, on the other hand, looked shocked. His gaze moved from Wynter to Charlotte to Wynter again, and when Wynter nodded meaningfully at him, Howard deflated like a ruptured pig's bladder. Wynter and Charlotte left him leaning out the door, watching after them.

Even that set Wynter's teeth on edge, and he was glad when the road turned and they were out of sight.

He recognized the tension, and he knew it had nothing to do with dislike and everything to do with a romance gone sour.

Rage swept through him. He wanted to take Charlotte to task, to demand an explanation, to force her to admit . . . something. That she'd been Howard's teacher and he'd kissed her. But no, Howard was older than Charlotte, and Charlotte had said she hadn't seen him for nine years. Perhaps she had lied or miscalculated. Maybe she had run into Howard at some great house and he'd forced his embrace on her. Or somewhere, sometime, he'd dallied with her.

Infuriated by the images, Wynter glanced at Charlotte.

She rode like a drone, intent on the task of controlling the horse, sitting erect in the saddle. So lacking in animation and color was she, Wynter realized if a vehicle had come barreling down the road now, it would have struck her before she realized it.

This wasn't a simple flirtation gone sour. She was devastated by the sight of Howard.

By God, she'd had an affair with him!

Wynter wanted to lift his head and roar like a wounded tiger. An affair? His future wife had had an affair?

Unthinkable.

She didn't notice him. He'd spent hours, days, making sure she noticed every move he made every time he was around her, and she didn't even take note of his righteous wrath. She still rode mechanically, her lips pressed tight together, little wrinkles between her brows as if she suffered some great, unspeakable pain.

And he . . . instead of ordering her from his home, he wanted to take her in his arms and comfort her. He wanted to thrash that blackguard Howard. What was wrong with him?

Had she loved Howard?

The two rode without speaking to the break in the

hedgerow where the horses could get through. Beyond was Wynter's land, a rolling expanse of meadow dotted with trees and a trickling brook, and Wynter breathed a sigh of relief as the hedgerow blocked their sight of the road.

No, Wynter told himself. No, she couldn't have loved a man like Howard. *Howard* was a chucklehead, a weakling—married! *She* was his lady who worshiped on the altar of propriety.

While keeping an eye on her, Wynter urged Mead straight toward the hill topped with a single ancient oak. Reaching the summit, Wynter stopped and dismounted while Charlotte stared at him unseeing. He tethered Mead and Charlotte's horse on separate low-hanging branches, then reached up to Charlotte. "Down, Lady Miss Charlotte."

She did as he commanded, slipping into his arms as smoothly as any willing woman. Held close, she didn't feel abstracted or brokenhearted or seduced. She felt very much like the lady he planned to marry.

He, Lord Ruskin—born of the loins of Adorna and Henry, adopted by the people of the desert, true-hearted warrior and master of the horse—he should not have to wed a female distracted by the memory of another man. She couldn't be his soulmate.

Yet still Wynter wished to marry her. He wished to cherish her. Perhaps the humid air of England had softened his brain.

"My lord, what are you doing?" Her voice was muffled against his chest.

He looked down, but all he could see was her hat, a stiff-brimmed, veiled contraption of annoying proportions. "Holding you." But he let her go and allowed her to step away from him. "All my life, this place has been a solace for my soul. See." He waved his arm toward the view.

"Yes." She walked toward the highest place and looked around. "It's beautiful. But a solace to you all your life? You haven't been here a good portion of your life."

Where the breeze touched her face, healthy color replaced the pale stiffness.

Crossing his arms over his chest, he said, "I came here in my memory. Always I could see it. The hills rolling softly like desert dunes of spring green. The pastures rich with life and green with grass, giving to the bees, the cattle, the horses with equal generosity. Homes and stables dotting the land, roads meandering in lazy loops and from everywhere the hum of life rising to pleasure the ear."

The words were torn from her. "I saw it, too. All those years of exile . . . I could close my eyes and see the land that I loved, and when I was alone, I cried for homesickness."

Wynter realized then: They gazed across the boundary of his land onto the land of the Earl of Porterbridge. They were looking on the place where she had grown up.

They'd both been exiled, but he had exulted in his freedom. She had been condemned to a prison. A prison that stifled the heart and spirit of a thoroughbred.

That must be why she had become involved with Howard. Perhaps Wynter could excuse her for not saving herself for him . . .

Impatient with the excuses he made for her, he turned his back. Her beauty muddled his usual good sense. Not everyone would consider her beautiful, of course. She *was* short. Her hair *was* red. She had a few freckles, which some men disdained, but which he thought rather winning. Yet there was also something about her that would set any man to attention. Look at what she had done to poor, drooling Howard. Her allure was, Wynter thought, that indefinable air of innocence.

He found himself facing her again. He narrowed his eyes at her, outlined against the sky, her veil flowing in the zephyr. How could he be wrong about her innocence? How could he be wrong at all?

"Tell me," he commanded, his voice so harsh it could have stripped flesh.

She didn't play the dunce with him, and he wondered if she had begun to notice him again, and notice that he was on the verge of an explosion.

She had better bloody well be noticing him.

"Lord Howard was the man my uncle wished me to marry."

"No." His denial came from instinct and confusion. "Howard? You loved Howard?"

Charlotte stared at him, her deceptively sweet face framed in that wretched hat. "What are you talking about? I never loved Lord Howard. I would have married him if I did."

"But you did love him. You saw him on the road. He stared at you with desire. You spoke coldly to him, but you clearly showed your pain at the meeting. It must have been love, or—" He caught himself in time.

She laughed. She didn't laugh often, and this laugh was no innocent, lighthearted fling at joy. This was a woman's laugh at a foolish man. At him. "I didn't marry Howard because I thought him a vapid, weak fool who imagined himself better than me because he was in line for a title and inheritance. I thought it likely he would waste the inheritance. I've heard I was right."

"Yes, you are right."

"He didn't take rejection well. After I had refused him, he kissed me. In public. In full view of everyone." Charlotte looked disgusted. "He thought to mark me as his own, to make me change my mind. I did not, although still there are those who turn from me as if I were a fallen woman."

"And you are not."

"Not unless one pinch-mouthed kiss makes me one."

Wynter relaxed, inexorably relieved by her confession, but still confused. "Yet you grieve." Grief. Yes. The sorrowing lines returned to mar her smooth skin.

"I don't grieve for Lord Howard. I grieve because . . ." She looked back out over the view to disguise the swim of tears in her eyes. "Today I saw the road I might have taken. Being married to him would have been . . . bearable. Women have suffered worse over the ages. After all, he never would have beat me, and I've been patronized more since I refused him than he ever could have done. If I'd married him, I would have had . . ." She swallowed. "I always thought I would be a good mother."

Relief burst on him. Children! She wanted children! Of course. All women wanted children.

He was potent. *He* could give her children. It would be a pleasure.

Walking to Charlotte, he wrapped her in his arms. She stood stiffly, not fighting him but not permitting, either. Women were supposed to have instincts, but Charlotte didn't even know how to accept solace.

He refrained from shouting instructions at her. Instead he drew her closer and rubbed his palm up and down her back.

She remained rigid for one more long moment. Gradually, she grew slightly, ever so slightly, relaxed.

He kept rubbing.

She leaned into him.

Her hat knocked his chin. He growled and tilted her chin up. "That contraption must go." He jerked the ribbons apart and found himself distracted. Distracted by her eyes, wide, green and fringed by dark, damp lashes. By her soft lips, slightly open. By the dimple in her chin and the way she watched him as if she *wanted* a kiss.

Of all the wishes she held undeclared in her bosom, that was the wish he best could fulfill. Gathering her closer, he touched his mouth to hers. Just a touch, as sweet as the first gleam of light on the swell of dunes.

Her mouth moved beneath his.

Response. Sweet response. His blood leaped in his veins. He moved to deepen the kiss . . . and bumped her hat.

It slid off the back of her head. She gasped. They both grabbed. He caught it by the ribbons. And, as the romantic moment vanished, they laughed.

Together, Wynter noted with satisfaction. They laughed together.

Handing her the hat, he said, "Come. We will return and see if the man you did not wish to marry has departed."

"Yes, you should return to spend time with your friend, my lord." She tied the bow beneath her chin. "But I am the governess. My place is in the schoolroom."

As Wynter helped her back into the saddle, he thought, *Not for long, Charlotte. Soon your place will be in my bedchamber.*

CHAPTER 21

"My mother has returned."

Wynter's observation transported Charlotte back to real life. It was true. Adorna stood on the terrace surrounded by bandboxes and scurrying servants.

"Darlings," Adorna called as they rode near. "What a lovely day to be out!"

Charlotte had been in service long enough to recognize a note of doubt in her employer's voice. Adorna was not particularly pleased to see her son with the governess, and from the way she observed them, it was obvious she noted a shift in their relationship. Charlotte glanced toward Wynter to see if he had taken note of his mother's disapproval.

He displayed only pleasure at seeing his mother again.

Perhaps he hadn't heard her questioning tone. Men were notorious for failing to observe the most obvious of evidence. Or perhaps he didn't care.

Charlotte glanced at him again. He caught her eye this time and smiled back warmly.

No, this man didn't care what his mother thought. He didn't care what anyone thought. He'd already proposed to her, Lady Charlotte Dalrumple, despite the

fact he was breaking every rule, and that he should—
and could—wed a wealthy and suitable debutante.

Footmen rushed to the mounting blocks to hold the
horses' heads.

"Yes, Lady Ruskin, a beautiful day for a ride,"
Charlotte said. "Lord Ruskin wished to check out my
skill before I assisted Leila in learning the sidesaddle."
She managed to get down off the gelding before Wynter could come to help her. She climbed the stairs to
the terrace. "I believe he is satisfied that I can instruct
that precious child."

Apparently offended by her independence, he
stalked after her.

Ignoring him, she stopped close beside Adorna.
"My lord, will I be allowed to start those lessons tomorrow?"

He glared at her from the other side of his mother.
"Of course. I will accompany you."

"Dear boy, how could you be free? People have
been asking for you ever since you left the city."
Adorna laid a hand on Charlotte's arm. "Your lessons
are working, Charlotte. He was so charming, all of
London wishes to meet him, especially the ladies. My
card salver is overflowing with invitations."

Without being told, Charlotte knew Adorna
schemed to find him that perfect wife. If only Adorna
realized how wholeheartedly Charlotte approved of
that plan. "Then he should certainly go to London tomorrow."

"Those people and what they want do not matter,
Mother." Wynter had an edge to his voice. "But I will
go for the business."

Charlotte deemed it a good time to slip away, murmuring, "If you would excuse me, I must go to the
children."

Inside the manor, she was walking slowly, allowing her eyes to adjust from the bright sunlight, when from the gallery she heard her name called.

"Charlotte!" Lord Howard hurried to stop her.

In the peaceful ride back from the hill, she'd forgotten he might be there. Now she wished she had bumbled along quickly to avoid what would surely be an uncomfortable encounter. "My lord, you found your way here. I hope you were given refreshments?"

"Yes, thank you, but I would like to—"

Courtesy be damned. She interrupted. "Your children were fed, too? And taken to the schoolroom?"

"Yes, thank you, they're upstairs playing, and I've been waiting to—"

"Then I should go to them at once. Children require constant supervision, my lord, and I treasure my position as governess here." She curtsied.

"You could take a position with me." He looked at her from great, sorrowful eyes, and his tone was that of a beggar. "I could make you happy."

She backed away from him, backed away from the insinuation that he wished to make her his mistress. He used to be comely and so overbearing about his background, title and eligibility, he had annoyed her without even speaking. Now drink had corrupted the handsomeness, some great misery had crushed the arrogance and she could feel nothing but pity for him. "Thank you, but I am quite satisfied with my current employment."

He followed. "I mean it. I'd hire you. As a governess, I mean. To my children."

She almost wished he still posed and strutted. It would be better than this dejection. How hideous was his marriage that he make such an offer, when nine years ago he had sworn, in an ugly scene, never to speak to her again?

"I will keep your offer in mind should my situation change." She sped up the stairs, knowing he watched her and wanting nothing more than to get away from the man whom she'd blamed for her tribulations. It had taken facing him to acknowledge that wasn't true; her uncle's determination to get her married without a season or a dowry and her stubborn resistance had combined to bring the disaster to pass.

Once out of sight she relaxed, and realized even that disquieting scene couldn't shake her. Funny, but the last few days had been so wretched with havoc, all caused by Wynter, and now Wynter's gentlemanly regard had soothed her. And how had Wynter soothed her? By simply holding her, not with rapacious intent, but by just . . . holding her. For one moment he had allowed himself to forget all his arrogance and intractable determination and just be . . . nice. Very nice. Even the kiss was nice, and if her hat hadn't fallen off . . .

Well, that didn't matter, she chided herself briskly. She hadn't really responded, so she was still innocent of enticement.

Opening the door to the schoolroom, she was greeted by a shout of joy from Leila and by Robbie begging her to rescue him from this invasion of girls.

She relaxed. Her life had returned to normal.

Lord Howard didn't immediately summon his daughters, so after Charlotte spoke to the drawing mistress, she organized a reading activity for the children. She hoped the presence of Lady Mary and Lady Emily would incite Leila to show off, but although Charlotte could have sworn Leila understood the letters and the words, the child sat mute.

Charlotte resolved to write Pamela for suggestions; Pamela regularly taught younger children, and she might know what would spur Leila to learn.

Then Charlotte looked for her copy of *The Arabian Nights' Entertainments*. Much to her surprise, the book wasn't in her bag, but on the floor beside it. "I have been careless," she said as she dusted off the leather binding. "Books shouldn't be left on the floor. You all know that, don't you?"

"Yes, Lady Miss Charlotte," Leila said. "Are you going to read to us?"

Charlotte brushed at strands that straggled from Leila's braid. "Would you like that?"

"I like that more than anything."

"Will I like the book?" young, sallow-skinned Lady Mary asked.

"You'll like it," Leila said.

Leila would make a good governess, Charlotte thought, amused. She told one what she expected in a clear and matter-of-fact manner. Opening the book, Charlotte allowed the children to settle around her. Robbie remained aloof, close enough to hear the tale but far enough back to avoid contamination from the girls. Leila pressed close, of course, but so did Lady Mary and Lady Emily. Charlotte watched them as she read; although Lady Mary was a child given to childish whining, and Lady Emily to world-weariness, at heart they were good children, eager to please. Charlotte's heart ached for them, but she couldn't give them what they needed—a mother who cared. Yes, she preferred her current position to any Lord Howard could offer.

The door to the schoolroom opened, and Miss Symes poked her head in. Charlotte expected a summons from Lord Howard for his children, but the housekeeper clearly had other matters on her mind. She glared from beneath a prominent brow, and her mouth puckered so tightly her thin mustache bristled. "Miss Dalrumple!" she snapped. "Lady Ruskin requires your presence in the gallery. At once!"

Startled by the housekeeper's tone, Charlotte rose. "Is there some difficulty involving the children?"

Miss Symes sniffed. "That's not for me to say."

"I can't leave the children without supervision," Charlotte said.

"The new nursemaid is on her way, and Lady Ruskin will allow no delay."

Something had happened. Charlotte's heart sank— had Wynter told Adorna of his proposal? That had to be it.

Charlotte could certainly reassure Adorna about that. She wouldn't marry an arrogant man like Wynter, no matter how much he stroked her back. But to be dismissed . . . to ruin the fragile reputation of their tiny business venture.

"Here she is," Miss Symes said, and ushered the nursemaid in. "Come along, Miss Dalrumple."

Charlotte marched along the corridor and down the stairs, Miss Symes on her heels like a goaler. Charlotte hesitated at the bottom. "Where . . . ?"

"In the long salon," Miss Symes said.

The private tête-à-tête Charlotte imagined could not take place there, especially not when, as they approached, she heard the hum of a dozen voices.

"Go in." Miss Symes sounded cold as ice. "They're waiting for you."

"Who?" Charlotte asked.

Miss Symes snorted. "You'll see."

The first person Charlotte saw as she stepped into the room was her uncle the Earl of Porterbridge, seated and swollen with glee. Her aunt sat there, too, as did the vicar and the vicar's wife, a half dozen of her uncle's sycophants, and Cousin Orford. In the middle of the group sat Adorna, biting her lip and staring about her with manifest repugnance.

At once, Charlotte became the cynosure of all eyes.

The look Adorna cast at her was compounded of equal parts of guilt and relief.

What had happened?

"Charlotte, dear." Adorna's usual allure seemed badly diminished.

"I always knew you'd come to a bad end, Charlotte," Aunt Piper announced.

Adorna turned on her and snapped, "Piper, silence! I will not allow mob rule."

Aunt Piper turned an ugly color of purple and subsided.

Satisfied that she'd brought the crowd under control, Adorna continued. "Charlotte, dear, these good people have come to me with a report that very much concerns me."

A report. Well, there was a list of indiscretions. So much *had* happened, all of it with Wynter. His scandalous conversation in the picture gallery. Their kiss in the old nursery. His scandalous almost-touch in his bedchamber . . .

"You were seen atop the hill kissing Wynter."

Charlotte stared blankly. "When?"

"Has it happened more than once?" Orford crowed.

Uncle's hand swung out and knuckled him beside the ear.

Adorna briefly touched her fingers to her temple. "Today, Charlotte, dear."

Today? With all the passionate moments that had

existed between her and Wynter, and a public outcry exploded over that chaste kiss?

"Is it true?" Adorna asked.

Still dumbfounded, Charlotte didn't answer.

"The vicar and his wife saw the whole sordid affair." Porterbridge sounded jovial. "Do you doubt their word?"

In that moment, Charlotte realized how thoroughly uncivilized contact with Wynter had made her. Any intimacy between a governess and a gentleman was unacceptable. *Any* intimacy, no matter how guileless. She would have been the first to say so . . . two months ago. Now she could only recall the more ardent moments she and Wynter had shared, and thank God no one had seen any of those.

For if they had, she wouldn't be able to stand, clear-eyed and unblushing, and admit, "Yes, it's true. Wynter kissed me this morning."

The uproar that followed reminded Charlotte of the fracas that had occurred when she refused to marry Lord Howard, only worse, for Wynter's reputation as a barbarian gave the affair a greater relish. Aunt Piper's shrill voice beat against Charlotte's ears like the shriek of a bird of prey. The vicar was pontificating on something. Adorna tried to make herself heard above the babble.

Charlotte met Uncle's gaze out of pure defiance, for this time there was no escape. No one would ever hire her again. She would have to find another vocation, or change her name, or leave the country.

The clamor had risen to a crescendo when a roar from the outer door brought it to an abrupt halt. In unison, everyone turned.

Wynter stood on the threshold. Howard stood in his shadow.

"Someone will tell me what is happening. You!" Wynter pointed at Aunt Piper. "You will tell me why you visit my house and why you speak so discordantly."

Aunt Piper loved to be the center of attention, but not necessarily from a man bristling with ill humor and tainted by foreign influences. "It's . . . ah . . . about your governess."

"Lady Miss Charlotte."

"Ah . . . yes. Ah . . . Lady Charlotte. Miss Dalrumple."

Charlotte was human, after all; she enjoyed watching Aunt Piper flounder beneath Wynter's focused attention.

"She . . . ah . . . was seen . . . ah . . ."

Orford couldn't bear his mother's dithering any longer. "Oh, for God's sake, Mum, he's almost a damned foreigner. She"—he pointed at Charlotte— "has again proved herself a wanton when she kissed you this morning and everyone saw it."

Lord Howard gasped and looked at Charlotte, his eyes as wide and accusing as a cuckolded husband's.

Wynter advanced into the long gallery and came to a halt before Charlotte's cousin. "I remember *you. You're* the boy who told me at my father's funeral that my father was a peasant and I was a bastard." Wynter's fist shot out and smashed into Orford's face. The women screamed. Wynter grabbed Orford by the collar before Orford fell. "That was for my father." He hit him again. "And that was for Lady Charlotte." He released him and Orford hit the floor, moaning, then tried to stagger to his feet. "If you get up, I will just have to knock you down again," Wynter warned.

Orford sank back into convenient unconsciousness. Wynter looked around. "Now. Someone will explain everything, for still I do not understand."

He cast a commanding glare around the room.

Adorna said, "A governess's reputation must be sacrosanct. Charlotte was seen kissing you this morning. This is not the first time she has kissed a man without benefit of matrimony, and since her reputation was already besmeared, she must be dismissed."

Wynter looked to Charlotte.

She nodded. "I'm afraid that's true, my lord. Our affectionate display was unacceptable, and cannot be forgiven."

Wynter frowned in bewilderment. "Still I am puzzled. Mother, you will explain to me. In English society a kiss on the hill will ruin Lady Miss Charlotte?"

Adorna wrung her hands. "That's right."

"Yet it is acceptable for her to be in my bedroom alone at night while I'm undressing?"

CHAPTER 22

"YOU COULDN'T KEEP THAT TIDBIT TO YOURSELF, could you?" Hot with rage, Charlotte hurried along the corridor and away from the fainting women and shocked whispers in the gallery. "You had to tell them I was in your bedchamber while you were undressing."

Wynter strode behind her toward the stairway. "I shouldn't have told them I was undressing?"

Taking one step up, she turned, gripping the newel post to keep from flailing at him. "You should have said *nothing*. Before you arrived, I feared I would have to leave England to find a position. Now I fear I will have to leave the continent."

"You do not need another position. I told you you could be my wife."

Standing on a higher step, she was eye-to-eye with Wynter. "I don't want to be your wife."

"When I announced I had proposed, all of the people in the long gallery were most impressed by my gallantry."

"And your charity." Hot rage faded, to be replaced by cold mortification. "Except, of course, for your mother, who couldn't have been more appalled."

"You exaggerate." He coaxed her with his smile. "I

have frequently seen her more appalled."

Suspicion grabbed her by the throat. "This artlessness is artificial, sprung from the same guile that leads you to ask foolish questions when you know the answers and make social mistakes when you know how you should behave."

"Ah." He spread his hands. "Sometimes a man can learn many things by allowing others to believe him imbecilic and inept."

Her suspicions confirmed, she flared with indignation. "You think this is amusing!"

His smile faded. "That my future wife does not wish to wed me? No, I do not think it amusing at all. I did not wish to ruin you so thoroughly, Lady Miss Charlotte, but instead of telling those people I would do you the honor of making you my wife, you talked about leaving. I had no choice."

"You *did* understand what you were doing."

"I admit, I think like a desert man, but, in English parlance, I am not a dunce."

"No. I'm the dunce." Passing her hand over her damp forehead, she fought this sense of entrapment. She hadn't really believed Wynter meant marriage. "Why? Why do you want to marry me? I have no money. I'm not a beauty. I've been on the shelf so long I'm dusty. Why *me*?"

"We have passion," he said simply.

"All men and women have passion!"

He chuckled. "There you do reveal your ignorance. Passion such as we have is rare, and that, added to the fact you love me, makes you the most suitable of wives."

When he talked like this, revealing how clearly he valued her as a *thing,* a possession, she could scarcely breathe. "I *don't* love you."

"No. You only love my children." He chuckled again.

He frustrated her so much. He controlled every situation, and those situations he didn't control he turned to his advantage. It never occurred to him to think what she wanted was important; his belief in himself was immutable. She had to do something, *say* something that would shake that execrable confidence. Any mad accusation would do, if only it would wipe that grin off his face and give him a taste of his own medicine. "You pursue me. You steal kisses from me. You"—she pointed her shaking finger at him—"*you* must love me."

He sobered, and his eyes narrowed as he studied her. "Charlotte."

She knew at once her volley had gone astray. His kind tone and the way his hand came up to frame her face warned her.

"I could tell you a falsehood, Charlotte, but that is a poor way to begin a pledging, and you are intelligent. Soon you would acquire the truth. Then you would truly be hurt." His fingers slipped around behind her neck to hold her in place. "It is a fact I learned in the desert which seems to be lost in this society of England. This talk of romance and true love between a man and a woman. It is nonsense."

"That is your fact?" she asked incredulously.

Several spectators had sidled from the gallery and stood watching. Her aunt. The vicar. Lord Howard.

Charlotte ought to be mortified, but she wasn't. A bubble of something, she didn't know what, had come to life and was rising inside her. "Men and women don't love each other?"

"Women *do* love. That is what women are good at." His fingers massaged the tense cord between her neck and her shoulder. "And a true man cares for his wife."

"Cares for his wife." The bubble expanded, choking out her remaining good sense.

"Cares deeply." His voice reverberated with earnest goodwill. "Barakah, my desert father, explained it best. A woman loves her man. Her life revolves around the sun that is her man. But a man, like the sun, does not love a woman. He shines on his woman, he warms his woman, he shelters his woman, but the sun does not love as a woman does."

"So to be warm and sheltered and shone on, I should wed you."

He looked delighted, and he gave her shoulder a little squeeze. "Now you understand!"

She would have done anything, paid anything, to scoff at him. But she'd lived in too many different households. She'd observed too many married couples. She'd seen the husband's indifference, the wife's disillusionment. "Do you think I don't know that a man cannot love a woman? That you not only don't love me, but can't love me?"

"You said—"

"I know what I said. It was as nothing, the wisps of a melancholy fantasy tearing apart and floating away." The bubble within her had burst, and all the pent-up years of cynicism and bitterness poured forth.

His accent grew crisp. "I do not understand."

"Of course you don't. You don't have to. You're the sun, and I'm a floating particle of dirt."

"This is not what I said."

"I apologize if I misinterpreted your golden pronouncement, Lord Sun." She swallowed, trying to rid her voice of that desperate tremor. "But even sorrier because I think I interpreted your words all too well."

"Your excessive distress is unacceptable." He took

both her shoulders in his hands, held her and looked right into her eyes. "You will explain it to me at once."

"For that, Lord Sun, you will have to imagine yourself down on my level. Down on the level of a lowly woman. A woman who has no choice in her husband, who is forced to marry because of ludicrous circumstances and who is expected to love a puffed-up, overgrown, oafish boy like you."

Wynter didn't respond to the insult. Maybe he was just astonished at her wondrous flow of words.

The speech had rather amazed her, too, stored up in her brain as it must have been. "But! Love will never live between us. The passion you feel for me is not in your heart, but in a different organ entirely. And when that organ is satisfied, I no longer have any useful function in your life, except as the mother of your children and perhaps as your hostess. You will not look forward to seeing me at the end of a day. I am supposed to pine for you during your business trips, but not burden you with excessive emotion. And certainly we must not embarrass proper English society by adoring each other in any manner, or even, God forbid, conversing with each other for any reason other than to pass the vegetables and complain about finances. Yes, my lord, surely I, like every woman, must look forward to the privilege of marrying a creature such as you."

He was blinking at her. "You're mad."

"Crazy or angry?"

"I don't know."

"Neither do I." She couldn't stand here looking at him any longer. He'd admitted he knew what he was doing when he compromised her, that he knew the harm he would cause when he spoke so disingenuously. The spectators stood listening to her impassioned speech with their mouths hanging open, and worst of all, pain was unfurling inside her, roiling in her blood.

Why? She should be inured to disappointment. She never should have had hope.

No. No hope. Of all the illusions a governess couldn't afford, hope was the shiniest and most tempting, and the one dream she could never, ever afford.

Apparently Charlotte's heart had forgotten that truth.

"History repeats itself." She pushed his hands off her shoulders and walked with an excess of dignity up a few steps.

Wynter caught her skirt. "What history? Whose history?"

She staggered to a halt. "Mine. I have to marry or I'll be a pariah. But yours, too. You're marrying a woman who won't have the right to demand anything from you, because you saved her. Never mind that you ruined her in the first place; you saved her when you could have let her sink, so all will admire you. You can pat yourself on the back for being so generous"—she looked down at his hand wrapped in her skirt—"oh, wait, you're already doing that! Ah, well, munificent, lucky you never have to waste another thought on your wife and her happiness. The privilege of being your wife and warming herself in your rays should be enough."

People were getting bold, stepping closer to hear every word. Charlotte saw her aunt leaning against the wall as if overcome by her niece's outspokenness, her uncle looking between his wife and Charlotte in button-bursting astonishment, Adorna with her hand over her mouth, Howard red-faced and wiping his brow.

In a distant part of her mind, Charlotte was aware

she was making the kind of scene that would go into the annals of inglorious English gossip. She didn't care a bit. There was some facet in her, in fact, some part normally shackled and confined, that seemed to be reveling in it. "I find myself thinking I have wasted the last nine years. I would be better off if I'd married Lord Howard in the first place!"

She saw at once she'd struck a chord.

Wynter bounded up the stairs to her side. His fair hair and his earring glittered almost white with his wrath. "You do not think that."

"I do think it." Charlotte tasted the gratification of a dramatic exhibition well done before an appreciative audience, and she now allowed herself to get carried away. At least, that was what she told herself later, because there was no other explanation for her reckless pronouncement. In a voice that projected over the crowd, she proclaimed, "I tell you this, Lord Ruskin, and I mean it—I will stand up with you before the vicar and speak my wedding vows, but I will never share your bed."

The white heat of Wynter's ire gradually faded. He didn't react to her challenge. Not by a word, not by an expression, not by a twitch.

His inaction drove Charlotte to greater histrionics. "Do you understand me? I do choose to wed you, but I will never become your wife in the full sense of the word."

Still he stood motionless.

Except for a faint twitch of his upper lip.

Once long ago her parents had taken her to London to see an exhibition of wild animals. The great maned lion had not moved while she watched it, yet it reverberated with intent. The intent to hunt and stalk the prey which dared to tweak his tail.

The same intent now sprang to life in Wynter. She had become a *fête champêtre* for the great beast.

Too late she realized what she had done. Too late she wished she could recall the words.

Miss Priss had just lost her temper. Taking one step up the stairs, then another, she kept him in sight.

The crowd in the corridor murmured, their faces upturned as they watched Charlotte retreat before the stone-still Wynter.

When she thought herself out of his immediate grasp, she took a chance and turned her back. She didn't waste time on dignity; she fled with unashamed terror down the corridor and away from their audience.

She couldn't hear him following. A glance from the top of the stairs proved he still stood and watched her. She hurried toward the nursery, changed her mind, swerved toward her bedchamber. She didn't hear anything behind her, but she knew that somehow, sometime, he would catch up with her and—

He caught her arm and swung her around, trapping her against the wall. His hands slapped the wall on either side of her head. "You have until our wedding night to resign yourself to being mine."

He infuriated her with his invidious confidence and overwhelming size. He frightened her for the same reasons. She challenged him with her stance, her upraised chin, her incensed gaze. "What will you do, rape me?"

"No." He bent his head so close his breath brushed her face, and he almost crooned. "Lady Miss Charlotte, I do not need to rape you. You forget, I have kissed you, and beneath your sturdy corset and rigid propriety lives a woman with rich red blood pulsating through her veins. Your lush mouth softened beneath mine, and opened on my command. You were eager as ever I was, and I wonder how many other men you have kissed to gain such experience."

He made her so angry. Angry for throwing her folly in her face, angry that he spoke so about a moment she would have treasured, if not for its dismal results. "Except for Howard, I have never kissed another man."

"Ahhh." He held her cheek in one hand. "A babe in the ways of men."

Had he trapped her into a confession she shouldn't have made? Surely not. He was crude, obvious, not subtle at all—or so she had always thought. Wrenching her head away, she sidled under his arm. The movement only brought her up against a small round table, a stand for a delicate porcelain vase of vibrant azure hues.

He moved with deceptive leisure, snaring her between wall and table before she could flee down the corridor. "Be careful, Lady Miss Charlotte. You wouldn't want to topple my mother's prized bit of trumpery." His fingers stroked her throat. "That would bring our guests running, for they badly want to observe our mating rites. You do not want that, do you?"

He smelled of leather and horses, and that put her in mind of the gentle kiss on the hill. This moment could not have been more distinctly different. She turned her head away. "No, I don't want that, but I seldom get what I want." She heard the bitterness and self-pity, and thought, just once, that she deserved to indulge herself.

He, of course, paid those fruitless emotions no heed, but leaned to look into her face. "My delight will be to give you what you want—on our wedding night." He smiled at her, a golden barbarian, a predatory lion. "By the time we have stood in the church and said our vows, you will be throbbing with need for me. I will have tasted each sweet corner of your body, kissed you with fervor and with passion, caressed you until your nipples tighten and the dampness blossoms between your legs."

Damn him! How could a woman maintain her equanimity in the face of such vulgarity? Worse, to hear such matters openly spoken of caused her nipples to tighten, and dampness did blossom between her legs. She exerted every ounce of willpower to hold his gaze, and she whispered fiercely, "This is the kind of improper conversation I have warned you against pursuing."

"Actually, Lady Miss Charlotte, I don't believe you ever broached such a matter." His brow wrinkled as he pretended to consider, and his fingers pressed against the place where her heart throbbed in her throat. "No. No. You warned me against too-specific compliments, against speaking my mind, against criticizing the English way of life, but never did you tell me I should not make love to my woman with words."

What to say? Which point to argue? And would her meager voice be up to a diatribe of the length and insistence she longed for? All she managed was, "I'm telling you now."

"You will tell me a great many things before our wedding night, Lady Miss Charlotte, and I will not listen. You will say no, then you will say maybe, then you will cry out for me, but your words will be as a woman's breath upon a glowing fire."

Her knees shook. He was so intent, so serious. Only the servants belowstairs indulged in such tawdry sensuality. But when he spoke, it didn't seem tawdry. It seemed . . . seemed . . . too thrilling.

"Do you know what the Bedouins call a dimple such as yours?" His fingers wandered up to press the indentation on her chin. "They call it an angel's kiss, and they say one so blessed will have a long and happy life. I will see to it."

"You will not—"

He kissed her, crushing her soft mouth beneath his. This wasn't the soft, eager, mutual kiss of this afternoon—but then everything had changed since that afternoon. Now she knew he was serious about wedding her. Now she had agreed to the ceremony.

Now he wasn't cruel, but he was definite, not allowing her to deny him. He wrapped her in his arms, threaded his hand into her hair and cupped her head. He closed his eyes as he kissed her, concentrating like a gourmet sampling vintage champagne. He surrounded her with his scent. Familiar arms, familiar scent, familiar Wynter, but different from every time that had come before.

He caught her lower lip in his teeth and, when she gasped, took her mouth with his tongue. He filled her with his flavor, probed her, enticed her, when all she wanted to do was get away. Desperate enough to try anything, she placed her fingers on his arms and dug them deep.

"Don't hurt me," he murmured against her lips.

As if she could. He was bigger and stronger.

More than that—as if she would. She didn't have the stomach for violence. She couldn't sustain a rage. She didn't want this battle, yet day after day Wynter brought turmoil into her peaceful existence. Damn him! Bunching her fists, she punched them into his sides.

He arched her form into his. Like a blacksmith's red-hot iron, his heat struck her. His hand in her hair, his mouth on hers, his arm around her waist, the length of him dominating, and her own body relaxing, tensing, reveling . . . betraying.

Embarrassed and enthralled, she whimpered.

His kiss lightened, became less imperious and more seductive. Slowly, he loosened his hold, easing her back against the wall, sliding his hand around to cup her chin, and, finally, lifting his mouth.

To her mortification, her lips clung to his.

She didn't dare open her eyes. She couldn't bear to look at him.

"I will not shame you, my darling. I will treat you with the utmost tenderness and care, and demand for you all the honor due my wife. But I will not be denied."

Blindly, she turned to flee. She struck the table. The vase wobbled, then smashed to the floor.

She stood, horrified, and stared at the shards scattered across the hardwood. This was what she had come to. Unrestrained panic, inelegant motion, and the ultimate social *faux pas*.

Her life was shattered into as many pieces as the vase, and all because of him.

His voice was smooth and deep as Lucifer's own. "Charlotte, my darling girl . . ."

As if a single endearment could mend the vase! Or her life.

She fled down the hallway to the sanctity of her bedchamber.

CHAPTER 23

My dear Pamela and Hannah,

I can think of no way to announce this with any amount of dignity or grace. Because of circumstances which occurred today, and which I assure you were most innocent, I am forced to marry. Lord Ruskin is my betrothed, and although in many ways he is a worthy man, he is also exasperating and I foresee no love in our future. The rush is obscene, the wedding is planned for the Monday morning after the last of the banns had been called, and might have been avoided if not for the Sereminian reception which looms one month after the nuptials!

As you can imagine, I miss you dreadfully, my dear friends. Not only for the reasons which you already know, but because I issued a most ridiculous challenge to Lord Ruskin and I fear he will feel he must answer it every chance he gets . . .

Never before had Charlotte thought twice when she crossed the long, shadowy gallery filled with portraits of stiffly posed, long-dead lords and ladies. Tonight, a mere twenty-four hours after the dreadful scene on the stairway, she was nervous.

She could admit the truth to herself, at least. *Wynter* made her nervous, relentlessly watching her from his portrait on the wall. She'd paid little heed to that picture of the youthful Wynter and his spaniel before. Now she couldn't stop glancing at it as she hurried from Adorna's apartments back to her own bedchamber.

Even though Wynter had left for London this morning, still he stalked her.

On her previous journeys along this very route, she had never wondered what hid behind the closed doors in the portrait wall. Tonight she was convinced something waited to spring out at her. And in fact one stood open . . .

She slowed as she approached. The darkness in that inner chamber was absolute, unilluminated by the feeble light of the candle in the wall sconce just outside, and even by straining her eyes she couldn't see within. Yet she wasn't a fanciful woman. She could think of a dozen reasons why the door would be open. Probably the maids had been cleaning. Or the children had been playing hide and seek. Or . . .

"Lady Miss Charlotte."

She shrieked.

She never shrieked.

But Wynter's voice coming from a darkened chair directly in front of her startled her so much— She clasped her hand to her chest. "What are you doing there? Here? Now?"

He rose, uncoiling his six-foot height as smoothly as any snake from the garden of Eden.

Charlotte rattled on. "I thought you were in London."

"I was." He snagged her wrist. "Did you think I would leave you for more than a day?"

She'd *hoped* he would. Indeed, she'd depended on his absence to recapture her equilibrium. Obviously, he hadn't been gone long enough—and, she suspected, it might not matter how long he was gone. She might never regain her equilibrium again.

Oh, dread thought! To have so lost herself!

He was drawing her toward him, a darkly golden male gleaming with intent.

She found herself bursting into speech. "My lord, it is not seemly that we be alone before our wedding."

"Or after it, so *you* say." He sounded amused, but in the feeble light she saw no smile on his lips. "Or have you forgotten that?"

"No."

"Have you changed your mind? Will you welcome me into your bed?"

She couldn't win; she knew it. He pulled her close against him as though he could overcome her objections with nothing more than his proximity. She craned her neck to see his face. His height was greater than hers, his strength far superior to her own.

The contrast between his power and hers was vast; even more weighty was the reality of the law. When Wynter was her husband he would have the right to do with her body as he wished. He could beat her, or lock her away. He wouldn't; she knew that. But he would take his conjugal rights, and if she dared complain or bemoan her fate, the men who made the laws would shrug and turn away. More important, hundreds of women less blessed in their mates would rise up against her and browbeat her into submission. She had no choice. He would have her.

Perhaps if she retracted her challenge, he might

leave her alone until her unhappy wedding night.

But she couldn't. When she thought about allowing him the freedom of her body . . . she just couldn't. Useless or not, she had to fight him, for if she didn't she would lose some vital piece of herself.

Even knowing he wouldn't understand, she spoke her mind. "If love were real, we would give our bodies to each other. But love isn't real, is it? You told me it was not. So I refuse to give you anything. Anything."

His arms tightened on her, and she felt frustration vibrating through him. "How do you dare defy me? I could crush you between my two hands should I desire, yet still you tilt your chin and tell me no."

"If I thought you would crush me, my lord, I would obey you out of fear of your brutality. But for what you wish of me, I believe you want me pink and healthy."

He smiled, a smooth half curl of his lips. "In that you are right, my light of the morning, my angel of desire." They might have been waltzing, so quickly and smoothly did he whirl her into the open chamber. He shut the door with his foot. The air inside was cool and still, and darkness pressed around them like a living entity.

She wasn't afraid of the darkness. Only fools and weaklings feared the night, but she didn't know what was in here. She couldn't make a move without Wynter. She depended on him totally, and that, she knew, must be his strategy. The warrior she had challenged contrived and executed his pursuit of her as surely as he plotted his desert battles.

Apparently his vision was unimpaired, for he seated himself on . . . something . . . and pulled her between his legs.

More for the form than because she thought it would do any good, she lodged a protest. "I'm not comfortable with our isolation, my lord."

His hands rested on her waist. "It is not our isolation which discomfits you, my sweetheart, my princess." He brought her closer to him. "It is your reliance on me."

She could have informed him that it was more than that. Shared with him that the warmth of the chamber, its closeness and night's dark shadows gave her a sense of security, as if they'd found a place apart from their day-to-day life where whatever they did would be between them only.

She was, she realized, weary of all the years of being on show. This lonely room fulfilled a compulsion she didn't even know existed.

As usual, she wore her sensible governess gown of dark blue with the white collar pinned close at the base of her throat. As he bent her over his arm, his breath touched her neck just below her ear. Merely the warmth and the air brought a chill to her skin.

She resisted him, not with struggles, but with her stiff and uncooperative body. "What is this place?"

"A guest room." One hand slid up to her breast. Not to touch it, but to circle like a hawk circling for a kill. "The maids have been working here, preparing for the wedding company."

She could smell the scent of beeswax and soap. She could also smell the scent of Wynter, of starch and clean flesh and knavery.

"There is an aired bed with clean linens waiting for us should we desire," he added.

Every muscle in her body clutched in panic. "You said I had until our wedding night."

He chuckled, a deep, warm puff of air against her

cheek. "So I did. But I will listen to pleas to take you now."

She fortified herself with scorn. "As if I would."

Putting his mouth against her ear, he breathed, "You will."

His hand cupped her. His fingers found her nipple and gently massaged.

She came up on her toes.

Her gaze searched the darkness, seeking something to fix on, something that would distract her from the rhythmic movement of his fingers. But it was so dark in here! And he was so insistent, caressing her as if he had the right to make her miserable. Or perhaps 'miserable' was the wrong word. Perhaps the word was . . . 'disturbed.' Restless. Desperate.

She shifted her weight, trying to move away from him.

He halted her before she had done more than shuffle. "Trying to escape already? Ah, Lady Miss Charlotte, we've barely begun."

She struggled to sound dignified and managed to sound unbearably stuffy. "I wish you would stop touching me there."

"As you command, oh siren most seductive." His hand slid up to her collar. He manipulated the brooch that held it together.

She relaxed and grinned. As if he could open the pin with one hand! She couldn't even open the pin with one hand, and she'd had years of—

Her collar loosened. Her brooch slipped away.

By what trick had he contrived that?

She grabbed, but she heard it drop to the floor. "That's mine!"

"I do not like such a restrictive decoration." He slid the collar from around her neck.

This time she better understood his dexterity, and clutched at his hand, but he unfastened the ivory buttons at a speed doubtless unrivaled by any libertine. "Stop that!" she said.

"As you command, oh mistress of my destiny."

He did do as she ordered, but only because he'd unbuttoned her bodice down almost to her waist. She pushed against his shoulders, but he clamped his legs together to hold her in place.

Air brushed her skin as he spread the cloth apart.

She aimed a clout at the side of his head, or where she thought his head might be—close to her chest. She guessed right, for her fist connected with the hard bone of his skull.

He grunted.

Wincing, she nursed her knuckles.

He toppled her sideways and down.

She clutched wildly, not knowing where she would land, but he cradled her until she rested on a soft, upholstered surface. A sofa. She flung her arm out. A sofa with no back. The end under her head was raised. A fainting couch.

He bent over her, an invisible shape formed of powerful threat and impossible passion. "Charlotte," he whispered as he slid an arm up her side to support her head. The location of his other hand remained a mystery. When she tried to wiggle away she found herself trapped by his knee on her skirt. More than that, she felt trapped by him and by . . . what? Desire? Expectation? She only knew the novelty of being this close to a man made her want to explore these inappropriate sensations.

If only she felt safe with him. If only she knew that when her limit had been reached, he would call a halt. But no. This man would always push her too far, too fast. She had to remember that now. She had to keep her head and not listen to the seduction of his accented voice as he called her name or deign to notice how his long fingers trailed across her skin at the edge of her chemise.

"Charlotte." His voice was closer, much closer.

She braced herself to ignore his kiss on her lips.

He kissed her bare breast.

"No." She grabbed handfuls of his hair and tugged. "Beast!" His lips closed around her nipple and he suckled, pulling the tip into his mouth and laving it with his tongue.

Her breath left her in a rush. Her hands flattened on his head. Her back arched. For one magnificent moment, she couldn't think. Sensation and instinct held her triumphant in their twin grip, and she gloried in the pleasure.

Then consciousness intruded. She held Wynter's head pressed to her. She wiggled against his mouth like a wanton. She moaned . . . had she really forgotten herself so much she moaned? But she knew she had; the sound still echoed in the still, dark room. Deep inside she hurt from craving him.

This was what he meant by making her beg. He would inflict intimacy on her until she lost her mind and her pride. She wouldn't do it. But oh—she smoothed her fingers through his hair—how much he made her want.

"That's enough, Wynter." She sounded remarkably strong for a woman in the throes of revelation. "You've proved your point, I believe."

His breath gusted over her damp breast. *He* was laughing.

She responded with a tightly puckered nipple and restless lower limbs.

"I have barely begun to prove my point, Charlotte." When he said her name, he made her sound like the most precious jewel of the universe. "There is so much more you don't know."

"I do too know. I am not ignorant." His fingers were massaging her scalp, making her very aware of the lie she told. For she had never been informed that a man could create pleasure with his touch on her head. Like a cat she relaxed into his touch. "I simply have no practical experience."

Disregarding her claim with the scorn it deserved, he said, "You are the brightest of shooting stars in a velvet sky." His restrictive knee rose off her skirt and he placed it on the other side of her. "I alone will catch and hold you." He straddled her, looming above like Zeus come to seduce in secret. His lips trailed lightly across her cheeks, her lips, her eyelids, bringing gifts of renewal to her starving senses.

She stilled. Like Alcmene, she allowed the sorcery, reveling in his delicate caress. Her eyes fluttered closed. She breathed deeply, concentrating on just that touch.

So his next tactic caught her unprepared. Somehow, his hand had reached under her skirt. Sliding his hand under her knee, he lifted it and curled his arm around her thigh so that he held her in place while his finger touched the most intimate part of her . . . drawers.

She tried to sit up, to dislodge him, but his upper body blocked her, his knee trapped her by her skirts and he whispered, "Shh." He delved into the slit in her underwear. "Don't move."

"Don't move?" She found herself whispering, too, but it was a furious whisper as she tried ineffectively to close her lower limbs. She found his second leg in the way. "This is unacceptable! You cannot just . . .

just put your hand wherever you want."

"I only want you." His contact was as subtle as that of his lips on her face.

But he was stroking the tips of the hair that covered her secret parts! She tried again to dissuade him, but her voice wobbled. "This isn't proper or acceptable."

"But agreeable, yes?" He sounded almost . . . curious, as though he didn't quite know that chills skittered over her skin, her toes curled, and deep inside, her womb clenched as though wanting a deeper bond.

She swallowed. "Please. Wynter."

His fingers opened her. His thumb slid up and down until he found the moisture she couldn't control. "Ah . . ."

She could *hear* his smile, and she wanted to smack it right off his face. Except she couldn't quite remember how to lift her arms.

Nuzzling her neck just behind her ear, he said, "Lady Miss Charlotte, I have pleasured you." His thumb touched a sensitive place. One that brought her to painful rigidity in his arms. "Think how much more you will be pleasured when I place my mouth here"— his thumb slid lower—"and kiss each place"—he penetrated her slightly—"and caress you with my tongue."

She tried not to listen, tried to fight the whimper that rose in her throat, but his stroking, combined with his words, created such pressure inside! Her womb felt heavy and needy. His thumb deliberately stroked in and out, each time delving deeper. She clutched at the edges of the couch as if some great quake threatened to toss her off, yet as her lower limbs moved aimlessly he anchored her ever more firmly with his weight.

"Think," he murmured, "how it will be on our wedding night when we are unencumbered by clothing, when we are twined together as bare as Adam and

Eve. You'll open your arms to me. I'll take my place between your legs. I'll enter you slowly"—with his thumb, he matched action to declaration—"and you . . ."

His whole hand pressed against her, cupping her, putting pressure where she needed it most.

She didn't understand . . . her lower body . . . no, her whole body lifted toward him. Her hands found his shoulders. She gripped with all her might and cried out, "Wynter!" Everything within her concentrated where his finger was . . . no, deeper . . . God, so deep . . . the spasms went on and on, encouraged by his touch, his voice, his weight.

And when the contractions finally halted, and she rested panting on the couch, he smoothed her loosened hair off her forehead and promised, "I'm going to make you do that again and again, until you submit and avow that you love me."

She didn't know where she drew the strength. She certainly couldn't lift her head or even raise a blush. But somehow she managed to whisper, "No."

He chuckled, a low, erotic sound of appreciation. "That's right, oh flower of the oasis. Fight me. Fight me with all your will. That will make the victory all the sweeter."

"Charlotte, I have brought you a gift."

Charlotte looked up from pouring tea to see Wynter posed in the doorway of the gallery. He wore his traveling clothes and, for a change, footwear, and held a flat box of carved and polished wood like a showpiece. The visiting ladies, numbering fourteen, murmured in curiosity.

Instinctively, Charlotte touched the broad ribbon she had pinned around her throat. It covered a brand he had placed with his mouth just last night. The round, purple mark looked painful, but she hadn't noticed his activity at the time. Or rather—she hadn't noticed that particular activity. Her attention had been wholly retained in trying to stop him from untying and lowering her drawers.

So now she wore a ribbon and resolved that, regardless of his sleight of hand, he would not unpin this brooch and embarrass her before their guests.

Adorna sat relaxed in a comfortable chair, indicating by her indolence her confidence in Charlotte's hostessing abilities. "Dear boy, I wondered why you rushed off to London again so abruptly. You went to purchase jewelry for your betrothed." To Charlotte, seated alone behind the tea table, she said, "You two are a perfect couple. I couldn't be more pleased."

She meant it, Charlotte knew. In the week since the engagement had been declared, Adorna's objections had vanished as if they had never been. Thank heavens, for the constant preparations and parties had proved exhausting for Charlotte, and without Adorna's support she might have collapsed.

"Can we all see, Wynter?" Adorna asked.

Of course they could all see. Charlotte should have known jewels would be his next ploy, for to the fullest of his ability, Wynter was making a spectacle of their engagement. He wished to make his possession of her so unequivocal as to be indisputable.

Placing the pot on the tray, Charlotte smiled, a mere movement of the lips to please their audience. "How kind of you, my lord. I am aquiver with excitement."

She had hoped to annoy him. Instead he smiled, a real smile that mocked her coolness. "That is exactly how I like to see you, Lady Miss Charlotte."

Someone gasped. Mrs. Burton smothered a chuckle.

Picking up the tea table, Wynter placed it off to the side, then knelt so close he pressed against Charlotte's knees. Even kneeling he was taller than she was, and over his shoulder she could see the ladies gaping at them in anticipation of a scene.

Worse, she feared they might get one, for Wynter continued to be ruthless in his pursuit of her. Every day and every night, wherever she was, whatever she was doing, he was there. In company he would rub her back or take her hand and press a passionate kiss on her fingers. Despite her best efforts, he seemed always to be able to catch her alone, and then the loving would begin in earnest. He held her against him, allowed his hands to roam where they would, allowed his mouth the freedom of her body and occasionally, just occasionally, made her shudder with that disreputable emotion.

But no matter what he did or how often he did it— or how much she responded—Charlotte still had not yielded her declaration of love.

She *thought* he might be getting a little frustrated. She *hoped* he would perish from discontent.

Soon.

Holding the box before her, Wynter opened the clasp.

Tawny yellow and beaten gold flashed in the light. As Charlotte focused, she saw a necklace and bracelet of polished amber set in gold, earrings in the same style and a ring that looked too big for her hand. In fact, everything looked too big for her, for the style was rough and almost medieval in its workmanship, yet . . . yet each piece embodied a particular stormy magic. Unwillingly drawn to them, Charlotte reached out one finger and touched a stone in the necklace.

The surface slid away like cool silk, and a fire of red licked at the saffron inside.

"Yes." Wynter spoke quietly, for her ears only. "I thought you would like them. I chose each stone remembering always the flame of your hair, and I insisted that the setting be like you—polished and crafted, yet always unique . . . and wild, Charlotte. You are so wild."

Enthralled by his deep, rough whisper, she looked up at him.

Fool! He captured her gaze, holding her hostage as he leaned toward her.

Unnoticed, the box slid off her lap.

His lips parted, his head tilted. He was going to kiss her, right here in front of the neighbors and the curiosity-seekers from London . . . and she was going to let him.

In one stratagem he had been successful. He had trained her body to desire at the mere sight of him.

Her eyelids fluttered shut as his mouth closed on hers. To the ladies seated around the circle, the kiss might have started out looking innocent, but his tongue touched Charlotte at once, opening her lips, sliding inside and filling her with the taste of him. Boldly he pressed her against the chair until her head rested on the back and illicit passions rioted through her veins. Her nipples—her *nipples*! she still couldn't believe she ever even thought the word—puckered so tightly as to be painful, and her fists rose from her lap and grasped the lapels of his jacket.

His marauding fingers slid into her hair, rumpling her carefully designed chignon, yet she thought of nothing but the pleasure of his touch. When at last he drew back, her eyes opened and she came to consciousness gradually.

Not a breath from the onlookers broke the silence. Not a sound could have distracted Charlotte from the sight of him. Of Wynter, his eyes alight with desire, his lips damp from hers, soft and red, lips made for kissing, his long fingers trembling as they slipped away from her face.

Perhaps he made a display of their craving to stamp her with his ownership, but as he taught her passion he drove himself as wild as he claimed she was. She knew as soon as he left she would be embarrassed by their exhibition, but right now . . . right now she just wanted to go with him to some private place and let him touch her where he'd touched her before.

His plan to conquer appeared to be working.

Her grip loosened from his jacket. Her hands fell limply into her lap.

"I wish you would leave your magnificent hair down for me." One of his hands tugged softly at a loose strand until it curled over her shoulder. "It contains the color of fire and the texture of silk, and I dream of our wedding night when I will spread it across a pillow and bury my face in its fragrance." Leaning over, he gathered the jewelry off the floor. He clasped the bracelet around her wrist, bestowing it with a kiss on her pulse.

She tried to take the earrings away from him, but he made it clear he would decorate her himself and she had no wish to lose both a wrestling match and her dignity. The kiss he placed at each earring barely touched the sensitive skin beneath, yet goose bumps skittered up her spine and she caught her breath.

Sliding his hands under her hair, he fastened the necklace around her throat; then, moving as smoothly as the lover in her private fantasy, he turned her head to one side and pressed a kiss on her throat. Her heart raced beneath his lips and she scarcely subdued a whimper as his mouth slipped lower, just to the edge of her collarbone. Would he have stopped there if her modest collar had not been in place?

His lids were heavy over his eyes as he reached for the last piece of jewelry. The ring. The band slid over her slender knuckle and settled solidly at the base of her finger. The amber stone blared its blatant message. Wynter's woman. Wynter's property. Too late she tried to wrench her hand away from his, but he took her fingers in both of his and brought them to his lips. The kisses he pressed to the ring, then to the tips of her fingers, then on her palm, bore no resemblance to his other, sweeter kisses. These kisses answered her challenge, telling her without words that he would woo her and he would take her whether she wished it or not.

He wrapped her fingers around the last kiss, forcing her to hold it close as if it weren't some ethereal possession. "Save my kiss for that moment in the night when I am alone in my bedchamber and you are alone in your virgin bed. Then take it and place it where you will, and imagine how my mouth will feel when at last I hold you in my arms, and love you beyond pleasure."

Graceful and passionate, he stood, still holding her hand. As if he could not resist, he bestowed one last kiss upon her fingers before letting them go. He backed away, then bowed to the ladies. At the door, he bowed to Charlotte, and somehow he imbued that simple obeisance with devotion, passion and stark hunger. As he left, the last thing he saw, Charlotte knew, was the blush that rose in her cheeks.

Crack! A dozen fans snapped open and flapped back and forth before their owners' flushed faces.

"Gracious." Adorna dabbed at her forehead with a lacy handkerchief. "Isn't it warm in here?"

Charlotte settled into bed, plumping the pillow beneath her head, wishing she could purge her mind of the memory of Wynter so she could just sleep without dreaming of him, his sudden appearances and unexpected tortures. Tortures that wrung unrestrained cries from her. From her, who had for so long taken pride in never speaking rashly or without forethought. Of course, he would laugh if he knew of the pride she'd taken in her own caution, and tell her that the noises she made during lovemaking were not words, only sounds that expressed her inner feelings.

Well, that was the problem, wasn't it? She didn't want him to know her inner feelings. Wasn't a woman allowed sanctuary even in her own mind?

Apparently not, for tonight she couldn't drive the thought of him out of her consciousness.

A sound on her balcony brought her up in the bed. The thunk of metal against wood. Straining, she could see, on the floor of the balcony, a four-sided hook attached to a rope draped over the railing.

Wynter. Wynter planned to climb the rope and invade her bedchamber.

Her heart jolted into the frenetic beat his closeness always caused. Dear God, did he plan to take her here, now? Or was this another of his long teases? She pressed her limbs together, trying to halt the dampness the thought caused. Just as he vowed, he was addicting her to his touch, and by the time the wedding occurred, she would be begging him to take her.

Just as now, she wanted to beg him to leave her alone.

The hook moved along the floor in little jerks,

pulled by the rope from below, until it rose and caught on the balustrade. Wynter jerked again, hard, to set the hooks—and with a creak and a groaning tear of wood, the railing toppled over the side.

For one second of horrified amazement, she stared at the empty place where the railing had been—then she heard a satisfying thunk, followed by a shower of splinters and one very succinct curse word.

Lying down again, she hoped Wynter hadn't been *badly* hurt.

Charlotte slept as she had not slept in a fortnight.

CHAPTER 24

"*I* TELL YOU, MY LADY, I THOUGHT IT A YOUNG GIRL'S hysteria, too, until I heard the sounds and saw that ghostly white form gliding down the corridor toward me." Miss Symes's fingers fretted the fringe of her knit wool shawl.

Adorna took that as an ominous sign, for Miss Symes was usually the most pragmatic of women. Clearly the ghost had her worried. "Dear Symes, I am not doubting you, I am simply saying a specter haunting the house while we prepare for the wedding is most inconvenient. The seamstress almost quit for fright, and dear Charlotte's dress only half done! She's not eating well, you know, so the seamstress had to take in the waist." Adorna couldn't keep the aggravation from her voice. She sat at her desk in her apartments, listing the tasks that needed to be completed and checking off those that were finished. In the rush to get Wynter and Charlotte married before the preparations for the Sereminian reception began, this haunting situation seemed almost farcical. "We've never had a ghost before. Can't you just make it go away?"

"I'm doing what I can, my lady. I set up watches,

but the men fall asleep or are so frightened they can't be trusted. And the maids are quitting so quickly the work is piling up, and with the wedding less than a week away . . ."

"I know, dear Symes, and you've been working like a zealot." Adorna took Miss Symes's thick hand and patted it. "Let me put my mind to the problem. I'm sure if I try, I could find someone who specializes in exorcism."

"Oh, dear, my lady!"

"What?"

"That seems a bit . . . extreme."

"I don't know why. How else does one rid one's home of a ghost? If we don't exterminate it, we shall have to train it." A thought occurred to Adorna. "Perhaps the ghost is just rude, like Wynter. Perhaps it needs a governess."

"A ghost governess?" Miss Symes repeated weakly.

"Or a good talking to." Adorna nodded, satisfied with her solution. "That's it! Leave the ghost to me. I'll have a stern word with it. But not now, dear Symes. I'm busy."

The housekeeper curtsied, leaving Adorna to her work again. The work she adored. Two grand parties in a row! A wedding and a royal reception. What could be more fun?

"Mother!" Wynter spoke from the doorway. "I have something I need to tell you."

"Dear, you're just the man I wanted to talk to. The invitations are sent—we're inviting everyone, darling, so promise me you'll remember your company manners. You're good with them when you choose. Uncle Ransom and Aunt Jane have returned from Italy—so fortuitous!—and will be here for the ceremony. Cook has the menu planned. The children are quite excited about the parties . . ." Adorna stopped checking off items on her list and stared at her son as he limped across to the fireplace. For a moment she wondered if Charlotte had caused his male organs to seize in the upright position. Then she realized one of his bare feet was wrapped in a white cloth. "Why are you walking like that?"

"It's nothing, Mother." Wynter frowned as if that would intimidate her. "It will be healed by the wedding day."

Adorna relaxed back in her delicate desk chair. "Did Charlotte finally put a dent in your . . . ah . . . infallibility?"

"Charlotte had nothing to do with it."

"What a lie, dear. With you, these days, Charlotte has everything to do with everything." Prudently, Adorna placed her pen on the blotter. "Doesn't she?"

"If she would just admit she loved me," he burst out. In a more temperate tone, he repeated, "If she would just admit she loves me, she would be happy."

How Adorna relished this! She hadn't planned that Charlotte should marry her son, yet now that the marriage had become inevitable she saw the rightness of it. They were good together!

Or rather, they would be once they'd smoothed out a few minor wrinkles. Wynter was so frustrated he was confiding in his mother, something he hadn't done since his eleventh birthday party when that dreadful, overgrown girl Prunella had punched him in the nose and made it bleed.

And Charlotte. The firm set of her chin could not fool Adorna; beneath her resigned exterior lurked rebellion and determination. Well, of course. Only look how she had thwarted her uncle's plans for her. Wynter was a stronger character than that weasel Porterbridge, but Adorna enjoyed watching such titans clash. "Charlotte is a sensible girl. If loving you would make her happy, I'm sure she'd admit it. Even if it weren't true."

"But it is true." He stood before the fireplace in Adorna's sitting room, legs apart like a sailor on the bridge, and arms crossed. "How could she not love a man of my stature and honorable nature?"

Adorna gave in to her mirth. She laughed a feminine version of Wynter's bellow, and when she stopped, one look at Wynter, glaring at her in disgust, sent her off again. "Wynter, dear, think! If that were true, every woman in England would be in love with you." She held up her hand before he could speak. "And they aren't. I assure you. I know quite a lot about romance."

She shouldn't have expected to laugh at him without retribution. "I do not understand, my mother, why you consider yourself an expert on this thing you call love. You do not seem to be overwhelmed with joy now that Lord Bucknell has ceased to visit."

She felt the pain of that thrust immediately. She hadn't really allowed herself to believe that he had stopped calling. She had hoped he was temporarily otherwise engaged. But she had to face the facts; he wouldn't take her on her terms, and she wouldn't take him on his. It was over. Even Wynter, self-absorbed as he was, knew it.

"Nonsense," she said stoutly. "I'm ecstatic that he has found something more satisfying to occupy his time." But she blinked rapidly to keep the tears off her cheeks.

Wynter was not fooled. "Has Bucknell been invited to the wedding?"

"Of course, dear." She attempted to smile with her usual ebullience. "We're *friends*."

"You were more than friends."

When had she lost control of the conversation? In fact, when had Wynter become perceptive about anything but horses and business? "Lord Bucknell has not the *joie de vivre* of your father."

"That, my mother, is a slight to one or the other."

"No, it's not. Each man has—or in your father's case, had—his appeal. Bucknell is rather sober." Before Wynter could taunt her again, she added, "And incredibly staid. But he couldn't stay away from me and I . . . well, for the first time since Papa's death, I found myself attracted." She saw a way to divert his attention from her and back to him, where it belonged. "One would wish one could be drawn to a mate with a little more dash, but it never seems to work that way, does it? Me and Lord Bucknell, you and Charlotte. Totally different people."

"My desert father told me that men and women are wholly diverse."

Some of the beliefs he'd come home with! She didn't envy Charlotte teaching him differently. "No, they aren't, dear. We all feel the same pain, enjoy the same pleasures, want with all our hearts. We just want different things, like you want Charlotte and Charlotte wants love." Let him ponder about *that* for a while. Turning back to the work spread out on her desk, she said, "I've been thinking."

He recognized her ploy. She'd used it often enough in his youth. She was going to change the subject, and right now he thought it a good idea. "Always a dangerous activity, Mother. What have you been thinking?"

"That embezzling in the business. It wasn't much, really."

Her comment, and especially with her warm, persuasive tone, surprised him. "It wasn't much?"

"Much money gone, silly. Whoever took the money didn't take much." Picking up her pen, she dipped it in the ink. "Did he?"

What was she getting at? "How can I tell? Every time I check the accounts the amount changes. The embezzler is worried and paying the money back."

"Yes, of *course* he is." She made a mark on the page before her. "There isn't one person in our organization who isn't a good soul, and if he took the money I'm sure he had a worthy reason. He was just borrowing it, really, and now he's just returning it."

Wynter stared at the back of Adorna's blond head. "And if he wishes to borrow it again, we should just let him? Mother, what are you saying?"

"That whoever did it is really, truly sorry."

Wynter adored his mother, but her mind had always been a mystery to everyone except his father, and even he had occasionally shaken his head and smiled. But this! "Mother, this is not some child with no sense of right or wrong who takes another's toy. This is a man who stole money—your money—and he must be punished."

"That seems so harsh." She sighed.

"There is no excuse for that kind of behavior."

"Oh, Wynter, you are such a man." Her laughter flowed like a babbling brook. "There is always an excuse. Do you have any suspects?"

"At one time, I had too many."

"Oh." She bent her head to her work again, and her pen whipped back and forth as she wrote. "Who's left?"

"Hodges, for one. He claims to adore you, and it's obvious he resents my return and the fact I will take over the reins. Shilbottle proclaims his worship of

Papa, and that could be viewed as suspect considering the embezzlement. The others either lack the chances or the intelligence to pull off such a clever scheme."

The busy pen paused. "Then you've given up Stewart as your suspect."

Wynter hated to tell her, but there was no keeping this secret from Adorna. "Stewart is my main suspect. I have set traps for him, and by the dunes, I will catch him."

Adorna swung back to face him, her hands clutching the back of her chair so tightly her knuckles turned white. "Stewart? Dear Stewart? How can you think that? He has always been my main support."

"Exactly." Wynter nodded. "He's had unlimited access to our funds."

"He's your cousin."

"He's a thief."

"Thief." She made a moue. "That is such a cold word, Wynter."

"Stealing is a cold art."

"Well." Adorna huffed strands of hair off her forehead. "You must keep me informed of everything you do."

He knew better than that. "So you can warn him, Mother? No, that seems unwise."

"But Wynter . . ." she wailed.

"But nothing." He had made it his mission to catch the swindler, and he would. As he limped toward the door, he grimaced at the pain in his foot.

"Wait! Wynter, what did you come by to tell me?" she asked.

He should have known she would drive all good sense from his mind. "Before the wedding we need to check the railings on all the balconies. The wood is rotted."

*   *   *

The morning of the wedding dawned clear and bright, thus proving to Charlotte that a man owned even the weather. In the last three weeks, she had been constantly buffeted by old and new emotions, and now she sat in a tub of warm, scented water and watched the sunshine creep down the wall to the floor. She was numb, resigned to her fate. She would marry Wynter. She would be properly grateful for his charity. And she would allow him to inflict himself on her . . .

Briskly, she picked up her washcloth and the milled soap Adorna had given her.

In theory, the wise thing to do was *allow* him the use of her indifferent flesh. In reality, she had little control over her body or its reactions. She might want to remain quiescent under his caresses. Doing so proved quite another thing.

"Charlotte, dear, don't tarry," Adorna called from the other side of the screen. "We have your dress laid out, but it will take time to do your hair. Of course, Wynter wants you to leave it down, but I told him he could have the pleasure of unpinning it tonight. Or at least, I think he'll have the pleasure, unless you decide to lock yourself in here and—" Charlotte heard Adorna's mouth snap shut.

Swiftly, Wynter's aunt Jane picked up the conversation. "The seamstress finished the last seams on the gown last night. Each stitch is in place, and the unornamented white satin is perfect with Charlotte's vibrant coloring. However did you realize that, dear Adorna?"

Charlotte grinned. Aunt Jane had arrived only yesterday, but already she had impressed Charlotte with her good sense and tart wit. Both women had impressed Charlotte with their kindness; in the absence of her own female relatives, they acted as her support on this important morning.

Adorna said loftily, "You give me too little credit, Jane."

Charlotte grinned more. The gown had been plainly constructed because Charlotte had insisted on it. A gown of furbelows such as Adorna had wanted would have overshadowed a woman of Charlotte's stature.

"The row of tiny buttons down the back is exquisite," Jane said, "but they'll be fiercely uncomfortable to sit on."

"Oh, I doubt if Wynter remains much past the luncheon," Adorna burbled. "You know how impatient he is."

Charlotte dropped the bar of soap with a splash.

Silence followed from beyond the screen.

Then Jane said, "What beautiful long sleeves. They give the gown a medieval flavor, and I recognize the veil."

"From two weddings," Adorna said.

They had both worn it, and Charlotte had been touched and honored when they'd offered it to her.

"Don't you love the jewelry? You should have been here when Wynter presented it to her!" Adorna giggled, then squawked as if she'd been elbowed.

Jane said, "The color of the amber reminds me of . . ." Her voice trailed off.

Charlotte stopped fishing for the soap and strained to hear. What did the color remind Jane of? Had Jane seen some mark on the gown? Had the moths eaten a previously unseen—

Wynter stepped around the screen.

Charlotte froze.

He was dressed as formally as any Englishman in his black, well-cut suit that hugged his shoulders and nipped at his waist. Yet his feet were bare—and he was in her bedchamber. As she bathed. And he watched her through eyes that glowed with ardor.

Adorna recovered her voice first. "Wynter, you come away from there immediately. It's bad luck to see the bride before the ceremony!"

"Adorna, dear." Jane sounded choked. "You're missing the larger repercussions of his actions."

Charlotte slapped the washcloth over her chest and sank down into the water. "Go away!" she whispered at her looming, impudent betrothed.

Strolling forward, he stood over her with a regal aura of privilege, looking right down into the water.

She tried to stretch the washcloth to cover all her vital parts, and discovered how truly futile that exercise was. "Go away," she repeated, and submerged far enough that the water lapped at her lips.

He knelt beside the tub and stirred the bath with his finger.

Charlotte saw an indignant Jane appear at the edge of the screen and start toward them. Adorna's arm snaked out, caught her, and pulled her back. She heard the flurry of whispers. But she couldn't truly comprehend anything but Wynter, large and wicked.

"What do you want?" she finally managed.

"Oh, Charlotte." His finger rose, dripping with water, and smoothed over her cheek. "You. I only want you. And today, I will have you." Leaning over the tub, he pressed a kiss to her forehead. "I didn't want you to forget."

CHAPTER 25

CHARLOTTE STOOD IN THE ANTECHAMBER OF THE church, holding a bouquet of white roses and listening impatiently as Lord Howard stammered, "Y-you don't have to marry him. I would give you anything you want if you would just come with me."

She glared at him, wondering what god she had offended to have to suffer such visits on her wedding day. First Wynter, arriving like some unruly satyr to stand over her nude body and tell her she would soon be his wife—as if she could forget that! Then Leila and Robbie, needing reassurance that all would be well—for them she had put aside her misgivings and, without regard to her elegant gown, hugged them until they broke into grins.

Now Lord Howard. In the voice of goaded patience she usually reserved for undertrained dance instructors, she said, "Why would I sell myself to you as your mistress? I wouldn't even sell myself to you as your wife. Go back to Lady Howard."

Head hung, Lord Howard stumbled out.

Charlotte turned to Mr. Burton, dressed in his best. "I never thought I would say this, but the sooner these nuptials take place, the happier I will be."

Stern of visage, Mr. Burton straightened his cuffs. "From what I've heard of Lord Ruskin's behavior, I must concur. That young man needs a thrashing."

It appeared Mr. Burton was not only taking her father's place in walking her down the aisle, but also in his ire about her groom and his everlasting arrogance. God bless Mr. Burton; how it mollified her that at least one other person thought Wynter's behavior was outrageous. Resting her hand on Mr. Burton's arm, she said, "Sir, I must extend my most sincere thanks to you for consenting to walk me down the aisle. It is a debt I can never repay."

"Ah, well." He cleared his throat uncomfortably. "I'm honored you asked me, Lady Charlotte. I remember your father and—"

A voice interrupted from the doorway. "I'll walk you down the aisle."

For one moment Charlotte heard her father's voice in the abrupt sentence. Then good sense resurrected itself, and she turned.

Her uncle stood there, trussed into a formal black jacket and purple silk waistcoat. The suit was done by a London tailor; she knew, for she remembered how he had groused at the cost when he bought it. He'd told Aunt Piper not to expect him to ever buy another, that he would be buried in that suit. It appeared that if his valet could pull his corset strings tight enough, he would keep his vow.

Why had Uncle come to the antechamber of the church? Surely not to give her a tongue-lashing. Not today. Charlotte said, "My lord, you should take your seat if you wish to watch the ceremony."

Mr. Burton looked from one to the other.

Uncle spoke to him, abrupt, loud and overbearing.

"I'm the Earl of Porterbridge, and this is my niece. I will walk her down the aisle."

"Lady Charlotte, what would you have me do?" Mr. Burton asked.

"You don't need to ask her," Uncle said. "She'll do as she's told."

She'll do as she's told. The phrase hung in the air. If she had done as she was told, he would have walked her down the aisle nine years ago and he'd be finished with her. But that hadn't happened, and now they were trapped by awkward emotions and uncomfortable disclosures.

Uncle scowled. "My brother would expect me to give his daughter away."

Her eyes widened. *Now* he worried about her father's wishes?

"He would," Uncle snapped. "I can do this right, at least."

The moment was poignant with astonishment, and Charlotte's realization that . . . good heavens, Uncle wanted to do right by her. She nodded to Mr. Burton, who bowed and left them.

An uneasy silence settled between uncle and niece. Charlotte, who prided herself on teaching even dunces what to say on every occasion, found herself searching for a topic that would not be incendiary. For the second time within a few moments, she found herself saying, "I appreciate your gesture in offering to walk me down the aisle, my lord."

He waved a brusque hand. "Had to do it. Didn't have a choice. You damn near got my head chopped off with that speech you gave about men not loving their wives."

She didn't understand. She didn't have the stamina to understand or even care right now. "I'm sorry you heard my outburst, Uncle. It was . . . an impulse."

"Don't apologize. That young whelp Ruskin deserved it." Uncle glared glumly forward. "Piper said I deserved it, too."

He captured her attention, something she didn't believe possible right now. "What? Deserved what?"

"She said you were right. She said I didn't love her, thought I was the sun and she was the dirt. Said she'd loved me when I had no prospects and she loved me since I was an earl and I'd been nothing but a jackass every minute."

Charlotte supposed she should murmur some politic denial, but she couldn't lie. Not in church.

"She said I didn't love her."

Recalling all the times he'd ignored Aunt Piper, blamed Aunt Piper, sneered at Aunt Piper, Charlotte found her palms inside her gloves grow damp. "Do you?"

"Of course I do, girl. She's my wife." He hesitated; then, as if this were the inarguable evidence, he added, "Haven't shared another bed for thirty-five years."

Charlotte almost laughed. Did every man in the world think alike? "Women don't consider fidelity the proof of love."

"Well, what the hell else would it be?" her uncle snapped.

"The proof of laziness," she snapped back.

"Your time away hasn't improved you, girl. You're damned cheeky." His gruff voice rose. "I'm the earl. I don't have to exert myself and go out looking for tail. Women come to me."

She nodded, her stomach tightening yet more. Trust her uncle to turn a reconciliatory gesture into a peep show which showed her own probable future. She was marrying a viscount who admitted he didn't love her and thought passion should be sufficient to make her happy. How could she go through with the ceremony?

Uncle apparently took her fright as contempt, for he said loudly, "All right. You women are all the same, wanting blood from a man. Your aunt's the only woman I've ever known. Some of the others have looked pretty damned good, too, Miss Sassymouth, so don't tell me it's just laziness. Piper's just the only one I've ever wanted to—"

She interrupted him hastily, not wanting to hear more. "I believe you, Uncle." Maybe she was wrong. Maybe, for a man, fidelity *was* the proof of love.

That uncomfortable silence fell again.

He cleared his throat. "Piper said a few other things."

Charlotte couldn't face much more. Hands trembling, she said, "Uncle, I appreciate your confidence, but I don't know if I dare listen to any further details about your marriage."

"She didn't talk about that. She talked about you."

"Oh." Charlotte had known her wedding day would be an ordeal, but not one of this magnitude.

"She said maybe we were a little rough on you, what with you having lost your parents. I said I'd lost my brother, and I thought the world of the man. Couldn't have found a better fellow. Good earl, too. Never thought I'd inherit the title."

Charlotte thought back to the days when her parents were alive and her uncle and his family had visited. Uncle had always been gruff and loud, but before he'd also been almost . . . kind.

"But Piper said losing a brother's not the same as losing parents, and any fool would know that." He faced forward and glowered. "Well, I didn't know it."

"Sometimes men are not insightful," Charlotte said in deliberate understatement.

"Well, how the hell are we supposed to know all this stuff about love and feelings? No one ever tells us until they're ready to run away. Anyway, Piper said we could have treated you better. Maybe let you have a season, like you wanted. She even said you were right about Howard. So what I'm trying to . . . it's been a few years, but I never meant . . . your father and I always . . ."

Uncle was a petty, uncouth tyrant, but he was trying to say he'd been wrong. Charlotte had met very few, young or old, rich or poor, who had the strength of character to admit that. In truth, she herself was rather lacking in that skill. Interrupting his halting flow of words, she said, "I understand. You did the best you could."

And, she supposed, given his character and expectations, he had.

Adorna was determined she would not cry. Weddings were joyous occasions, not the funeral dirges so many reveled in thinking them. She would just sit here in the family pew, waiting for Charlotte to walk down the aisle, and while she did she would think cheerful thoughts. After all, she never had cried at a wedding before . . .

"Grandmama?" Leila's small gloved hand tugged cautiously at the sky-blue silk and lace-trimmed skirt of Adorna's gown. "Why is Papa standing up in front looking so mad?"

Adorna looked down at the fingers wrinkling her garment.

Leila whisked her hand away.

Then Adorna shifted her gaze to the child seated on

the pew beside her. "He's not mad, he's happy."

Leila shook her head. Except for the crumpled white rose from Charlotte's bouquet, she looked quite respectable in her pink velvet gown. "He doesn't look happy."

"Well, he is," Adorna snapped. She intercepted a shocked glance from Aunt Jane, and collected herself. "He's just determined."

Robbie leaned across Leila and whispered loudly, "Why isn't he happy?"

"He is happy," Adorna repeated. "He's just . . . men really like it when the wedding part is over."

"Oh." Robbie nodded wisely. "So the mating can begin."

Uncle Ransom smothered his smile with his hand.

Adorna put on her most helpless act and gestured for Uncle Ransom to deal with Robbie. Uncle Ransom ignored her. He'd not only *seen* Adorna's helpless act before, he'd seen *through* it almost at once.

"It's all right, Grandmama." Leila patted her hand. "You don't need to be afraid. You don't have to get up in front of everyone and talk so they laugh at you."

At first Adorna thought how charming it was that Leila thought she should comfort her. Then she thought—"Wait. Who has laughed at you?"

Someone shushed them from behind. Probably Lord Bucknell, suffering from an attack of bellicose propriety. Adorna ignored him. "Has someone teased you, dear?"

"Not really." Leila's lip quivered. "Just a little."

Robbie leaned over again. "It was the vicar's son. Alfred made fun of her accent and made her cry." He leaned back again, crossing his arms over his chest. Apparently brotherly love won out over young friendship, especially when Alfred vexed her about the very quirk she shared with Robbie.

"I didn't cry," Leila said.

Robbie rolled his eyes.

"Maybe once, but not for long," she conceded. "That stupid boy can't make me cry."

Looking at Leila's thin chin, pointed into the air, at her tall, scrawny body, at her dark thick hair, Adorna was struck by her resemblance to Aunt Jane. Aunt Jane, whom Adorna revered for her courage, her stubborn integrity and her capacity to love. All characteristics Leila contained in abundance.

And Robbie. In his profile, Adorna saw Wynter's stubborn, outthrust lip, his brooding search for stability and . . . his ability with a blade. Closing her eyes, she remembered how nine-year-old Wynter had carved her table with *his* knife. Back then, she had laughed.

She heard her own dear husband's voice in her head. *Adorna, without a child's love, you'll shrivel and grow old.* Loving a child, laughing at its antics . . . that was Henry's prescription to combat age, and it had worked. Until the day of his death, he had retained a youthful spirit, and for that, she had loved him.

Of course, these children were mischievous and a trial for a woman used to her own way. But Adorna had always doted on children. She looked toward Wynter, handsome and shod, his gaze fixed to the door at the back of the church. Behind him, the ancient stained-glass window gleamed, rich with colors. Tears prickled in Adorna's eyes. She swallowed. She was *not* going to cry.

She was not going to dwell on the fact that this wedding was a culmination of dreams going back to the day she'd rocked Wynter in *his* cradle. She'd feared those dreams could never be fulfilled during the empty years of his absence, but soon . . . oh, soon she would have other grandchildren to pamper.

From the corners of her eyes, she saw Robbie slide his arm around Leila's shoulders.

The other grandchildren wouldn't speak with an accent. Their coloring would be similar to everyone else's in England. They'd have both a father and a mother.

They wouldn't need Adorna.

Robbie needed her. Leila needed her. Adorna stifled a surprise sob with her gloved fingers.

"Grandmama?" Leila whispered.

Adorna struggled to respond, to behave as if tears weren't trickling down her cheeks.

"What's wrong with her?" Robbie forgot they were in church, and he spoke out loud.

Aunt Jane shushed him. "She's happy," she explained.

"People here really act funny when they're happy," Robbie said in boyish disgust. But his hand softly touched Adorna's shoulder.

And Leila planted a kiss on her arm.

The organist began to play. The soprano began to sing. Charlotte stood at the back of the church with . . . the Earl of Porterbridge? Adorna blinked, dabbed her eyes with her handkerchief, then shrugged and moved aside to allow Leila and Robbie the best view.

"There's Lady Miss Charlotte. She is so beautiful." Leila spoke so quietly Adorna had to lean down to hear her. "After she's married Papa, do you think she'll still be nice to me?"

Her subdued question tore at Adorna's heart. How could a child residing in *her* household be so unsure of herself? Especially her own granddaughter? Leaning over, she hugged Leila to her. "Of course she'll still be nice to you, darling. She loves you—and so do I."

CHAPTER 26

*T*HE WEDDING HAD BEEN A TRIUMPH.

Wynter had listened intently while Charlotte whispered her vows. Then he'd proclaimed his fidelity and loyalty to her in firm tones that resounded throughout the church. In this manner, he had assured her he not only understood the oaths they took, but that he intended to keep them. He would not be neglectful, cruel or unfaithful. He knew she must have been pleased and gratified by his sensitivity.

The reception, staged in the ballroom and long salon of Austinpark Manor, was less of a triumph. He knew Charlotte thought so, too, because the smile he adored was artificial and strained. They had to stand in line with his mother and Porterbridge, murmuring polite nothings at guests he wished to Gehenna. Howard and his harpy of a wife. Lady Smithwick and her very disappointed daughter. Hodges and Shilbottle. Drakely and Read. Stewart.

Stewart . . .

"Cousin." Stewart shook Wynter's hand firmly. "Congratulations on your marriage to such a lovely, accomplished Englishwoman. Now you'll settle down and be in the office every day, eh?"

The trouble with Stewart, Wynter thought, was that he looked completely sincere. His compliment to Charlotte sounded free of mockery, and he behaved as if he really hoped Wynter *would* come into the office every day. The man was a gifted actor—for an embezzler. "Thank you, cousin," Wynter said gravely. "But I must take my honeymoon first, and teach my bride the pleasures of love."

Next to him, Charlotte gasped. Down the receiving line, Mrs. Morant fainted. Adorna giggled.

Leaning close to Charlotte's ear, Wynter asked, "Was that a personal comment?"

"One doesn't speak of the honeymoon in mixed company." Her voice was steady, but her gaze slid away from his.

"Then I will not do so again." Not when it made her lose the little color still highlighting her cheeks. Raising his voice, he called to the people remaining in the receiving line, "My bride is tiring. We shall cease greeting now so she may sit and you may dine and consume intoxicating beverages. Later we shall start again."

Laughter rippled among the crowd, but they dispersed at record speed.

"That was not . . ." Charlotte sighed and gave up.

"I know." Wynter took her arm. "But you are not a blushing bride. You are pale."

"I say well done. My feet hurt, and I have to find Piper. See if she's still mad at me." Porterbridge shambled off.

"Your years in the desert certainly gave you an attitude of command, dear." Adorna smiled at him, then stroked Charlotte's cheek. "You *are* wan, Charlotte. A plate of food and a little brandy would do you wonders."

Wynter had made it his business to know what she liked. "She does not like brandy. Nor does she like coffee. She shall have tea."

"Actually, I'd like a glass of wine," Charlotte said.

"No. No wine." He noted Charlotte glared at him as if he were dictatorial, when actually he had her best interests at heart. "No wine today, oh blossom of the desert. I do not wish you impaired for our true union later."

Now the color swept into her cheeks.

Satisfied that his ruse had worked, he led her to an upholstered chair, ousted the occupant and placed her in it. "Sit. I have an offering for my bride."

"Wynter."

She used his first name. That pleased him.

"There will be no union later."

Still she challenged him. That displeased him. Going down on his knees before her, he lifted her hand and showed her the wedding band of plain gold he had placed there only hours earlier. "I pledged you my troth. You will accept it." With a kiss on her fingers, he rose and left.

He had a gift for her. A very special gift. The best he could give her, one that signified his commitment to her happiness. For she would be happy in this marriage, of that he was determined.

As he strode toward the stairway, he noticed Bucknell standing stiffly near the doorway, staring at Adorna. Just staring. Not moving toward her, not leaving.

And Adorna—she stood near the doorway on the opposite side of the ballroom, ignoring Bucknell with all her might.

This Bucknell had made his mother cry. Wynter hated to take the time now, but later he would be distracted, and as Adorna's son it was up to him to take Bucknell vigorously to task.

Veering toward the tedious nobleman, with a jerk of his head he indicated Bucknell should come with him. Bucknell followed, as Wynter knew he would. Leading Bucknell into the library, Wynter marched to his desk and stood beside it, stiff and tall. "Sir, you will tell me if your intentions toward my mother are honorable, or if you are merely toying with her heart."

Bucknell puffed up like a dueling moorfowl. "Honorable? Of course my intentions are honorable. She will have none of them."

Which left Wynter with nothing to say for a few very critical moments.

"Adorna—your mother—Lady Ruskin—"

"I know who she is," Wynter said dryly.

"She refuses to marry me. I have begged, I have pleaded, I have pointed out the benefits of such union to us both, but she wants . . ." Bucknell turned a ruddy red. "She wants an affair."

"An affair?" Wynter should have known. When had his mother ever done anything in the customary way?

"As distressing as it is to me, she will not wed. She says we are too different for our marriage to be successful. She says we're not suited for a lasting relationship. She says our only recourse is . . ." Bucknell's cravat seemed to be choking him. "Bedsport."

Wynter was fascinated. "But she adores you. I have seen it."

"I thought so, too, and I assure you, Lord Ruskin, I worship her with all my heart." Bucknell paced across the library, hands behind his back. "But I am an honorable man, and I will not so disgrace my name and hers with such irregular behavior."

Wynter wouldn't have thought the older man would

need guidance, but obviously he did. "This determination for an affair is very wrong-headed of her."

Obviously pleased that he and Wynter agreed on one thing, at least, Bucknell trumpeted, "Just what I told her."

"So you must steal her."

"Steal her?" Wynter saw the moment Bucknell understood, for he stiffened as if he were a corpse. "You mean, kidnap her?"

Wynter thought about it. "Yes. I believe that is the word."

"I say, kidnapping might be the way to get a bride in your desert, but we don't perform such barbaric acts in England."

"Really?" Wynter hoped Bucknell didn't suffer an attack of apoplexy. "I didn't believe this was a cultural matter, but a matter of human nature. My wife, whom I always turn to for advice and guidance, has told me that men and women are no different in their ability to learn."

"Harrumph. Well, I wouldn't say that. Most women are delicate flowers—"

"Most women, but not our women. My wife and your beloved have proven themselves in the most difficult of conditions. My wife during her years as a governess, your beloved when she guided our business during my absence."

"Yes, yes, both the Lady Ruskins are extraordinary women, but—"

"My wife"—Wynter enjoyed repeating that word— "has also told me that the women in El Bahar are the same as the women in this country, and if given the same opportunities to learn and be independent, they would be as Englishwomen. Is this not so?"

"I suppose," Bucknell said grudgingly.

"Thus, it makes sense that Englishwomen, if treated the same as women in El Bahar, would respond in much the same way. I must tell you, when a Bedouin woman meets a man she desires but who is of a different tribe, the Bedouin man will kidnap her and take her into the desert, keeping her until her protestations have died beneath the barrage of ardor he showers on her. It is well-known that these are the true love matches among the Arabs, for the woman is pleased by her husband's boldness and devotion to her."

"Young man, that is just unacceptable."

"No. Unhappiness for the rest of your life is unacceptable." No wonder his mother hadn't wanted to marry Bucknell! No desert man would provide his woman so uncertain a wooing, and this proved that such pallid civilized English courtship was not effective. "Taking action to secure your happiness, and hers, is the only sensible recourse."

"Your mother wouldn't respond to such barbarity."

"Indeed, my mother is a woman who admires daring, yet it appears she is unable to ascertain the difference between mere lust and a man's deep love and admiration. If both love and daring are combined, she would be willing to ride into the desert with her kidnapper." Wynter frowned as if the thought had just occurred to him. "As you have undoubtedly noticed, my mother is a woman who attracts men like a flower attracts bees. I am surprised no one has kidnapped her previously."

"Englishmen do not kidnap their brides."

Bucknell sounded as if he were trying to convince himself, now. Well, Wynter had done what he could. "It is, of course, your decision, but please note, my lord, you have my permission to kidnap my mother at any time."

He left Bucknell sputtering.

*   *   *

The wedding had been an ordeal.

Wynter had been so intent he'd leaned close to hear Charlotte whisper her vows, then proclaimed his fidelity and loyalty to her in firm tones that resounded throughout the church. The reception was equally distressing, with guests consuming an amazing amount of food and drink, and as the liquor disappeared their reticence had, too. They had openly reminisced about her original inglorious refusal of Lord Howard, then compared it to the current scandal with Wynter. Predictably, they hadn't censured either Lord Howard, who was drunk as a stevedore and staring at her broodingly, or Wynter, who had disappeared for over half an hour. No, each weighty sin had been placed squarely on her shoulders, and she, Miss Priss, couldn't answer with the pithy responses she wished. Instead she had to sit politely and smile at the guests' ill-timed quips.

"Here comes the groom. 'Bout time he returned." Mr. Read squinted through his alcoholic fog. "Uh-oh."

"What's wrong?" Cousin Stewart asked.

"He's got a couple of women with him," Mr. Read answered.

Mr. Read was obviously a disagreeable man in need of a sharp rap across the knuckles.

Cousin Stewart, on the other hand, chuckled softly. "If there is one thing I have learned about Wynter in the last few weeks, it is that he's a single-minded man. And only a simpleton would imagine that he is anything but devoted to the new Lady Ruskin."

Looking down at her new rings, Charlotte thought how true his statement was. Wynter was devoted to her. As devoted as any man could be who kept his heart untouched and his wife in her place. Even her aunt Piper had a better lot than that, although it had taken thirty-five years of living with Uncle to get it.

"Charlotte, see your gift." Wynter sounded proud of himself, as proud as Leila when she brought her a bouquet of wildflowers.

"Charlotte!"

She recognized the voice, but thought she was dreaming.

"Charlotte, we came for your wedding!"

Pamela's voice. Hannah's voice. She looked up and saw them, her two best friends, one on each of Wynter's arms. She stared, thinking she was hallucinating, thinking this was impossible and too wonderful for words. She wanted to sing and shout, to hug them and tell them how happy she was to see them.

Instead, she burst into tears.

CHAPTER 27

CHARLOTTE SAT ON HER DRESSING STOOL IN HER BED-chamber while Pamela and Hannah removed her ivory veil and gloves, and put wet cloths on her forehead. This was no small storm, but a great breaking of the dam of grief she had stored up for nine years. Or even since the death of her parents. Heaven knew she hadn't cried like this within her memory.

When the worst of the tears had passed, she hic-cuped, "I'm . . . sorry."

"Don't you apologize," Hannah said.

"Don't try to stop, either." Pamela sounded furious. "That husband of yours . . . did you see him? When we carried you off, I thought he was going to come in here with us and demand you be delighted."

A huge sob escaped from Charlotte.

Pamela handed her a clean handkerchief. "I told Hannah you must be disconsolate at being forced to marry, but we had no idea . . . we would have come sooner . . ."

"I never thought . . . you would come . . ."

"*He* insisted." In an exasperated gesture, Hannah pushed her own hair back. "We liked him for that! He sent his own carriage to get us here for the wedding.

But we couldn't leave immediately. We have found Pamela a position, and—"

"A . . . position?" Charlotte took a quivering breath. "Oh, Pamela . . . what?"

"For Lord Kerrich." Pamela shrugged uncomfortably. "Very temporary, but very lucrative."

"A shabby conspiracy, if you ask me," Hannah said.

"If I can succeed, I'll earn as much in two months as I did all last year, and while caring for *one* small child." Pamela's smile broke through at the thought of so much money. "Hannah, you must see why I've taken it!"

"I understand," Hannah said darkly. "But I don't approve."

Alarmed, Charlotte asked, "Is it legal?"

"Yes," both the friends said together.

"You're not to worry." Wringing out a cloth, Hannah knelt at Charlotte's side and pressed it to Charlotte's wrist. "You know I would never allow Pamela to do anything disreputable, no matter how much money was offered." She shot a glare at Pamela.

Pamela flounced to a seat.

"But after one encounter with Kerrich," Hannah continued, "I can assure you he is a man so spoiled by wealth and privilege he never thinks of another's feelings."

"No one will get hurt," Pamela said. "You must trust me."

Charlotte and Hannah exchanged a troubled glance. Pamela's family had been well-bred and wealthy. Then, in a dreadful turn of events, they had lost everything. Her mother had died from lack of care, and from heartbreak. That left Pamela more determined to succeed than either of them put together. Nevertheless,

Charlotte and Hannah worried that someday Pamela's ambition would lead her astray.

Not this time, Charlotte prayed.

"Besides, we're here for Charlotte's sake, not to talk about me and my assignment." Pamela came and knelt beside Hannah at Charlotte's feet. "This is a beautiful manor, Charlotte, and you must be very rich now."

Hannah elbowed her. "Money does not buy happiness."

"No, but it certainly helps get you into the better shops."

"Pamela!" Hannah snapped. Pamela subsided, and Hannah turned back to Charlotte. "Has Ruskin . . . hurt you?"

"No, of course not." Blowing her nose into a final handkerchief, Charlotte dropped it on the pile on the dressing table. "Only at first when he started talking marriage, I thought he was jesting, or trying to seduce me. Then he deliberately compromised me, and I discovered he was serious, and there I was right back where I started. Facing marriage to a man who would do no more than tolerate me."

Now Hannah and Pamela exchanged a glance.

"A remarkable tolerance that sends such a beautiful carriage to get your friends to your wedding." Hannah picked her way through a perplexing situation. "The carriage broke down, you know, or we would have been here on time. When we didn't arrive, he worried and sent a second vehicle to rescue us . . . Charlotte, he seems thoughtful and kind."

"He is," Charlotte exclaimed. "I don't mean to malign him! He is . . . he tries . . . he has kindness in him."

"Is it the children?" Pamela asked. "Do they resent you?"

"I love the children, and they love me." Charlotte thought of how perfect they'd looked today and how well they'd behaved. This was their debut, and forever they would be remembered for how they deported themselves at her wedding. Right now they were hosting their own children's reception in the playroom, and she had the satisfaction of knowing she'd helped them to blend in and never, ever become objects of scorn.

Hannah's mouth drooped. "Then, Charlotte, I must suppose you are unhappy because you hold in your heart a secret desire that he love you."

"It is no secret," Charlotte answered.

"You don't want that," Hannah said. "A man doesn't love like a woman does. When a man loves, he wants you to do as he says without question. He wants you to exist for him only. He is an autocrat of the worst kind."

"You just described Wynter." Charlotte swallowed yet another sob. "And I assure you, he doesn't love me."

Pamela was looking at Hannah strangely, but now she turned to Charlotte. "How do you know?"

"He told me."

"You thought he was trying to seduce you by telling you he didn't love you?" Pamela tried to remain solemn, but her natural grin broke through. "Someone is bewildered. Me, for one."

"You don't understand." And the situation was too complex for Charlotte to explain. "Anyway, it doesn't matter. I've wed him, and as Pamela says, my future is secure. I've been too often without resources to dismiss that." A thought struck her. "What will happen to the Governess School?"

"We were talking about that on the journey here."

Pamela rose and with mock sternness said, "We're going to cut you out as a proprietress."

"So I can't come back to teach others how to be governesses?" Charlotte pulled a long face.

"But we will allow you to be our patron." Hannah rose, too.

"I would like that."

"You'll be needing a new governess for your stepchildren," Pamela said, "and we know a place which provides expert placement."

Charlotte laughed, startling her nervous system with the abrupt change between tears and amusement. "We're going to need a tutor for Robbie soon, too. Can you handle that?"

"Absolutely," Hannah said happily. "With your help, I foresee many placements."

"From the look of Lord Ruskin, I think she'll need a nursery maid within the year, too," Pamela said softly.

The three friends struggled to comprehend that one of them could be a mother.

Charlotte struggled to comprehend that she might someday cradle a life within her womb.

"Charlotte, try to be happy," Pamela begged.

"Don't ask for so much," Hannah added. "You have his name and his fortune, you say he's kind and his children love you. Settle for that."

Put like that, it seemed logical. But—"I can't. I want everything."

"Of course she does." Pamela embraced her. "And she'll get it, too. Charlotte's strong."

"So she is." Hannah was troubled, but she put her arms around both of them and hugged them tight. Then she said, "Pamela, we should go and enjoy the reception, and allow Charlotte to tidy herself."

"I'm not returning," Charlotte answered. "I shall stay here—all night." She saw the glance Pamela and Hannah exchanged, and held up her hand. "Don't try and talk me out of it. I know what I'm doing."

"Aren't you afraid Lord Ruskin will turn to another?" Pamela asked.

"No." Of that Charlotte was sure.

Hannah said, "Aren't you afraid he—"

"I'm not afraid of him at all."

Her two friends nodded, and tumbled out the door as if they couldn't wait to escape. Apparently Charlotte was the only one not frightened by Wynter's mystique.

As soon as they left the bedchamber, she turned the key in the lock. The thick door was strong oak. The hinges and lock were sturdy iron. She was safe here.

The lengthy storm of tears left her calm and resolute. She was married. She'd been left with no choice in the matter. But she didn't care how much Wynter seduced, persuaded and insisted, she was not going to allow him in her bed. The struggle between them had come down to this, and if she succumbed to his blandishments, she would be the loser. She couldn't give him what he wanted—a wife who willingly surrendered to him in every instance.

Besides, when she thought about the passion he had taught her . . . but she couldn't think about that. When she imagined how his nude body would feel against hers, he had already won.

Her things had been removed from this chamber. She peeked under the comforter. But the bedding remained on the bed. She had nothing to drink or eat, but such craven attention to physical needs never won a battle. Most prisoners of principle were not so fortunate in their lodging.

She shrugged uncomfortably under the weight of the gown. She couldn't loosen the tiny buttons down the back, and must therefore sleep swathed in the weight of heavy satin, but she could remove her shoes and stockings. Sitting in the window seat, she took them off and sighed at the relief of wiggling her toes in the plush rug.

And her petticoats. She would be much more comfortable without them. It was too bad that she couldn't, as Wynter always advised, remove her corset, but—

No. She wouldn't think about Wynter's advice, or the way his voice lowered to a husky whisper when he tried to coax her out of her clothes. He was her husband. That gave him enough authority without allowing him the freedom of her mind.

Standing, she untied the petticoats from around her waist. She let them drop to the floor, and promptly felt so much lighter she could almost dance to the tune drifting up from the ballroom. She used to be quite a good dancer—

Someone tried to turn the doorknob. Something thudded against the door.

She jumped so hard she bit her tongue.

Then a hard knock reverberated throughout the room.

She hadn't a doubt who stood on the other side of the door. She had, she realized, been waiting for him. But she hadn't expected he would arrive quite so quickly. *Be firm,* she cautioned herself. *Remember your resolution.* "Yes?" She *sounded* firm and resolute.

"Lady Miss Charlotte." He sounded firm and resolute, too. In fact, he sounded rather harsh and furious, and her fortitude quailed. "Open the door at once."

"I will not. I told you I wouldn't share your bed, and I mean it."

"I told you you had until the wedding day to prepare yourself, and I am a man of my word."

"Yes. Well." She grinned at the sturdy, locked door in a sudden attack of lightness. Not even a big, muscled, irate barbarian could get through that door. "You don't have a lot of choice, do you?"

He struck the door with his knuckles. "Open at once."

"No."

"You do not care what our guests think of your obstinacy?"

"No." In fact, in the most wicked corner of her soul, she reveled in besting him.

"So you refuse?"

"Yes."

"I thought you might." He sounded grimly pleased. "Charlotte, stand as far away from the door as you can."

She didn't answer. She didn't understand what he meant or why he said that.

"Charlotte? Are you standing back?"

"Y-yes."

The blast shook the floor and shattered her eardrums. The lock fell away and splinters went flying. Wynter kicked the door so hard it bounced against the wall. And there he stood wearing his djellaba—and holding a smoking pistol.

CHAPTER 28

"MY LORD?" CHARLOTTE QUAVERED.

Her new husband swept into the room with the speed and fury of a wind off the desert.

"Wynter?"

Never slowing, he tossed the pistol onto her marble dressing table and removed one of the gold cords around his waist. She tried to scramble aside, but he caught her wrists. He tied them together, twirled her around, and bound a soft scarlet cloth around her eyes. Before she could catch her breath to berate him, he turned her again. He dipped, and with his shoulder in her midsection, he picked her up and headed for . . . where?

"What are you . . . you can't . . ."

He maneuvered out the door. She felt the twist of his muscles as he turned sideways and realized the care he exerted so that she wouldn't strike the door-frame.

"My lord, this isn't . . ." Her head hung down his back. She kept trying to push herself up by her elbows, as if that would somehow allow her to see past the blindfold.

A blindfold. She was blindfolded and trussed. He'd had a gun.

He'd expected her to lock herself in. He'd been prepared!

The first uproar of her agitation was replaced by trepidation, although she tried very hard to make it indignation. "What are you doing?" She gasped for breath. "This is outrageous!"

He didn't respond, but strode along silently... somewhere. Again she struggled to bring her arms up. If she could just grasp her blindfold and fling it off! Then from below she heard someone call, "I tell you, I heard a gunshot."

Incredulity struck. They were approaching the stairway. "My lord, where are you taking me?"

His voice resounded with tenacity and composure. "I am kidnapping my wife."

She began to struggle in earnest. "Where are you taking me?"

"I have prepared a place."

"But you're not to go through..."

He took the first steps down, and she stilled. She didn't want to fall off his shoulder and roll down the stairs. Only one thing could be more scandalous. "Wynter, I forbid you to do this!"

He ignored her, but all the while he moved carefully, cradling her against the worst of the jolts as he descended the stairs.

The sound of voices grew louder, and a male voice—Lord Bucknell's?—exclaimed, "By Jove!"

Her fears were all the more horrible for being well grounded. Wynter was headed for the reception.

"Look at that!" A woman tittered.

"Wynter, please don't show me to the guests," she pleaded.

"It will be a brief showing," he assured her.

The buzz of conversation grew louder.

Panicking, Charlotte asked Wynter, "What purpose will that serve?"

"I must go this direction to take you to the place I've prepared."

Individual voices began to impugn on Charlotte's sensibilities.

Cousin Stewart stammered, "Wha-what is Cousin Wynter doing?"

"Isn't that sweet?" Adorna trilled. "Wynter is so fond of our dear Charlotte, and they do enjoy playing their little games."

Charlotte didn't think it was sweet, and she wasn't playing a game. Digging her fingers into his back, she said, "You could go another direction!"

"This is the direct route."

"You are humiliating me."

He stopped. "This is not about humiliation, Lady Miss Charlotte." He smoothed a possessive hand over her buttocks. "You are a maiden with a maiden's fears. I am a man and I will cajole you out of them. You will admit your love for me. We will live happily ever after."

Whatever alarm she felt faded in her rise of indignation. "You make this exhibition sound like a normal incident."

"Today, Bucknell reminded me that reluctant maidens should be kidnapped."

Her mouth would have dropped open if she hadn't been hanging upside down She struggled to raise her head. "Lord Bucknell reminded you of that?"

"Yes." Wynter walked on as if he'd explained everything.

Conversation had halted. Wynter must have walked

past the reception, although she couldn't trace his route in her mind. She got her hands up to her blindfold at last, and shoved it up on her forehead—and saw that they moved right through the ballroom and long salon. People were standing, hands hanging at their sides, wide-eyed, watching her. Watching *them* as Wynter strode through the reception and toward the outer doors.

She pulled the blindfold back over her eyes and drooped down on Wynter's back. Miss Priss? After the scandal of her engagement and this spectacle, she would never be known as a maven of civility again.

She heard the door open. She smelled fresh air and felt sunshine on her back.

She relaxed. What a relief to be out of the house even though she knew, without even looking back, that every guest from her wedding stood in the open doors and observed them leaving the manor.

She heard the horse whinnying, and she struggled again. "My lord, please. I don't want to ride on your back on a horse. I'll suffocate. Wynter?"

He righted her. The horse was right there; she smelled its equine odor, felt its heat. Wynter took a step up, placed her into the saddle, put her hands on the saddle horn and while she wavered, mounted the horse behind her.

She hated this whole scene. She hated it and yet— she felt so alive. Her heart pounded, her muscles tingled. Behind her, Wynter warmed her back. His arm encircled her waist. When had her incredulous embarrassment become excitement? Or were they one and the same? They rode for perhaps a quarter of an hour, galloping sporadically, and walking frequently. Occasionally the hooves tossed up gravel. Occasionally she smelled the scent of grass as the horse crushed the stalks beneath its hooves. She lifted her hands toward her blindfold, but he caught the cord that bound her and held it. She was not to know where he was taking her, where Wynter had "prepared a place."

"We're here," he announced.

She could scarcely catch her breath as he slid out of the saddle, reached up and pulled her down into his arms. This time he held her with one arm under her back, one under her knees, and as he walked away from the horse, Wynter laughed. Laughed right out loud, and raised her up as though showing the world his newest acquisition.

She jabbed at him with her elbow.

He huffed when she connected with his sternum, and said, "Lady Miss Charlotte, if you are not cooperative I will tie you hand and foot."

"You will not!"

"This is my day. You are my wife. I will do with you as I please."

He hadn't stopped walking to produce his ludicrous pronouncement, and through the blindfold Charlotte saw the alteration in light that indicated they'd entered a building. She felt the temperature change, and she smelled sweet scents. Rose, lemon and a warm spicy fragrance she couldn't identify.

Wynter kicked the door shut, then put her on her feet. He untied her wrists. He pushed the blindfold off her eyes and dropped it to the ground. Hands on hips, he stood smiling at her as if he were the pirate king and she the captive princess.

She had never felt less like a princess—or more like a captive.

The chamber wasn't one that she recognized, but she guessed it must be in a home somewhere on the estate, for it was of large proportions with tall ceilings.

The drapes were closed over the windows. There was no furniture.

But most important, dominating the room was a tent. A huge tent formed of white and pale pink silk. The door flap was swept aside, revealing an inner room large enough to stand in, with carpets on the floor and—she ducked her head and looked inside— a bed. A mattress, really, made up and massive and strewn with velvet pillows and softly draped sheets.

A woman could be debauched in that bed.

She tried to back up, but Wynter stood right behind her. Catching her, he propelled her remorselessly toward the opening. "I have prepared this place for you. You will find it enjoyable to lose your virginity within."

She stumbled on the edge of the carpet as she entered at his behest. "I won't."

"You sound like a child, saying, 'no,' and 'won't,' and 'don't,' in defiance of something that will bring you great joy."

Her bare feet sank into the lush carpet. The bed was even bigger than she realized. "You will never bring me great joy."

He turned her to face him and held her shoulders. "It will be *my* great joy to prove you a liar."

She glared at him. A silly, futile reaction, but what was she supposed to do? Strike out at him as if she were Leila? She'd already cried like a child; she didn't need to act like one, too.

"Take down your hair."

Her hands went to the flattering chignon created by Adorna's *femme de chambre.*

He surveyed her figure, shown clearly by her up-raised arms, with flattering appreciation. "If I have not yet told you, this wedding gown is lovely. How do I take it off of you?"

Retain some maturity, she warned herself as she lowered her arms. "*You* don't." So much for the maturity.

Leaning down, he drew a knife from his boot.

She knew he wasn't going to hurt her, and she was determined not to let him frighten her. "Is there some food you wished to slice?"

"Not at all." Even in the dim light, the curved edge gleamed as he hooked it in the high, unadorned neckline. "I'm going to remove your dress."

She couldn't move. Not with the tip pressing so close to her skin. "Don't be childish. Just because you're not going to get your way—"

The satin tugged, then gave with a rich ripping sound as the knife sliced through it.

"You cut my gown!"

"My knife is very sharp, Lady Miss Charlotte. Don't distract me." The blade slid downward.

"There are buttons!"

"Too many to cut off." He split open the fitted bodice, the waistline, the beginning of the skirt.

She stared at the ruin of her wedding dress in dumbfounded astonishment.

"Charlotte." He used that conspicuously seductive croon when he said her name. "You wear no petticoats." He cut with a great sweep of his knife, leaving the tatters of her dress hanging off her shoulders. "You have no stockings."

When he looked up at her, his brown eyes flickered with an inner flame. His chest rose and fell in forceful breaths.

He'd been playing before. Playing with a knife, yes, but he had always been completely in control of him-

self and his infantile kidnapping. Now . . . now he had
seen her bare legs and he knew that at last he had her
in such a place that he could thrust the seal of his
possession within her body.

He removed his boots. She stepped backward. He
pointed his knife at her. She gave in to panic and ran.

She tripped on the drooping hem at once, falling
half on the bed. He grabbed her skirt and tugged. She
wiggled her shoulders free and stripped her arms out
of her sleeves.

He laughed.

Of course he would, the crafty blackguard. He'd
tricked her out of her gown. She scrambled toward the
back of the tent, thinking if she could lift the silk she
could crawl under and be free.

Picking her up by the waist, he tossed her on the
bed. "Lady Miss Charlotte, I have told you time and
again you should leave off your corset. Now"—he
knelt on the mattress beside her, that wicked blade
gleefully shivering—"I will enforce my wishes." He
turned her over, anchored her with his knee right on
her derriere and started cutting.

She didn't care about the danger anymore. He just
made her so angry! She clawed at the bedcoverings,
but everything was silk and satin, slippery and soft.
The mattress was feathers, impossibly thick and deep.
She got nowhere. Meanwhile, one by one, all of her
corset strings were popping and half her hairpins falling. That left her clad in a thin lawn chemise with a
partial tumble of shining red curls around her shoulders.

She could do nothing about the hair, but she wasn't
giving up the chemise—although how she was going
to stop him from doing as he wished, she didn't know.

Cunning. He was cunning, but she could be, too.

She shoved a pillow out of her face. "This is not fair. I'm to be naked and you have your clothes on!"

The last corset string burst. He pulled on the edge to remove it from beneath her, flipping her over at the same time. Her chemise was hiked to her thighs and she knew it was almost transparent, but for some reason he kept his gaze on her face. "I remove all of my clothing on your command."

The gold cords were tied in a simple knot, and when he eliminated the first one, Charlotte realized she might have outsmarted herself. "No. Wynter . . ."

He tossed the second cord aside. He opened his djellaba. And her curiosity was answered at last. He wore nothing underneath.

Any proper maiden would have covered her eyes.

Charlotte looked. She'd seen his chest twice before, and in a primitive way found it appealing. But below the waist was a whole different matter. A very large, very straight, very smooth and frightening matter.

He allowed djellaba to drop off his arms and let her look her fill. "You tell me as my governess it is rude to point, but as your husband, I tell you—this kind of pointing is gallant, and a compliment."

He might have been speaking in jest, but she couldn't tell. Obnoxious man, he was as proud of himself as if he had created his own body rather than receiving it as a gift from God. She couldn't lift her gaze from that . . . organ.

While she was staring, he sliced the slender sleeves of her chemise.

She was glad for an excuse to look away. Smacking at his hand, she said, "You dare!"

"It was *your* dare. Your challenge. I only answered it." He made one last cut in the neckline, then took careful aim and threw the knife. It stuck in the side of a low table across the tent, quivering and quite out of reach. With one last tear of the fragile material, he would have her freed of clothing and laid out for his delectation.

Cunning? If she had any at all, now was the time to show it. Holding the neckline together, she slid back from him. More hair came tumbling down, the chemise slithered down her back, but she managed to speak as judiciously as she did when supervising any scholarly competition. "I admit. You've won. We're done."

His fingers clamped onto her ankle, and his laughter mocked her propriety. "We have not even started."

She tried to kick herself free.

He crawled up her body, hand over hand, touching her calf, her thigh, her waist. He didn't even bother to wrest her grip from her chemise. He rose above her, straddled her and taunted her with his grin. Hooking his hand at the place where the cloth was torn, he said, "You are a good"—*rip!*—"civilized"—*rip!*—"dutiful lady of England." Yanking his hand back, he tore the chemise clear to the hem.

At his first sight of her bare body, his eyes widened, he drew an audible breath and he was blessedly silent. But not for long. He smoothed his palms between her breasts and down her belly to cover her hipbones. There he pressed her into the mattress. "You will submit to your husband as the law and custom demand."

She didn't care how much bigger he was. She didn't care that he was right. She didn't care what the law and custom demanded. She would not give in.

Balling her fists, she struck at his inner elbows. He collapsed, then caught himself. She rolled against his arm, and he fell all the way down, half on her, but she was out from underneath. The chemise got caught under him, and she was crawling toward the door.

The element of surprise, she thought triumphantly.

But he caught her easily and pressed her to the floor, like a lion playing with a mouse.

He was heavy. He was naked. He was aroused.

The carpet prickled at her bare belly. Her breasts were crushed beneath her. And between them rested his organ, hard and very definitely seeking.

A proper Englishwoman would be shocked and helpless. She was just enraged. Wynter was larger and stronger, yes. But that didn't give him the right to always win. "Get off me, you big oaf." She reached back, trying to grab his hair.

He pulled away, straddling her thighs. "With just a little adjustment, I could . . ." Slowly, he slid a finger between her buttocks and down to that place he loved to touch.

For the last three weeks, every chance he could, he had slid a finger inside of her. He had caressed each fold, each mound, finding her secret places and seizing control, regardless of her resolution to remain unmoved. She had moaned and whimpered, shuddered and undulated on his command, and never, ever, had he been similarly overcome. Now here he was again, overpowering her, holding her against her will, making her want more than him—and now, as her husband, he had the right.

It wasn't fair. She was already damp. She was already ready. He still retained mastery of himself.

She didn't have to put up with this.

Kicking and twisting, she challenged his domination. She turned over, sat up and shoved him as hard as she could. He went over backward, falling on the mattress like a great toppling tree, and she went after him. She jumped on him without concern to any body part, his or hers. *She* straddled *him,* groin to groin, and glared at him. "You think because I'm civilized I have to yield to a savage like you?"

His hands rose toward her breasts.

She grabbed his wrists. "I don't care what the law says. I'm not just your wife, an extension of you. I'm a person." She slammed his wrists to the mattress. "And I will not submit!"

He gave a roar like a wounded lion, came up from underneath her and tumbled her sideways and over onto her back. She kicked out, gained purchase against the mattress and kept the momentum going. They were rolling, over and over. She caught whirling glimpses of the white and pink tent walls, then the ceiling, then the silk bedcovers, then the walls . . . then the ceiling.

They'd come to a halt. She was on her back, her legs around him. He was still grinning, but no longer in a mocking manner. No, this was the grin of a warrior in combat, and she realized she grinned in just the same way. Blood thundered through her veins. Her muscles strained. She panted for breath, fighting for air so she could live to fight again.

Live. Yes, she felt so alive.

His hips and chest pressed her down into the feathers, but she still held his wrists. He couldn't touch her *there*.

But he did. Just like before, he began to penetrate her body . . . only not just like before. This wasn't his finger. This . . . this was large, stinging, directed by the gradual flex of his hips.

She dropped his wrists and grabbed his shoulders, lunging toward him—and screamed.

She'd pushed him farther inside. He threw his head back, eyes closed, teeth clenched, groaning, "Charlotte. Oh, sweet God, Charlotte."

How dare he look as if *he* were in pain? She *burned* with pain . . . surely this was pain. She wanted him all the way inside. She hurt and she . . . she bit his shoulder, sinking her teeth deep.

His eyes opened; he looked incredulously at her, at the mark on his skin. And she saw it happen. He lost control.

He plunged all the way inside, clearing the way for himself, making himself at home in her body. Tears sprang to her eyes, but when he pulled away she wrapped her legs around him. He came back, sliding more easily this time. She whimpered, her inner muscles flexing and releasing.

"Charlotte." His voice was dark and rich, flavored with the desert language. "You are so beautiful, Charlotte."

He moved between her legs. Driving in, touching deep, then gliding out. Her feet stirred restlessly across his buttocks, feeling the labor of his muscles. He encircled her with his body, enveloped her in his pleasure and she loved it. She rose beneath him, learning to match his rhythm. Learning that her movement could make him groan her name again and again.

His hands skated into her hair, every strand loosened in their struggle. He held her head and brought his lips to her face, showering kisses on her. Kisses that fell so lightly she couldn't catch them, but kisses that told more clearly than words his delight in her.

She wrapped her arms around his shoulders. The pain—or was it ecstasy?—increased as his tempo increased. She recognized the sensation; he'd brought her to this peak of exhilaration time and time again in the last weeks.

But this was more. With him inside her, touching

the deepest part of her, *being* a part of her, the loneliness of a lifetime vanished.

Close against her ear, she heard the catch of his breath. The momentum increased. Excitement thrummed through her, rising inexorably with each stroke and kiss. Each whisper of her name became a groan. She raced toward the tumult with him in her arms, cradled by him. Yet inside her womb was stillness . . . waiting. Waiting.

The waiting ended. Deep inside, the spasms started, growing, pulling at him. He panted, thrusting into her as if heat would make them one. Planting her feet on the bed, she lifted and lifted her hips—and froze as surges of rapture shook her. Again she screamed, this time not in pain but in bliss.

He continued, then halted. His face above her revealed a man transported by euphoria. The muscles of his thighs contracted once, twice, three times. Tiny movements, nudging as deep inside her as he could be, filling her with his seed.

Closing her eyes, she luxuriated in the scent of him, the weight of him, the full satisfaction of urges she'd realized only with him. Trembling and ecstatic, she savored the last moments of fulfillment.

"Charlotte," he whispered. "My wife. At last."

Then, languidly, they sank to the bed.

For a blessed long time, her mind was empty of worry or guilt or . . .

My God, what had she done?

CHAPTER 29

CHARLOTTE HAD WRESTLED WITH WYNTER AS IF SHE thought herself some kind of warrior.

She *had* thought herself some kind of warrior. For some reason, he'd let her tussle with him, hold his wrists, imagine she had a chance of winning. And she had fought him until vigor had swept her mind clear of thought and left her only her instincts. Instincts which had led her to this . . . mating.

Merciful heavens, she had screamed in the throes. Twice.

His voice rumbled through his chest to hers. "I was hoping you would drop off to sleep and not be troubled by vexsome cares, my rose sweet with petals of flame."

He hadn't moved. He remained a weight atop her, his head resting beside hers and turned away, so how did he know?

"You . . ."

"Yes?"

She didn't know what to say to him. What did one say to a man when one had experienced such an amazing activity in his arms? "You must think I'm a woman of easy virtue."

"Easy?" He reared back and stared down at her, the portrait of righteous indignation. "I'm married to you and I still had to shoot off the lock!"

She tried to look straight at him, she really did, but her eyes swam with tears.

"Ah, woman." Gently he lifted himself away from her.

To her distress, her body objected, pulsing around his organ as if providing a lingering kiss.

"Dear lord." He sounded hoarse, tormented. "You are . . . wonderful."

Wonderful wasn't what he had been going to say, she was sure. Wanton? Maybe.

Where he had been pressed against her skin, the air felt cool, and the chill revived her brain yet more. How could she have been so gullible as to think she might have a chance against him?

Slowly, as if he hadn't yet recovered his vitality, he stretched out on his back beside her. Painstakingly, he wrapped his arm under her shoulders and around her hips and pulled her against him.

She hadn't grown used to this nudity, his or hers, and now that passion and wrath no longer tumbled through her, she was painfully aware. Her head rested in the hollow of his shoulder. Her hands . . . where did she rest her hands? One underneath him, of course, but the other? He caught it as it hovered and placed it on his chest. The front of her rested against his side, and she didn't dare move. That would attract his attention and . . . and what? She didn't know what happened next. She only knew that as he held her close, the chill faded.

Catching a blanket, he pulled it over them. Tilting up her chin, he looked into her eyes. "Now. You are thinking: He played me for a fool, pretending to wrestle with me. But you must think with my mind, Lady Wife. I have wanted you since I saw you standing on the portico with your carpetbag at your feet. I was determined to be strong and not take advantage of my children's governess, but you tempted me."

The heat of vexation dried her tears. "I never tempted you!"

"But you did. You walked, you breathed, you smiled." He traced the curve of her cheek, the shape of her lips, and it felt remarkably like affection. "Too seldom you smiled, Lady Wife. When my mother decided you should teach me, I decided to surrender to your wiles."

"I don't have any wiles."

He smiled down at her. "Your *unconscious* wiles. I could not be a cad and seduce you, so I determined to wed you."

"You could have warned me," she muttered.

"So you could fight me more? I do not think so. My conceit lies in tatters as it is."

That made her laugh. Just a chuckle, brief but reviving.

"Then—I have convinced you to marry me—"

"Blackmail!"

"And you challenged me. Me!" He thumped his chest. "I answered your challenge, finding you, teaching you to accept my touch, bringing you to ecstasy."

She tried to bury her head in his chest, but he still held her chin.

"No. Don't turn away. It is a good thing for a wary woman to find pleasure in her man's caresses." He took an exasperated breath. "But it is very, very difficult for the man."

"Really?" Such a thought had never occurred to her. "Did you suffer?"

"Yes."

She liked that. She liked that very, very much. "How charming."

Now he chuckled, but darkly. "If I had managed to climb up to your bedchamber, I doubt I could have kept my vow to consummate our marriage after the ceremony, for you had strained my resolution to the limit. I would have taken you then." He glared at her to give his words more impact. "*I* would have taken *you*."

Her fingers flexed on his chest. Her legs moved in a restless movement. Just as she had responded to his coercive seductions, now she responded to the fact he had wished to dominate her. What kind of primitive creature lived in her heart, craving his mastery?

"Your railing gave way, thus proving God was watching over us." He tipped her over on her back as he came up on his elbow. Leaning over her, darkly golden and insistent, he said, "Today I did not take you, Lady Wife. We struggled. We fought. We took each other. Never lie to yourself about that." He cupped his hand over her shoulder and shook her slightly. "Promise me."

So. He had tricked her. He had known he would possess her—truth to tell, she had known it, too—but he'd refused to allow her the easy way out. She could never say she had been unwilling. She had been a participant in their joining. "You know me very well," she said.

He towered over her, rugged, hearty, male and completely convinced of his superiority. "A wise hunter knows his prey."

She knew him very well, too. "Everything has come out just as you intended." Her throat hurt with holding back tears, but she had to bring forth the words. She had to tell the whole truth, and thus comprehend exactly what she had done. "I will now be your wife. You will take care of me. And I will love your children—and you."

"Yes!" His eyes shone with approbation. "You see at last my wisdom and the wisdom of my desert father."

She'd said it. She'd admitted that she loved him. She'd admitted it to him and to herself. And he did not reciprocate. His only thought was that he had been proved right. That she had become a creature of his design. A woman like any other.

The press of tears eased, for what had she to cry about? Her life was settled. She'd had to surrender the one principle that had molded her character. She'd fallen in love with a man who didn't love her and become, not the center of his universe, but a convenience to make his life easier, a mere planet dependent on the mighty sun. She had lost herself.

Ironic, that he had come from the dry and arid desert and brought the desert to her. "As you say, you didn't take me, we took each other," she said. "I can't lie to myself about that, and I never will. I promise."

He kissed her forehead and smiled at her, the most beautiful smile in the world. "You are everything I have ever wanted. Sensible, hardworking and pleasing to gaze upon."

She watched him, in awe of his handsome face and impregnable conceit. "Such praise will turn my head."

For a moment he frowned, uncomprehending. Then a gentle smile lifted his lips. "You are the light of my eyes, the dawn of spring, the—"

She interrupted. "And you are the custodian of worthless compliments. I liked being sensible, hardworking and pleasing to gaze upon better."

"You do not like my tributes?"

She couldn't contain her distress. "You already have me. There's no use wasting them."

"But to me you are the dawn of spring," he said.

Absurdly, she thrilled to his words.

"I am happy, and you are happy. When I have recovered, and this may be"—he lifted his hand, fingers spread—"a year from now, I will wake you, and we will again take each other. Now, sleep, Charlotte, my wife."

They settled together, shoulder to shoulder.

He thought he'd won.

She knew he had.

CHAPTER 30

*T*HE WEDDING A MONTH AGO HAD BEEN A RESOUNDING success, and everyone in the *ton* was obsequiously mindful that Adorna had made it so.

The ceremony had been poignant, the food and drink had received high praise, the orchestra had played the night away, Wynter's departure with Charlotte had caused an immense amount of satisfying gossip and the *ton* now waited anxiously to see how Adorna would top that on the morrow during the Sereminian reception. Adorna smiled as she walked toward the stairway. As if there could be doubt.

"M'lady, m'lady!" The poor dear footman Harris rushed toward her. "Cook says th' ducks haven't arrived from London yet." He looked absolutely beleaguered with his hair standing on end.

Adorna patted his arm soothingly. "If there are no ducks for the dinner, then Cook shall dig a pit and roast an oxen. I'm sure the Sereminian delegation will enjoy it."

Harris nodded, bowed and rushed back toward the kitchens.

Adorna climbed the steps.

The skeptics didn't know her. When the Sereminian

royal family left Austinpark Manor, they would be charmed and entertained, Queen Victoria would be gratified and Adorna would be the most celebrated hostess in England.

Adorna quite looked forward to that.

"My lady!" Miss Symes hurried down the corridor toward her. "Someone at the wedding stole the linens in the west wing and we can't make up all the beds."

"At least this time they didn't steal the silver." Adorna put her arm around the housekeeper. "Queen Victoria's whole idea is to give the Sereminian delegation a short tour of the English countryside and entertainment in a casual setting. Her Majesty, Prince Albert, the court and the Sereminians are coming in the morning and returning to London late in the afternoon. We don't need beds made up."

Miss Symes pulled a disgusted face. "You know some of them will get tiddly and they'll have to stay over."

"But not all, dear, and we have enough linens for the east wing, don't we?"

"Yes."

"There. You see. We shall be fine."

Miss Symes wasn't happy; she hated to be in any way unprepared. "Thank you, my lady. I'll make up every chamber in the east wing at once." But she didn't curtsy. Instead, she looked off to the side as if she were embarrassed. "Have you . . . given thought about what to do about the ghost?"

"Oh, yes." Adorna touched her finger to her cheek. "I suppose when the Sereminians are gone, I will have to do something about our little spook, won't I?"

"If you want to have any upstairs maids left, you will, my lady."

"I'll take care of it, Miss Symes." Adorna sent her

on her way. Miss Symes was a dear to worry so. Too bad that all of Adorna's reassurances that some grand merriment would arise had not reassured her.

Of course, Adorna *would* think of something special to entertain the delegation, and if she didn't, without a doubt some bit of excitement *would* turn up. After all, she hadn't actually *planned* for Wynter to blow the lock off Charlotte's door. That had been pure serendipity. Adorna always had been lucky that way.

Except with Lord Bucknell. She set her teeth and walked more quickly. He had disappeared during the wedding reception and never returned. She'd not heard one word from him, not even when she sent around a little note inquiring with the greatest delicacy about his health. Vile man. She didn't know how she had ever thought she liked him. She certainly didn't understand why she missed him.

The door of the nursery stood open, and from inside Adorna could hear Charlotte speaking. The sweet girl insisted on working with Robbie and Leila on their manners every day, ignoring Adorna's reassurances that the children had been exemplary at the wedding.

Charlotte was a dear, but subdued since she'd returned from the hunting lodge with Wynter.

If Wynter would only stop searching for the embezzler! He went to London every day. He was there now. Adorna had thought his marriage would keep him home, but he matter-of-factly kissed Charlotte every morning and rode off to the city. Why, when Adorna had married Henry, he hadn't been able to stay away for more than two hours at a time, and he'd been in his seventies!

Young people just didn't have that spark anymore.

Pausing in the doorway, Adorna saw that Charlotte read from that book the children adored so—*The Ara-*

bian Nights' Entertainments, it was called, and they seemed to be in quite an exciting part. At least, it appeared to be exciting to Charlotte and Robbie. They sat side by side in chairs, hunched over the book, as Charlotte read faster and faster.

Leila, on the other hand, sat droopy-eyed on the floor, tracing the pattern in the carpet. Suddenly lifting her head, she said, "Lady Miss Charlotte, can we call you *Mama* now?"

Robbie turned on his little sister. "Leila. For the last time, be quiet! I want to know what happens."

Leila flopped back on the floor in a huff.

Charlotte looked at a loss. "Of course you may call me *Mama.* That would make me very happy."

Adorna moved then, and Charlotte noticed her.

Robbie noticed her, too, and in obvious disgust tumbled to the floor beside Leila.

Leila grinned, lay down and drummed her heels on the carpet.

"May I come in and listen?" Adorna hadn't planned to attend them, but the household could run without her for a few minutes, and she sympathized with her grandson's impatience.

Charlotte accepted her presence calmly, but then Charlotte accepted everything calmly these days. It was as if the tumult before the wedding had never occurred, and without a murmur of protest she had settled into being the wife Wynter had wanted. "Of course, Mother, we'd be glad to have you join us. Robbie"—Charlotte touched his shoulder—"set a chair for your grandmama. She wants to hear the rest of the story."

Robbie flashed Adorna a smile as he placed a chair on the other side of Charlotte. Since the wedding, she and her grandson had come to an accord of sorts. He didn't throw his knife at her wallpaper, and she pretended not to notice when he sneaked out to play with his new friends. That included a rather subdued vicar's son, who apparently made no more slurs about people's accents or backgrounds.

A valuable lesson for both the lads, but the turn of events left Leila alone again.

Adorna seated herself and pretended to listen while Charlotte took up the thread of the story. In actuality, she watched Leila. Leila, who made a production of not listening. Leila, who played with the wooden horse Charlotte had given her, yet never complained that her riding lessons had been set back once again.

Leila. Adorna seldom found herself at a loss with other people, but Leila puzzled her. She was hiding something, of that Adorna was certain. But what? What secret could a child of Leila's age keep from every loving adult? Why did Leila smile slyly when she thought herself unwatched? Why, when she talked about El Bahar, did she call it *home*? And why had Adorna once seen her helping herself to Cook's homemade rolls, tying them into a handkerchief and sneaking them upstairs?

Adorna intended to find out—after the Sereminian reception.

Adorna realized the story had ended while she contemplated the enigma of her granddaughter, and Robbie watched her expectantly. "Very good," she exclaimed. "If every tale is as exciting as that one, I will have to read the whole book myself."

"I want to," Robbie said. "But I don't. I like to hear M-mama read them."

Charlotte's face lit up in tangible pleasure, and she embraced Robbie.

Leila sat up. "I wanted to call her that!"

Charlotte opened her other arm to Leila. "I'll be *Mama* to both of you."

Leila came to Charlotte's side and accepted the hug, but all the while she moved nervously as if she were a thoroughbred waiting for the start of a race.

"Charlotte, dear, do you know anything about Sereminia?" Adorna asked brightly.

"Why, yes, we all do." Charlotte put on her governess face. "When we studied Europe, we discovered that Sereminia is a small country in the Pyrenees on the border between France and Spain. What is their official language, Leila?"

Leila sniffed, but obediently answered, "Their official language is Baminian."

"Robbie, what are the names of their rulers?"

"They are ruled by King Danior and Queen Evangeline, and—"

Leila interrupted. "Why can't *you* still be our governess? I don't want a new governess."

Looking troubled, Charlotte took a deep breath. "I'll still supervise your lessons."

"Why can't *you* teach us?"

Robbie couldn't stand his sister's badgering anymore. "Because she'll be having a baby, dunderhead."

"No . . ." Charlotte said.

"I want to be the youngest." Leila's lower lip trembled.

Charlotte was blushing. "I'm not . . ."

As a tear trickled down Leila's cheek, she turned to Robbie. "Will she have a baby *soon*?"

"Real soon," Robbie confirmed. "Papa is potent!"

Even the tip of Charlotte's nose blushed. Adorna had to walk to the window to hide her irrepressible laughter, but when she turned back, she clearly saw the expression on Charlotte's face. What she had previously suspected was confirmed. Charlotte was unhappy. Unhappy and determined to endure.

No unruly child ever put that sorrow on a woman's face. This was Wynter's fault.

Adorna sighed. She didn't want to interfere, but if her son was as oblivious and complacent as he appeared, she would be forced to—after the Sereminian reception.

The thought recalled Adorna to the reason she had come. "Do you scholars know anything about Sereminian traditions? I wish to arrange some appropriate entertainment for them."

Charlotte was patting Leila on the back, even though Charlotte looked as if she badly needed her own back patted. "Sereminian women are known for being adventurous. In her youth Queen Evangeline was quite a daring woman, given to rowing on rough rivers and climbing steep mountains."

Adorna covered her cheeks. "That doesn't help."

"Queen Evangeline is also known throughout Europe as a gourmet," Charlotte offered.

"What about King Danior? Hopefully he's as dull as Prince Albert."

Regretfully, Charlotte shook her head. "That is not his reputation. I'm sorry I can't help you more, Mother."

"Actually . . ." Adorna thought about what she'd learned and smiled. "You helped me quite a lot."

CHAPTER 31

Wynter stood in his traveling garments and watched as an army of house servants placed chairs and tables in comfortable groupings on the wide portico. Workmen spread a golden awning over a wooden frame to provide shade and protect the royal parties from sun or rain. Inside, he knew, local help was cleaning and scrubbing until everything gleamed in sparkling perfection.

A wise man would stay far, far away. Barakah would have stayed far, far away.

Wynter wasn't Barakah.

His mother stepped out the door, a sheaf of papers in hand, looking bright and summery in a grass-green dress few women could have worn. He told himself he should be grateful he had a youthful mother he could apply to in her wisdom. Yet he didn't feel grateful. He just felt disoriented, like a man whose shelter was disappearing in a great, irrevocable sandstorm.

Adorna stopped, clearly startled to see him. "Wynter. Dear. I thought you'd gone to London for the day."

"I did."

She glanced toward the sun. "But it can't be more than one o'clock. It's a two-hour ride."

"I can make it in an hour and a half." Galloping and with a change of horses, but he didn't have to tell her that.

"But an hour and a half there, an hour and a half back—you can't have spent more than two hours there." She brightened. "You didn't go to the office, did you?"

"I did."

Her face fell.

"I couldn't concentrate." He hated to do this. Hated it so much, he almost changed his mind. But he'd searched for other options, and he couldn't come up with any. "Mother, I want to talk to you."

Adorna's hand went to her chest and clutched the stretch of smooth material in her fist. "Dear, what I did was necessary."

"What you did?" Why was she talking about *her*? "What did you do?"

She stared at him, wide-eyed, then took great pains to smooth the wrinkles out of her gown. "I spent over four thousand pounds on this reception."

Why was she babbling about the reception? "Fine. That's fine." He glanced around the portico, which was teaming with workers. "Could we go somewhere private?"

"Of course." Adorna indicated he should walk into the house ahead of her. "I think my study is probably the only place where we can be alone today."

As they passed a mirror, he glanced to one side and caught her dabbing her brow with her handkerchief. "Did you really think I would care?" he asked, trying to give heed to her concerns when he wanted only to talk about his own.

"Yes. Yes, I did." Her voice quavered.

"The money from the business is your money."

Taking her arm, he led her around the kneeling forms of two housemaids, both polishing the lowest step until it shone. "I am not your husband to check your accounts. I am your son. And not a good son, either. If I were, I would have been here for you after Father's death. You would not have had to work so hard to run the business. We would not now be searching for the identity of an embezzler."

She gripped his hand as they climbed the stairs. "Dear, you can't be serious! You don't really think that. Why, you're the best son any woman could ask for! Interesting, exotic, masterful—a man in fulfillment of his destiny. I don't want you to be anything but what you are. I might have wished for you to come home sooner, but . . . you don't really think you have anything to make up to me, do you?"

Today he was grimly aware of his faults. "Mother, while I always knew you could run the business, to leave you to bear the burden for so many years was not right."

"But I like running the business. Your father taught me so much, and I enjoy putting his lessons to use." She sounded faintly pleading. "Oh, dear, I never thought you would take this embezzlement so seriously."

He suspected they were talking at cross-purposes again, but he didn't have time to question her about her misgivings. Not when they were entering her apartments. At last he could talk to the one woman he knew would understand about the one woman he did *not* understand. Hands on his hips, he said, "She isn't working out the way I'd planned."

Adorna's brow knitted. "Who, dear?"

"My wife, of course."

Adorna sank down on her sofa and stared at him.

"She has ceased her senseless defiance. She has admitted my wisdom in bringing about our marriage. She thanks me for my gifts of clothing and jewelry. Yet"—he could scarcely stand to admit this—"yet she is not happy." He paced across to the window, then paced back. "Mother, why is she not happy?"

"Some wives"—Adorna seemed to carefully pick her words—"don't find pleasure in the marital bed. Is Charlotte one such woman?"

He had no time for this English delicacy about perfectly natural functions. "Barakah, my desert father, taught me that if a wife does not find pleasure in the marital bed, it is the husband's duty to discover what will pleasure her."

"The old blackguard was right about that, at least."

"Charlotte and I find much gratification in each other. She brings me ecstasy, and I do the same for her. Many times. Often. I bring her to the peak often because . . ."

Adorna was clearly fascinated. "Because?"

"At night, when she thinks I am asleep, she weeps."

Adorna's face fell.

He gritted his teeth, then told it all. "This morning, after the sun rose and I had brought her much bliss, she turned her back to me and cried."

Adorna shook her head. "Oh, Wynter."

"My appeals for elucidation proved fruitless. She will not talk to me."

"Never?"

"Not as she used to. Even when I eat with my fingers, she says nothing!" That was the worst—he'd performed the most heinously improper act of which he could think, and Charlotte hadn't reprimanded him! "She said she loved me."

"Yes . . ." Adorna appeared to be deep in thought.

"A woman is fulfilled when she loves a man."

Adorna choked.

"So why is she not happy?"

Leaning back into the corner of her sofa, Adorna asked in a sarcastic tone, "I don't know, Wynter, why isn't she?"

"Because she wants me to love her!" He paced across the room.

"Charlotte is a very loveable woman," Adorna pointed out.

"A real man does not love a woman. So my desert father Barakah taught me."

"Wynter!" Standing, his mother snapped out his name as if he were six years old and embroiled in a fistfight. "You tell me that this Barakah, this desert father of yours, said a *real* man does not love his wife. Do you remember your *own* father at all?"

Her vehemence startled him. "Yes, of course. I honor his memory."

She stood there, staring at him, waiting as if he were supposed to know something he didn't.

At last she made a sound of disgust. "Could you be any more stupid?" Placing her hand to her forehead, she said, "I don't understand what you want from me. Do you want me to tell you how to make Charlotte happy?"

His mother had to know. She had to, for where else could he turn? "Well . . . yes."

"It seems to me Charlotte has already told you how to make her happy, but in case you need to hear it again"—she gestured—"perhaps you should ask her."

Charlotte stood framed in the doorway. She wore one of the gowns he had bought her, a simple white cotton, and even with the mark of Leila's sole upon it, she looked most ravishing. Her hair was down, as he preferred, and was caught back in a clip of blue diamonds set in platinum. She looked like a sweet and gentle angel. An angel who was glaring at him.

He didn't know why, but she was angry with him.

Anger was better than that awful resignation and sadness.

"I came looking for you to tell you how concerned I was about Leila," she said. "And I find you discussing me with your *mother*?"

He looked to Adorna for guidance, but she had disappeared. "I did not know what to do about you."

"*About* me? You didn't know what to do *about* me? Am I a child to be handled?"

"Not a child, no. But certainly a woman who doesn't know what she wants."

Her fists balled at her side. "I don't know what I want? I am not the one who had to come to my mother for advice."

He blinked in amazement. "Coming to my mother was the logical course to take. Our union is not proceeding as I had foreseen."

Her skirts rustled as she strode into the room. "It is, too."

"This is an untruth. You are not happy as you should be."

"Why would I be happy?" Coming to him, she placed her hands on his arms and looked up at him earnestly. "My life is just what I feared it would be. At least before, I was a governess. I worked for my keep. My labor had worth. Now I need do nothing. I *am* nothing. I am a possession to be tended as long as I give pleasure."

"A wife is more than a possession."

"Like a horse is more than a possession?" She must have seen the answer in his face, for she flung out her hands. "I'm not a horse. I'm not a dog. I'm a human being and I want to be valued for that. I want to be . . ."

Her eyes must have been filling up with tears again, for she turned away. Had he ever seen her cry before their wedding? No. And since then she had not stopped. Not to control him, as Barakah had warned him some women did, but out of some deep-held pain.

Barakah would have told him that a woman's pain was a trivial matter, and she should be left alone to heal. But something in Wynter demanded that he help with the burden of Charlotte's pain. If he didn't, he thought she might bear it forever. He repeated, "You want to be . . . loved?"

Leaning her shoulder against the wall, she groped for her handkerchief. "He comprehends!"

"But it is enough that you love me."

She blew her nose. "Apparently not."

He experienced confusion. He did not like confusion. He liked life to proceed as it should according to the laws and traditions set down by the men who were his elders. "A real man does not—"

She swung on him like an avenging goddess. "I'll tell you what you can do. You real men can just go to—"

"Papa!" Robbie appeared in the doorway, eyes wide and horrified, holding a piece of paper. "Papa, Leila's run away."

CHAPTER 32

CHARLOTTE SNATCHED THE NOTE AND IN DESPAIR READ the childish scrawl.

"Run away?" Wynter stared at Robbie. "Run away where?"

Hoarsely, Charlotte said, "Home. She says she's gone home."

She had never seen Wynter turn pale, but he paled now. "To El Bahar." He stood as if turned to stone, then seized Charlotte's hand. "You were going to speak to me about Leila."

"Yes. Yes." She scrambled to collect her thoughts. "As we got busy preparing for the Sereminian reception, I've grown worried about her. I suspect she feels neglected. She's cheerful, then ill-natured—"

"Really crabby," Robbie interjected.

"Yes," Charlotte agreed. "I don't think she's sleeping well, and while she was always a challenge, she just isn't her usual exuberant self."

Wynter nodded curtly. "Robbie, would she try to run away to El Bahar?"

"Yes. She's so dumb she might not remember how far it is. She'd try to go back." Robbie grimaced as if trying to contain tears. "She hasn't been happy about

330

me playing with my friends. This is my fault."

"You're not responsible, son, I am." Wynter placed a hand on Robbie's shoulder and squeezed. "Very well. Robbie, go to the stables and speak to Fletcher. See if Leila has been there. Charlotte, send someone to the hostelry and see if she's boarded the coach." His face took on a grim cast. "I'll go to London and search the docks."

"No, you won't." Charlotte twirled and strode out the door. "At least . . . not alone."

Wynter finished talking to the sea captain he had collared, and realized with a start that Charlotte had vanished from his side.

It was a pitch-dark night on the London docks, his wife and his daughter had both disappeared and he could have howled from a fear that ate at his guts. He was going to lose Leila, or Charlotte, or both of them, and this time he couldn't run far enough to cover the pain. This crisis was nothing like his father's death. This time Wynter was an adult, a man responsible for the well-being of his family, and he was failing in every way.

How was this possible? He had lived by the truths as he understood them, taking responsibility, behaving honorably, acting always in an upright manner. What had gone wrong?

In the darkness, he appealed to the sheikh who had guided him into manhood and taught him his hunting skills. "Barakah, please help me find them."

He took a few steps along the wall of a tavern, using every sense to locate his wife. She couldn't have gone far. She'd just been here.

Then he heard her. Charlotte's voice, asking, "If you see a girl walking alone, will you let me know?"

Wynter leaned against the tavern wall, which was damp from the fog and permeated with the stench of old ale, and passed a shaking hand over his forehead.

"Aye, miss, but . . . lots o' girls walkin' alone down 'ere, miss, an' none o' 'em fer a good reason."

Wynter followed the voices down a fetid alleyway, taking care to make no noise.

"I know, but this girl is special," Charlotte said urgently. "This is my daughter."

Wynter clamped his hands on her shoulders. "What are you doing, Charlotte?"

The prostitute shrieked at his sudden appearance and stumbled into a pile of rubbish.

Charlotte leaned back as if she never had a doubt who stood behind her.

He slid one arm around her, feeling the firm combination of skin and muscle that was Charlotte. He needed this. He needed her; worried as he was about Leila, dismayed as he was at having his wife along on his hunt, still he took comfort in her presence. She gave him hope.

Barakah would be amazed at her strength.

"This young lady is out in this alley all night long." Charlotte sounded unruffled, as if she regularly spoke to prostitutes in the lowest dive in London. "She has kindly consented to watch for Leila."

Charlotte had a good idea, Wynter admitted. Alert the prostitutes to watch for Leila. But he didn't think he could survive very many more of Charlotte's good ideas. Not if they involved her disappearing into the night.

"I'll pay you well," he told the prostitute. He could scarcely see her in the spill of the tavern light behind him, and he knew he was nothing more than a hulking brute to her. But she saw the gleam of his coin as he extended it, and at once it disappeared up her sleeve. "There's more where that came from if you see her. Come to the Ruskin Shipping Company. We'll be there."

"No." Charlotte grabbed his arm. "We can't stop looking now."

"The sun set two hours ago. The fog's thickening, and we're just as likely to get our throats cut as find Leila." *And I need to stash you somewhere safe.* But he didn't say that. She had insisted on coming to London. She would resist any attempt to search without her. And in truth, hunting now was foolish for just the reasons he listed, even for him. He herded Charlotte toward the street. "We need to rest so we can search again in the morning."

"What if Leila's out here alone?" Charlotte asked in a low voice.

"At the age of five, she survived a raid on our camp." He reminded himself of that often. "She is wary and wily, and if she is hunkered down somewhere, we could never find her anyway." Charlotte didn't know it, but he held his knife unsheathed in his right hand. "She might not even be out here. The girl they said took the London coach did not match her description."

"Leila could have worn one of your mother's wigs."

"I know." Of course he knew. Leila could do anything when she set her mind to it. "Grip my coattails," he instructed. "I will lead us back to Ruskin Shipping."

To the best of his ability, he kept to the deepest shadows, hearing the grunts of the working prostitutes, the snores of the drunks, the occasional whimper of a soul in distress. The thought of Leila out here ate at him. In the morning . . .

"There are lights on in your building," Charlotte

said. "I thought everyone would have gone home by now."

Wynter stared at the blank front of Ruskin Shipping. She was right. A candle flickered in Wynter's personal second-story office.

Someone was in there. A thief? Or—he took a hard breath—an embezzler?

Had one good thing come of this debacle after all?

"Quietly," he warned Charlotte as he eased the door open. But her skirts rustled as she moved, a womanly sound he usually relished and which now could betray him. He led her through the darkened warehouse, with its wooden crates and spicy scents, to the bottom of the staircase. "Stay here." Moving with the stealth of a desert warrior, he crept up toward the one lit office, knife in hand, his whole being focused on that criminal within.

Whoever he was, Wynter was going to kill him.

Halting, he took a breath to calm his murderous rage. Perhaps killing the embezzler would be disproportionate. But given his gnawing fear about Leila, his frustration with his failure to find the embezzler and Charlotte's unreasonable behavior, bloodshed sounded quite desirable.

Hearing a board creak and a rustle on the dark stairs behind him, he swiveled, knifepoint out.

"Wynter," Charlotte whispered, a pale silhouette against the night. "I just thought—would Leila have known to come here?"

The hand that held the knife shook as he sheathed it. "I don't know." Leila *had* been here on their way through London to Austinpark Manor. Perhaps his resourceful daughter had found her way to the safety of her family's property.

Charlotte groped for his hand. "I want to come with you."

He couldn't send her back down. Even as his eyes adjusted to the dark, he could scarcely make out the multitude of obstacles. So he led her forward. "When we get up there," he murmured, "stay out of the way."

"Yes."

As they reached the upper corridor, he saw that the door to his office stood open.

His fatherly hope died. It wasn't Leila. He knew it wasn't. His vigilant daughter would never be so foolish as to leave herself exposed in such a manner.

Releasing Charlotte, he brought forth his knife and crept forward toward the light. On the threshold he stopped and took in the scene, lit by two candelabras.

Stewart, dear innocent-looking Cousin Stewart, sat at Wynter's desk, spectacles perched on his nose, account book open and neat stacks of pound notes around him.

Wynter made no sound, and Stewart muttered as he worked, but some other sense must have alerted him, for he looked up suddenly. He jumped, spattering ink across the scribbles on the page and exclaimed, "Cousin!" For one moment, he looked almost pleased to see Wynter. Then Wynter saw the guilt set in, for he put his hand over the book. "This isn't what it looks like."

"Oh?" Deliberately, Wynter opened his hand to release the knife. It clattered to the floor. "What does it look like?"

Stewart's gaze fixed on the knife, and he seemed unable to raise his eyes. "I didn't . . . that is, there's a good reason . . ." His thin, gnarled fingers trembled. "I'm your cousin. You won't kill me, will you?"

"If I was going to kill you"—Wynter sprang forward, grabbed him by the cravat and lifted him to his feet—"I wouldn't have dropped the knife." He dragged Stewart over the top of the desk. Books and papers scattered, ink spilled, his flailing feet sent the chair flying.

"Wynter!"

He heard Charlotte's cry, but he paid her no heed. Stewart, his cousin, had taken advantage of Adorna, his mother. He had stolen from the family business, the business that had provided him a living all of his adult years. Stewart's eyes bulged as Wynter swung him up against a file cabinet and tightened his grip around Stewart's throat.

"Wynter, what are you doing?" Charlotte tugged at his arm.

"Why?" Wynter demanded of Stewart. "Why did you steal from my mother?"

A woman spoke from the doorway. "He didn't."

Wynter recognized that voice. He should; it had sung his lullabies.

"Let go of Stewart," Adorna commanded. "He didn't embezzle from the business."

Wynter released Stewart, an awful suspicion springing to life. Turning to face the door, he saw his mother, dressed for traveling and drawn up to her full height. "Who did, Mother?"

She lifted her chin proudly. "I did."

CHAPTER 33

CHARLOTTE HAD NEVER FELT SO LEFT OUT, SO UNIN-formed, so orphaned in her whole life. Wynter had thought someone was embezzling from his business? And he had never told her? But of course, she realized, he had never thought to tell her anything.

And Adorna had done the embezzling?

Nothing could have made it clearer to Charlotte: She was not a part of this family.

Then behind Adorna, something moved. A face peeked around the doorway.

And Charlotte forgot her sense of abandonment on a surge of joy. "Leila."

The little girl looked at her and smiled tentatively.

Dropping to her knees, Charlotte held out her arms. Leila wiggled around Adorna's full skirts and into Charlotte's embrace. Leila hugged Charlotte with all her might; Charlotte squeezed the thin body, murmuring, "Leila. My dear little Leila."

Somehow Wynter got there, too, on his knees, arms around them both, rocking them in his hold.

Later, Charlotte thought he had been crying. At that moment, nothing mattered but the return of her child.

Unfortunately, reality returned on a father's growl.

"Leila. Fruit of my loins, you have much explaining to do."

Leila did have explaining to do, Charlotte realized. Like her grandmother, she was dressed in traveling clothes. She didn't look frightened. She wasn't dirty or bruised. All of which made Charlotte thankful, and at the same time ready to shake her. "Leila, young lady, where have you been?"

Leila's lip trembled, and Adorna intervened. "Do you want me to tell you about that first, or explain about the embezzling?"

Charlotte stared at her mother-in-law, who appeared fresh and beautiful while Charlotte resembled a London alley in both odor and aspect. Then she looked at Wynter. Smudges marked his skin, his golden hair was dingy and in the scuffle with Stewart he'd split his wide lower lip. Blood dried on his chin, but he kept his arms around his wife and his daughter, and glared at his mother.

"Leila first," he said.

Wynter and Charlotte had already left for London when the cause of the uproar reached Adorna in the formal dining chamber.

"My lady, have you heard? The little lass ran away to be with her infidel husband," Miss Symes told her.

Adorna stopped counting the table linens and asked impatiently, "Symes, what are you babbling about?"

"Miss Leila. She's gone."

Adorna gave Miss Symes a look, the one that demanded facts and not speculation.

Miss Symes straightened to almost military attention. "She left a note. She said she was going home."

"To her infidel husband?"

Miss Symes squirmed. "Well . . . no."

"Hmm." Adorna went back to counting the table linens.

"My lady, aren't you worried about her? Your own granddaughter?"

"Hmm." Miss Symes left Adorna thinking, and thinking hard, and when she had finished counting, she also had solved the puzzle that was Leila. She had Cook pack a basket. She climbed the stairs to the second floor. Then to the third floor . . . then, very quietly, to the attic.

Carefully, she opened the door to the main room. Not surprisingly, it echoed, barren and empty. But Adorna noted the floor, dust-free in front of one of the corridors that led away into the attic chambers. As silently as she could, she crept down that hallway, and at a door near the end, she found the clue she needed. A single piece of straw.

Straightening—after all, there was no use in stealth now—she flung wide the portal and announced, "Your grandmama is here with provisions."

"Yipe!" Leila curled into a little ball.

"Good heavens," Adorna exclaimed, gazing around her. "No wonder the ghost made so much noise."

The child had done a marvelous job of re-creating her home in El Bahar. The stolen linens from the west wing had been draped around to create a tentlike atmosphere, with an opening at the window for light and air. Leila had found an old carpet and placed it over the squeaky floorboards, and she'd made up a bed of straw from the stables. In the place of honor, in the center of the chamber by the pretend campfire, stood the wooden horse Charlotte had given her and an open book.

"You can't tell me she didn't drop straw anywhere else," Adorna muttered. Then she saw Leila's expres-

sion of defiance and misery, and hastily she changed from disapproving homeowner to indulgent grandparent.

Opening the basket, she lowered it so the child seated on the cushions could see the contents. "I brought cold meats, hard-boiled eggs, the choicest strawberries and sweetened cream to dip them in." Pointing at the little pile of stale rolls Leila had hoarded, she said, "With your bread, we could have a real feast." She smiled charmingly. "Won't you invite me into your tent, oh mistress of the desert?"

"So she never left the house." Charlotte could have kissed Adorna, but she still knelt on the floor in Wynter's office, clasped in both Wynter's and Leila's arms. So she hugged Leila again. "Sweetheart, what made you think of going up there?"

Leila took a big breath and confessed, "I needed someplace to hide so I could read your book."

"What book?" Charlotte asked.

"The Arabian Nights' Entertainments."

"You didn't have to hide to read it. I would have given . . . ohh." Charlotte understood now. "But if you knew how to read, why did you tell me you didn't?"

"I thought you'd stop reading to me." Leila looked sideways at her father. "Like after he'd taught me to ride, Papa stopped riding with me."

"No, you don't, monkey. You can't make me guilty to get out of punishment for this." Without the hint of a smile, Wynter looked at his daughter. "Frightening us like this was wrong, and you knew it."

"Yes," Leila said in a little voice.

"But you are a child. You are learning right from wrong." Releasing his grip on Charlotte and Leila, Wynter rose to his feet. "Your grandmother, on the other hand, is an adult who should have known better than to embezzle from her own company. Mother, what possible excuse do you have for this reprehensible behavior?"

Adorna took a step back from his rapidly increasing volume. "I wanted you to come home."

Wynter was struck speechless.

"From the way Stewart was acting, I knew he had had some kind of contact with you."

Charlotte glanced over at Stewart.

He was massaging his throat and smiling nervously. "A letter," he croaked.

"Yes, I had sent a letter," Wynter confirmed, "to tell him I was alive and to prepare you for my eventual return."

"After I confronted him, he did tell me. I was very happy you were alive." Walking to him, Adorna rested her gloved palm on his cheek. "But he said you weren't coming back right away."

"I didn't tell her immediately," Stewart said, "because I knew she would be unhappy that you delayed your return."

"Ah." Wynter nodded. "I stayed for the children's sake, Mother."

Adorna snatched her hand away. "The children are my grandchildren, and they belong in England."

Charlotte looked into Leila's eyes and saw the delight there. It would seem granddaughter and grandmother were reconciled at last.

Charlotte rose and stood on aching knees.

"So you wanted us to return to England, and knew appeals would have no results, so you and Stewart hatched a plan to make it look as if someone were embezzling from the business," Wynter deduced.

"Stewart is the most honorable, sweetest man in the

world," Adorna said. "He would have never done anything so underhanded. It was all me."

Wynter turned to Stewart, who shrugged in embarrassment. "I wrote you that letter thinking I needed to alert you of a serious threat to the family business."

Both men scrutinized Adorna. "I suppose you could say you did," Wynter said.

Charlotte didn't think Adorna's wide-eyed innocence could have been faked. She had truly done what she thought best, and she didn't regret it a bit.

All women could learn a lot from Adorna.

"Poor Stewart didn't find out what I'd done until after you were home, and he was very disapproving, Wynter." Adorna shook a stern finger at her son. "You owe Stewart an apology for choking him."

"Sorry, old fellow." Wynter extended his hand.

"No apology needed. I'd have done the same." Stewart shook hands with Wynter.

Wynter was putting it all together now. "So, Stew, when you deduced who the villain was, you ended up trying to put the money back."

"Yes. She's done so much for me over the years." Stewart's spectacles sat crooked on his nose, and he tried to straighten them. "I owed her that much. But she didn't ever seem to comprehend the seriousness of her felony!"

Charlotte felt moved to point out the obvious. "Stealing from herself is not a felony."

"Thank you, Charlotte," Adorna said.

"I thought I could finish the job tonight, because I was sure you wouldn't be in town. Not with the Sereminian reception tomorrow." Stewart looked them all over. "What *are* you doing here?"

"Oh, dear." Adorna looked at the clockpiece on the shelf. "We need to get back to Austinpark Manor at

once. Queen Victoria and the royal party will be there
in about nine hours. Get the candles, Stewart." She
took Leila's hand and Stewart's arm, and led them
toward the door. "What an evening this has been! But
at least I have a special entertainment planned for
Their Majesties, thanks to my dear granddaughter."

The light disappeared down the corridor, leaving
Charlotte and Wynter alone. She shook out her skirts
and started to follow her mother-in-law, daughter and
cousin. *They* were her family. She understood
Adorna's embezzling activities. She comprehended
Leila's childish rebellion. She admired Stewart's
staunch protection of Adorna. Whatever grief they had
caused her, she could forgive.

But Wynter . . . she paused and eyed her husband
with intense disfavor. She'd cried over this man. She'd
moped about his detachment. Now she knew he'd
been busy trying to find an embezzler, but she didn't
know why she had cared. She would just walk away
from him and never concern herself with him again.
Give him a taste of his own medicine. She would just
walk away . . .

She snapped, "At least now I know why you have
spent all your time in London. I suppose I should be
grateful for that."

Folding his arms over his chest, he took his desert
prince stance, complete with hair, earring and scar.
"You missed me?"

She took a quivering breath. Why was she talking
to him? She should leave. She shouldn't allow herself
to feel emotions so similar to the ones she experienced
with Leila—worry, exasperation and, of course, love.

Love. Not like the indulgent, anxious love of a parent, but this inconvenient passion that brought her
physical fulfillment night after night and left her days

empty and lonely. "You thought someone was embezzling from your business—and you never even gave me a clue."

He recited one of his moronic adages. "A woman is not interested in business."

"A wife is interested in her husband's activities," she countered. "Married couples should talk."

"Talk?" He had the nerve to knit his brow as if he'd never heard the word. "Lady Wife, I think you should remember. You have never been married before. I have, and I assure you, married couples do not talk."

"And men do not love." How did she fight him? Why did she even try? "You didn't love your first wife."

"No." He sounded positive of that.

"But she loved you."

"Yes." He sounded less certain.

"She chose you because she thought you would save her life. That would seem to be a pragmatic decision. So maybe she didn't love you, she only loved the security you provided for her. A lot of marriages are like that, Wynter."

"It was a good marriage," Wynter reminded her. "Placid and uneventful."

"And that's what you want again." Charlotte nodded. "As you wish. I am resigned to such a union. You can do—you have done—what every other man does, and put me into a compartment in your mind. The compartment marked *wife*. And it'll be one of many compartments, and some will be more important that others. *Business*, for instance, will be a big one. So will *horses*, and *male friends*. And you'll glance at the compartment marked *wife*, and as long as there's no fuss going on there, you'll think you have what you want. You'll think I'm happy, that you knew best, and that the only compartment in my mind is the one marked *Wynter*. But it's not, because I'm going to find other interests, other activities. If you won't give me any of you, then I will keep all of myself. And one day you'll wake up and look in my compartment, and I won't even be there."

He moved so quickly she gasped when he gripped her by the arms. "You can't leave me."

Maybe he *did* care. Maybe he *was* listening. "I don't have to leave you. I'll just be like all the other wives, Wynter. My husband won't be important to me at all."

He stared down at her as if he couldn't believe she could defy him so completely.

Then, throwing back his head, he laughed.

Laughed! Again she had tried to communicate with him. Again she had bared her soul. And he laughed?

"You! You think you can be like this? You, who loved my children from the first moment of meeting? You, this creature of passion who every night opens her arms and legs to me with all the generosity of her soul?" Wrapping his arms around her, he brought her close to the heat of him and glared hotly down into her eyes. "What do you gain from this . . . resignation? Yes, I understand you were disappointed in the first man who wished to marry you. Yes, I understand you were abandoned by your family. But this has nothing to do with us. Nothing!"

Her muscles clenched from the hurt of his laughter, from the way he twisted her words . . . from the clarity of his vision. He saw through her and her defenses. He stripped them away and left her naked and shivering. "I am what my upbringing has made me!"

"So you are. You are a woman who has much love, stored up and overflowing, and all the resignation in the world will not change that." With cupped hand, he smoothed her hair away from her face. "You love me. You fight it because I do not love you. But is not love a giving of oneself, the taking of a chance, a gamble so big that the result could be true love forever?"

She took a quick, startled breath as he scored a direct hit.

"I demand happiness for you," he said. "I will settle for no less than happiness."

$\mathcal{T}$HE RETURN TO AUSTINPARK MANOR IN THE DARK was a grueling one, hampered by several downpours that turned the turnpike to mud and made Wynter swear he would start taking that newfangled train.

He knew he wouldn't. He liked his horses too much.

But the whole family arrived in time to snatch a few hours' sleep before they had to rise with the radiant sun and prepare for the Sereminian reception.

Predictably, Queen Victoria, Prince Albert, King Danior and Queen Evangeline, the English court and all of the Sereminian delegation arrived promptly at nine in the morning.

Robbie and Leila had been in charge of taking the Sereminian royal children off to play, and they offered hospitality so graciously Charlotte had glowed with pride. Then Adorna had taken over and the royal party had been ruthlessly beguiled. They were given a tour of the house and the gardens, fed and chatted up.

Now they were seated in rows on the portico, waiting to be entertained.

So Wynter found himself in the stable, arrayed in his white djellaba, a turban wrapped around his head. Robbie was dressed like a miniature version of his father. And Leila wore sky blue, the feminine version of the traditional garb.

Leila preened with delight. She was going to get to ride again, not in the hated sidesaddle, but astride or standing, shooting a pistol and showing off her greatest accomplishments. Best of all, she had her grandmama's encouragement.

Under Adorna's tending, Leila would now bloom like a rose in the soil of England.

Wynter had no more worries about his children.

Only about himself. And Charlotte, who would scarcely look at him and claimed she was becoming resigned. Charlotte, who still failed to realize that a man's reasoning was superior to a woman's emotion. Charlotte, who made him experience such . . . well . . . frustration.

Yes. What she made him experience *was* frustration.

He wanted to talk to her, and the damned reception would not end for hours. So he resolved not to think of her now.

Naturally, Robbie stood in the middle of the stable and asked, "Papa, why aren't you and Lady Miss Charlotte happy?"

Wynter grimaced. "I shall explain at some other time."

"I thought you told me I could ask you anything and you would answer," Robbie said.

Yes. Wynter had said that. But he had thought his son would ask about girls of his own age, not Wynter's own unsettled marriage. He wanted to say again, *No, not now*. He wanted to tell Robbie he had appalling timing. That Fletcher and his assistants were walking the horses to warm their muscles. That their grand-mother depended on them for international amusement. That Charlotte had not yet become the wife Wynter knew she should be.

But Robbie and Leila looked up at him as if Wynter could explain everything in the universe, and Wynter was loath to disillusion them. So briefly he tried to clarify the situation. "Charlotte is being stubborn. She loves me, yet doesn't accept this as her destiny, so she is not a happy or fulfilled woman."

Leila said what Wynter desperately wanted to hear. "But she *does* love you, Papa. Why doesn't that make her happy?"

Wynter found himself remembering the prediction of an old wise woman at Leila's cradle. The old lady had said Leila would grow in wisdom and in beauty. Right now, Wynter hoped Leila spoke wisdom. "Charlotte is an Englishwoman," he said, "and in many ways Englishwomen are foolish. She refuses to be happy in her love for me until I say I love her."

Leila tied a sky-blue scarf over her braided hair. "Why won't you tell her?"

"I cannot build a marriage on a falsehood."

"What falsehood?"

"That I love her."

"But, Papa, you do love her!"

He abruptly experienced an unmanly set of weak knees, and sank down on a wooden crate. "Men do not love women."

Leila's nose wrinkled. "That's stupid. Who told you that?"

"Barakah, my desert father," Wynter replied with crushing finality.

Coming to lean on his shoulder, Leila pronounced, "He was wrong. Look at that Lord Bucknell. He loves Grandmama."

Robbie joined them, leaning on Wynter's other

shoulder. "Papa, you know he does. He watches her all moony-eyed." He did an imitation of Bucknell wishing after Adorna.

"Besides, if it's true men don't fall in love"—Leila crossed her skinny arms across her chest—"then I will never fall in love."

Pulling her onto his knee, Wynter explained, "A woman must fall in love to be happy."

Leila pointed her thumb at her chest. "*I'm* not going to get all sappy after some man who thinks he's the sun or something and wants me to spread rose petals for him to walk on."

Robbie sang, "Rose petals, rose petals, Leila's going to spread rose petals."

"I have never asked for rose petals," Wynter said stiffly.

"No, you just want Mama"—Leila paused, tilting her chin—"my new mama to adore you while you don't have to pay her a lot of attention."

"I like that!" Robbie said. "I'm glad I'm a man."

Wynter glared at his son, then turned back to Leila, who had become an exasperating woman-child while he wasn't watching. "That is not true."

"You'd like that, Papa," she said. "You could be lazy. She'd have to do all the work, and if your marriage wasn't good you could blame her."

"You are a child. You do not understand."

"I understand." She had an expression on her face he'd seen before, and he recognized it. This was the look of the wise old woman. "I understand too well. Barakah was wrong. Men do love women."

"Barakah was a leader of the desert men."

"But you're not a desert man, Papa," Robbie said. "You're an Englishman."

"And you love Charlotte." Taking Wynter's face in

her hands, Leila turned it toward her. "You love her very much. Even dumb ol' Robbie can see that."

Robbie didn't take umbrage at the epithet. He just nodded agreement.

An Englishman. Wynter was an Englishman. The years he'd spent in the desert had taught him much, yes, but no influence could ever supersede the original influence of those who had borne him. His mother . . . and his father.

His father. Henry, Viscount Ruskin. It had been so many years ago, yet . . . yes, he remembered him. Old and tottering, yet more intensely alive than any man Wynter had met before or since. In the long days and evenings they had spent together, his father had told Wynter so much. How to calculate numbers in his head, how to behave during business dealings, what kind of horse to buy. But he'd taught him by example, too.

Closing his eyes, Wynter remembered the way his father had looked at his mother.

His father had adored Adorna. And he was as much a real man as Barakah had ever been.

Barakah had been a wise and brave man. But in this matter, at least, he had been a foolish coward.

He had never *dared* love a woman.

"Papa?" Leila pushed his hair back and toyed with his earring. "Are you suffering from wind?"

Opening his eyes, he looked at his daughter. "What if I am?"

"Then I'm leavin'."

Laughing, he kissed her forehead. He ruffled his son's hair. And he said, "Here's what I plan for us to do."

* * *

The first time Wynter slipped off the bare back of his horse and rode between the galloping legs, Charlotte shrieked.

Queen Victoria looked at her in spartan amazement.

Adorna pretended not to be amused.

Queen Evangeline said, "Lady Ruskin, that must be your husband."

"Yes, Your Majesty." Charlotte's voice wasn't working right. Even to herself, it sounded a little high. The three horses galloped at a great speed, around and around the open area in front of the portico. Targets had been placed, for what reason Charlotte scarcely dared imagine, and Wynter, Robbie and Leila rode like maniacs in their desert garb.

Leila stood up on the horse and traveled around the circle as lightly as a fairy.

The Sereminian children oohed in admiration.

Charlotte ripped her handkerchief in half.

King Danior patted her on the shoulder. "Great riding. Is that your son?"

"Daughter," Charlotte squeaked.

"You'll forgive Lady Ruskin, *Your Majesty*." Queen Victoria emphasized his title. "She seems to have forgotten her manners."

King Danior chuckled. "Not at all. If my daughter"—he glared at Queen Evangeline meaningfully—"or my wife rode like that, I would forget my very name."

"I can't do those tricks!" Queen Evangeline answered.

"Nor I, Your Majesty," Adorna said. "But I would love to learn."

Charlotte could scarcely believe that Adorna would say such a thing. Love to learn? *That?* As if Charlotte weren't frightened enough having her husband and two little children performing maneuvers that would bring on palpitations! Soon. She would keel over from fear.

"Yes, indeed." Queen Evangeline beamed. "I, too, would love to learn."

"Really?" Queen Victoria turned in her purple velvet chair and stared at Queen Evangeline. "You would try that?"

"Of course." The queen of Sereminia was in her forties, a beautiful woman resplendent with content. "What is the use of being queen if one can't enjoy oneself?"

"And give your husband gray hairs," King Danior interceded.

Prince Albert harrumphed. "I say, yes."

"No, Evangeline." King Danior sounded both stern and apprehensive. "You have wanted to return to England for years, but we cannot dally here forever. It would be a strain on our gracious hosts if you were laid up indefinitely with a cracked skull."

"I suppose." Evangeline turned back to the show, shoulders slumped. Then she leaped to her feet and clapped her hands. "Look at that!"

The horses looked as if they would collide, then Leila hurtled from her gelding to Wynter's stallion.

Charlotte slithered out of her seat onto the floor. She wanted to close her eyes so badly, or hide behind one of the uprights on the balustrade, but she couldn't take her gaze off the magnificent creatures racing before them.

"Dear Lady Ruskin, do rise," Queen Victoria said. "Your family seems most accomplished at this fascinating endeavor, and you do them an injustice with your excessive anxiety."

"Sorry." Charlotte climbed back into her chair. "Sorry, Your Majesty, I just—"

Leila still held the reins to her mount, and she returned to it with a bound while at the same time Robbie jumped on the broad horse's back behind his father.

Charlotte whimpered.

Then the target shooting began.

By the time the three horses, with their riders, were lined up before the portico, Charlotte's hair had somehow fallen out of its coiffure, her handkerchief was in shreds and she was hoarse from trying to contain her screams.

"Before her marriage to Wynter, our dear Charlotte used to be known as Miss Priss, a most excellent finishing governess," Adorna announced—an uncalled-for comment, in Charlotte's opinion.

Each rider held a bouquet of blossoms from Austinpark Manor's garden, reaped one by one through an exercise wherein the rider leaned off the horse and snatched it out of a maidservant's extended hand.

Charlotte was miserably aware that the flowers looked better than she did.

Leila removed the scarf, revealing her braid. Under her urging, her horse bowed before the company. Being on a horse lifted Leila to almost the same level as the company on the portico, and so she was able to extend her bouquet to Queen Evangeline. The queen took it with thanks, and Charlotte thought the pleased grins of child and queen were almost identical.

Robbie repeated the exercise to Queen Victoria, removing his turban, bowing with his horse and extending his bouquet. Queen Victoria did not grin, but her cheeks were rosy with the excitement she had finally been unable to suppress.

Then Wynter moved into place before Charlotte.

Charlotte glanced at Adorna, trying to tell him he was making a mistake, that propriety demanded he give the bouquet to his mother, the hostess.

She should have remembered that Wynter never did anything he didn't want to, and for some reason, he wanted Charlotte to have the flowers.

He removed his turban, displaying his mussed hair and his barbaric earring. He bowed with his horse, a gracious motion of the upper body. And when he reached out with his bouquet, he said, "I offer this to my lady wife, who with her beauty puts the first flower of spring to shame, who with her knowledge has brought my children and I into the arms of civilization"—he looked into her eyes—"and who with her love has conquered my heart."

She had started to extend her hand, but now she drew back. "No, I haven't."

"*She* was a finishing governess?" she heard Queen Victoria ask incredulously.

"All my heart," Wynter clarified. "My *whole* heart. My whole heart, which beats only for you, oh dearest and most brilliant star in my sky."

He didn't mean it. He couldn't have changed his mind in so little time. Yet he looked earnest enough, and she couldn't imagine why he would lie. Not this man, who insisted on honor in all things.

Charlotte clasped her hands together. "Really?"

"If you will not believe me," he replied, "ask my children."

Both Robbie and Leila nodded their heads enthusiastically.

"For you," Wynter vowed, "I will get my hair cut. I will remove my earring. I will wear proper English clothing at all times and always sit in a chair."

"I don't want that." Charlotte's voice rasped in her throat. "I just want you to say it, plainly."

He smiled at her. Only at her. "Lady Miss Charlotte Wife, I love you."

Never, not even in her dreams, had she imagined happiness like this. "I love you, too." Extending her hand, she reached for the flowers. She got them, as well as his fingers clasping hers. He brought his horse alongside the railing, and carried her hand to his lips, and kissed it passionately.

"Well! This has been most entertaining," Queen Victoria said. "We thank both the Lady Ruskins, and Lord Ruskin, of course, and his children, who are most talented. But if we are to get back to London before dark, we should start at once."

Prince Albert harrumphed. "Yes, indeed."

Charlotte managed to wrestle her hand away from Wynter's and turn to face the company.

"Most entertaining." King Danior sounded as if he were amused.

"I never imagined being this entertained." Queen Evangeline leaned against King Danior's shoulder.

"Thank you, thank you." Adorna fairly gushed with pleasure. "I always try to make my galas memorable."

"I think we can safely agree you have done that," Queen Evangeline said.

Wynter, Robbie and Leila dismounted. They gave their horses over to the stableboys and climbed the stairs. The royal children surrounded Robbie and Leila at once. Wynter never took his gaze away from Charlotte, and no one got between them as he made his way to her side.

The royal leave-taking proceeded around them, and Charlotte stared at him, still not quite believing. He didn't touch her. She didn't touch him. They didn't dare, or she knew they would behave in an even more improper manner than they already had, and dimly, in some now-unexercised corner of her mind, Charlotte was aware they had behaved most improperly, indeed.

"Dears," Adorna trilled. "Their Majesties are departing!"

Side by side, Wynter and Charlotte walked to Adorna. Charlotte curtsied and took personal pride in Wynter's elegant bow. Smiling and waving, they observed as the royal party stepped into open carriages and at last, at long last, drove away.

Blessed silence fell. Adorna, the children, the servants were watching Wynter and Charlotte. Charlotte knew it, but she didn't care. All of England could discover how much she loved her husband, and she didn't mind, because he loved her back. She had everything she could ever want.

"I will make you happy," Wynter vowed. "I will pleasure you every night."

Adorna sighed. "That might make up for being such a jackass," she murmured. Lifting her voice, she said, "Come, children. I'll teach you how to play whist."

As she began to herd Robbie and Leila toward the house, Wynter and Charlotte reached out to each other—and heard the sound of carriage wheels returning on the gravel drive.

Wynter's hand dropped. "They forgot something."

"I suppose." Adorna sounded disgusted. "I would have sent it on."

But Charlotte didn't recognize the coach that drove up. It was closed, for one thing, and draped red silk covered the door as if concealing a crest. The coachman wore red, too, an eighteenth-century oddly mismatched nobleman's costume. He grinned at the assemblage as he pulled the vehicle to a halt.

The door was flung wide. A masked man dressed all in black leaped to the ground.

He wore a short cape, a doublet, tights and leather gauntlets. He strode up the terrace steps with an arrogant gait, and at the top slung his cape over one shoulder and stood, fists on hips, glaring at Adorna through the slits in his mask.

"Grandmama, who is that man?" Leila asked.

Adorna stared, head tilted, and finally guessed, "Lord Bucknell?"

Beside Charlotte, Wynter gave a slight and almost silent chuckle.

"Lord Bucknell?" Adorna sounded a little surer this time. "What are you . . . ?"

The masked man didn't answer. Instead, he walked to Adorna, bent and picked her up.

As she hung over his shoulder, she shrieked.

Charlotte stiffened. What had Wynter said when he carried her off to their wedding bower? *Bucknell reminded me that reluctant maidens should be kidnapped.*

Lord Bucknell was carrying away her mother-in-law.

As he stuffed Adorna into the coach, she shrieked again, but it sounded as if she were laughing.

Her abductor leaped inside. He shut the door. The coachman whipped up the horses, and they were gone.

Shocked, Charlotte stared after them.

"Mama, why did Lord Bucknell take Grandmama?" Leila asked.

As generations of parents had done before her, Charlotte replied, "I'll tell you when you're older."

"Come on. Let's go get something to eat." Robbie put his arm around Leila's shoulder and led her away. "And I'll explain."

Pointing a shaking finger down the drive, Charlotte said, "My lord husband, I recognize your fine hand in this scandal."

"Yes." Wynter couldn't have sounded more delighted. "Bucknell will make my mother very happy."

She despaired of ever making him understand, but as the former Miss Priss, she had to try. "You must realize that in civilized society you cannot indulge in the kind of barbarism you so relish."

Leaning against the railing, he crossed his arms over his chest and stared at her challengingly. "Why not? Bucknell's barbaric behavior succeeded where his domesticated courtship did not, and in the struggle between you and me, dear wife, it is obvious who is the victor."

Charlotte almost chocked on her indignation. "The victor? I prefer to think that there is no *victor* between us."

"You are right. We do not have to say there is a victor." He straightened up and moved toward her. "As long as we are agreed I always get to win."

She stood her ground. "In marriage, there is no winner and no loser, no right and no wrong."

Seductively, he crooned, "We can go upstairs. You can take off your shoes, Lady Miss Charlotte, and I will massage your feet."

"It is obvious to me that removing one's shoes is a symptom of—" Now she backed away from his looming figure, excitement beginning to banish wrath. "—of the kind of crude and uncultured comportment which will result in illicit passion—"

Wrapping his arms around her stiff form, Wynter brought her close to him and sought her lips with his. At last she collapsed against his warm body and let him kiss her. Kiss her until she was pliant, inarticulate and quite improperly passionate.

"Then I submit that more Englishmen should remove their shoes, so they can be as happy as we are." He smiled down at her. "My dearest and only love."

DO YOU REMEMBER
THE FIRST TIME . . .

. . . you saw **him?** *Perhaps your eyes met across a crowded room . . . and you knew he was the one destined to change your life. Or was the* **last** *person you thought you'd fall for . . . the one all your friends warned you about. Infuriating, fascinating, and ultimately irresistible . . . he's the man who can rouse your passions as no other.*

Now, come meet six unforgettable men . . . cowboys and rakes, both honorable and scandalous (and some a bit of both!), as created by your favorite writers: Barbara Freethy, Cathy Maxwell, Christina Dodd, Lorraine Heath, Susan Andersen and Kathleen Eagle.

Turn the page—you could be meeting the man you've been waiting for all your life. . . .

Katherine Whitfield thought she'd found herself a cowboy on the wrong side of the Mississippi. There she was, stranded on a Kentucky roadside, with no one to help her but lean, sexy Zach Tyler. Trouble is, Zach might be easy on the eyes, but he had the most annoying habit of telling her what to do. And although it soon became clear that he had a gentle hand with horses and a slow hand with women, Katherine sure didn't want him to get the upper hand with her!

ALMOST HOME
by Barbara Freethy

COMING IN JANUARY 2000

𝒦ATHERINE SHOOK HER HEAD, TRYING TO FIGURE OUT where she was and who was yelling at her. There was a man—a tall, dark-haired man with burning black eyes standing next to her car window. He was pulling on the door handle and yelling all sorts of absurdities that seemed to have less to do with her and more to do with a horse.

She roused herself enough to unlock the door. She pushed on it as the man pulled on it, sending her stumbling into his arms.

He caught her with a sureness, a strength that made her want to sink into his embrace and rest for a moment. She needed to catch her breath. She needed to feel safe.

"You could have killed my horse," he ground out angrily, his rough-edged voice right next to her ear. "Driving like a maniac. What were you thinking about?"

Katherine could barely keep up with his surge of angry words. "Let me go."

His grip eased slightly, but he didn't let go.

They stared at each other, their breaths coming in matching frightened gasps. Dressed in faded blue jeans and a white shirt with the sleeves rolled up to the forearms, the man towered over Katherine. His eyes were fierce and his thick dark hair looked like he'd run his fingers through it all day long. His face was too rugged to be handsome, but it was compelling, strong, stubborn, determined . . .

Good heavens—she had the distinct feeling she'd found herself a cowboy.

Forced to rusticate in the country to hide the disgraceful results of her elopement, Leah Carrollton is utterly dismayed to see Devon Marshall striding toward her across the English countryside. The beautiful debutante had fled the wagging tongues of London's ton *and an arranged marriage to another, but could marrying Devon truly save her from scandal?*

A SCANDALOUS MARRIAGE
by Cathy Maxwell

COMING IN FEBRUARY 2000

LEAH HAD BEEN STANDING A STEP APART FROM A group of other debutantes. They'd all worn pastels and smelled of rosewater. Their claim to conversation had been self-conscious giggles. She was one of them, and yet alone.

He instantly recognized a kindred soul. He understood. She wanted, no, *had* to be accepted by the group but exerted her own independence.

She sensed him staring at her. She turned, searching, and then looked straight at him.

In that moment, time halted. He even stopped breathing, knowing he still lived only because his heart pounded in his ears, its pulse abnormally fast. Cupid's famed arrow had found a mark.

For the first time in his adventurous life, he felt the sweaty palms and the singing in his blood of a man smitten beyond reason by the mere presence of a woman. The poets had been right!

Oh, she was lovely to look at. Petite, buxom, rounded. He could have spanned her waist with his two hands.

Her heavy black hair styled in a simple, elegant chignon held in place by gold pearl-tipped pins emphasized the slender grace of her neck. He imagined himself pulling those pins from her hair one by one. It would fall in a graceful, swinging curtain down to her waist. Her eyes were so dark and exotic they reminded him of full moons, Spanish dancers, and velvety nights.

But it wasn't her beauty that drew him. No, it was something deeper. Something he'd never felt before. He wasn't a fanciful man but he could swear he'd been waiting for her to walk into his life.

She smiled. The most charming dimple appeared at the corner of her mouth and his feet began moving of their own volition. He wasn't even conscious that he was walking until he stood in front of her.

"Dance with me." He held out his hand.

Carefully, as if she, too, understood the importance of her actions, she placed her hand in his. It was a magic moment. He felt changed in some indefinable way.